THE FOUNTAIN

THE FOUNTAIN

A Novel

CASEY SCIESZKA

HARPER

An Imprint of HarperCollins*Publishers*

This is a work of fiction. Names, characters, places, and incidents are products of the author's imagination or are used fictitiously and are not to be construed as real. Any resemblance to actual events, locales, organizations, or persons, living or dead, is entirely coincidental.

Without limiting the exclusive rights of any author, contributor or the publisher of this publication, any unauthorized use of this publication to train generative artificial intelligence (AI) technologies is expressly prohibited. HarperCollins also exercise their rights under Article 4(3) of the Digital Single Market Directive 2019/790 and expressly reserve this publication from the text and data mining exception.

THE FOUNTAIN. Copyright © 2026 by Casey Scieszka. All rights reserved. Printed in the United States of America. No part of this book may be used or reproduced in any manner whatsoever without written permission except in the case of brief quotations embodied in critical articles and reviews. For information, address HarperCollins Publishers, 195 Broadway, New York, NY 10007. In Europe, HarperCollins Publishers, Macken House, 39/40 Mayor Street Upper, Dublin 1, D01 C9W8, Ireland.

HarperCollins books may be purchased for educational, business, or sales promotional use. For information, please email the Special Markets Department at SPsales@harpercollins.com.

hc.com

FIRST EDITION

Designed by Bonni Leon-Berman

Library of Congress Cataloging-in-Publication Data has been applied for.

ISBN 978-0-06-339340-0

25 26 27 28 29 LBC 5 4 3 2 1

For Tracy Kennard

THE FOUNTAIN

1

April 2014

Vera is losing her grip on time. She's been driving all night, for days even, she can't say.

She pulls over onto the shoulder of road next to the creek, her wheels rumbling across a muddy lump of plowed snow as she comes to a stop. What sunlight reaches over the mountains feels thin and weak. She gets out of the car, leaves it running, then hurriedly makes her way down the rocky bank to the icy edges of moving water and steps in.

The current presses against her shins. Her feet go numb almost immediately. It's shallow, too shallow. She'll have to lie down to fully submerge herself. Will be able to sit up too easily once her lungs give out.

"Goddamnit," she says aloud to no one.

Wind lashes her hair across her face. She knows there are houses upstream and downstream from here, but at this vantage in the brook all she can see is water, rock, and ridge. It could be a hundred years ago, two hundred. Only the rumble of her Subaru's engine behind her spoils the effect, her jeans and boots if she looks down, but her eyes are now set on the peaks ahead of her. On the notch between them where the turnoff for The Road begins.

Vera has broken a lot of promises over the years. She'll write, she'll call, she'll see you Monday. But she's never broken the promise she, her brother Eli, and Ma made to each other until now. The transgression felt theoretical and distant as she packed up her life once again last week. But standing here today beneath the eerily familiar faces of these mountains, some tendril of feeling is pushing its way up through her exhaustion, and it unsettles her.

She could turn around right now. She's expected for her first day of work at Forest Ranger Headquarters tomorrow but she could disappear, it's something she's very good at after all. No one will know where to start looking, if they even bother. She's driven cross-country, the search area will be too large. Besides, no one will be that surprised to hear she's vanished. There's always been something strange about Vera, and it only got worse after the incident in the desert. "Poor girl" they'll say after trading their few and paltry memories of her then immediately get on with what's left of their short lives.

Vera takes a pistol out from the waistband of her pants.

A memory of standing barefoot in this creek with Eli appears like a scrim in front of her vision. The tip of her rod curving with the trout she hooked. Her brother shouting directions excitedly as she struggled to keep her footing. Sun hot, water gushing, the promise of a glistening reward if she could listen to the pull of the line and respond calmly, if she could just be steady and patient.

It was hardly a mile upstream from here but lifetimes ago.

The sour tang of bile rises in her throat.

This was a mistake, Vera thinks and pulls the safety.

There's a reason they made this promise. There will never be any answers, never be any reprieve. How stupid and naive to return, how horrifically pointless, all of this. All of her life.

She touches the barrel to her chin, to her temple, back to her chin. She braces herself for the shock of it. She hopes for the thousandth time, millionth time, for some relief.

"You OK down there?"

Vera whips around to see a middle-aged woman standing at the top of the creek bank above her.

"I'm fine!" Vera yelps as she quickly slips the firearm back into her jeans and pulls her sweater over its grip. Her heart spasms in her chest.

The woman crosses her arms, considers what she's looking at, what she thinks she saw.

"Your car is running, I was guessing maybe you had a flat or—oh my god, what're you doing in the water you'll freeze to death!"

"Just scouting some fishing holes, got waterproof boots on," Vera lies, suddenly very cold and very anxious to be out of the creek and far away from here. The woman looks at her with a certain wariness Vera knows too well, then into the rear window of the parked Subaru.

"You got a lot of stuff in there," she says matter-of-factly. She's wearing a sweatshirt, gray as the scene around them. Her short blond hair stands up with a gust of wind as she peers into Vera's car.

"I'm moving," Vera says, trying the truth this time. It's the easiest way to keep her story straight. To tell the truth, but as little of it as necessary.

She should climb out of the stream and talk. But then the woman will see she lied about her boots and she has to be careful, always so careful.

Vera has grown sloppy recently, careless. There have always been phases, times when her burden has felt heavier, when the tides of her pain have washed higher. But in the past few months it's become harder to reason with herself. Harder to keep a hold on herself even when she tries.

What was she thinking climbing down here with her car still running? Taking out her *gun*?

"Moving? Ah OK, where to? There's no cell service out here so don't even bother with your GPS but you got lucky, I'm the postmaster! Janet." The woman points a thumb at her chest. "You couldn't find someone who knows this area better than me if you tried."

Vera forces a tight smile.

She found the place on Airbnb, brand-new listing, no reviews. The address was hidden but she recognized it right away because there in the pictures was the meadow of goldenrod and aster, the small stony creek, the specific humped ridge of the mountain to the south. Her mouth went dry at the shock of seeing it again even through the small square of a computer screen. At least half of the apple trees were gone, and for a moment she feared the house and barn were, too, replaced by this little cottage with its fake wood-paneled walls and brown wall-to-wall carpeting. But in her messages with the owner it became clear that the old white farmhouse still stands. That it's where the owners live, just out of frame of the photographs.

Vera is loath to give out her exact address even though she knows that if this town is like every other small town she's ever lived in, the whole neighborhood will know in a matter of days anyway.

"It's a cottage, about a mile down that road up there."

"Oh, Cate and Brian's! You must be the new ranger."

She could still leave. Forget the whole bad idea and just go, gone again. Vera flashes forward in the fantasy and finds herself working as a cleaner at a roadside motel somewhere in Pennsylvania. She knows that life. She's lived dozens and dozens of them. It could be fine. She could be fine. She could just continue to live cycles of small, modest existences, one after another after another, passing through and through and through.

But she can't anymore.

She takes a deep breath—forget Ma, forget Eli—and tells the postmaster, "Yes, I'm the new ranger. I'm Vera." The sound of her real name feels foreign in her own mouth, it's been so long.

Janet beams, hands on her hips, so pleased to have put the pieces together. She gives Vera directions—half a mile straight ahead then a left at the flagpole, past the post office and the church, four, five, yes the fifth house down on the right.

"Thank you, Janet," Vera says as she begins to make her way carefully to the edge of the creek, her legs entirely numb now.

"If you cross a bridge you've gone too far," Janet continues, satisfied to finally be of help to the newcomer. "It's a beautiful spot, the valley really opens up there."

"I know," she says, the small slip hanging between them.

Janet doesn't notice, says she'll start getting Vera's P.O. Box ready, does she want a small one? One of the medium-size ones? Does she have mail forwarding already? She should come by once she's settled and get set up.

"I will," Vera tells her, repressing a shiver through another gust of wind.

"Well, welcome to town, Vera!" Janet says. Then she nods good-bye with a smile and leaves Vera standing in the creek.

*

Back in the car, heat blasting, Vera's teeth chatter and she shivers violently but it's the kind of pain she is well versed at weathering. Vera shifts into drive and moves forward. The mountains loom closer. At the flagpole, she grips the wheel and turns onto The Road.

It's like a mirage, actual déjà vu, *now* and *then* collapsing on top of each other.

Here are the same white clapboard houses, the post office, the church. Here is the same roll of mountains behind them. There's the little parsonage, more weathered white clapboard houses. Everything remarkably well kept. Time has added a few garages, telephone wires, asphalt, and two stripes of yellow down the middle of The Road, but it's startling, downright amazing how little has changed since Vera was last here.

Her breath grows shallow through her chattering teeth as she continues to look out her window.

White hills undulate like waves behind the houses, shaggy snow-crusted pines texturing the vista. Hints of angelic blue glow through the soft patches of gray clouds. It's not as grand as the Rockies, not as stunningly desolate as the Mojave. It is so modest in comparison to all things west but her eyes are feasting, greedily taking in this familiar landscape. That same tendril of emotion pushes up and reaches, brushing something inside her that speeds her pulse again.

Vera rounds a gentle bend. The old general store comes into view, empty now from the looks of it, then a stand of trees.

And suddenly, there it is.

The house is the same white box. Same porch, too, or "stoop" as they used to call it—not because her family once lived in New York City, but because it's the old Dutch word for "porch." The door is different, blue with gridded windows, and there's an exterior light now that wasn't there before. But it's unmistakably the house.

Her house.

So pulled by the familiar draw of it, Vera nearly misses the split in the gravel driveway that leads to the little white cottage tucked into the shade of the encroaching pines. She puts on her blinker, for who she doesn't know, and turns left into this new place.

The wheels grind on the gravel as she comes to a stop in front of the screen door. She turns off the ignition, then everything is quiet. She can hear a faint ringing in her ears, the sigh of the engine cooling down. She zips up her jacket and gets out of the car. The cold covers her immediately and completely. She breathes it in, the pines and mineral hint of snow. She steps toward the front door, her wet boots crunching noisily in the patches of icy white, a sound she's almost forgotten after so many years in deserts.

"Hey there!" someone calls from behind her. Vera turns around.

"Cate?" she asks, even though she knows from the little bit of googling she did before arriving here that this is definitely Cate Bennington. Tall and sturdy, early thirties. She's in a thick white sweater and the kind of black leggings that can pass for pants these days. Mass-produced moccasins, a mess of brown hair tied up. A smooth, peaches and cream complexion that was once so hard to attain but can now be easily achieved with makeup.

Vera herself looks about twenty-six. She's small, pale, and plain, with unremarkable features and straight brown hair. All in all, unmemorable-looking, which has been a unique blessing for her unique condition. The few people who truly know her, though, could spot her immediately by the way her right front tooth overlaps with the left just a touch, by the way she chews her cheeks when deep in thought and cracks her knuckles when frustrated. How her eyes alight into a particular hazel when excited. How dimmed and dulled they can become. Vera herself rarely looks in the mirror anymore. She knows what she looks like by now all too well.

"Yes! You're Vera, right? Let me get my boots one sec, I'll show you in," Cate says and disappears into the house before Vera can answer back.

Vera stamps her feet and rolls her stiff neck. When she sighs a big puff of condensation fills the air in front of her. She looks at her house again and something in her flutters. It's still here, after all these years. Never once moving as Vera herself has scuttled across the country, this place to that.

How badly Vera wants to go in. She feels it like an ache in her abdomen. Then again, maybe that's the cold of her soaked pants, or the fact that she hasn't eaten in at least forty-eight hours, hasn't slept in just as long. She can't untangle any of her senses these days. All of it a heavy fog punctured only occasionally by piercing panic.

The door to the house moans open in need of a little oil and Cate reappears in large, fur-lined boots but no jacket.

"I guess you found the place OK? I turned the heat up for you last night—" and on Cate talks. Happy, empty talk of weather and travel and their communication leading up to Vera's arrival. Cate's husband, Brian, ran into town, she's sorry she hadn't thought to ask Vera if she needed anything, she could probably get a hold of him although service out here is spotty.

"That's OK," Vera says as Cate unlocks the door and holds it open for her.

They tour the cottage. Living room and kitchen here, bedroom here, bathroom here. Cate's sorry there's no dishwasher or washing machine but at least there's a bathtub. The place is dated—built in the sixties and hardly touched since then—but it's clean. Vera's never been one to focus on material comforts. Born first from a need to be frugal and invisible, it's morphed from a coping mechanism to a point of pride. Unlike the decadence of her brother with the private planes and sea yachts and bags that cost ten, twenty, thirty times more than they should simply because they've been stamped with a certain logo. Eli would never live here, but for Vera it will do. Besides, she didn't choose this place for anything but its location. The cottage, the new job—none of that is what matters to Vera right now. All of it just a means to an end.

"Your name sounds kinda familiar," Cate says interrupting her own monologue on frozen pipes and how much woodstove heat dries out her skin.

"My name?"

Vera suddenly regrets her rash and sentimental choice to use her real name. It had felt so bold as to feel safe. Like a deer standing still in the wide open, counting on being downwind of its predators. No one who was alive then would be alive now, and her brother would never look for her under their family name. She hasn't been Vera Van Valkenburgh in a very long time.

"Yeah, I think—oh crap!" Cate cries. She forgot she has a phone call with a client. Wedding invitations, she explains. She's a graphic designer. "Give a holler if you need anything!" Then she's off, closing the cheap door behind her with a hollow slam.

Vera startles at the sound. Her heart surges into her throat, her limbs flash full with sour adrenaline.

"Get it together," she hisses at herself. She runs her hands over her face and can feel they are shaking.

She needs to get out of these wet clothes. She needs to sleep.

She needs to end this.

It takes Vera two trips to gather all her worldly possessions from the car. She unpacks only what she'll use tonight, she'll deal with the rest tomorrow, then she draws a bath. She peels her soaked jeans from her clammy legs. She yanks at her saturated socks. The steam begins to billow and fogs the tiny window that looks into the backyard—apple trees, pines, the mountains, all cast in shadow, now that the sun has finally set on the day.

Naked, she steps into the tub and sinks down. The heat scorches her but she doesn't cry out or lift a limb. When the water reaches her chin she turns off the faucet with her foot and the comparative silence is striking.

Pink and warm, Vera reaches for her razor. She's never shaved her legs or armpits with any regularity. She has fine, downy hair and a dislike for that kind of modern female grooming.

Jacob rises, unbidden, to the forefront of her mind. Years and years since she's allowed herself to think of him. It rushes her— yellow coneflowers in his hands and the musk of sun-warmed hay, the big domed bowl of blue sky they once shared. That laugh. For a moment Vera can feel all the old hope, all her old plans for how things could have maybe, finally been different. It steadies the churn and rock within her now. She thinks she can even taste it, that stubborn will to believe.

And then the present returns.

No anger, no joy, no sadness, she opens her veins.

Her thoughts loosen and swirl as she listens to the small plops of the leaky spout. She weakens and drifts until finally, she is emptied. She touches the edge of the void—there—

One brief moment of ecstatic nothingness.

And then, her mind gains traction, her body burns and tightens as it heals itself.

Returned, as always, Vera sighs, an exhale of exhaustion.

Then she stands and runs the shower as the tub drains red.

2

May 2014

Winter has thawed and hesitantly offers a muddy spring. Hopeful clusters of daffodils have pushed up around the village and the last of the hardened, gravel-pocked snow piles at the end of everyone's driveways have finally melted. The difference a few weeks can make out here.

Vera feels herself breaking into a proper sweat as she climbs the mountain steadily, one foot, the other, her breathing audible but not completely labored. Her new coworker, Ranger Daniel Lopez, keeps pace at her side, an excited bounce in each step despite the steep grade of the rocky trail.

"You're gonna love it," Lopez tells her. "It's beautiful. Such a clear day, we're gonna be able to see for miles."

Vera puts on a smile of acknowledgment. The sun breaks out from behind a puffy cloud and bores down on her shoulders, the dark green of her uniform shirt warming in the rays.

"You settling in OK?" he asks her, his third variation on the question since they set out on the trail together an hour ago for their rounds. His need to be welcoming radiates from him like a heat. She's looking forward to her training period coming to an end in a few weeks. She tried to get out of it—ranger work is ranger work, and she already has three years under her belt—but her new captain is a stickler for rules and protocol, and Vera isn't here to make a scene.

"Yup," Vera answers again.

"California, that's cool," Lopez says, referencing the little bit of her biography she parted with earlier on the trail. He says he's never been, would like to go one day.

"You should."

"What park were you stationed at again?" he asks, as if she'd mentioned it to him before even though she hasn't. She hasn't told any of her coworkers where she came from, why she left, why she transferred here of all places. In fact, there's not a single soul besides Vera who knows what she's really up to.

Vera needs to change the subject.

"Did you grow up around here?" she asks Lopez brightly.

He grabs on to the question with the enthusiasm she hoped he would and tells her he was born an hour and a half south in Newburgh, almost enlisted in the army out of high school but went to community college instead. Transferred to SUNY New Paltz and got a degree in environmental science before becoming a ranger. It's his fifth year on the force. He lives outside Tannersville now with his wife, Jenny, who works at a local bank, but his mom and two of his three sisters live in Newburgh, the third in Poughkeepsie. His dad is out of the picture, he died when Lopez was in his teens.

"Mine, too," Vera tells him, surprising herself for voluntarily bringing it up. But being home again these past few weeks has brought all of them so close to the surface. Pa, Ma, her brother, Eli, his wife, Lotte. She is swimming in them. Maybe drowning.

"Shit, I'm sorry," Lopez says, slowing slightly.

"You didn't do it," Vera deadpans, and for a moment Lopez hesitates then laughs heartily, his dark eyes crinkling.

"Dang Van Valkenburgh, was that a joke?" He takes off his hat and fans himself.

A genuine smile tugs at Vera's lips. There was once a time when her disarming humor opened doors for her, when it worked as the sleight of hand they all needed to get by. But these days it's taking so much to simply rise each morning. To put on the uniform, drive to work. To remember to feed herself. To act out a life.

Vera breathes in deeply and realizes from the scent of it that they've crossed up into the higher elevation of the firs, where it always smells like Christmas no matter the time of year.

"Still, I'm sorry," Lopez says as they continue, their steps almost in unison. He's strong, but not particularly tall. Five foot eight maybe. "I was gutted when my dad died. Cancer, snuck up on him real quick." He looks at her expectantly.

"A logging accident," Vera says, which is mostly true. It was a rotted chestnut he was felling alone. It should have been easy. He'd cleared the whole meadow by himself without so much as a scratch. But accidents happen, and Pa, it turned out, wasn't like the rest of them.

"Damn." Lopez holds his khaki hat to his chest. His slick, black hair glistens in the sunlight.

"How much farther?" Vera asks, but she knows. These mountains are still an extension of herself. Even with the slopes now covered in budding foliage and brush, all evidence of the sheep and sawmills, the tanneries and quarries, long gone. People get sentimental about the wilderness, as if this version of flora and fauna is how it has existed for all time. They forget the past so easily. Accidentally, willfully.

"Only twenty more minutes," Lopez promises.

The steep trail crests and flattens out the last quarter mile as it follows the gentle humps of the summit's ridge. Suddenly the path gives way to a clearing of ragged grass, more brown and yellow than green, and there, the fire tower and its cabin. Vera tilts her head back, shades her eyes, and looks up at the empty observation box above.

She's about to start walking over to it when Lopez stops.

"I have a confession," he says. Vera turns to face him, raises her eyebrows in question, braces herself. Sometimes people can smell the secrets on her and it makes them want to confess their own. It can be useful. It can also be heavy, dangerous.

"I'm afraid of heights."

"Lots of people are," she tells him, momentarily relieved. Then she starts for the tower.

"What are *you* afraid of?" he asks from behind her, and Vera looks at him again quickly, some kind of frown apparent on her face because he decides to reword the question. "I mean, do you have any kind of irrational phobia?"

"Snakes," she says, because she can't tell him "the dark." Can't tell him "infinity."

"Yeah, snakes are creepy," he agrees. He puts his hands on his hips and explains that he has to run up the stairs if he's going to make it all the way. "Got to force my body to do it before my mind realizes what's happening."

Vera nods, a veteran of so many kinds of fear.

He crouches like a football player or a track and field runner waiting for the starting gun, not an ounce of humor in his performance, then he bolts. She follows behind him at a quick walking pace.

His boots clang loudly on each metal step above, hers echoing below, as they both follow the tight little spiral around and around up the sixty-something feet to the tip of the hundred-year-old fire tower.

Vera finds him at the top, gripping the railing with both hands, looking east. A satisfied smile on his face.

He was right, they can see for miles. Rolling hills and cradled valleys are dotted with miniature white buildings. The stretches of pines are jagged and emerald, the rest of the trees and meadows a hazy mix of brown and yellow and green. A pack of cumulus clouds glides slowly west across the expanse of the blue sky toward the Hudson River. There are no cooking fires in sight anymore, and nearly all the farmland and grazing pastures have reforested, but this is the place. Home.

"It's something, right?" Lopez asks her quietly with palpable reverence. She nods in agreement, not trusting her voice to hold. Lopez extends his hand, palm up. "Gimme your phone."

"Why?"

"So we can take a pic."

Vera shakes her head, says she doesn't have a smartphone, besides she doesn't like having her picture taken.

"Aw man, you're like Jenny. She *hates* when people take her picture." Lopez rummages in the cargo pockets of his uniform pants, pulls out his own, and hands it to Vera. "Take one of me then." He leans against the railing with extravagant, put-upon casualness, and smiles. Through his gritted teeth he says, ventriloquist style, "Just try not to capture the total terror in my eyes!"

Vera takes the picture and as soon as Lopez hears the digital click he bolts up to look. She hands it over and watches him as he squints and zooms in on his own face.

"Nailed it. Jenny's gonna be proud." He returns the phone to his pocket and looks out once again at the bright expanse around them. "All right, I think that's enough conquering-my-fears for today. See you down there? We've got two more lean-tos and the campground to check. I'll show you this other spot where people are always trying to set up tents too close to the trail for regulation."

Vera nods, and he clangs back down the stairs, the tower jolting slightly with each of his steps.

She crosses the small deck, facing south now, and considers the landscape once again. So lush compared to the desert, even in this partial, springtime state. Dense, fecund. A warm wind picks up and ruffles the stray hairs that have escaped her braid. She pulls her brimmed, uniform hat more firmly onto her head so it won't fly off, looks down to the clearing below where Lopez is now sitting on top of a picnic table. She considers how badly it would hurt to jump. She hasn't done something that extravagant in a while, the world more filled with witnesses than ever before. That, or maybe she's grown weak, soft, accustomed to her razors and her pills. Warm, gentle deaths. A shudder runs up her spine. She steps away from the railing and hurries down the stairs.

Back on the trail with Lopez, Vera stops at a spring to refill her water bottle. She squats, cups her hands into the current, and drinks.

"I wouldn't do that any lower down the mountain unless you want giardia," he warns.

Water has been Vera and Eli's theory for a while now. Some literal fountain of youth in a natural spring. It's what all the old stories speak of—floods and violet-scented waters that bestow eternal health and youth. Maybe that night they all went swimming by the falls and the moon was full? It's one of the only times they can think of where the three of them—Vera, Eli, and Ma—were somewhere all together without Pa or Lotte doing anything out of the ordinary.

"Giardia's a nasty one," Vera agrees, even though she's immune to waterborne diseases. All diseases in fact.

Imagine if this is the source, she thinks to herself as she fills her bottle from the spring. Because that's her plan, in as much as she has one: to re-create whatever phenomena did this to her and, in doing so, reverse her condition. To hunt for the fountain and drink from it again. A flimsy theory perhaps. But it's one of the least ridiculous she's entertained over the years, and it has taken ahold of her with a conviction of its own. She needs to start *somewhere*. This needs to end.

*

After work, Vera finds a note from Cate slid under the front door inviting her over that evening for drinks on the back patio. She's foggy and exhausted, hasn't slept through the night in months, and a day of small talk with Lopez has left her almost fully drained, but she knows she should accept. Besides, she wants to go inside her house.

"Here she is!" Her landlord bolts up from her chair as she spots Vera walking around the side of the building, a bundle of backyard-foraged daffodils in her hands. "I can't believe we haven't had you over until now, we've just been so busy!"

Cate takes the flowers, thanking her profusely, and ushers Vera to a flimsy lawn chair on the other side of the small, rusted firepit under a string of lights. Vera sits. Cate asks if she's chilly, if she minds being outside.

"The second it gets above fifty degrees we start acting like it's summer. All winter we're cooped up in that damn house." Cate gestures behind herself to the house in question.

"I'm fine, this is great," Vera says as she looks at her childhood home somewhat warily, aware now that any facade of having kept her promise to Eli and Ma has vanished entirely.

The back door opens and she almost expects to see one of them emerge, but it's Cate's husband, Brian, wearing athletic shorts and a T-shirt, a baseball hat over his short, sandy hair. He's holding a bottle of rosé.

"What's up," he says to Vera, not quite a question, as he pours three full glasses.

"How's settling in going? I remember when we first moved here I was like, *Dear god, what have we done?*" Cate cups her own pink cheeks dramatically. "It was such a change of pace from the city."

"New York City?" Vera asks, redirecting the conversation as she takes a sip of the cold wine. It's good. Refreshingly tart with a smooth, peachy finish. People have no idea how much better their booze options are today than ever before. The barrels of absolute swill Vera has drunk over her lifetimes, and all to chase a high that never lasts more than a few minutes, the chemistry of her body righting itself too quickly.

Cate nods. "Brooklyn," she clarifies. It was fun for the first five years, but after a while they realized they weren't taking advantage of everything the city supposedly has to offer—galleries, restaurants, shows. Everything was too expensive, and they were so burned-out from their office jobs. "It's shameful how many nights we spent on the couch shoveling takeout into our faces with the TV on. In New York City!" Cate rolls her eyes at her old self, though Vera knows for a fact they still watch at least one hour if not two of television every night. She can see the electronic glow of it from the cottage. Sometimes Brian comes down in the middle of the night and watches more. A fellow insomniac of sorts.

"How'd you find the place?" Vera asks, nodding toward her house. She'll ask to use the bathroom after this glass of wine, that's how she'll get in.

"It's been in Brian's family for generations," Cate says triumphantly.

"More like two generations," Brian says.

"Three! You, your parents, your grandparents—"

"My parents never lived—"

"His grandparents left it to him." Cate turns to Vera to explain. "Totally furnished. Some of it was the most awful old lady stuff, no offense, Bubby!" She raises her head to the sky, hands pressed in prayer.

"The bones of it are great though, lots of character. But let's just say it was in dire need of an update."

"Do you know much about the history of it before them?" Vera asks, as casually as she can manage. She's embarrassed how her heart bucks at the question.

"I think my grandparents told me it was built in 1805," Brian says.

Vera resists the urge to correct him and restore the first five years of her life.

"Probably Dutch people," Cate adds. "There were a lot of Dutch people in the Catskills back in the day. I think that's why I thought your name sounded familiar. There's a million Van Something or Other roads around here."

Vera nods, holding her face as neutrally as she can, though she feels a flush of nervous color rising in her cheeks. *I'm a tenant interested in local history, nothing unusual about that*, she reminds herself. There's no reason for Cate or Brian to suspect the truth when the truth itself is so outrageous.

"We have some news," Cate says suddenly, her jovial tone changing to a more nervous pitch. Vera's mind quickly combs over the announcements that usually follow this kind of introduction. A wedding? No. A baby? Maybe. A move? It seems too soon to evict her, she only arrived last month.

Cate looks to her husband, as if asking him if he'd like to be the one to tell. He nods his head back at her, *You do it*.

"I hope you aren't going to be mad," Cate begins, setting down her wineglass and lacing her fingers together. Vera takes another sip from her own glass. "We never thought we were going to do something like this when we drew up the lease in March, everything's been moving so fast and we'll *totally* understand if you want to break the lease and move out once things get going because it might—"

"We're opening a cidery," Brian interrupts, bringing all of them to the point.

"We're opening a cidery!" Cate parrots with much more enthusiasm. "God, it sounds so weird to say. *We're opening a cidery*. Like a brewery! But cider instead of beer."

"Here?" Vera asks, still trying to parse what precisely this news has to do with her living in the cottage.

"In the old barn," Cate says, gesturing to the 213-year-old structure still standing in the meadow a couple hundred feet away, its red paint peeling off to reveal the bare, battered planks beneath. It used to be whitewashed every spring. Vera wonders if the same hand-hewn hemlock beams still hold up the roof, if the swallows still nest in the center rafter each thaw. She wonders if it smells the same—dry wood and hay and animal dung.

As Vera gazes at the barn, Cate continues to explain how she and Brian didn't know what they were going to do when they moved up here last year after inheriting the house. How the remote freelance work has been OK money but is honestly kind of boring and they want to get their hands dirty, really build something, be a part of the community. They considered reopening the old general store next door and made an offer but that fell through and so, with the wind let out of their sails, they looked around at all their apple trees and the barn—

"And it all came together in an epiphany, like bang! Let's open a cidery right here in this place we already own!"

"Congratulations," Vera says, lifting her glass.

"You're not mad?" Cate asks, genuine surprise in her dark brown eyes.

"Why would I be mad?"

Cate says the construction might be loud, and once it's open people are going to be coming and going.

"That won't be for at least a year, babe, probably more like a year and a half," Brian interjects, pouring himself another glass, his first apparently already downed.

"I'm hoping I won't be here longer than a year anyway," Vera says, and it's true. God she hopes it won't take that long to find what she's looking for. Is desperate about it, really. Time has been different for her than it is for everyone else for a while now, but ever since the incident it's become unbearable. The years used to rush by like days, a rapid current. Now the hours are days, the minutes—alone, at night, in the dark—are months, *years*. She knows she will break if she has to continue on like this.

No, she knows she is already broken. That there is no way she can go on like this, forever.

Vera throws back the rest of her wine without tasting it. Wordlessly, Brian refills her glass, too.

"Oh my god, I'm so relieved!" Cate says and launches herself at Vera, covering her in an awkward but enthusiastic crouched hug. The tightness of it makes Vera's chest seize. She pushes her way out of it, spilling some of Cate's wine down her own back in the process, splashing some of her glass onto the patio, too.

"I'm sorry—"

"I'm so sorry! I—here—let me—"

Vera stands. They shake the rosé off their hands.

"Is there a bathroom I—"

"No, let me get you a towel, don't move. Brian?" And he's off, inside, the door already closing behind him.

"I'm sorry, I'm a hugger. And a klutz!" Cate holds her dripping hands in front of her. "I'm just so glad you're down with this whole thing. I would feel so bad if you moved out here only to—"

Vera cuts Cate off and insists she doesn't mind. "I don't care about the noise. I've worked in construction before."

"OMG, can we hire you? I'm joking, I know you already have a *much* cooler job than helping us turn that ancient tinderbox into a taproom."

Vera considers the badly veiled ask and surprises herself with the fact that she is imagining what it would be like to help Cate restore Pa's barn. That some part of her is in fact drawn to the idea. To do it for Pa. But no, that's not why she came here.

Brian returns with two checkered kitchen towels. Vera and Cate wipe their hands and set the towels on the side table, then all three of them look out into the meadow toward the barn and the mountains. The grass is bright green down here in the valley, still short enough to not yet need a mow. A few yellow bursts of dandelions dot the expanse. The maples are partially leaved, and the ashes, mulberries, and apple trees have tiny buds. The whole place feels on the cusp, waiting to explode into blossom and greenery. This time of year was always such a relief, even if it meant the hard work of the fields was upon them once again. The smell of thawed soil. It was a triumph. Another year survived.

An airplane moans above them. The first Vera's ever seen over the valley. She watches its white contrail streak the sky.

"I'm so glad we're doing the cidery instead of the general store," Cate says dreamily, breaking the silence, and Brian grunts in agreement. "Such a blessing in disguise that we got outbid by those Fountain of Eternal Youth idiots."

Vera's glass of wine stops midway to her mouth. "Fountain of?"

"Fountain of Eternal Youth LLC," Cate says and rolls her eyes then brushes something invisible off her pants. "Must be a cult."

"Promising eternal youth?" Brian scoffs. "Who would ever buy into that?"

Vera sets down her glass of wine. Her eyes flick toward the old general store to their right then back to the barn.

She suddenly feels very exposed.

"I should get going."

"Already?"

"Early start tomorrow."

She stands up. They say their goodbyes, they hug, they agree this was fun they should do it again. Then Vera forces herself to slowly walk back to her cottage even though everything in her body is screaming *run*.

3

May 2014

Unlike her brother, Vera doesn't enjoy parties. But she accepts the invite to Stan's annual Memorial Day bash that weekend via Cate because there are things Vera needs to know and she's come against the edge of her own inadequate, amateur detective skills. Over the past few days, she's gleaned nothing about Fountain of Eternal Youth LLC beyond the fact that it's registered to the address of an office park in Palo Alto, California. No names of members, no statement of purpose. No hint of what on earth they want with this corner of the Catskills. Whether it might in fact be the very same thing Vera is seeking. She feels hunted and a little frantic. She needs to know more. Surely other people in town are also curious and better at googling than she is.

"So you're the mysterious ranger!" a neighbor says, the seventh or eighth time she's heard something of the like since arriving at the party twenty minutes ago.

"That's me," she answers again. This neighbor introduces himself as Sam, that's his wife, Eliza, across the way in the blue dress. Just about everyone at the party appears to be in their fifties or sixties and white—this is the whitest place Vera has lived in ages. She recognizes a few faces from her drives down The Road. The ones who spend their time outside gardening, mowing, sorting wood, generally fussing about with their property.

"We're weekenders," says Sam, like it's a confession he wishes to have out of the way. He smooths the front of his green T-shirt, which is tucked into belted jeans. "But we're hoping to move up here full-time, that's the dream right? Four more years until I retire. D'you have a retirement package with the Parks? Government jobs are great that way."

"Is this the ranger?" asks another fifty-something woman in a purple dress as she appears next to Sam. "You're so cute! Look at you!"

Vera feels herself balking at the effusive attention. She regrets having made the effort to put on her one nice blouse. Wishes she were in her usual jeans and T-shirt instead. Her derringer is warm against the skin of her lower back, tucked into her pants as it almost always is these days, even though she knows it's reckless. Still it's a small, old comfort, and she hasn't been able to bring herself to stop since she picked it back up a couple months ago. She holds out her hand, introduces herself.

"And I'm Wanda. So much young blood on The Road now!" Wanda coos in what Vera guesses is a Queens or Long Island accent.

"The Road?" Vera asks.

"That's what we call it," explains Sam.

Vera smiles at the coincidence, at the possibility that the simple nickname has been passed down this long.

Wanda says she still calls it "the block" by accident sometimes, once a city girl always a city girl. She laughs at her own joke. "You live with Cate and Brian?"

"In their rental cottage," Sam answers for her.

"I'm so excited for the cider place—the cider—" Wanda scrunches her face in puzzlement as she tries to find the proper word. "It's not a brewery."

"Cidery," say Sam and Vera at the same time.

"My daughter-in-law is gluten-free, she's going to love it. Do you think—"

Sam and Wanda continue to fawn over the prospect of having a cidery on The Road. A place to run into people that isn't the post office, a bar less than a thirty-minute drive away, maybe food or live music on the weekends. They're hoping for a fireplace, too, or at the very least an outdoor firepit for winter nights. Wanda's husband, Bill, built one with fireproof bricks, and they use it all the time, just love it.

"I heard someone bought the old general store next door to where the cidery will be," Vera says, and lets it dangle.

"Yeah. Barbara is selling to them, too." Wanda sighs.

"Barbara went for it?" Sam asks.

"Sorry, they're buying more than the old store?" Vera says. A high-pitched ring sounds in her ears.

Wanda opens her mouth to say something but is interrupted by the entrance of another neighbor, gleeful hugs and compliments exchanged. Vera is introduced once more and the talk turns to where the arrivals should set down the guacamole they brought, if someone else in particular is already here.

The moment to ask more has passed.

Reluctantly, Vera slips off. She keeps her eyes down as she nudges her way through the crowd to the sunny back deck, where a bucket of bottles are sweating on ice next to a tray of stemless wineglasses and a partially demolished plate of crudités. Two clean-shaven men are on the other side of the patio enjoying themselves as they argue about whether or not Republicans will take the Senate in the fall. Vera's never voted, mostly because up until recently it had been a long time since she legally existed. But really she finds it hard to get excited about a bunch of old white men in suits making promises they never seem to keep.

She lifts a green bottle from the ice and sets it back down, lifts another. She pours herself a tester sip and feels a hand on her shoulder.

"You must be the ranger," says the voice as she turns to see a trim Asian man in his late forties. He's dressed like everyone in town, but the cut of his plaid shirt is slim and his jeans are distressed in such a manner that say money more than manual labor. His skin is flawless.

"You're Stan."

"Guilty as charged," says the host, and his very white smile widens—oh the improvements in dental hygiene Vera has seen over her lifetimes. He takes his hand off her shoulder and says it's Riesling, quite dry, she'll like it. Vera pours herself a cupful then takes a sip as Stan watches.

"Good right?"

"It is," she says, not to please him but because it is. He asks if she likes wine or knows much about it. "My brother's a bit of a sommelier. I've learned a thing or two from him."

"I used to be in finance so wine came with the territory. Much like golf, unfortunately."

"You're here full-time now?" Vera asks, even though Cate has already told her that he is.

"Yes, I made the move after nine-eleven. Couldn't stomach any of it after that." Stan pauses, his eyes glazing slightly. "Built the garden, got the horse." He lifts his chin in the direction of the impeccably maintained barn next to the pond.

"Your place is beautiful, thank you for inviting me," Vera says gently.

"Ah! You found each other!" Cate calls from the doorway. She walks over and drapes an arm around Vera's shoulder, a full head taller, enveloping her in perfume and friendly affection. If friendship is what this can be called so soon, though Vera has interacted with Cate in some form every day since she was invited over for that first backyard drink. On Wednesday a knock to see if she needed anything from town. On Thursday an offer to join them for tacos at Paco's Cantina. And on Friday a drop-off of three Catskills history books Cate thought Vera might be interested in. It's an affection that's appeared suddenly and fully formed, as if it's always existed and Cate has simply been waiting for Vera to come around and open the door to it.

"I hope he's not torturing you already, is he? Are you? I told you to be gentle with her! This group can come on a little strong."

"Whatever do you mean?" Stan asks batting his eyelashes with cartoonish naiveté, playfulness having returned to his demeanor.

"Oh please, you were all practically vampires for me and Brian when we first arrived," Cate scoffs and takes Vera's cup out of her hand to have a sip. "Is this the Riesling you had the other weekend? It's good. We might serve a red and a white at the cidery, too, I'm not sure yet." Stan asks when everyone is going to get to try their cider. Cate laughs and returns the cup to Vera, says he'll have to talk to Brian about it, that's his job.

"You're not going to make the cider with him?" Vera asks. She pictures her own family gathering apples, taking turns at the press, sealing the bottles. It was festive and less grueling than farmwork but grueling nonetheless. A very physical endeavor. There must be more mechanized and streamlined production techniques available these days, but it'll never be anything more than a tiny, backyard operation if Brian attempts it alone. Now that Vera thinks about it more, even two people hardly seem enough for the scale Cate has been describing to her. A full tasting room in the barn with a patio, multiple draft lines, bottles and cans distributed wholesale to bars and restaurants in the area and down in New York City, reserve bottles aged in oak and bourbon barrels—

"Of course I'll help! It's just the actual cider is his baby. He could give a crap about the tables or the taproom or whatever, but you know he's going to personally fondle every apple that goes into it. You've seen what a nerd he is about his home brewing."

"I was about to open one of his saisons," Stan says, and he reaches for an unmarked brown bottle from the ice bucket. Cate takes her arm off Vera's shoulder, steps up to the little bar, and pours herself a cup of white wine as they continue to chat about the likely division of labor at the cidery, the possibility of employees once the operation is underway, what the timeline for pressing and opening could be. A few other partygoers join them and the merry little group crowds around the bar and the appetizers, the news, and the newcomer.

"This place is heaven," a man named Phil announces, looking off the deck into the mountains, and they all agree by touching drinks.

"It's a special valley," Eliza chimes in. "It's the east-west axis, very unusual."

"Sunshine all day," says a guy named Pete.

"Can't find another place like it," Wanda adds.

"Actually, Ojai is another east-west valley—"

"And that's why I sure as shit am *not* selling to some Fountain of Immortal—"

"Of *Eternal*—"

"Of *Eternal* Youth, whatever the hell they're called," Phil concludes.

Vera lowers her drink, her attention refocusing tightly.

"They offered to buy you out, too?" Stan asks Phil.

"No, but I wouldn't bite."

"I would never either," Cate insists.

"Wanda mentioned someone named Barbara Johnson sold to them, too," Vera says, hoping her voice doesn't betray the deep level of her interest. "Where is her house?"

"Right next door to the general store, on the other side." Eliza leans in and lowers her voice to a stage whisper. "Apparently they offered her double the appraised value."

A few people gasp. Someone mumbles, "Good for her."

"Brian thinks they're a cult," Cate tells the small crowd. The song inside changes to a bass-heavy dance number. Someone whoops with delight. "You don't actually think they're a cult, right?"

"OK, I didn't want to fan the flames of rampant speculation today," Stan says, even though it's clear he's about to revel in doing exactly that. A few people move in closer. "But I had an old friend do some digging and the long and short of it is, Matthew Barbery is behind it."

At this, everyone within earshot gasps. Everyone except Vera.

"Who's that?" she asks, hoping her cultural ignorance won't be noteworthy. There is simply too much to keep up with these days, new generations of celebrities constantly popping up like weeds.

Everyone tries to explain to her at once. The billionaire, no multi-millionaire. He just sold that app. He's brilliant, no, just another tech bro who got lucky. He's not even forty!

"The LLC itself is registered to a nobody, some woman named Lydia Kirke," Stan continues firmly and the other voices die down. Vera thinks the name might sound familiar but can't pinpoint it.

"Who is she?" Wanda asks.

"A nobody, that's the point, it's a shell, I don't know why. But I have it on good authority that she's working for Matthew Barbery. Don't ask me how I know, I swore on my life I wouldn't tell." Stan holds his hands in the air like it's a stickup.

"How do you know?" Phil asks anyway and Wanda swats his shoulder.

Figuring she's gathered as much information as she's going to get from this crowd, Vera tries to leave the party a few minutes later, but Stan and Cate will hear nothing of it.

"We haven't even put the meat on the grill yet!" Stan says. "Let me show you the barn. I'll introduce you to the love of my life."

"He means his horse," Cate clarifies.

"Buttercup is hardly just a horse! Vera, have you ever been in love?" he asks as they follow him out the side door into a little vegetable garden. Smoke from the double grill on the deck wafts across the breeze.

"Yes," Vera answers and it comes out tight and clipped. Jacob's face rises to the forefront of her mind. Jacob's hands—

She pushes the vision away. She needs to find out more about whoever Matthew Barbery and Lydia Kirke are right now! She doesn't need to be swooning over someone long gone, or looking at a vanity project horse. She suddenly feels like she's wasting time, it seeping rapidly, irreversibly, through her fingers. It's only been three weeks since she arrived but still, she has nothing to show for it.

"Oh you're too young to be heartbroken!" Stan says, misunderstanding her grimace. "You'll find love again, I promise you will."

A movement behind the barn catches Vera's eye but not in time for her to make sense of it. A raccoon probably, or a rabbit. Maybe nothing. She can no longer trust her senses. Something is *happening* and she needs to wake up and pay attention. She needs to—

Call her brother?

They haven't spoken since the desert. And she can't tell him she came home. But maybe she could tell him about the LLC some other way. He'd want to know, wouldn't he? It could all mean nothing, but then again—

"Are you one hundred percent certain it's Matthew Barbery who's behind the cult?" Cate asks Stan, linking arms with him at the elbows. "I don't get it. What would someone like him want with this town?"

"Darling," he says, squeezing her closer as they continue across the grass. "If there's anything I learned from Wall Street it's this: extremely wealthy people are, quite frankly, extremely bizarre." Maybe it's a tax dodge, he speculates. Or maybe the Lydia woman is actually just a mistress who likes to ski. Maybe he lost a bet. Stan doesn't have the same sway he used to, so all he knows is Barbery is involved somehow. "If it makes you feel better though, I sincerely doubt it's a cult, given that the buildings are *right* on The Road. The other thing wealthy people will always pay out the nose for is privacy and there's—"

A startled neigh from inside the barn abruptly silences him.

"What was that?" Cate asks.

They stop walking and strain their ears over the sounds of the party drifting out from the house.

There it is, again, louder now.

Vera is the first to take off running to the barn. Stan follows.

A moment later, at the barn door, they hear the thuds of the horse's flank banging against the stall.

"She's cornered," Vera says.

Stan slides open the heavy door as quickly as he can. It rumbles along the steel track loudly. The contrast of the summery afternoon with the dim darkness inside the barn makes it impossible to see what's going on at first, everything a hazy gray as Vera's eyes try to adjust.

"Buttercup, I'm here! What's wrong, baby?" Stan calls as he jogs toward a stall at the end.

Vera feels it on the back of her neck before she hears it—a growl that stops them both right where they are.

"Don't move, Stan," Vera orders, her pistol out now. She takes a low and slow step forward, releases the safety.

The creature growls again and Buttercup kicks at the stall, her white mane catching the light from the window behind her, dust and hay particles swirling.

"It's OK, girl," Stan says softly from where he's frozen. Buttercup bucks and whinnies again at the danger she knows is near.

"What's going on?" Cate asks from the doorway behind them, having caught up.

"Stay back," Vera says without taking her eyes off the beast she can finally see.

There used to be wolves in the valley. Vera's family built fires to keep them at bay in the early years, never walked alone at night unarmed. Eventually the wolves were pushed north and west. There are coyotes nowadays. But they almost never come out during the day.

Unless they're sick.

Vera sees its eyes glint yellow. Its fur is matted, mangey.

"Stan, without turning around, I need you to get behind me."

Stan obeys, slowly backing his way to Vera whose heartbeat now pulses in her ears. She's not worried for her own safety. But Stan, Cate, Buttercup. There's nothing less predictable than a rabid animal.

"Is that a *gun*?" Cate whispers.

The creature growls again and takes a listing step to the side. Teeth bared, foam at the corners of its mouth.

"Buttercup is safe as long as she stays in her stall," Vera says quietly, her pistol following the ill creature's erratic movements as it paces along the row of doors. "I need you two to back away, get outside the barn. I'm going to shoot it once it—"

But before Vera can finish her sentence the beast lunges for Buttercup's door. There's an explosion of splinters, whinnies, and snarls as the frightened horse smashes through the wooden door. Vera hears Stan and Cate both scream behind her.

She doesn't have a clean shot in the chaos.

"Run!" Vera cries as she does the same, back out into the blinding daylight, the pounding of panicked hooves at her heels.

In her mind she sees Jacob again. His grin the first time she succeeded after those weeks of trying, the hours upon hours spent in the dusty corral together. *I knew you could do it*, he'd told her, then kissed her square on the mouth, changing everything.

Vera shoves the pistol into her pants as she sprints across the meadow. It's been so long—more than one hundred years—but some things never leave your body. Some loves, some miseries, some very particular skills. She feels the wind of the mare approaching behind her as she continues to run. She turns and—

Vera jumps.

The split second she's airborne an eternity.

Then her hands make contact with Buttercup's neck and she holds mightily, pulls herself up and over, swift and smooth, the warm muscle of the galloping horse beneath her now. Time releases again, hooves pounding. She grips Buttercup's flanks with her thighs, raising her hips with the movement. She takes out her pistol and whips around. *Where did it go?*

It's running fast, charging straight for them, well past Cate and Stan and the barn. Vera aims, a decent shot. But Buttercup spots the crowd spilling out of the house and bucks. Vera grabs her mane with one hand and holds on fiercely as she's tipped back, the snarling beast gaining on them, closer. Vera can feel Buttercup about to come down on her front hooves again, a certain stillness, like being at the very top of a Ferris wheel. She steadies her other hand out, trains it on the sprinting coyote, takes aim between its eyes, and pulls the trigger.

The shot rings out precisely across the valley. Someone screams.

*

The party rages. The shock turns into glee, the incident quickly ballooning into a tall tale right here among everyone who saw, facts growing fanciful and embellished as they always do. Vera knows the story will continue to swell. That this tale will stick to her now. It's exactly the kind of thing that once made Ma nervous, causing such a notable splash. Exactly the kind of thing that once made Eli proud, or Jacob.

No one cares about Fountain of Eternal Youth LLC anymore tonight.

Vera stays long enough to eat a veggie burger and accept some adulation. She toasts everyone with a beer she never finishes. Tells them all she grew up riding, mostly out west, yes. No one asks her why she had a gun.

By the end of the evening she's been invited to Wanda and Bill's for s'mores next Friday, to Sam and Eliza's thirtieth wedding anniversary at the end of the month, and to Pete and Judy's third annual barn party in August where there'll be line dancing and a proper Catskills caller. To Dorothy and Phil's cabin for a dip in their swimming hole, to Nancy's for martinis on her spectacular deck, she has the best view on The Road everyone insists, she really does, and to Stan's for "anything ever" as he insisted emphatically several times, he's so grateful.

Before she leaves, Vera makes sure Buttercup is settled in her new stall. She's relieved to find the mare unafraid of her touch. Then she loads the dead coyote into her trunk—everyone assuming she's operating under some forest ranger protocol—and drives off in the twilight as they cheer for her from the deck like she's won a championship game or an election.

Back home, in the meadow behind the cottage, under the sliver of a crescent moon, she digs a hole as deep as she is tall. The physical labor of it blunts the scattered, frantic tenor of her mind, adrenaline still sending waves of aftershock through her eternally unharmed body.

She remembers watching Eli dig Pa's grave, hardly a hundred feet from here, the stone marker now lost to weather, erosion, time. How Eli sweat through his shirt entirely, wouldn't accept any help. How she climbed up a scraggly, nearby apple tree and waited because her brother might change his mind and let her dig, too, because she couldn't bear waiting in the house with Ma and Lotte. She remembers thinking of her own death then, wondering if she, too, would be buried in this meadow. How much the idea scared her at the time. How much she longs for it now.

There is always Plan B, she thinks as her shovel hits another rock. Although, even after nearly two hundred years of contemplation, it remains more of a question than an answer.

See, so far they have found no limit to what their bodies can recover from—deprivations, wounds, amputations. Not only do they not age, they are truly miraculous healers. Yet through all the injuries there has always been some percentage of their bodies that stayed intact enough to remain the home of their soul, their consciousness, whatever word one might choose for the sentience that is attached to their bodies.

But what if they become so thoroughly exploded, so minutely divided, that there are thousands of pieces of them? Millions? What would regrow then? To what pieces would their souls hold on?

Could the answer be *nothing*?

So far it has never felt worth the risk to any of them. And the fear—

beyond the pain of the explosion itself—is that the pain will be eternal. A scalding thrum felt as not a person, but as millions of unconnected pieces, forever and absolutely ever. A never-ending cry heard by no one.

A terrifying possibility, but still more theoretical than anything. Until the desert. It was hardly a taste, but.

No, Vera tells herself. There are other options before Plan B. She will find the source. That will be the answer. It has to be.

Vera has no words for the coyote as she covers it with the dirt and rock she only just dug up. She has no particular love for it either. It was sick and it needed to die.

It was lucky.

4

June 2014

In principle the Parks Department is pleased by the growing popularity of the Preserve. These lands are public so that they can be enjoyed by everyone. However, the summer litter at the swimming holes in particular is becoming a problem of a magnitude never experienced in the Catskills before. And people, like Captain Newsman, are not happy about it. There's talk of fining overflow cars illegally parked, organizing trash pickup. Maybe even limiting the number of visitors with ticketed entrance times.

Everyone is startled when Newsman clicks to the next slide of his presentation—side-by-side photographs of the Peekamoose Blue Hole on Memorial Day last year versus last weekend. Food wrappers, beer cans, soda bottles, plastic shopping bags, even a dirty diaper, all strewn across rocks and grass and propped up against trees in overflowing piles, as if that were better. The world's litter is becoming more colorful and long-lasting and unfortunately that second piece is the biggest problem. Vera looks at the images and considers not for the first time that she will be the only one in the room to outlast it all. To be buried in a world of it. It's hard to convince herself that any of her own actions—her pescatarianism, her obsessive reusing and recycling, her edible gardens, her mending—will amount to anything against all *this*.

"Trail logs have shown us that most visitors are coming from New York City and—"

"It's those people," interrupts Ranger O'Donnell, and everyone turns their heads his way in unison. Vera feels Lopez steel himself beside her, but Captain Newsman goes on before anyone else can continue, announcing that there's going to be a volunteer-based cleanup effort supervised by the Catskill Interpretive Center. That they are going to start with the Blue Hole this week.

They move on to review the three rescue operations that took place since their last meeting—all minor lower-body injuries on trails close to parking lots—then the repairs scheduled for a portion of the Devil's Path, parking lot expansion petitions from the towns of Lexington and Big Indian. They're assigned their rounds for the next month, and finally there's a reminder that everyone needs to file their overtime online by 11:59 p.m. on Wednesdays or else the paperwork is a nightmare for Linda in HR, then they're free.

Vera catches up with Lopez in the parking lot as he lights a cigarette by his truck.

"Don't tell the wife," he says, clicking the lighter twice before it catches. The craving for nicotine rises in Vera's body and makes her veins acute with anticipation even though she quit ages ago, back when it seemed like more people smoked than not. It felt unfair for her to share a vice with those who could actually die from it.

"How is—Jenny, right?" Vera asks. Lopez smiles as he exhales a plume of smoke into the air over his shoulder away from her.

"She's dying to meet you. Thinks I'm lying about there being a girl on the force. Doesn't help that you don't have Facebook or anything." He takes another drag and Vera pulls her sunglasses out of her shirt pocket, puts them on. She can tell by the way he holds the cigarette, how he savors the inhale and expertly redirects the exhale, that this is an old habit of his. "What'd you do for the holiday on your day off? You hit up any barbecues?"

"I went to a party," she answers.

"Good for you. You're too young to not be out partying with friends. How old are you anyway?"

"O'Donnell seems like a piece of work," Vera says instead, steering them to the safety of a shared adversary.

"The guy acts like it's the freaking fifties." Lopez blows another stream of smoke out his nostrils. "I swear to god, if he brings up the border with Mexico around me one more time—"

"You said you're from Newburgh, right?"

"Yes! *And* my mom *and* my dad. Not to mention my grandparents are actually Dominican, German, and Italian but, whatever, forget him—you hear Lieutenant Rogers is transferring?"

Vera shakes her head no. She isn't sure which one Rogers is. The hierarchy spreads high and wide across the region and administrative duties are her least favorite part of the job, so she spends as little time as possible in the office. Lopez pulls another drag and the smoke comes out with his words as he explains that the lieutenant's transfer means there'll be some reshuffling, maybe a promotion for someone.

"You trying for a promotion, Ranger?"

"Well—" He looks over his shoulder to the sterile building behind them and the empty lot. "I'm not supposed to tell anyone yet, but you seem like someone with secrets so—"

Before Vera can balk at the accusation Lopez corrects himself quickly.

"Like someone who's *good* with secrets! Sorry, I—Jenny's pregnant!"

Vera's face flushes at the accidental accusation. But she knows Lopez will assume any emotional reaction from her is the normal, delighted one of a young woman hearing news of a welcomed pregnancy.

"Congratulations!" she says and is suddenly, unexpectedly, enveloped in a hug.

"I'm so freaking excited! I've always wanted to be a dad," he says into the top of her head and squeezes her harder. Vera feels her body involuntarily stiffen and her windpipe begin to close. The panic, always so near the surface now.

Lopez releases her with a laugh. She takes in a lungful of air, looks to the open sky. She's OK, she's OK.

"I really shouldn't have told you. I haven't even told my mom yet!"

Vera smooths her hair and aims to be casual. She deadpans, "Well, I'm someone with a lot of secrets so you can trust me."

"I'm sorry! That was awkward. You know what I meant, right?"

She plucks the cigarette out of his fingers, takes a long drag, then drops it on the ground between them, and puts it out with her boot. She picks up the extinguished butt and hands it back to him.

"You should quit for real this time, Dad."

*

After her shift, Vera spends the rest of the day in her small garden, then in the woods, collecting more water samples from nearby springs.

In the five weeks since she's arrived, she's tried twenty-two sources her family might have drunk from once upon a time then ended herself after each. But her body continues to rebound. The frustration and despair rising with every fresh failure.

Vera is not convinced this is the most scientifically sound path forward but cannot come up with a better approach either. So, she continues this way.

New samples tucked into her bag, she follows a trickling tributary down the mountainside to where it joins the stream, then pulls out her collapsable fishing rod. The last of the day's sun warms her bare shoulders as the warblers and kingfishers chitter above her. She's hardly three miles from where the creek's headwaters flow out of the land, which means down here the water is always cold, just the way these hardy little brook trout like it.

She walks upstream slowly, stepping carefully so as to not disturb the fish she is stalking or slip on the stones. When she wears waders she feels disconnected and clumsy. Whenever she can, she fishes like this, like she used to—barefoot, toes gripping the rocks and river weeds. After so many years out west, she'd almost forgotten the pleasure of fishing tight little feeder creeks like this one. Hardly any space to back-cast, but an endless array of small eddies tucked under rocks. The shape of the stream has shifted some, but in spirit, in experience, it's exactly like it used to be.

Vera catches about a dozen brook trout and releases them all. The sun is nearly behind the mountains now. She tells herself one more hole then she'll call it a day.

Three holes later, she catches an absolute beauty. Gold and dark green—the exact shade of the shadowy pools around her—with a yellow underbelly, orange-tipped fins, and cadmium red dots surrounded in ghostly blue halos. She has the impulse to show it to Pa and Eli. Even looks up as if either of them might actually be on the water with her.

Swiftly, she is knocked back with sadness, then, after a moment, suffused with the anger and impatience that are her new, near constant companions. She releases the fish gently then telescopes her rod back down, rough.

Usually she waits to try her samples until she's home, but Vera feels herself boiling and craves release. Feels the rash desire to drink one now and finish herself right here on the creek.

She looks around. Fill her pockets with rocks? Take a tumble off a boulder? She begins to move again, her legs splashing through the current, no more care about spooking the fish. She rounds a bend and spots a figure a hundred feet upstream. Instinctually she crouches into the greenery behind her. She looks again.

Jacob?

Of course not. It's just another brown-haired man. Similar stature, similar strong build. He's fishing, changing out his fly, too focused on the task at hand to notice her yet. Vera stands to retreat, admonishing herself for even considering doing this here—did she not learn her lesson that first day with Janet?

She peers at the man again.

It's uncanny. The bridge of his nose, the jut of his jaw, the way his hair falls—

He looks up swiftly, like a deer who's heard a snap of a branch in the woods. Then he turns and sees her. His face softens.

"Hi," he says, one hand up in an open wave.

Vera waves back but doesn't say anything. Instead, she spins around and walks in the other direction as quickly as she can across the slippery rocks, back around the bend, out of sight.

Three years together in Wyoming at the turn of the century, both of them ranch hands who smelled like dust and hay and the soft musk of the creatures they tended. She loved Jacob. He loved her. She was with him for her hundredth birthday. Bourbon and pie and sex on a scratchy wool blanket under the kind of Milky Way you don't see much anymore.

He talked about their future together incessantly. The stretch of land they'd one day buy for themselves, the house they'd build together. Their own ranch, their own horses. The mountains, the meadows, the enormous blue sky. Every day for just the two of them. She was dreading her family's inevitable exit—Jacob's sharp grief if she staged her own death, a longer soupy sadness if she disappeared. Vera wished she were a vampire, endowed with the ability to turn another into her kind. She would have done it, as cruel as it would have been, that's how much she loved him. How real the impossible future he promised her seemed.

"I hope you're not making things unnecessarily hard for yourself," Ma warned her one morning after she'd traipsed in at sunrise having clearly spent the night with Jacob yet again, and it irked Vera. That Ma would treat her like a child still after so many years. That she never said anything like that to Eli. The letters and trinkets and lipstick-stained kerchiefs, the faint whiff of someone else's perfume ever present. Such a long trail of women behind him. Vera was always more discreet than her brother, and never felt anything close to love for the men she briefly shared her bed with. Until Jacob. Which is what Ma was trying to say, but still, Vera didn't want to hear it. It was different with Jacob. Or it could be.

"Don't worry yourself about me," Vera said to her mother, then turned heel, out to the corral, without staying for breakfast.

Riding the ridge with Jacob that afternoon Vera almost told him the truth of it all, the temptation so near she could taste its metallic edge. Figured maybe if she explained the situation he would understand why she was going to have to leave town soon.

Figured maybe—maybe—they could decide to do something different this time, together.

What Vera hadn't figured was that Jacob might die before they even had a chance for any of it.

It's just ghosts, Vera tells herself now as she continues to hurry in the opposite direction, downstream. Ghosts everywhere now that she's home. She's spent centuries putting people and places behind her, purposefully forgetting it all. But now that she's back her entire past has been set loose and is jostling around in her head. Too many memories for any single brain to handle, this accumulation of all her small lives, beginning over and over again. Her body can survive forever, but who's to say what might happen to her mind?

Half a mile later, she hoists herself up the rocky bank and onto the warm grass. From across the meadow she hears the back door of the house creak open, sees Cate standing in its frame.

"Oh my god, you fish, too? What are you, an actual fucking cowboy?" Cate calls across the open field. Vera walks the rest of the way to her landlord, who's now standing barefoot on the stone patio, eyes closed, face pointing to the last of the sun. "I've been inside all day doing stupid paperwork and scanning photos," she moans dramatically.

"I had a meeting at headquarters today, too. A shame when the weather is so nice."

"I'm *this* close to being finished. Keep me company?" Cate asks, already making her way to the door.

Vera leaves her sling pack of rod, flies, and water samples on the back patio next to the kitchen door then wordlessly, she follows.

"Sorry this place is a pit. I spent all morning on the phone with our lawyer—"

As Cate continues to complain jovially about the level of financial documentation required to apply for a liquor license, Vera reminds herself to breathe.

She's inside. She's home.

It feels smaller and larger at the same time. Heart-warmingly familiar and heart-stompingly *un*familiar, too. The floorboards in the living room are the very ones her parents planed all those years ago—she can see the circular burn mark where she set down a pan of corn cakes she'd grabbed from the hearth, realizing too late it was too hot to hold. Someone installed beadboard between the old ceiling beams, which brightens up the whole place, and there are modern additions everywhere—baseboard heat, a new woodstove, so many electric lights, bookshelves, a television. It's a normal-looking house but to her it feels crowded, overcostumed. Like a plain girl wearing too much makeup for her age. A sour taste rises in her stomach.

"My office is on the second floor. Watch the stairs though," Cate warns. "Brian ate it on them this morning and almost broke his back. They're crazy steep."

Vera balks internally at the insult—because that's what it feels like. To insult the house's construction is to insult her and her family and all of their hard work. *You try to build a two-story house with nothing but a bunch of trees*, she wants to say. But she dutifully holds the railing, follows Cate's clean, bare feet up the stairs to the second floor and into Eli's old room.

There's new drywall, molding, and trim. A table strewn with papers, a large desktop computer. The walls are lined with framed art, which upon closer inspection reveal themselves to be invitations and event posters designed by Cate.

Vera can picture Eli's low bed, the wobbly side table he made for himself when he was small, his blue quilt.

"I'm about halfway done with the photos," Cate explains as she moves a pile of them from her stool to the top of a cream-colored filing cabinet.

Vera picks up a stack of black-and-white photographs. The notch road that cuts between the mountains, the old De Vries home, a gathering of children in aprons outside the one-room schoolhouse. The church in the village, a church a town over. Three women in the grass in white dresses holding parasols, only one of them laughing.

Vera knows there won't be a picture of herself in here—photography wasn't yet invented when they left, but still. She's disconcertingly nervous. It seems all too possible that the ghost of her old self might reappear.

"I'm such a sucker for vintage photos. I could spend days looking at them, making up lives for the dead people. Brian had to drag me to bed last night."

"Where'd you get these?"

"Anna Dunham, the general store lady." Vera's heart rate ticks higher at the mention of the store. Cate continues. Eighty years old, Anna grew up in town but lives in Florida now. Her parents ran the general store through the tourism booms of the fifties, sixties, and seventies. But it's been left vacant since the eighties when the region took a downturn in popularity. Anna inherited the building when her parents died but she'd already moved away, had a family of her own, so she left it as is. Cate was able to look her up in the tax records and find her online this past winter when she and Brian first had the idea to reopen it.

"Sweetest old lady ever," Cate gushes declaratively, a hand over her heart. "We weren't even in contract yet, but she said we could take whatever we wanted from the building. That's where I found this box."

Vera steadies herself and asks, "So how'd the Fountain of Eternal Youth people find the general store if it wasn't for sale?"

"Freaky timing," Cate says with a shrug over the high-pitched hum of her scanner. A few weeks after Cate found Anna online, the LLC's lawyer did, too. Anna called Cate to apologize. Didn't tell her the exact final figure, but did say it was "shamefully high" and that she would have been a fool to refuse it. "But it's better this way," Cate insists.

"You heard anything more about them?" Vera presses.

"Nah," Cate says and tucks some of her wavy mass of hair behind her ears.

Vera knows it will look too suspicious to push any further, and it doesn't sound like Cate knows anything else anyway. So she forces herself to surrender for the moment and quietly flips through the rest of the photographs. Faces she's seen a thousand times before. Not that she recognizes any of these in particular, they're simply the same kind of hardscrabble souls she's spent lifetimes with in other small towns across the country. She knows the fashions, too, of course. Can remember the itch of a starched petticoat, the slickness of a leather sole worn too thin. How it felt to have her hair tied up in that Victorian pile, lace for special occasions. Elastic is a revelation.

Cate continues to scan photo after photo, chattering on about how she plans to use them for labels and tasting room decor. Vera looks at each one and flips them over, attempting to decipher the scrawl of old cursive she's no longer used to reading. She picks up another—

Lotte!

Vera must have gasped aloud because Cate asks her, "What?"

"Something in my throat."

When Cate turns around to lift the scanner and place another in the machine, Vera tucks the picture in her back pocket.

Gravity and time did their usual damage but Vera is certain: of the two women in this photograph, one of them is Eli's wife.

"Beer?" Brian asks, suddenly at the door's threshold, holding an amber bottle.

"Oh my god no, I think I'm still hungover from Sunday," Cate says, then turns to Vera. "Consider yourself lucky you left when you did, Stan broke out the good stuff. I think he must have toasted you six hundred more times after you left."

"You want one?" Brian asks Vera, who shakes her head no. "I talked to Joan," he tells Cate. "She thinks we're crazy."

"Well, she never liked it here so obviously she thinks we're crazy."

"Joan's his mom. She thinks we're throwing our lives away out here. Well, Brian's life. The wasted potential!" she mocks in a falsetto as she takes another photograph off the pile and places it in the machine. "Did she bring up your master's?"

Brian gives an almost imperceptible nod.

"Like a master's in English from City College is a law degree from Harvard or something! No offense, darling."

"Never any taken," he says, and Vera is surprised to find herself possibly believing him. Some people play the part of the unruffled boy well enough, but most of them are faking it to a degree. Brian is extremely stoic. Though perhaps boring might be another word for it.

"You swear you don't hate me for taking your room? This is Brian's childhood room. I stole it from him."

"You lived here, too?"

It escapes before Vera can catch it—that "too"—but neither of them seem to notice.

"Only summers."

"His Bubby and Grampy passed away the winter before last. They died within a week of each other, old people do that you know, the ones who are truly in love?" Cate throws her arms around Brian and kisses him on the lips. "Let's go that way, too, OK?" she says in a baby voice, and the whole display makes Vera look to the floor then down the hall to where her old room is. The door is closed.

"So what should we call this thing?" Cate asks, as if that's what they'd just been discussing. She rattles off a list of possibilities that all sound the same to Vera: Catskills Cidery, The Cidery, Catskills Cider Co. Cate moves more photos through the machine and continues to talk about color schemes, fonts, screen printing. Then she announces they're done with the scans.

"One more," says Brian, and he plucks the photograph of Lotte from Vera's back pocket.

She grabs his wrist before she has time to think about it. Pure reaction, reflexes precisely honed after so many years. They make eye contact and Vera lets go as quickly as she'd seized him.

"Oops! Thank you," sings Cate, and she turns around to take the photograph from Brian's outstretched hand then sets it on top of her pile. She didn't see anything. And now Brian's looking away, out the window into the meadow, the bottom of his beer tilted up.

Cate's computer makes a disappointed beep.

"Come on Photoshop," she growls. "I'm so close, please let me finish this."

Brian downs his bottle. "Another round?" he asks the room.

"I should go," Vera says because she's too jumpy and she's had enough of being inside this house. Because Brian will be watching her now.

"Already? Aww." Cate leans in and gives her a European-style cheek-to-cheek air kiss, tells Brian she thinks she does want a beer after all, then turns back to her machine, mumbling about a reboot.

Vera lets Brian leave the room first. Then she swipes the photo from the top of Cate's last pile and slips it under her T-shirt into the front of her waistband. One swift, easy motion and she's off. The sheer number of things she's stolen out of necessity over the years.

"Bye, Cate."

"Bye, girl!"

Vera follows behind Brian, watching his head bounce down the stairs, which he takes at remarkable speed. No wonder he fell this morning. He rounds the corner to go to the back of the house where the kitchen is, but Vera can't stand to be inside a moment longer, so she lets herself out the front door at the bottom of the stairs. She's almost to her cottage when she hears it creak open again.

"Vera?"

She turns around. Brian leans out the door.

"Yeah?" She waits.

So he's the first to wonder.

"You forgot this."

He holds out her sling pack.

Back in the cottage Vera puts the new water samples with the others on the shelf in her hall closet. She returns to the kitchen to unpack her rod and flies and glances out her window. Brian is sitting on the front stoop, watching The Road. Watching the cottage.

5

June 2014

Vera does her usual shift but without Lopez, finally. She walks three trails on the north end of the Preserve, checks in with two of the more popular car-access campsites, and sends a bear-sighting report to the Department of Environmental Conservation. She collects four new water samples and marks them on the map she keeps folded in her pocket.

At the end of the day, she takes her rod to a shaded patch of the Schoharie Creek, where she catches two good-size brookies—ten-inchers—plus a thirteen-inch brown. She releases the brookies but clubs the brown on a warm rock—it's an invasive species, introduced sometime after they left, and could edge out the native brook trout. She guts and rinses it in the stream.

Back home, she dusts it with flour, salt, and pepper, and gives it a quick fry like they used to. Then she pours herself a glass of rye and calls her brother.

It's almost two weeks early, but she can't make herself wait any longer.

They used to mark the anniversary with more than a phone call, back when Vera and Eli lived together. Some years it was a somber event, the weight of their strange predicament heavy. Other times it was light and festive, playful even. A chance to revel in the absurdity of it all and laugh until their sides hurt, wipe happy salt from the corners of their eyes.

Ma started the tradition. Early on, Vera and Eli both balked at the whole thing. At being forced to think about a past they could not and should not access. Why pretend to *celebrate* it, they demanded.

"Ceremony, respect. Something did this to us, we might say thank you," Ma answered one year in the plains of Nebraska, an especially brutal winter just behind them, and Vera was so disgusted at the idea of gratitude for this that she went and threw herself off the roof of the barn.

It hurt like hell, but she didn't cry out as she lay there on her shattered back looking up at the wisps of clouds thinly veiling the stars. She was fine within a few minutes, walked back in without so much as a limp, said good night to her mother and brother at the table, and went to bed.

The worst was 1917, their first as just a twosome. God were they wrecked.

After a while, a year got shorter and shorter, and by the time July 10th rolled around they would both think, *Already?* Time beginning to speed, hurrying on to nowhere.

He picks up after one ring.

"Hello?"

"It's me."

There's a pause and she realizes he was expecting a call from someone else.

"Hi!" he finally says, the usual gaiety returning to his voice. "New number. You're early!"

"I know, I was thinking about you. Why wait?" She spins her glass of rye slowly between her thumb and middle finger, looks out the small window over her kitchen sink to their house illuminated in the twilight.

"Where are you?"

"Home."

She says it noncommittally. Like maybe she just means she's at her house for the day's end. She wants him to figure it out. To force her hand.

"Me, too," he says, and she hears him turn on a faucet, a static-y gush.

"What're you making?"

"Pasta."

Vera thinks of the boxes of dried macaroni in her cabinets. Or maybe she ate them already, she can't remember. Feeding herself sits low on her list of priorities these days. But when Eli says "pasta" he means hand-folded ravioli stuffed with summer squash and goat cheese. He means fresh-made fettuccine with cream and bacon and peas from the garden. He means meals that could outshine a Michelin-starred restaurant.

"So what's up?" he asks as he clangs around with a pan. "It's been a little while."

"It has."

Suddenly Vera knows she's not going to tell him a thing. It's like a door has slammed. She feels a nauseating mix of rage and despair. Hearing his voice for the first time since the desert. And being here now without him—188 years is a long time to keep a promise. You need a real good reason to break it. Which she has, she knows in her heart she has. But she also knows that she can't tell her brother about the LLC. Cannot tell him she's come home to die.

She's going to have to do this on her own.

"You still out there with Yogi Bear?" Eli asks. She hears another kitchen instrument clang. The faucet turns off.

"Still working for the Parks, yeah. You?"

Vera opens a kitchen drawer, sees the photograph she swiped yesterday of old Lotte with a young woman on the steps of the general store and turns it facedown. She doesn't want Lotte looking at her right now. Lotte who they left behind.

Lotte & Lyd, 1861, the faded, delicate cursive on the back of the photograph says.

So she made it to at least—Vera does the math quickly in her head—sixty-two years old. Considerable enough back then. She'll send Eli the photograph before all this ends. He'll want to know Lotte lived on. He'll want to see her face again, even hollowed with age.

Perhaps especially so. He's always been the one to hold on to trinkets and charms from past lives. To save pictures of friends, and collect newspaper clippings that mentioned their own miraculous survival of something. For the first ten years on the run together he had a little box of all of it that Vera poked sisterly fun of, not realizing she was accidentally fanning the flames of Ma's fear.

"You shouldn't keep all that," Ma told Eli one evening as he had it out on the kitchen table, idly flipping through. "You're collecting the evidence someone else will use against us one day."

He blew her off, said she was being paranoid, he'd keep it safe.

The next day it was gone.

"What'd you do with it, Ma?" he shouted, and it scared Vera. It takes so much to anger Eli. Affable Eli, life-of-the-party Eli, can-turn-anything-into-a joke Eli. But his eyes were animal-wide, his face pink with rage.

"We're safer without it," Ma said, her voice firm, no hint of regret or apology. Vera left the room to put another log on the fire, to stay out of the one that was about to erupt between her brother and mother. Then she saw it, in the orange coals—one charred corner of the box. She placed a new log on top and buried it in the ash.

"I got back from Idaho this morning," Eli tells her now. A friend of his has a place in Sun Valley, Vera won't believe how pricey the real estate is there these days. As he talks about the acreage and multiple hot tubs and size of the wine cellar, Vera cracks her knuckles one by one. Now that she knows she isn't going to tell her brother anything she wants to get off the phone. She prefers plausible deniability. She switches the receiver to her other ear.

"Oh dude!" Eli interrupts himself. "I never asked, how was the end of the trip?"

"What trip?" she says, playing dumb very badly, her voice sliding up into a high, desperate squeak as it closes in on her. She's instantly parched.

"Joshua Tree! I feel bad I had to bug out early."

The rumble and the crash and the darkness. The scorching pain.

"It was fine."

"Fine?"

Vera closes the drawer a little harder than she means to.

"Yeah it was fine," she insists, willing herself steady now, but she's shaking and her chest is constricting, sweat forming on her forehead.

"Look, I know we kinda got into it out there but I didn't think you were still mad at me. *Are* you still mad at me?"

"No, I—"

She closes her eyes, squeezes them shut as hard as she can, then opens them into the light. Her chest palpitates desperately.

"I'm sorry, I didn't mean half the shit I said about—"

"Look I've got to go, I'm meeting someone for dinner," she interrupts her brother. Ears ringing, heart wild under her ribs, not enough air in her lungs.

"Early bird special!" Eli laughs and Vera realizes too late it's only 4 p.m. on the West Coast.

"Happy hour."

"OK, cool, no worries. I'm glad you called! I've been thinking about you, too. I've got this opportunity lining up and I want to onboard you when the time is right."

"Like an investment? Eli, you know I don't have that kind of money." She wills her heart to slow down, this phone call to end.

"This'll be more like sweat equity but you won't have to do a thing."

"Sounds too good to be true," she says, her voice clipped.

"I've always got your back. You know that, Wolven." He's suddenly serious.

"I know," she says and downs the glass of rye before her throat closes completely.

"For fucking *ever*, Wolven."

She nods even though she knows he can't see her.

That night in the bathtub Vera drinks from one of her samples then tries to conjure the good times. Fleeting moments, but moments nonetheless. Fishing with Pa, bringing the horses in with Jacob. But as her consciousness brushes with the edge, all she can summon is the darkness.

Vera pulls onto The Road and sees a sandwich sign by the flagpole with an arrow pointing to the Volunteer Fire Department's Annual Chicken BBQ Dinner. *$10 PER PLATE, EAT IN OR TO-GO*. She doesn't eat meat anymore, but she knows it will be good to widen her circle. She needs to reach out, include the fire department, the churchgoers, the old-timers who will surely be there. Vera has lived in enough small towns to understand that if she doesn't ingratiate herself now, she'll be forever lumped in with "the weekenders" and city transplants. Besides, maybe someone here knows something about the LLC.

She parks next to the church on the trimmed lawn with the other overflow cars. WHERE WILL YOU BE SITTING FOR ETERNITY? SMOKING OR NON? the little black-and-white marquee sign asks. Vera walks over to a folding table being manned by two pale, white-haired women in pastel T-shirts. In front of a metal cash box there's a roll of red raffle tickets.

Vera tips her ranger hat. "Afternoon."

"Welcome!" says the rounder and rosier of the two. "Thank you for supporting our volunteers! We—"

"How many?" the other asks.

Her friend scowls at her, clearly thinking it was rude to interrupt like that.

"Three please," Vera says, deciding she'll surprise Cate and Brian with a plate each. Not to mention, there's a direct correlation between how much people like you and how much you donate to their hobbies, clubs, and belief systems.

"That'll be thirty."

Vera briefly considers giving the women two twenties and telling them to keep the change, but that's the kind of thing Eli can pull off, not her. Instead, she removes one twenty and one ten from her wallet—she always has cash on hand, managed to avoid debit and credit cards for years—and gives the bills to the grumpy woman whose wrinkled hand is outstretched.

"You're the ranger," says the first, tearing off three tickets and sliding them across the table to Vera.

"I am. Vera. Nice to meet you."

"I'm Sue, this is Beverly. Our boys Paul and George are both part of the volunteer team."

Sue explains that their sons have been with the Volunteer Fire Department for six years. Her son, Paul, is an EMT, Beverly's son, George, works for the Highway Department. Beverly here made the potato salad, Kathryn made the desserts. She points to a different white-haired woman sitting with another elderly couple at one of the tables placed in the shade. Cushy white sneakers abound.

"I'm looking forward to trying it all, thank you."

"No thank *you*! I'm so glad we finally got to meet you. I've seen your truck around town. You live at the old Hoffman place, right?"

"Can't say for sure, ma'am, were those Brian's—"

"Ruth and Joe, may they rest in peace," says Sue, clutching her hands together. "Little Brian's grandparents. *Little*, listen to me! He's all grown up now, naturally. So nice that he and his wife have moved in. We *love* to see young folks here again. But look at me babbling on! We should let you get your plates. God bless, hon. Don't forget to pick a dessert."

Vera thanks them and walks around the side of the white clapboard church to its backyard, where Sue's and Beverly's sons are squinting over the large smoking barbecue. Lines of splayed half chickens lie in neat rows. The men wear matching blue Volunteer Fire Department shirts. They're sweating.

Vera recognizes one of them.

"Pass me the tongs?" asks the fisherman from yesterday.

A young woman with blond, hair-sprayed curls stands in front of another table with several towers of Styrofoam clamshells stacked around her like a wobbly castle.

"Ticket please," the woman says and Vera hands hers over and is given three warm boxes of chicken in return. "You can pick out your own desserts, too."

Vera surveys the individual plastic baggies of cookies and brownies as the wind shifts and the smoke wafts over them. She looks up at the man again.

"Paul, please, you're killing me!" says the woman as she waves ineffectually in front of her face, her charm bracelet jingling.

He laughs, hands the tongs to the other man, and opens four new clamshells. Vera watches as he scoops Beverly's gelatinous potato salad into each of them then waits for the next round to be done. He wipes his brow with his muscled forearm then looks up, meets Vera's eyes, smiles at her. Then his face freezes as he tries to place how he knows her.

Vera looks down, eyeing the dessert table again as something inside her hurries, floats, warms. She chooses three brownies and piles them on top of her boxes.

"Need any forks?" the woman asks her. "Jayden, no! Get down from there!" Vera turns just in time to watch a little boy launch himself off a tabletop into the grass, where he rolls several times then stands with a pleased grin. "Boys," the woman says and shrugs.

Vera thinks of the many times she was reprimanded by Ma and Pa when she was little for climbing the apple trees, the hayloft, the wagon. Family lore had it, she scaled the entire set of stairs to the second floor one morning without anyone noticing until she'd made it to the top and *that* was how they figured out she'd learned to crawl. It's no wonder she climbs mountains for a living now, really.

"I think I saw you fishing," Paul says, and Vera looks up.

His features are strong, almost hawkish. His eyes a surprising blue. He's probably only thirty but looks weather-worn and strong.

Vera likes to think she doesn't have a type.

"On the creek here? Yesterday?" Paul prods.

"Yup, that was me," she says and adjusts her hat.

"You catch anything?" he asks.

"Nope," Vera lies, like she always does.

"Me neither."

"He's full of crap," his friend says, and Paul mimes mock horror, his eyes wide, mouth open in a perfect O. "He just says that so no one else will fish the holes he likes."

"George! You never give away an angler's spots, come *on*!" Paul shoves his much broader friend playfully and he hardly budges. Vera finds herself smiling.

"Whatever, I bet she caught a dozen, too," George says and looks to Vera. "Am I right?"

Vera shrugs, her smile turning sly.

"Told you," George says, not at all unkindly, bumping his shoulder into Paul's who doesn't break eye contact with Vera despite the jostle.

"I'm Jocelyn," the woman introduces herself. Vera breaks the gaze first, turns to shake the woman's hand.

"Vera."

"That's my husband, George, and that there is the pain in the ass otherwise known as Paul. You're living down the road at the Hoffman place, yeah?"

The women exchange basic get-to-know-you facts and Vera gathers that all three of them grew up here. That Jocelyn and George are high school sweethearts and have two kids, Jayden and Ella. That George and Paul have been friends since elementary school. Answering their questions Vera tells them yes, she came from California, yes, she's been here about two months now, yes she likes the area just fine. Then Jocelyn asks if Vera's landlords are in fact opening a cidery.

"That's the plan."

"That'll be a lot of traffic."

"Oh come on, you love hard cider," says George, making it clear he's been listening to the women's conversation this whole time. Jocelyn agrees that she likes cider but counters that she doesn't like the idea of people getting drunk then driving, they already drive too fast, look. And as if on cue, a white truck whizzes by at least fifteen miles per hour over the village speed limit of thirty-five. Vera wonders where exactly on The Road Jocelyn and George live. Surely they've seen her speed by before, conspicuous in her ranger truck. Then again, maybe Jocelyn doesn't mind if Vera speeds. People have an unfortunate tolerance for unlawful behavior from law enforcement.

"They gonna have beer, too? I heard he makes beer," says Paul, clicking the metal tongs.

Vera nods, surprised by how tongue-tied she is right now, a little irritated at herself for it even. He just spooked her looking so much like Jacob she tells herself, that's all. She unwraps her brownie and eats it as the group continues to talk. Paul says it was a bad apple year last year, which will be good news for Cate and Brian because the pattern goes every other year. George says he thinks his mom, Beverly, has an antique cider press in her basement, maybe they could use it or put it on display somewhere. Jocelyn wonders if they're going to host weddings because those also bring a lot of traffic and are loud, but maybe won't be too bad if there are only one or two a year. A girlfriend from her beautician's license course got married at a vineyard on the other side of the river and it was beautiful.

"All those fall colors and french braids and these super cute little plaid shawls for the bridesmaids. Are you married?"

"Nope."

"I didn't think so. How old are you anyway? You look like you're twelve."

Twenty-six used to be old. Half the village thought Vera was a lost cause before they disappeared.

"I get that a lot," Vera says because she does. From men and women, from children. This particular vein of it though—passive-aggressive questions from another relatively young woman—is one of the more tedious. If only because it's often followed up with questions about her nonexistent skin care routine and can easily slide into how skinny Vera is for how much she can eat, and if it was boring the first time it's definitely boring the three thousandth time. In her more charitable moods, Vera feels bad for the women she's met over the centuries who've wasted so much of their brief time worrying about their appearance, desperately trying to stave off the inevitable. But most of the time it makes her mad. The stupid waste of it. Especially when hundreds of years of experience have shown her that men will have sex with practically anything.

"What about the general store people?" Vera prompts. "Do you think they'll be opening up something, too?"

"They just bought more land behind it," Jocelyn says.

"Barbara Johnson's place?" Vera asks.

"I hear Mrs. Johnson's going to retire a *very* happy lady with the deal they're giving her," George says.

"*I* hear we should probably mind our own business," Paul chides through a smile as he waves to an older couple in accidentally matching blue plaid coming around the bend.

"Not Mrs. Johnson's, the old Galloway land," Jocelyn explains, undeterred. "There's no house on it, just acreage. It's on the other side of your place."

"On the other side of *me*?" Vera asks, panic rising. Always so close to the surface now. She adjusts her hat.

"Sounds like your landlords might make more money selling than they would opening the cidery," George jokes.

"Mr. Ricci, Mrs. Ricci, hello!" Paul says loudly.

Vera stands there, unfinished brownie in hand as Jocelyn, Paul, and George serve the couple.

The general store, Mrs. Johnson's, this other piece of land. They're surrounding her.

She moves to leave and accidentally catches Paul's eye.

"See you on the creek sometime?" he asks, open clamshell in one hand, tongs in the other.

She nods, feels a flutter on top of her nerves, then hurries away with her boxes.

Back on the other side of the church she sees Janet, red ticket in hand.

"Well, you loaded up! Save any for me?" the postmaster asks with a laugh. "Hey, I hear you put on a real rodeo show at Stan's last weekend!"

"It was nothing, just did what had to be done," Vera says with a forced smile and keeps walking.

"Ah OK, the humble type," Janet jokes. "I'd promise not to tell anyone else but I think you and I both know it won't be true!"

Janet continues around the bend toward the grills. Vera gives a wave to Beverly and Sue as she passes their table.

"You're a Van Valkenburgh, right?" Beverly asks.

"I am," Vera says, and she stops and nods down toward her badge.

She was Vanessa Smith back in California most recently. But she doesn't want to die as Vanessa Smith. She wants to die as who she really is, as she was born. As Vera Van Valkenburgh.

"You know, it was Van Valkenburghs who built the house right next to your cottage."

She holds herself steady and says what she imagines someone else might say. "Very cool."

"Is that so, Beverly?" chimes in Sue, genuinely charmed. "Do Cate and Brian know? Oh, we should tell them if they don't!"

"It's funny 'cause the new general store gal, she's a Kirke," Beverly continues. "Another neighborhood name coming home to roost."

"Really?" Vera asks and something inside her pings.

"Kirke, Dunham, Shoemakker," Sue lists, counting names on her fingers.

"Bakker," Beverly adds.

"Yes, Bakker," Sue says and sticks out another finger. "Van De Vries. Lots of old families here still."

"Well, who would ever leave a place like this?" Beverly asks.

"I should get these back before they're cold," Vera says, then she jogs to her truck because something has just come together for her.

*

When Vera gets home she yanks open the kitchen drawer by the old telephone, grabs the photograph of Lotte, and turns it over.

Lotte and Lyd, 1861.

She flips it back.

KIRKE'S GENERAL STORE says the hand-painted sign above them.

Lydia Kirke.

6

July 2014

Vera doesn't want to call from her landline or flip phone, and it's near impossible to find a pay phone these days, so here she is at a gas station using the cordless one from behind the counter.

"Hello?" a man answers after just one ring.

"Hi, I'm hoping to talk to someone about selling my land. It's near the parcels your company recently purchased."

A pop song blares above her on the radio and the door chime rings. The clerk continues restocking chewing tobacco tins. She can see Lopez filling the tank outside in the drizzling rain.

Earlier that morning, in uniform, Vera stopped at Barbara Johnson's and asked for the contact of the buyer. Told her big buyers like this are also often great philanthropists and the Preserve would like to get in touch with them. The old woman didn't see through Vera's lie, or perhaps she did and didn't care, either way.

Vera tucks the sticky note with the number back into her uniform pocket and plugs her other ear with her finger.

"What's your name?" the man asks.

"Ah sorry, can't tell you. See the rest of the family isn't exactly on board yet and I have a few questions first. You know how it is."

"Which parcel is this?"

"May I speak with Lydia Kirke?"

Her heart gives a gallop under her shirt just to say her name.

Lydia is one of us, she thinks for the thousandth time in less than twenty-four hours. The possibility thrills and spooks her.

No, Lydia might *be one of us*, she corrects herself. Because all of this might be just a coincidence. It might be just a coincidence that Matthew Barbery's company is called Fountain of Eternal Youth LLC. Just a coincidence that the company's supposed straw man is named Lydia Kirke. Just a coincidence that they bought the old general store that shares her name, right next to Vera's old house, plus two more properties surrounding it.

Vera knows she can be paranoid to a fault. Then again, it's kept her safe this long.

"I'm the person authorized to discuss all details pertaining to possible land transfers," the man says. He must be their lawyer.

"OK, well, can you tell me what they're planning on doing with these properties?"

Vera watches Lopez return the gas pump to its slot as the light patter of rain begins to pick up.

"I'm not at liberty to discuss that."

"It would help me convince my husband," she says. "There's a lot of rumors going around town and people are starting to worry. I think if you all were a little less cloak-and-dagger and told everyone what you were up to, well, you'd have more offers to sell than you'd know what to do with."

She can see Lopez looking around for her. They make eye contact and she holds up a finger, *One minute*.

"Consider it noted," the lawyer says.

Lopez begins to walk toward the door.

"Never mind then. Thanks for your time."

The chime sounds again.

"Your phone dead? You coulda used mine," Lopez says, brushing drops off the shoulders of his uniform.

"I'm good. Where to next?"

Back in the truck Vera fiddles with the radio and eventually lands on 89.1 FM.

"God, you and your classical music," Lopez moans.

"What? Everybody likes classical," Vera says confidently because she knows music is the one place her tastes can remain anachronistic but not suspiciously so. Beethoven, Mozart, Vivaldi, Chopin. She wishes she could play. She's tried—piano, cello, violin, the flute. It turns out some skills do in fact require something more than simply practice. Vera is many things, but not an artist.

"You're such an old man," Lopez teases as he reaches for the buttons and switches through the static to 100.7 FM. The cab fills with the bass of the same pop song that was playing inside the gas station.

Normally Vera might fight harder for her station, but she's distracted now. Disappointed. Not that she really believed Lydia Kirke would come on the phone and confess but, well. She hadn't anticipated being so thoroughly snubbed. All this poking around, plus this new discovery, and she still hasn't made any *real* headway.

"My little sister got engaged yesterday," Lopez says as they pull out of the gas station.

"Congratulations," Vera replies automatically, her eyes out the window on the glistening, leafy trees, the rain picking up even more.

"Thanks, but he's kind of a douche." Not a bad guy per se, totally fine on paper Lopez explains, but he tries too hard, it's annoying. "And the more he tries to win me over the more I'm like, bro, get away from me."

Vera says she knows the type.

"Yeah?"

Lotte Janssen was beautiful, if your tastes run toward delicate and fair. Corn silk hair, creamy skin, lips that always looked like she'd just finished eating summer berries. Her father was Preacher Janssen, the first behind the pulpit at the new church in town. He was arrogant, quick to tell you the meek will inherit the earth while never sharing more than a single potato without expecting something from you in return. That wasn't the way of life back then. It wasn't that people were more virtuous, they just understood how much they needed each other to survive. He was a difficult man to please, obviously, so Eli didn't try. Didn't have to. Turned out Preacher Janssen was also the type of man who found it nearly impossible to deny his only daughter what she wished, and what Lotte wished for more than anything else the summer she turned twenty-one was to marry Eli.

At the time Vera herself was twenty. Barely a year younger than Lotte but whole worlds apart, and marriage—serving a man and bearing his children and probably dying from it—was something Vera was dead set against. A conviction Ma and Pa were, for at least that moment, still willing to go along with as she was integral to operating the farm and didn't have any prospects knocking down their door.

Vera can admit now that she never gave Lotte a fair chance. That when Lotte arrived, overbearing in her be-my-sister attention and her visible, arduous striving to be a "good wife," Vera didn't want any of it. Didn't like that it threatened to take away her best friend either, Eli saying they would build their own place once a child or two came along. Ma made a good show of it, but Vera could tell her mother was also not as enthralled with Lotte as Eli, Pa, and the rest of the neighbors were. Vera nurtured that seedling of a feeling in Ma, carefully, purposefully.

"My brother's wife," Vera says with a sigh. "She was very over the top with me and my mom. Like she was always trying to prove something."

Vera pictures Lotte—in the kitchen trying to perfect Ma's apple pie, on her knees scouring the stairs, in the doorway of Vera's room holding out a blue silk ribbon, a matching one woven through her own blond braid.

Standing outside the steps of the general store with Lydia Kirke.

"Yes, dude, exactly like that!" Lopez says. "I want my sister to be happy but it's annoying. I'm thinking about saying something."

An old but familiar tug of guilt pulls at Vera.

"Just remember, whatever you say you won't be able to take back and you'll all have to live with it forever."

"So they're still together?" he asks, changing the speed of the windshield wipers to match the increasing rain.

Vera wonders for the millionth time: How different might things have been if Lotte had carried any of her pregnancies to term and bore children with Eli those five years together? If Pa hadn't died and saddled Eli with three women? If Lotte had turned out to be like them and they hadn't left her behind that summer morning in 1826?

"No, she's long gone."

Lopez takes his eyes off the road and looks to Vera to see if she's joking then breaks into a delighted laugh.

"So you're saying there's hope for me?" He laughs again and Vera puts on a smile then looks back out the rain-streaked window.

The song ends and another overproduced and equally forgettable one begins.

"Hey, can I ask you something?" Lopez says, turning down the music, his tone suddenly gentle. Vera braces herself. She shouldn't have said those things about Lotte. Some people are happy with scraps. Others, you give them a little taste and it awakens a whole appetite for more.

"Sure," she says. Not too curt, not too inviting.

"Did you know the guy who got trapped in the landslide?"

Vera's ears go cottony. She keeps her eyes on the window but can no longer see clearly, her vision blurring, darkening.

"I know the memo said the ranger wanted to remain anonymous, but you had to have known him, right? It was Joshua Tree. That was your park, I heard you talking to Captain Newsman about the rattlesnakes out there."

Vera can't breathe properly. She grips her thighs. Tries to open her window but it's locked, the button useless.

"Sorry, I—I shouldn't have asked," Lopez says next to her. "Jesus, I can really put my foot in my mouth sometimes."

Vera manages to choke out something that sounds like "It's OK" as the darkness continues to take over her vision, as everything rings and tightens and overheats.

"I just keeping thinking about it." Lopez is almost whispering now, his voice barely audible over the wooshing of her own ears. "Imagine being trapped like that? Pinned under all those rocks in total freaking darkness, never knowing if someone is going to find you or if you're just going to—"

Or if you're just going to stay trapped there.

Forever.

Vera gets through the rest of the long, soggy day of work on autopilot then drives home. As she gets out of her work truck, the front door of the house whines open and Brian appears, shirtless in athletic shorts, skinny and hairless, his chest concave.

"Vera, come here a sec," he calls to her from the doorway. Rain runs off the porch's roof into the grass. The gutters are gurgling.

Vera is fairly certain Brian has pinpointed *something* is off about her. But like most people, he has no idea what to do with this intuitive feeling. She could misdirect his suspicions and sleight of hand his attention to something safe that would "explain" her strangeness. A mysterious and possibly abusive ex she's avoiding, a vaguely shameful habit like, say, compulsive gambling. But he ranks low on her list of worries at the moment.

She closes her truck door, walks up the steps. "What can I do for you?" she asks briskly, still in ranger mode, still chewing over Lydia Kirke. Still pushing the darkness from the edges of her vision.

"Somebody dropped something off for you," he says and walks back into the house. Vera stays on the porch, since she's muddy and doesn't want to linger. She wants to get inside her cottage to her bath and her bottle. Needs to scratch at the never-ending itch of her existence and clear her mind if only for a flash.

"Babe? You talking to me?" Cate calls from upstairs.

Brian shouts back that it's Vera.

"Vera!" she cries brightly then pounds down the stairs. "We're on the agenda for the Planning Board meeting next Tuesday, you have to come! It's the public hearing for the special permit, the one to operate the cidery. I don't think people are going to oppose it, but Stan says you never know, sometimes locals come to these meetings and it can get a little people-out-with-their-pitchforks if you know what I mean."

"Sure," Vera agrees, willing this interaction to come to a close quickly.

"Thank you! I think it will help our case to have the famous rodeo ranger on our side," Cate tells her with a smile.

"The cult's on the agenda, too," Brian says.

"What?" Cate cries and whips around to face him.

"That's what Paul said."

Vera's attention flickers at his name.

"Why'd he tell you and not me?" Cate wants to know.

"I think you'd gone upstairs to get the demo label." Brian shrugs. Vera can see he's holding a small box now. Is that for her?

"Will Matthew Barbery be there?" Cate asks her husband.

Or Lydia Kirke? Vera adds silently.

Cate's phone dings and she pulls it out.

"Paul thinks probably just the lawyer," Brian answers. "That's usually how rich people do stuff."

"Oh shit," Cate says, eyes still on her phone. Brian asks what it is, leans over to look.

"Stan just sent this to me." Cate rotates her phone sideways so they can all see.

There's a man at a podium. Cameras click and flash. His teeth are luminous, his hair shines. The skin against his white, unbuttoned shirt collar is disconcertingly tan. His blue suit gleams, his enormous watch catches the lights. He is the picture of wealth, of health.

Vera reads the ticker below him and her breath catches in her throat.

Matthew Barbery announces his next venture FOUNTAIN.

"Let's call aging what it is," he tells the reporters, the cameras snapping and illuminating him in bright snippets. "A *disease*. And what if—" He allows for a long, purposeful pause. "What if I told you I'm going to cure it?"

Reporters interrupt with questions, clarifications. Cure wrinkles and balding? Alzheimer's? Cancer?

"All of it. Fountain will disrupt death itself."

The room clamors for more, a chaotic pitch that goes silent as he leans down toward the microphones again.

"That's as much as I can say today, just know, whatever you're imagining right now? It's going to be possible with Fountain."

"What in the actual fuck?" Cate says as the clip ends.

Vera feels the blood throbbing in her temples. "Crazy," she says, her voice a hoarse whisper.

"Of course it's crazy! Which means we're going to have 'crazy' for a neighbor! God I'm *so* mad. Of *all* the places? Here? *Here?* And now everyone and their mother is going to come out for these eternal youth idiots at the meeting and they're going to be all riled up and we're going to be collateral damage!"

"If anything we'll look like the good guys in comparison," Brian says. "Just a little mom-and-pop operation versus some billionaire's freaky weird side project."

"We better hope so," Cate says, tightening her bun. "Disrupt death. I think that's *the* grossest tech nonsense I've heard in my entire life."

"Can I have the—" Vera begins as she reaches for the box. She needs to get out of here. Brian hands it over as Cate restarts the clip.

"Thanks for this," Vera says and turns to go.

"Oh, and he said to tell you he got twelve," Brian adds.

"Who did?" Cate asks.

"Paul," Brian answers.

"Twelve what?"

Vera opens the box. It's five small flies. Beaded Prince Nymphs, Wooly Buggers, a few originals she's never seen before. Each perfect for catching dozens of fish on these waters.

*

All week Vera steers herself toward Tuesday. All day she steers herself toward six thirty, but still she's late for the Planning Board meeting. The last of her paperwork, the construction on Route 23. She's hardly slept, hardly eaten, all of it—her usual pain, Lydia Kirke, Matthew Barbery's announcement—boring a hole in her head. But she's here now. She scuttles into the meeting and slinks into the empty folding chair next to Cate that's been saved for her. The room is crowded and stuffy.

"Girl, I thought you weren't coming—"

"Please rise for the Pledge of Allegiance," says the man in the front of the room, and everyone stands and turns to face the American flag in the corner, fifty stars now. They recite the poem in a rumbling unison, hats and hands over their hearts. Vera tries to look around the room discreetly. There are so many faces. She wonders which one is Barbery's lawyer.

Chairs creak and whine as they all sit back down. Stewart Rhodes, the cue ball–bald sixty-something chairman of the Town Planning Board sits in the middle of the table between Paul and the other four members of the board and a woman taking notes. Stewart makes the mandatory joke about the weather, thanks everyone for coming out, then gets straight to it.

"Tonight we've got some exciting business. I love to see a full house like this! We'll open with the public hearing on the Catskills Cider Co. operation. They'll present—you have a little something prepared, yes?"

"Yes, sir." Cate nods eagerly, mock-ups of the barn and logo designs in a neat pile in her lap.

"Great! So they'll present first and then we can open the floor for questions. If we can reach an agreement tonight, they'll go home with a permit. If the community has concerns that still need to be addressed, well, we'll see." Stewart picks up the printed agenda in front of him, puts on the reading glasses from his shirt pocket, and continues. "After that we've got a request to redraw lot lines down in the village, well"—he squints at the paper. "It's actually to *join* three parcels owned by the same persons, Fountain of Eternal Youth LLC—"

The audience chuckles, not particularly warmly.

"It's quite a name," Stewart says as he peers over his glasses. They all follow his eyes to the back of the room.

"I know," says a woman's voice, and Vera cranes past Cate to see a young couple smiling.

It's Lydia Kirke, of course. That doesn't surprise her. But the man sitting next to her does.

Eli.

7

July 2014

Ma killed Eli and Vera, Eli killed Vera and Ma, and Vera killed Ma, but never once has she killed Eli. Each time was an honest accident on a farm, a ranch, the frontier. Some slip of machinery or beast the other was responsible for that would have finished any normal human. Perhaps they were sloppier than most, knowing they were unsusceptible to death, but of course the pain is real, even when the recovery is short, so they've always done their best to avoid unnecessary danger.

Vera can't speak for Ma or Eli, but she felt wretched after accidentally doing in Ma with the tractor, even though she was assured there were no hard feelings. Vera silently vowed to be more careful, but her discomfort must have been potent because Eli sensed it, and in the long tradition of older brothers needling their younger sisters, he razzed her about it for years, feigning fear at her completing the loop of manslaughter. *Uh-oh, you gonna murder me over it?*

Eventually Vera was able to laugh about it, gallows humor being key to surviving a predicament like theirs.

But when Vera spots Eli across the room at the Planning Board meeting, her first thought is: *I'm going to kill him.* And she isn't entirely sure if her mind is joking.

Her second thought is: *I need to leave before he sees me.* But she knows that's impossible, given how small the room is, the layout, where she's sitting. Maybe if she scuttles by with her hat pulled down he won't notice her. He certainly won't be expecting to see her here of all places. But the chance of someone else bidding her goodbye by name is too high. Stan, Sue, and Beverly are all in the row behind her, and besides, what does she have to hide compared to whatever he's been up to? Breaking their promise, for *this*? She isn't the one who should be running away.

Vera sits stone-still through the board's brief presentation of Cate and Brian's proposed signage, external lighting, parking lot layout, building specs. A few minutes later, when the time comes for comments from the public, Cate and Brian are called upon to stand, at which point all eyes in the meeting turn to them. Vera looks down into her lap and pulls her hair from behind her ears to curtain her face.

There's a handful of concerned citizens who always attend these meetings. Mostly a mix of elderly old-timers and people who bought second homes in the area about five years ago. And while these two groups of people have probably never voted for the same presidential candidate, tonight, they are united.

"This town has always been a quiet, residential place," says a man who introduces himself as Richard Dwight, a weekender recently turned full-timer who bought his place on The Road three years ago. "We have to be careful about maintaining its original character," he says, fussing with the zipper on his unblemished Carhartt vest.

Vera doubts Richard would be pleased if the original sawmill returned. The one that was right next to where his house sits now.

For better or worse, everyone's more specific concerns are issues that cannot be addressed by this board. Drunk driving, lowering the speed limit on The Road. Cate swears up and down they'll never overserve their patrons, that they'll do their absolute best to encourage safe driving. In fact, if any of them want to petition the county to lower the speed limit they'll happily sign on, don't forget they also live on The Road and hope to have a family one day.

"I might be new here in the scheme of things, but my dream is to plant deep, long-lasting roots, and to honor Brian's family and those who came before us in doing so," says Cate, a line she clearly practiced in the shower.

Half the room claps. Beverly audibly groans behind her.

"Well, I think everyone's been heard. We'll put the ten p.m. noise statute in, parking limited to fifty."

"Dark sky lights—"

"Yes 'dark sky' downward-facing lights. Your contractor will know what we're talking about, this is pretty standard stuff. Can I get a motion to approve and move on to the next order of business?" Stewart looks up and down the tables to his left and right.

"Motion to approve," Paul says.

"I'll second."

"All in favor?" A series of ayes. "All opposed?" Silence.

"Thank you," Cate says, trying to hold back a grin. She and Brian worm through the rows to their empty chairs. Cate sits and takes Vera's hand in her lap, squeezing it tightly as she keeps her gaze straight ahead. It feels warm and sweaty, like her own. Vera squeezes back.

"OK! Moving on. Fountain of Eternal Youth LLC has purchased three properties in the village hamlet right next door to these fine folks, and they're looking to redraw the lot lines and turn it into one large plot. We're usually in the business of approving subdivisions, so this is a new one for us. In fact, I'm not sure you need a special permit, there's nothing specific in our zoning laws against this kind of request that I could find. Board? Any concerns?"

Deborah Dunham, a slight woman in her mid-fifties with a red nose raises a hand and says that joining three properties with two houses could make reselling it down the line an issue which could then lead to abandonment.

"We don't intend to ever sell," says Lydia from the audience.

Everyone turns around again. Stewart looks up.

This woman is also immortal, Vera thinks again. Someone other than Vera or Eli or Ma is also immortal and she is standing right here.

"I'll remind everyone that this portion of the meeting is for discussion from the Planning Board only. Time for presentations and public comment will come after. I'll let you know when that begins."

Lydia smiles and mouths *I'm sorry*. Eli puts a hand on his heart in apology.

His wavy, light brown hair is longer than it was when she saw him in the desert a few months ago, tucked behind his ears now. His beard is trimmed short. He's wearing a blue button-down shirt with fitted jeans, gleaming leather "work" boots that haven't seen a lick of mud. His legs are crossed at the knee and he has an arm around the back of Lydia's chair. He looks handsome and urban, confident and rich, distant and above the fray. Vera feels suddenly small and mousy and matted, like she always does around him, but now it feels like a power.

Has Eli completely forgotten what it's like to make a first impression in a small town?

Deborah continues. If they do decide to leave—you never know, never say never—who would want a parcel with two houses? Two wells? Two septics? A few other board members nod. Paul flips to a new page in the large binder in front of him and squints at the print. Donald Filson, another board member, leans back in his chair, hands in the front pocket of his neon-yellow MOUNTAINTOP CONTRACTING sweatshirt and says they might turn it into a single-structure lot, demo one of them, would that be any better? Probably wouldn't want that either. Both buildings have been in the town for hundreds of years.

There are more nods from the board and audience. A few look to Eli and Lydia, who are listening patiently, their lips pursed.

"Only specific hitch in the zoning I can find is that we technically allow only one residential structure per lot," Paul says, his blue eyes bright against the navy of his EMT uniform. Some of the crowd murmurs, the legal sticking point having finally been found. "But they might have plans for one of the buildings that's not residential so, Stu, what do you think about opening up the floor so we can hear from the owners themselves?"

Stewart nods at Paul, asks Lydia and Eli to rise, and as they do, her brother scans the room with a gentle smile and there—

He sees her.

His eyes widen a fraction, then he continues the sweep of his gaze until it settles at last upon Lydia next to him.

Vera can feel every hair on her head.

"Good evening. My name is Lydia Kirke. First off, let me say thank you to the board for taking the time to review this proposal." She laces her manicured hands together as she beams at the members.

"It's our job," says Donald with a shrug. Half the audience chuckles.

"And same to the rest of you for coming tonight," says Eli as he holds his arms out to the audience. "Lydia and I are psyched to be here and to get to know all of you. It's so rad to see we're becoming part of a community that really cares." He smiles his bright white Hollywood grin, and Vera feels a different half of the room soften.

"So where's the billionaire?" asks Donald, hands still in his sweatshirt, unwilling to be impressed or lose the room. "He figure out how to outlive us all yet?"

Vera wasn't sure how much of this crowd had heard the news. There was the usual media splash the day of the press conference last week, but she hasn't seen anything about it since, the whole thing seemingly filed away with other silly rich people's announcements about wanting to live on the moon and such. Clearly word of it *has* spread through town though.

"Matthew's in California," Lydia answers. "That's where his company is based and will continue to operate. We are working on something together at the moment it's true, though I'm not at liberty to divulge the specifics. What's most important is that this gentleman is right—" And at this she gestures with an open palm to Paul. "The old general store will be my office and my partner, Eli, and I will live in the house."

"Business partner?" Deborah asks, head cocked to the side.

"Life partner," Eli answers.

"Boyfriend," Donald concludes.

She looks exactly like her picture, it's undeniable. The curls, the straight nose, the long neck, the deep-set eyes. But instead of a drab dress buttoned up to her chin, she has on a floral sundress with an alluringly low but technically classy neckline. She's wearing lipstick. Vera checks for a diamond or gold band on her left hand and is relieved to see there isn't one.

"What kind of office?" Deborah asks.

"A lab," Eli answers for her.

"We talking chemical waste?" Donald asks. "Could be dangerous—"

"No, no. I work in biomedical engineering and biotechnology. Honestly, most of my time is spent sorting through spreadsheets of other people's data, coordinating with my off-site team. It's like everyone else's office but with a few more computers and a refrigerator or two for the occasional bio specimen."

"Is he really going to cure death?" Deborah asks, a distinct pitch of hope in her tone despite her skeptical frown.

"Matthew's a visionary," Lydia says fondly. "And also a bit of a showman if you know what I mean."

"So he's lying," Donald says.

"He's shooting for the stars," Lydia counters.

"Not a Planning Board specific question, but I'm curious—why here?" Stewart asks, and everyone tunes in closer.

"Well, when Eli and I first found out that we both have roots in the area—"

"R'you the same Kirke as old general store Kirkes?" Beverly interrupts, her frown ever present, but clearly excited to play town genealogist.

"We're related," Lydia answers carefully, and Vera feels her pulse quicken. The delicate but precise evasion. The exact kind she herself has used so many times before. "The work I do requires focus and concentration, sometimes deep isolation, and that kind of quiet can be all but impossible to find in Silicon Valley these days," Lydia elaborates.

Donald asks one more time whether Matthew Barbery himself will ever live or work here.

"No, it's just us," Lydia insists. She puts her hand on Eli's chest and smiles. He clutches his hand over hers.

"Ah," says Stewart, expressing everyone's simultaneous relief and mild disappointment.

Beverly raises her hand and begins talking before Stewart calls on her. "What're *your* local 'roots'?" she asks Eli.

"I'm a Van Valkenburgh."

"No shit," she says, and at this the whole room laughs, except for Vera and Lydia.

"*OMG!*" whispers Cate as she grabs Vera's hand again. Even Brian looks over at her. Vera gives her best what-are-the-chances smile. Stewart bangs the table with the heel of his hand and pleads for everyone to keep the language G-rated, even though he seems to be enjoying the turn of events, too.

"Apologies, Stu, and Lord forgive me for the cussing, it's just that we've got an invasion of the Van Valkenburghs on our hands. We've got the ranger over here"—Beverly nods toward Vera and all eyes follow her way—"and now you."

"You're a Van Valkenburgh as well?" Lydia asks as she trains her eyes on Vera.

"I am." Her heart is a beast in her chest. "First name's Vera."

"Is it now?" Lydia says. Then she turns to Eli. "What a coincidence."

*

When the meeting adjourns, everyone stands and the crowded little room fills with neighborly chatter. Vera sees in her peripheral vision the circle of people who have formed around her brother and his new girlfriend.

"Congratulations you two," Sue tells Brian and Cate across a row of now empty folding chairs between them. "I know Ruth and Joe would be so proud."

"Thank you, Mrs. Adams," Brian replies, his demeanor suddenly that of a cooperating child. How quickly people revert to old roles.

"Sue! Please, sweetheart, I've been telling you for years, call me Sue."

"Thank you, Sue," Cate says, slipping her arm into her husband's. "We're *so* excited."

Vera is sweating now. From the stuffy room, from the nerves. She fans herself with the brim of her hat, allows her gaze to raise over Cate's and Brian's heads to her brother, who's laughing gallantly at something Beverly has said. The sight of it makes Vera feel an entirely uneasy mix of fury and relief.

How dare he break their promise and come back here for this, so cavalier.

Thank god he's here.

Vera's eyes flick over to Lydia, who's laughing, too, as she holds Eli's arm, a mirror image of Cate and Brian, everyone claiming each other.

Who *is* this woman?

"Well, if you'll excuse me, I'm going to go introduce myself," Sue tells them, quickly cupping the back of her short, gray hair. She doesn't have to specify who she's talking about.

"We'll come, too," Cate says, happy, so happy now that they've received their permit, and pleased to go meet the new neighbors she has otherwise been fearing and building up in her own head for weeks.

Vera hesitates, pretending to brush something off her hat as the others migrate to the opposite side of the room. She doesn't know exactly how she wants to play this. Generally oblivious of course, as a stranger as far as anyone can tell. She and her brother have done this dance a few times before, arriving to town a handful of days apart, pretending they don't know each other. It's been a necessary tactic to cover their tracks once in a while when things went awry. *That brother-sister pair who suddenly skipped town last month? The card counter and the girl who's too good with a gun for it to be quite proper? Nope, haven't seen a duo like that around here.*

But they've always made a plan for it beforehand, together. And they never did it in a place where they were planning to stay for any significant stretch of time. It's a hard ruse to keep up, pretending to be strangers after two centuries of being family.

And now, there's Lydia. And whatever Eli has or hasn't told her about his sister.

"Vera, you coming?" Cate calls, and Vera sees both Eli and Lydia turn their heads at the sound of her name. Their eyes fix on her, animallike in their attention. Predatory. Eli is the first to look away, back to Beverly. Lydia's gaze doesn't flicker.

Vera crosses the room into the fray.

Sue introduces herself first, followed by Cate, who also does the honors for Brian.

"We're your neighbors! Right next door. I mean duh, you already know that," Cate says and laughs at herself.

"You're Vera," Lydia says, not a question, manicured hand extended.

Vera grasps it firmly but not overly so. The woman's skin is soft and cool to the touch. Vera forces her features to relax into a practiced, gentle smile which Lydia matches, but above her smile, Lydia's deep brown eyes are dark with intensity. Vera represses the urge to shiver.

Lydia knows something about her. But clearly not everything. The look is one of assessment, gathering. Is she tallying all the tiny ways she and Eli look alike once you know what you're looking for? The shape of their eyebrows, the high set of their ears. Can Lydia somehow sense, beyond any coincidence of names, that Vera, too, is immortal?

Vera lets go first and turns to her brother.

"Eli," he says, hand extended. Vera shakes it and looks into his green eyes, bright and hopeful as always. Familiarity floods over her and she feels the corners of her mouth involuntarily pulling into a grin, which she overcorrects and has to pass off as the pressing together of chapped lips. She nods, not trusting her voice yet.

To think, she'd been telling herself she would never see him again. Not if things went according to plan. She sees now that she was right to have skipped a visit to San Francisco to say goodbye. She might have said too much, hesitated. Might have backed out of the move, backed out of her whole plan, his presence a force as strong as gravity, always pulling her back into orbit to spin on.

Eli being here changes everything.

No, not everything. She's just going to have to work a little harder to stay on track. To not be fooled by his foolishness. Sure he loves her in his way, but he hasn't truly cared for anyone but himself in too long.

"Vera lives with us," Cate says, draping an arm over her shoulder.

"In the old house?" Eli asks, looking between Vera and Cate, unable to contain his surprise. Brian clarifies that his wife means the cottage on-site. Their property includes the house, a cottage, and the barn where the cidery will be.

"Lucky you, a bar right in your backyard," Eli tells his sister, regaining his usual composure.

"And lucky you, a bar right next door," Vera says to him, the volley between them so easy. Too easy?

"Have you been here long?" Lydia asks. A perfectly acceptable question. A perfectly impossible question. Vera doesn't fidget or blink.

"Couple months."

"What brought you to the area?"

She puts on her ranger hat. "Work."

"You dig it out here?" Eli asks, and Vera knows what he's really asking. *Are you happy? Are you OK?*

"It feels like home," Vera tells him.

Eli smiles in genuine amusement. He's always enjoyed being in on the dramatic irony of their narrative, still hasn't tired of the inside joke of their existence. Vera finds herself feeling bolstered by their hiding-in-plain-sight dance. She is still in control.

"Awwww," Cate says, and she pulls Vera in closer with a squeeze. "Best tenant ever, never leave, OK? You're gonna help us pioneer this place. You'll be able to say you knew it when!"

"I'm sorry to break things up, but we need to close the building and get poor Ellen home, we've kept her here long enough," Stu says, friendly but stern, the formality of his leadership role still in the tenor of his voice despite the fact that the meeting is over.

"Forgive us, Ellen!" Eli calls to the board secretary with a smile and an overly formal, playful bow of his head. "I'll get these loiterers out of your hair!" He puts his palm on Lydia's back and offers the crook of his elbow to Sue, who accepts and coos about what a gentleman he is.

Vera swears she can feel Lydia's eyes on her own back as she and Beverly lead the small crowd down the short, tiled hallway, their voices echoing as the chatter continues, through the double doors, and into the cool of the evening parking lot.

"Well, we'll see you around," Beverly tells the group, then turns to Eli in particular. "And I'll put in a word with Bobby Shoemakker about getting a deal on the dumpster. He can be a righteous old grump but he won't be able to turn down a Van Valkenburgh!"

Eli thanks her. Everyone says their goodbyes. Sue and Beverly walk off toward their cars.

"You guys *have* to come over for a drink sometime," Cate tells the new neighbors, now ebullient in hospitable affection after her win.

"How about now?" Eli asks and the suggestion has the exact effect his suggestions almost always do. *What spontaneous fun!* their faces all say. *Why* not *right now?*

All except Lydia's.

"Darling, it's been such a long day," she begins, outwardly gentle, but with the stern undercurrent used by so many partners of extroverts. "And we have that call in the morning."

Vera watches Eli quickly calculate the situation. There is no call. But there is obviously a lot he and Lydia need to discuss tonight.

Whatever their plan is, Vera being here was not a part of it.

A large white truck approaches the group and everyone falls silent as they step aside to let it pass. Instead, it stops, its headlights illuminating the flagpole, the trees. The window lowers. Vera's equilibrium falters again briefly at the face now looking at her.

"You get my flies?" Paul asks her.

"I did, thank you! Sorry, I meant to—"

He interrupts to ask if she's used them yet. Vera is acutely aware that everyone is watching them. She says she hasn't had the time.

"How about Thursday?"

"Thursday?" Vera parrots, unable to remember a thing about her schedule. Doing something as simple as going fishing sounds impossible right now. Laughable. Her 219-year-old brother just arrived to town with his also-immortal girlfriend, can't he see?

"Rain's got the water running nice and high and the runoff will be settled by then. Shouldn't be too turbid," Paul presses, a soft hint of vulnerability appearing between his words. He tilts his head to the side slightly and runs a knuckle against the scruff of his chin and Vera finds her insides flutter a little at the gesture. The way he touches himself making her wonder how he might touch her.

She feels an elbow in her back that must belong to Cate.

"I'll be there, six o'clock," Paul says and gives the side of his truck a pat out the window. "Think about it, no worries if you can't make it. You know where to find me if you want."

"Bye, Paul," Cate says sweetly. "Thank you *so* much for our permit. You won't regret it."

"What's to regret about free cider for life?" he asks. Cate begins to laugh but it catches in her throat. "I'm kidding! Think we forgot to put that in the stipulations. See you around!"

"Bye," they all say in unison as he drives off.

"Well, as usual, the lady's right," Eli says, putting an arm around Lydia. "Think it's best we tuck it in early tonight, but let's take a raincheck, OK?"

"A rain check," Lydia echoes, nodding and smiling demurely. "I'm very curious to see your operation."

"See you later!" Eli says with a wave to the group, his eyes lingering on Vera's for half a count longer than anyone else's, making sure his sister understands what he's telling her.

*

It's just after midnight when he finally raps on the back door, two quick knocks followed by two long. The knock they've always used.

Vera turns off the lamp, lets him in quickly, quietly, the only sound the swoosh of the sliding door opening then closing behind him.

"Returning to your no-electricity roots?" he jokes of the darkness.

"Yes. I'm also shitting in a hole outside. Indoor plumbing is overrated."

Her brother laughs and Vera finds herself smiling despite the fact that she's spent the past four hours waiting for him, swinging through a full range of dangerous emotions. This has always been his magic trick. His mere presence wiping the slate clean. How hard it suddenly is to remember precisely what you were so worked up about once you're looking at his joyful face.

He's enormous in the small room, his head hardly a foot from the cheap drop ceiling. He smooths his hair back with two hands and takes in the space through the shadows.

"Cozy," he concludes, though the place is obviously unremarkable. "Have you been inside the house yet?" He looks out the kitchen window toward it. "I don't—"

"Who's Lydia?" she interrupts.

"One of us."

"What does she know about me?"

Eli steps closer and puts a hand on his sister's shoulder, two. He pulls her in for a hug. As he holds her he says he swears he didn't tell her, Lydia figured it out at the meeting when she heard Vera's name, when he couldn't hide his own reaction, she's not stupid. Lydia knew he had a sister named Vera, he'd told her that much but *not* that she was still alive. Lydia is one of them, they can trust her. Vera should trust her.

Vera wriggles out of the hug and steps back again. "She know about Ma?"

"Yes. We're looking for her. Got a PI on the case."

"Why are you using your real name?"

"Why are you? Look it's *here*, whatever did this to all of us, and we're going to find it and we're going to use it to cure cancer and every other horrible disease people die from. Lydia is an actual genius, you'll see." She's a scientist who's spent lifetimes amassing knowledge about longevity and regeneration, he explains. She's cautious and extremely private. They were introduced this fall in San Francisco at a house party of a mutual friend—Matthew.

"You're friends with Matthew Barbery?"

"I've invested with him before." Eli shrugs. "We met at Burning Man a couple years ago."

Lydia told Eli about her antiaging work, but not that she was immortal. Not until Eli told her the truth about himself, so convinced was he that his confession would change everyone's lives for the better once it was in her hands.

"Her entire life is a quest to create a future without suffering," he tells Vera, wide-eyed, evangelical. "She's a legit visionary, Wolven. I'd follow her to the ends of the earth to help, I really would."

"So you're in love."

"That's not the point!"

It isn't, but it will certainly complicate things, Vera thinks as she walks over to the kitchen sink.

"Who else knows? Does Matthew—"

"No one!"

"When were you going to tell me?"

"Tomorrow."

She laughs, an ugly squawk. "Bullshit."

"No, it's not bullshit, tomorrow's the tenth."

She turns and looks at him again, realizes he's telling the truth.

It's Eli. It's really Eli. Here, at home. They're home—188 years later, they're home.

"You broke the pact," Vera tells her brother.

"I did, but I can see we both agree it outlived its usefulness." He holds his hands palms up, like them standing there is proof.

Vera asks what he means. She's being stubborn she knows, but she feels like she's owed answers right now. Any kind of answer.

"When we first made it, it was to keep ourselves safe, right? But everyone died who'd have ever heard of us, and we still kept up the charade. It became sentimental bullshit."

"It wasn't bullshit, it was a promise. A promise we made to Ma, too."

"Ma's the one who left us, we don't owe her anything." His voice has turned bitter. It will be ninety-eight years this Christmas, but there it is, still an open wound. The sting of being left behind.

And yet he had no problem turning around and doing the exact same thing to Vera, twice.

Vera opens her mouth to say something, but he beats her to it.

"Why am I the one getting grilled? You're here, too! Clearly you thought it didn't matter anymore either."

"I'm sorry," she says. Because she won't argue, won't explain. She can't. She needs to keep the focus on him. She looks out the kitchen window again. "Why didn't you buy our house, too?"

"They turned our man down."

"Really?" Vera can't quite picture Cate turning down the cash, doesn't totally believe Cate would be able to keep that nugget from Vera either. One of them is lying.

"We'll get it back eventually. We've got the time." Eli winks at her and smiles, then straightens his face again. "So will you help us?"

"Help you what," Vera says to the darkness outside the window.

"Help us save the fucking world."

8

July 2014

"We've already been able to induce totipotency in cells that have matured into pluripotency, all of which is integral to approaching cell immortality in a regenerative capacity. When you combine this with a targeted DNA sequence attack on senescent cells then we're talking about not just organizing, proliferating, and vascularizing cellular material but actually reprogramming fundamental instructions for longevity."

Vera looks to her brother, who's perched on top of a folding table behind Lydia, one leg up on a chair, grinning. He raises his eyebrows in such a way as to say, *See? Isn't she smart? Isn't this exciting?* Vera maintains her stoic expression and looks back to Lydia as she continues, the sterile light of the long fluorescent bulbs shining on the tattered insides of the old general store. Empty shelves line the walls. A few pots of dust-caked plastic flowers sit in the painted-over windows. The counter on which Vera is perched has a pile of yellowed papers and an elaborate brass cash register with big, circular buttons.

"The FDA is in a complicated place with stem cells and is dragging its feet on re-categorizing aging as a disease, which will make all the difference in the rollout of our therapies. But the WHO has at least had the foresight to switch, so the right dominos are falling."

Lydia is calm and confident, brimming over with expertise. She is significantly less warm than she was at the Planning Board meeting last night. Perhaps Vera is not worthy of the same pleasantries behind closed doors. Perhaps Vera should be flattered by this. That here, in her family's old store, Lydia can simply be the brilliant immortal scientist that she is.

Vera folds her legs up and under herself and does her best to follow along as Lydia explains that while lifespans in America have nearly doubled since the 1800s, once you remove deaths from the top eight infectious diseases—which have all but disappeared thanks to antibiotics and improved sanitation—our overall longevity has in fact barely increased at all.

"Modern medicine has done a fantastic job eliminating the fast deaths, but not the slow," Eli chimes in with a tone that feels rehearsed. Like he's been pitching people on this idea elsewhere. "What still kills people is *aging*."

"Cardiovascular disease, neurogenerative disease, type 2 diabetes, and cancer to be precise," Lydia adds, then continues her monologue on preventing, eliminating, revitalizing, and reversing. On epigenetics, morphallaxis, the Hayflick limit, apoptosis, necrosis, chromosomes, and proteins. On data sets, controls, samples, variables, regression analysis, and model systems. Acceptance criteria, in vivo trials, the IRB, pharmacodynamics, and pharmacokinetics. Funding, valuation, allocation, control rights, NDAs, and IPOs. And finally water—aquifers, glacial epochs, alluvium, hydraulic action, watersheds, and osmosis.

Finally Lydia stops—twenty, thirty minutes later?—clasps her hands together and asks Vera, "Do you have any questions for me at this point?"

So many. Too many. But they're all irrelevant until Lydia answers one.

"Forgive my bluntness as I put this in layman's terms," Vera begins. "But you're not just going to bottle this up and sell it to the highest bidder, are you?"

"Can you imagine!" Lydia scoffs, and Eli takes her hand in his and kisses her knuckles. Lydia's face softens into a smile in that shy, delighted way that Vera has seen on so many other women standing next to her brother so many times before. Vera barely holds back her own grimace at the display.

"I need you to say no," she presses.

Eli tries to shoot his sister a look, which she carefully avoids. Instead, her eyes train on Lydia in her most practiced, cold stare. The one that adds centuries of gravitas to her delivery. The one that always inspires fear and submission. The one that says: *I am something you don't even know.*

But Lydia returns it, unflinching, and for the first time in years—decades, a century—Vera feels exposed. It's like a winter wind, the crack of ice right before it all caves in beneath you.

This woman knows Vera's secret. The one Vera has protected, despised, and wielded for nearly two hundred years. Because this woman has protected, despised, and wielded it, too.

For the first time ever, the fight is finally fair which, absurdly enough, strikes Vera as deeply unfair.

"No," Lydia answers in a tone more grave than she's used all morning. "Obviously this is not the type of technology that can wind up in just anybody's hands, which is why we've taken careful steps to secure a vigorous—"

"I'm not one of your investors, just give it to me straight," Vera interrupts.

Lydia purses her red lips, holding back a frustrated sigh. She smooths the front of her not remotely wrinkled dress and turns a bracelet around her wrist. She clearly doesn't want to have to convince anyone right now of the value of her work. Especially not someone like Vera, who is neither investor, nor scientist, nor average mortal citizen looking to get five to ten more good years out of their life.

"I think Lydia laid out Fountain's values and their path to market pretty clearly here," Eli says, using a tone Vera knows he usually reserves for professional situations. No one knows what to do with her right now. "This is going to change the world," he adds more cheerily, eager to steer the conversation back to how they're going to be saviors.

"I know it will," Vera says as she jumps down from the counter. "This is basically a weapon."

"A weapon against aging and senseless death," Lydia says.

"That's how *you*'d use it."

"Look, we cannot hoard knowledge," Lydia tells her firmly. "Knowledge—even possibly dangerous knowledge—should never be censored. It's an immoral and not to mention impossible task."

"Sounds noble," Vera replies, and she hates herself a little for being petulant, but what this woman is talking about is extremely dangerous. *Eternally* dangerous. "You sure you're going to feel the same way when some psychotic despot builds an immortal army?"

"That's a little extreme," Eli says.

"I'd say Matthew Barbery's goal to 'end death once and for all' is pretty extreme. Are you going to make more of us or not?" Vera asks Lydia, taking a step closer to her.

"It's not that simple."

"Why not?"

"Maybe one day there will be an opportunity to offer targeted radical repair or indefinite life extension comparable to our experience via multifaceted senolytic—" Lydia's jargon makes Vera grind her teeth. Lydia stops and huffs. "Vera, have you of all people not already witnessed enough pointless suffering and death?"

The question catches Vera, hitches against her momentum. The framing of it this way, it feels unfair.

"But is it *reversible*?" Vera insists, and her voice rises like it's full of fight but really it's fear. Because this is what Vera needs to know more than anything else—is their condition reversible?

She braces herself.

"Quite possibly," Lydia says.

Vera holds as motionless as she can. Wills her expression to lay inscrutable on her face when inside there is now a tumult, an absolute explosion of possibility.

Lydia senses that she finally holds the room, and so, she walks over to Eli slowly, stands next to where he's sitting, and sets a hand on his shoulder as if posing for a formal portrait.

"I won't bore you with the science of it, since that appears to be of little interest to you," Lydia begins, and Vera bristles at the insult while simultaneously realizing it's true. She doesn't want more lab talk, she wants plain answers. "Essentially, being able to isolate the source itself should provide a formula that can be not only re-created but also reversed."

Vera's mouth dries.

"Well, that changes everything," she says. She puts her hands on her hips, drops them to her side.

"Does it now?" Lydia asks, one penciled-in eyebrow raised.

Vera folds her arms across her chest, even though she knows it's a classic defensive tell, but she can't help herself. She needs to hold it all in. Suddenly Eli bolts up and squeezes her in a crushing hug.

"I knew you'd come around, Wolven!"

Eli, so willing to imagine the best, even after all these years.

Vera can feel Lydia watching them. She endures the pressure of Eli's hug despite the tightening in her chest, the wobbling of her vision. She arranges her face into a placid smile as she resurfaces to Lydia's cold gaze.

Then she realizes she does in fact have another question.

"You seem certain it's water. Why?"

"The average adult human body is between fifty-two and sixty percent water, depending on one's fat-to-muscle ratio. Plainly speaking, we are water," Lydia explains. "Not to mention when considering a basic literature review, the source of immortality is most frequently water. Look at Gilgamesh, Herodotus, the tales of Bimini. So many floods and fountains, often paired with an element of earthly alchemy like in, say, the philosopher's stone. Stories are data points, too. There's almost always an essential truth being passed down in them."

Vera feels justified to have her own hunch confirmed yet still asks, "But if it was in the water, wouldn't it have happened to the whole town?"

"Clearly it's not as simple as that. There are literal *millions* of contingencies to take into account. This is exactly what I was saying earlier about running multiple models of regression analysis simultaneously in order—" Lydia stops herself and gives her curls a little shake. "Never mind. I see the apple didn't fall far from the tree." She looks back and forth between the siblings.

"She's my little sister, not my child," her brother says.

"You know what I mean." Lydia waves her hand in their direction. "You're very much alike."

They frown at each other. *Alike?*

Eli is the first to shrug and clap his hands together.

"Well, dang. Let's do this!"

That's so him, Vera thinks. To just cheerfully go along. To gallivant around as if this whole thing were some silly, whimsical puzzle they're all going to have so much fun figuring out together.

But it's not a terrible tactic.

She'll do it, Vera decides, the conclusion sudden, swift. She'll help them with their research. Help them find the source. She'll let them think she, too, is doing it to help others and cure the world of its many diseases. No one needs to know what she really wants. And by the time they unleash the whole thing? Well, she finally won't have to care anymore.

She'll finally be dead.

Vera smiles, and it's a sickening hybrid of performance and authenticity. To be beaming with her brother but at the prospect of something so different from the cause of his own magnetic grin.

"Yes. Let's do this," she repeats after him, looking in his bright eyes, feeling Lydia's on her, hunting, assessing.

"Get in here!" Eli says lifting both his arms. Vera settles under one, and together they look to Lydia. "You too, babe," he beckons and Lydia hesitates. It's brief, a small flash. But Vera's certain she's seen it. A hesitation to join them.

"Let's do this," Lydia echoes them, cheerful now, as she takes the few steps over and tucks herself under Eli's other arm. "We'll start next week."

*

Vera straightens her ranger hat. The green ferns wiggle and wave in the breeze along the narrow ridgeline. Lopez sets the pace ahead of her. In their companionable silence, her thoughts continue to loop as they have all day:

Someone else is immortal.

If we find the source, it's reversible.
If we find the source, I can die.
She can die.

It makes her feel fluttery and light-headed in an almost illicit way. No more hiding and lying. No more running away. No more wondering about Plan B. No more worrying that something like what happened back in California might happen again.

"Could we see your place from here if the trees weren't leafed?" Lopez asks, taking her out of her own mind again.

"Yeah, I'm straight down there." Vera points off the trail into the bowl of the valley. Together they peer into the rocks and trees.

"So freaking stunning." Lopez sighs, his appreciation of the region's natural beauty always so genuine. "You're lucky you landed a spot like that."

When Vera, Eli, and Ma left that summer day in 1826, they walked south across the meadow, through the creek, and up this mountain past where she and Lopez are standing right now. They moved leisurely in case any neighbors might have happened by and spotted them, in case Lotte was watching from the laundry line or the well. Of the three of them, only Eli was weak enough—or maybe it was strong enough—to look back at the house one last time before they entered the tree line.

A picnic, at Pa's favorite lookout. That's what they had told Lotte that morning. A thing for just the three of them. That was fine, she'd said. She was going to visit her mother and father that afternoon, might stay the night, would that be all right?

"Take your time, dear," Ma told her, the basket of their supplies already on her arm.

"I can prepare supper for you before I go," Lotte offered.

"Don't worry about us," Eli said, his voice nearly swallowing itself.

The way he kissed her, quickly, but on the mouth, in front of all of them. The look of embarrassed, pleasant surprise on Lotte's face.

Once under the cover of the hemlocks, chestnuts, and maples, the three of them hurried their pace. The plan was to get as far northwest as quickly as they could. To travel faster than the news of their disappearance. They considered splitting up. On their own they'd be less recognizable than as a trio. But in the end, they decided to stay together, no reason necessary beyond the fact that they were leaving everything and everyone they knew behind forever.

They stuck to the deep woods along the southern ridge of the valley. After an hour walking as quickly as they could, they found the tree where Eli had hidden a second blanket, a canteen of brandy, and a larger bag of rations for their journey. More bread, corn cakes, sausage, and cheese. They picked raspberries and blackberries along the way, successfully crossed the notch road without being spotted by anyone. When night fell, they stopped somewhere past what's now called Halcott Mountain but didn't light a fire.

"This is for the best," Ma said to the darkness as they lay three in a row on a bed of pine needles. Neither Vera nor Eli said anything either way. An unfathomable future ahead of them.

They woke at first light to the snapping of a twig nearby and bolted up in unison to find not another villager but a young stag, its horns velvet and small. It looked at them with its blank, water-deep eyes. After a time that felt longer than it was, it hopped away. Wordlessly they rose, bundled their things, and started walking again.

At midday they tacked north, picking their way along what they were hoping was Roxbury Creek. They'd brought a map Eli had secured from a fur trader he'd met outside the new general store. But none of them had been this far west before and couldn't be sure.

When they stopped for a lunch break Eli said, "Someone has to be looking for us by now."

Initially, Eli wanted to stage their deaths. Send Lotte on an errand and turn the house inside out, blood everywhere, make it look like they'd been sacked by Mohicans. But Vera and Ma didn't like it. It would spook the whole village. Besides, the Mohicans had always left them alone in the valley. People wouldn't believe it or worse, if they did, might go seeking misguided revenge.

Vera suggested a fire. It would account for the lack of bodies. The trouble was it would leave Lotte homeless, though in all likelihood Lotte was probably going to be taken back in by her parents, being widowed and childless and all.

"She'll find someone else soon enough," Ma had assured Eli in the barn one morning before they left. The three of them were forking hay in the loft together, trying to set Lotte up for success after they were gone without bringing too much attention to their prepping. Vera watched what was supposed to be a comfort land like a punch, Eli's face contorting in some mixture of private pain.

A fire was entertained for a full week before Ma said conclusively that she could not abide by wasting Pa's work. "It would kill him all over again," she declared.

So a picnic it was. Lunch and a wrong turn, maybe a bear. As long as they kept moving it would work, no one would ever find them. They swore to each other they would never return.

"Want to bushwhack back?" Lopez asks, whipping Vera to the present. "Cut off trail and head straight down? I'm kind of curious to see this part."

"Sure," Vera says tentatively. She can't help but feel like he's somehow been listening to her thoughts.

Together, they weave through tree trunks and hop over rocks as they poke their way down the mountainside that used to belong to Vera's family.

Moving easily among the pines and maples, she wonders who decided to sell this part off and when. Why.

"When exactly was the Preserve established again?" she asks over the crunching of their footsteps.

"That was 1885. Ranger, you gotta know your history! Article fourteen of the State Constitution declares that these acres be 'forever kept as wild forest land,'" Lopez explains in his most authoritative voice. "Originally established with thirty-four thousand acres, it's grown to nearly three hundred thousand since then."

"It used to be clear-cut here," Vera says. Every single maple, elm, mulberry, chestnut, and hemlock was harvested for their lumber or firewood. The lower half of the mountain shorn down to trimmed clover and fragrant thyme by their grazing sheep who dotted the green hillside like little white clouds.

"Logging and other rampant resource extraction was one of the main reasons the Preserve was created."

"OK, professor," Vera says and decides to not clarify that she was talking about the small-scale clear-cutting of lower elevations in the early 1800s, not the industrial scale of what came in the years after she and her family had already left—forests decimated for commercial tanneries and sawmills, for more and more settlers.

"Lots of mountainsides around here were replanted with red pines in the thirties as WPA projects when the state was trying to make jobs for people during the Great Depression and all that."

This Vera didn't know, but it makes sense. How else would a forest this homogeneous have appeared so quickly?

They continue downhill in silence once again, weaving through the tree trunks, stepping steadily on dirt and pine needles, over boggy spots and piles of deer and bear scat. Vera's mind now coursing through memories of the parched thirties spent with Eli moving town to town, relying on some of their less-than-admirable skills—petty thieving, card counting, and such.

After about twenty minutes, Lopez stops and leans against a rock wall, then pulls out his water bottle and takes a drink. At this quick pace and on this straight trajectory, the trip down the mountain will be three times faster than the one up.

"Who do you think made these?" he asks and nods toward the waist-high stack of stones he's resting on that runs in a line down the mountain. She doesn't answer, waits for him to tell her what he thinks. "Some people say it was Native Americans. Others say—"

"Farmers," Vera says, thinking they'll say it at the same time.

"I was going to say ancient aliens."

"What?" Vera laughs and shakes her head as she remembers the drudgery of digging, hauling, and stacking all those stones. Every year they rose in the thin soil like some Devil's crop set to destroy their own. Every year the Van Valkenburghs removed them to make way for the potatoes and hay and what not, dragging them in sleds behind horses, moving and stacking for hours upon hours. They marked their property line. They crossed the ridge to contain the sheep. They piled them into people-height domes when they had no more use for lines yet still more stones.

"Laugh all you want," Lopez says, vigorously screwing closed the top of his water bottle. "But a lot of these walls line up with a certain electromagnetic current that runs through this valley."

"You can't be serious."

For someone with an undeniably supernatural existence, Vera is deeply disinclined to believe in almost anything else even vaguely occult.

"As a heart attack! And the cairns? The big circular piles of them? Some of them align with the sunrise on the equinox." His voice is breathy with wonder.

"I'm not so sure about that," Vera says and she starts to walk again, Lopez now following behind.

"Jenny doesn't believe any of it either. My mom's real deep into this stuff though. Psychics, tarot, destiny, crystals." He says she always knew she'd have three daughters and one son. Had a vision of the dogwood in their backyard before she even laid eyes the house, that's how she knew it was the right place when the real estate agent showed it to her. Knew Jenny was the one for him because she kept seeing the number 1212 in the month before he met her and it turns out that's her birthday, December twelfth.

"Did she know about the baby before you told her?" Vera asks. She doesn't believe any of this but does enjoy the pleasure he's taking in sharing it with her. People find evidence of what's important to them in all kinds of ways. Proof that what feels special to them is in fact so.

"Claims she had a vision of a little girl the night before we told her! Jenny was *pissed*. She didn't want to know the baby's sex."

"But Jenny doesn't believe."

"Yeah, but my mom's rarely wrong about this stuff. Except—" He holds a finger in the air. Vera can see through the trees, now that they're almost to the creek. "She keeps asking me about an older woman. Says in all her readings lately I've got this old lady looking out for me."

Vera's neck tingles a little. She cracks the knuckles of her left hand in one swift movement and asks if Jenny's older than him.

"Younger. I was telling my mom maybe *she's* the old lady, but she didn't like that." He laughs again. Vera cracks the knuckles on her other hand. Dismisses the coincidence of Lopez's mother's vision as just that—a coincidence. She knows better.

"The creek's ahead," she says as the ribbon of it comes into view.

"Hot damn that was fast."

They hurry the last hundred feet and emerge from the shadow of the trees into the late afternoon sun. The water sparkles and gushes, bounty and relief. Always a comforting sight for Vera.

"You came!" a voice calls, and they both turn to see who it is.

It's 6 p.m., Thursday.

Paul is exactly where she saw him the first time. Again, he's wearing waders, standing in the water, rod tucked into the crook of his arm. The delight so obviously apparent in his animated face.

The way he looks at her, just like Jacob. It's so familiar it spooks her once more. She takes a step back and bumps into Lopez.

"You brought a friend," Paul says, spotting her partner, not entirely able to hide the disappointment in his expression now.

"You know this guy?" Lopez asks quietly behind her.

"I'm sorry, I—we—" Vera stumbles through an explanation that brings Lopez and Paul both up to speed about their patrol and bushwhacking and Paul's open-invite to meet on the creek today.

"Stay and fish, I know my way from here," Lopez tells her, trying to appear casual but clearly delighting in the idea of Vera having a date.

"No, we have to pick up your truck in the lot—"

"Nah, I've got it," he tells her, then turns to Paul. "You got your fishing license on hand?" Paul's face freezes. "I'm just messing with you!" The men laugh. "But seriously, you've got a license, right?"

Paul looks to Vera as if to ask *Does he really need to take out his license for them right now?* She smiles some, and gives her head a little shake no. The small intimacy of it—communicating with no words—makes her feel warm but exposed.

"Alrighty then," Lopez says, stepping out onto a boulder midstream. "I'll catch you at headquarters, Van Valkenburgh. What do you say to fishermen, good luck? It's not break a leg."

"Tight lines," Vera and Paul answer in unison.

Lopez gives a wave, another hop, then scrambles up the opposite bank, and is gone.

Vera looks to Paul. "I don't have my rod. Should I—"

"Use mine." He holds it out to her like an offering.

*

The canopy of green sways gently above them, fat maple leaves fanned out against the blue sky.

"Watch and learn," Vera says.

"Ho ho! I see how it is." Paul smiles with his whole face. "I wouldn't have pegged you for a shit talker, but I can dance."

"I'd prefer to fish," she says playfully, then casts over him upstream, placing the fly in a dark little eddy she knows the brookies favor. She gives one, two light tugs and there—a bite. She lifts the tip of the rod, quick and firm but not too high, and sets the hook.

"You did not just do that," Paul says, genuine surprise turning his face into wide eyes, an open mouth.

Vera is an amazing angler with twenty decades of fishing under her belt. But even she thinks she got a little lucky just then.

She pushes back her grin.

"You want to net me?" she asks and he looks at her willingly but still slightly dumbfounded. Vera keeps her gaze on her line as it tugs in the water, the trout darting and pulling as it tries to free itself. She begins to gently reel in her catch. In her peripheral vision she sees Paul fumble to unclip the small net off the back of his fishing vest. He's a little clumsier than Jacob ever was, she notes, skittish. Then again, Jacob had the steadiest hand Vera's ever known. It was why the horses loved him. One of the reasons she loved him, too. It always seemed like things would be OK when she was with him. Until they weren't.

"I'm ready," Paul says, crouching next to her, water running over the knees of his waders. Vera guides her catch in closer, closer, then, at just the right moment, Paul nets the trout. The fish continues to thrash but it's theirs now.

"Thank you," she says and squats down at Paul's level. She can smell him. Fresh laundry and something earthy. She's suddenly aware she could use a shower after today's rounds, her uniform a wash.

She refocuses. Balancing the rod against her shoulder, she takes the slick body of the fish in her hands, holding it with the precise amount of pressure she knows she needs to use—firm enough to keep it in her grasp, but not so firm as to injure or further panic it. In one smooth motion she deftly removes the hook from its mouth, then holds the fish under an inch or so of water, tilting it on its side so they can take in the intricate beauty of its skin, its colors.

"I'd call that a thirteen-incher," Paul says, stretching out his hands to measure the length of her catch. His thumb grazes the inside of her wrist and her veins are shot through with an instant and startling longing she hasn't felt in years.

She bolts up quickly and holds out the fish.

"And I'd call you an exaggerator, that's ten at best."

Paul laughs and stands, above her now. He probably has a whole foot on her. The trout's gills open and close silently. Vera bends back down and cups it in the creek, releasing her grip slowly, letting the creature readjust to the water. It begins to wiggle, realizes it's free, then darts out of sight to live another day. When she looks up at Paul, he's not looking where the fish went. He's looking at her.

"Well, I guess it's my turn to embarrass myself," he says after a beat, and steps backward toward the shore, the rocks clacking against each other as he accidentally kicks them over. He tries to reattach the net to the back of his vest but can't reach, starts turning like a dog might begin to chase its own tail.

"Here, I'll take it," Vera says, holding her hand out for the net. "You should try that pool again. I'm sure there's something else in there."

Paul does, and Vera is right. This time he brings in an honest twelve-incher. She points him to another eddy five feet up from the first and he lands another, this one smaller but its colors nearly tropical in their decadence. She shows him a third and again he hooks a beauty.

"Damn, Vera, how'd you learn to read the water like this?" His voice is full of unabashed awe.

"Practice."

He asks if she grew up fishing, she says yes. He asks who taught her, her dad? Yes. Where?

"On a creek like this one. Out west a little, too."

She wants to tell him more about all the waters she's fished. But she does not explain how much of the 1840s she spent catching dinner in what's now Montana because money was tight, Eli having risked it all on a big fur buy that went bust then a cattle drive of dubious origin. She does not go into her time in the 1970s riverboat guiding in Big Bend, Texas, through parts that were still Mexico back when she'd first seen it. Doesn't tell him how many days and days she's spent on this very creek lifetimes ago.

"I hear you ride horses, too."

She looks at him, and he's grinning.

"Did Janet—"

"Janet, Stan, even my *mom* asked if I'd heard about how the new ranger saved a whole party from a rabid coyote by catching a runaway horse with her bare hands and shooting—"

Vera waves him off, says everybody's exaggerating.

"What about you? Who taught you to fish this well?" she asks.

"My dad, but he left when I was twelve, so." Paul shrugs his shoulders and Vera recognizes the hidden hurt beneath his nonchalance. "Mostly I learned by doing. Trial and error."

"Sure," Vera says, nodding earnestly, because that's the only way she's learned anything over the past two centuries. By trying and failing. Trying and failing and leaving and trying somewhere else again.

"I've read some books about it, too, because I'm a nerd at heart. You're looking at the salutatorian of the Hunter-Tannersville Central High School's class of 2000 right here." He holds himself with exaggerated pride, like a statue portraying a grand victory.

Vera does the math she does all the time. He's thirty-one. Too young for her by about 180 years. Five years older than she'll ever get to be.

"I would have been valedictorian," he continues, pulling out a small box of flies from the chest pocket of his vest. "But my girlfriend bagged some extra credit from an independent study last-minute and totally stole it from me."

"Your high school girlfriend?" Vera asks as she watches his fingers sort through the feathered flies.

"High school girlfriend, college girlfriend, med-school girlfriend," he lists, and Vera begins to feel taken for a fool. "Hell, she was even my fiancée for a minute there." He laughs tightly.

Was. Like she's gone now. But in a moved-out-of-town way, not dead-for-a-century way.

"OK, your turn! Wanna try one of these I made last night?" he asks, animated once more, nodding at the small tufted fly sitting in the open palm of his outstretched hand. His hair falls across his eyes briefly before he shakes it back. *Jacob*, she almost says aloud because it is so uncanny. "If it won't work for you, I know it won't work for anybody," he tells her.

She looks at his lips, the corner of his mouth. She knows how it will feel. That soft scratch of two-day stubble. A warm, firm hand cupped on the nape of her neck, her back, her ass. His fingers grazing her nipples as he presses against her—

"I should go," she says, and it's abrupt and awkward and she should do a better job of pretending to be normal but she can't.

"Already?" Paul asks, rightfully confused. Is that disappointment she hears in his voice, too?

"I've got—I forgot I've got this thing—"

Now she's the one clumsily grabbing her boots and hat, stumbling over the rocks, crushing her toes and holding back a wince or a howl. Holding back everything, like she's always done, like she's always had to do. Keep it in, shove it down, run away.

"I'll see you around!" she tells him, already hurrying off.

"OK?" he says, and it comes out like a question. Like he has something else he wants to ask.

9

July 2014

Vera has never heard of Summer Friendsgiving until she's invited to Stan's.

Beer in hand, she watches Lydia explain for the twelfth, fifteenth, twentieth time to different smiling faces how she and Eli wound up here of all places. That, yes, she's a Kirke, like the old Kirke's General Store. No, sorry, they aren't going to reopen it. Yes, she's a scientist working for Matthew Barbery. Yes, Eli is in finance, venture capitalism.

"And quite the chef! Did you try his squash risotto?" Wanda moans and closes her eyes in exaggerated pleasure as she eats another bite.

"He made the chocolate soufflé, too," Nancy says, pointing with her fork at her now empty dessert plate.

Vera watches as the women of the valley work themselves into a lather over Eli's various talents. She spots him across the room with Stan, Bill, and Pete, their noses pointing into their wineglasses, careful frowns of concentration as Eli leads them through tasting notes.

Everyone loves Eli, they always do. Usually it's Vera who basks in the reflective glow near his side, however that's Lydia's place now and to Vera she seems hesitant, even put out by it.

It's hypocritical of Vera, of course. How many times has she herself begrudged Eli his social attentions and distractions out of fear or jealousy or some shameful combination of both? But as people have known for eons, there are things you can dislike about your own family, however that rarely means you'll appreciate hearing those same things pointed out by someone else.

Vera has been staying near Lydia out of a sense of duty. No, curiosity. But her patience for the repeating introductions has run its course. She wants to be with Eli but keeps reminding herself she has time—they'll have plenty of time. People might get the wrong idea if she hangs around him too much too soon.

"So how are you liking country life?" Nancy asks Lydia, blinking to reveal heavy brown eye shadow. There aren't many occasions to dress up out here, so the weekend crew takes what opportunities they can to demonstrate that they don't always exist in a sea of flannel, they clean up nicely, too.

"I'm a city girl at heart, but I'm making do," Lydia answers with a smile. She looks glamorous tonight. Sleek and chic in her tight black dress, deep red lipstick, her dark hair pinned back revealing her long, slim neck. Vera herself is wearing jeans and the one nice blouse she wore last time she was here. She hasn't owned a dress since the eighties. Certainly not lipstick.

"Do you miss takeout? I miss takeout," Wanda says wistfully. "Though maybe you don't if your man cooks for you like this all the time!" And at that the three women laugh together with more gusto and follow Lydia's gaze across the room to the man in question who, sensing their eyes upon him, looks up and gives a dashing wink.

Nancy asks Lydia if she's from San Francisco.

"That's where I was most recently, but I've lived in New York and Philadelphia, Chicago, Seattle, LA . . ."

With each city Lydia lists, Vera conjures a flash of some Hollywood-worthy life. Lydia holding a lace parasol strolling Central Park arm in arm with a man in a top hat. Lydia in a little flapper's cloche drinking champagne in a smoky jazz bar. Lydia in a bright scarf behind the wheel of a convertible on Route 1. Ridiculous she knows. Why should she think Lydia's lives have been any easier than hers? Lydia was living in the same world. And she was living in it alone.

The realization stops Vera, catches her breath tightly in her throat.

To have been completely alone in this for that long.

Then to find out there was someone else like her, finally. And that of all the people in the world that someone was Eli.

"My goodness, you've moved a lot!" Nancy says. "Was this when you were a kid—"

"No, my parents moved once right before I was born then never left that town. In fact, they thought I was quite mad to leave when I did."

"They still there?" Wanda asks, poking at what remains on her plate.

"They died many years ago."

Nancy and Wanda both express their condolences.

"Thank you, that's very kind. But to tell you the truth, we weren't close. I was always the black sheep of the family."

"How so?" Vera asks because she can't help herself.

Lydia appears to suddenly remember the multilayered nature of this conversation with Vera in the audience and she pauses as she brings her wineglass to her red lips. She takes a sip. Vera, Nancy, and Wanda all wait expectantly.

"Oh, the usual story. I had a bit too much ambition for their liking, no interest in settling down. I think they felt my desire to leave was an insult to their way of life, something I'd never intended and yet—" Lydia lets her sentence hang there unfinished.

"And yet now you find yourself back in a small town," Nancy says. "Funny how what we want in life changes, right?"

Wanda hmm's in agreement, nodding.

"My parents would certainly be surprised to learn how things have turned out for me," Lydia says, and Vera can't tell if her voice is mournful or wry. She doesn't understand this woman yet. Certainly doesn't trust her. What on earth did her brother see in her that made him share his most dangerous secret? *Their* secret?

Lydia finally laughs, breaking the tension in the air for the other women, who politely follow suit.

"How did you start working for Matthew Barbery?" Nancy asks, her tone slightly conspiratorial now in a gossipy, friendly way.

"*I* approached *him* when I heard he was moving into the radical longevity sector. I was initially in nursing, but I've always wanted to be on the forefront of this kind of cutting-edge research."

Lydia explains to the women that there is a misconception about the longevity movement. That's it's focused on selfish, frivolous things like antiaging skin care for vain celebrities and keeping ancient millionaires alive so they can amass even more money for themselves.

"But none of that is the point. It's certainly not why I've dedicated my life to it," she says with a hand over her ever-beating heart. "It's about giving people the longest possible *health*-span, not just lifespan. Who wants to live to one hundred if you're physically miserable for the last twenty years of it?" The women nod along vigorously, agreeing. "Ultimately, I feel I have a responsibility to do everything in my power to eliminate the unnecessary pain of aging as much as possible for as many people as possible."

"That is *so* admirable," says Wanda. "Good for you!"

"Anyone need a drink from the bar?" Vera asks because she can't help but feel that Lydia's little speech was partially directed at her, and now she wants to get away.

"Another punch please, thank you, cutie," Wanda says.

"And a white wine!" Nancy adds.

"Anything for you?" Vera asks Lydia. She's the only one among them whose glass is empty.

"No thank you," Lydia says without making eye contact, her attention now locked on Eli across the room.

Vera finds Cate at the ice bucket describing to Phil the cider making equipment that arrived this morning.

"We didn't think it would come this fast, we only *just* got the permit, but—"

"You ever run a bar before? Let me tell you something," Phil begins with a finger in the air, and both women steady themselves for the supposedly friendly, always uninvited, and rarely helpful advice that follows that kind of introduction from men his age. "You can't let people take advantage of you. You're a friendly young woman, people are going to think they can." Cate nods. Vera grabs a bottle of beer and opens it with her pocketknife then reaches for the white wine and pours a glass. "You've got to stand up for yourself, young lady!" he continues.

"Absolutely. I've been running my own graphic design business for—"

"And tell the drunks they're cut off when they've had too much! Bees to honey, you don't want the locals coming around thinking they can get a discount or a pass to drive wasted on The Road!"

Vera ladles out a cup of punch, asks Cate in gesture if she wants one, too, who mouths *yes please*. She hands it off, scoops another, and leaves Cate to endure Phil's cascading monologues alone because he's right about one thing—Cate will have to learn when to cut off certain locals.

Vera delivers the drinks. The party continues and everyone takes turns flocking to the newcomers. She gives them space. She talks fishing with Pete, gardens with Nancy, skiing with Stan, classical music with Wanda. It's been hardly six weeks since she came to the Memorial Day party here, but already it feels like she's been home for years. Time always stretching and collapsing around her.

As the party nears a pitch, Stan lowers the music, and turns to the crowd.

"Now I know at last year's Summer Friendsgiving I swore I wouldn't make you do it again but, like the pilgrims, I'm going back on my word!" Some people laugh and a few others groan. "It won't take long I promise! Not if you all cooperate."

"I'd be 'grateful' if we skipped this part!" calls Phil, hands cupped around his mouth like he's at a game taunting the opposition.

"All right, it looks like Phil got us started," says Stan, taking the jeers in stride. He lifts his glass in the air and everyone hushes. "This year I'm grateful for friendships—the old and *especially* the new." A few people take mock offense and he raises his eyebrows playfully. "To Cate and Brian and their chutzpah to dream big in a small town—" A few hoots and hollers break out with dampened, one-handed applause since everyone is holding a drink or a plate or both. Cate puts her head on Brian's shoulder and beams, the bashful bride. Stan continues. "To Vera and her careful stewardship of these beautiful lands we're all so lucky to call home—" There are hmm's and sage nods as Vera tips an invisible hat. "Not to mention her incredible Annie Oakley skills!" At this the crowd breaks into wild cheers and Vera looks toward the floor and shakes her head, can see Eli and Lydia out of the corner of her eye listening to Wanda as she excitedly explains what happened last time with the coyote.

"Buttercup and I will be forever grateful," Stan says with a hand on his chest. "And to Lydia and Eli—" he continues. All heads swing around to the newest of the newcomers, who look up at the attending eyes. "We've only just met, but it's my most sincere hope that you feel welcomed here and that you'll stay a long time. Cheers!"

They all clink glasses with the people at their shoulders and drink, the mood swelling. Look at this town, off to such great things. Cider-makers and scientists, horseback-riding rangers and handsome venture capitalists.

"Am I next?" Bill asks at Stan's other side. He looks down to his shoes then up to the ceiling. "OK. I'm grateful for my new granddaughter, Maeve."

A round of awws and more cheers.

They circle the whole party, everyone announcing their genuine gratitude, their self-conscious jokes in the face of such an earnest exercise, their mixes of both. Good health, a chance to see Italy again after having last gone as a teenager. The passing of a mother who had been in pain, it was her time. Finally getting Internet up here that's fast enough to stream movies.

When it's Eli turn, Wanda shouts out she's grateful for his risotto.

"And I'm grateful to have a new bunch of recipe guinea pigs! How do you all feel about venison lasagna? I hear Sam's still got some of that eight-pointer he bagged last year in his freezer! Should we help out Eliza and make some room in there?"

"He should be a politician," someone murmurs behind Vera, who's heard this sentiment before.

"But seriously? I'm grateful for so many things right now. Most of all that I get to be here with all of you in this place that meant so much to my family back in the day." He and Vera make brief eye contact as there's more cheering and clinking of glasses, then all eyes settle on Lydia at his side. They wait as she smiles and looks around the room, considering what to say. She smooths the sides of her already sleek dress with both hands. She looks so urban and elegant. An alien in high heels. No one would ever guess she was born in a place like this. In *this* place.

"Well? I'm grateful to Eli for restoring my faith in humanity."

There's a pause, so grand and personal is her gratitude. Even Vera is momentarily thrown by the magnitude of it. Then Phil shouts, "And his risotto!" And everyone laughs and wishes that they had someone like Eli in their lives, then they all remember that now they do.

A handful more people speak until it's Vera's turn last, having been on the other side of Stan when the circle first began fifteen minutes ago. She should have been thinking of what to say but she was so content listening. People usually spend so much time complaining. It's a form of gentle bonding—*oh this terrible weather, oh my mother-in-law is driving me crazy, oh this good-for-nothing government*—and Vera does it, too. In fact, it's the polite thing to do. But it gets heavy when it accumulates. When you spend hundreds of years listening to the banal complaints of people who should be perfectly happy because they are warm and dry and safe and mortal. Which means moments like this—pure appreciation—do something to Vera that briefly lightens that load.

She raises her glass of wine, still uncertain what she will declare. She looks at the small crowd, watching her so expectantly. She says what's true:

"I'm grateful this place is home."

Everyone cheers heartily. Someone says Amen. Stan turns up the music and a page in the party is turned.

The festivities devolve joyously.

Around 1 a.m., Lydia finds Eli in the kitchen with Vera, Stan, and Wanda, where Eli and Vera have been throwing back triple shots of whiskey to outpace their rapidly healing bodies best they can, inebriation always hard to maintain for more than a few minutes at a time.

"Darling, I'm pretty tired, shall we?" Lydia asks him.

"Oh, we can't go already! It's so early!"

Vera's been on the other side of this scene one thousand times before. Eli is impossible to extricate from a party he's enjoying. She wants to tell Lydia to not bother.

"Take the car! I'll walk later. It's so close, and there's no wolves to get us anymore!" He slurs that last part a little as he looks to his sister and grins.

"I'll walk with him," Vera tells Lydia, whose concern is radiating off her like a low hum. *Wolves? Anymore?* "With Cate and Brian, too," Vera adds for the sake of decorum.

"I love you," Eli tells Lydia as he leans in and kisses her on the cheek. He seems briefly, instantly sober again. Devout.

"Thank you for the lovely time," Lydia tells Stan instead of replying to Eli and she hugs the host delicately. "Good night, everyone."

Vera forces herself to not watch Lydia as she leaves.

"Who's hungry?" Eli asks suddenly. Everyone who hears him raises their hands.

Eli enlists his sister to help him make a pantry pasta of ingredients from Stan's well-appointed kitchen for the rest of the drunken revelers. Together they dice onions and squeeze lemons, peel sticks of butter and pry open bottles of capers. They dance to the disco Eli loved so much when it was new. Their hips swivel, their heads bounce as they slice and stir. Wanda is pink in the face from happy exertion, Cate is sweating, her hands above her head as she twirls. Stan has an unlit cigar in his mouth he occasionally takes out to gesticulate with enthusiastically. It's fun, so fun, and they are all drunk and happy and distracted. Which is how, in the middle of a particularly enthusiastic moment of dancing to "Staying Alive" while chopping up parsley, Eli accidentally slices off his entire left pointer finger at the knuckle.

"Aw shit," he says, like he's just spilled a glass of something. Disappointed but by no means bereft.

Wanda spots the blood first and faints immediately. Vera catches her in time, a little inebriated but her reflexes ever present. The song continues to blast as Vera lays Wanda down on the smooth floor behind the kitchen island, no one else appearing to notice, drunk as they are. Crouched there, Vera spots her brother's finger on the floor and grabs it, tucking it quickly into her back pocket.

"Did you seriously just put my finger in your pocket?" Eli asks, and together they laugh uproariously, gagging and gasping, tears in their eyes.

When they stand, he knocks over a glass of red wine—purposefully now, it will distract from the blood. Wordlessly, without having to make a plan, they clean the small mess, they revive Wanda and tell her it was only a little cut, show her his intact finger, find a new bunch of parsley, all before the end of the next song, before anyone can begin to wonder if something strange just happened. A perfect team. Again. Like the best of the old days.

They continue to dance into the night.

Everyone loves the pasta.

*

The next morning, Vera finds herself playing head contractor.

"Might be worth double-checking that post isn't load-bearing before we knock it out," she says as she moves between Cate's friend Emma and the post in question, which is most definitely bearing the weight of the barn's middle beam, which in turn is holding up the roof.

Both Eli and Vera have become serviceable carpenters over time, as well as competent plumbers and basic electricians. They built themselves several small houses over the years. But it's a depth and array of skills that's unlikely for someone her "age" or profession, so Vera is currently doing her best to limit her input to only when strictly essential.

"But I agree with Cate. An open floor plan is so much better for this space," says Emma, gripping the maul over her shoulder like a baseball bat. Her girlfriend, Faye, nods next to her enthusiastically.

It isn't that Vera thinks Cate and her new friends from a few towns over are dumb, they just haven't had the centuries of experience Vera has. Surely she was equally unknowledgeable when she was young, too. This is the ever-recurring annoyance with being secretly old. The sensation that everyone around you is a child, even those who aren't. There was a brief spell when Vera hoped surrounding herself with older people would make her feel better. But they were always trying to explain the ways of the world to her to save her from future heartbreak and such. *You're young, one day you'll see*, they told her, which only made it worse.

"Cate, can you walk us through the plan again?" Vera asks, but it's only to buy time so she can figure out a safer way to begin the demolition with her crew of liabilities.

Cate moves around the room as she describes which half of the barn will hold the cider press, where the bottling facility will be, the barrels for aging, the layout of the tasting room. She carries herself off in a long description of things Vera has seen at bars and breweries across the country over the past ten, twenty years: repurposed wood, Edison bulbs, chalkboards, minimalist draft taps, vintage photographs, maybe—

"Or maybe we should hook up the actual cider vats before we get lost in extraneous crap like what the menus look like," Brian interrupts, then turns to the rest of the women he's hoping will support this sentiment. His hangover is the worst of everyone's, Vera's being nonexistent, and Cate's comparatively mild, having switched to water once Stan brought out the twenty-year-old Scotch.

"You cannot underestimate the impact design details have on the customer experience," Faye says with authority. "Successful hospitality is *always* in the details."

"I'm just saying, we can't put the horse before the cart," Brian tries again.

They used to keep horses in here. And oxen, cows, sheep, chickens, and briefly once, an ornery pig. They built the barn that second summer, after the sawmill downstream opened and the logs could be locally planed. The beams were hewn by hand with adzes, colossal hemlocks that took the entire neighborhood to move.

Not that Vera herself remembers this. At the time she was much too young to be anything but a nuisance during construction, a year and a half old or so. *A little sprite who took off running the moment your toes touched the ground,* Ma used to say. And a climber. Always up a tree, up a rock wall, a fence, the leg of a neighbor who stopped by with news of another family come to town or a new tavern opened in Woodstock.

While Vera didn't build the structure herself, she has spent many, many hours of her life in this barn tending to the creatures in it. Milking, feeding, brushing, helping Ma with a complicated birth of a calf or foal or lamb. It was bitter cold in the winter. Even inside the houses, it was frigid unless you were settled right up next to the woodstove. The horses wore blankets and you could see the big puffs of their breath in the moonlight, but they were always warm to the touch. Vera fell asleep more than once leaned up against the flank of a colt only to be woken by the disgruntled moo of a cow nearby about to burst with milk.

It's a testament to Pa's precision that the barn has stood so firm and square all these years later. The house, too. His refusal to do things any way but the right way always frustrated Vera, made her feel flighty and irritated, impatient and a little less-than because neither she nor Eli had inherited this trait. All of which made the tragedy of his accidental death feel that much more unfair. It seemed so unlikely, or at the least so undeserved. But Vera knew it took only one slip to end it all. Normally, that is.

"What'd your grandparents keep in here?" Emma asks Brian.

"It was my grandpa's woodshop. No animals, but I think the people they bought from had cows or maybe goats?"

"Thank god it doesn't smell like animal crap," Cate declares. "I don't know what we'd do to get rid of that."

A power wash, Vera thinks and realizes that Cate really doesn't understand how complicated and expensive the barn conversion is going to be. Vera worked with a carpentry team on one in Montana about twenty years ago. She knows Cate and Brian will have to decide how to heat the space in such a manner that it doesn't float up to the unoccupied top half of the open structure and triple their bills. How to insulate it without losing the look of the interior wood. How to pipe the water and electricity discreetly, not to mention where the septic tank and distribution boxes and leach field are all going to be placed so that they're far enough from the house's existing system and the creek. The building inspector might also require a sophisticated fire-suppression system, not a terrible idea, considering the structure is essentially one large tinderbox of perfectly aged wood.

Still, Vera bristles a little on Cate's behalf at the possibility of all these regulations because she's of the opinion that life these days is a little overregulated. Sure, some of it is in the name of safety. There's no denying certain modern standards have saved countless lives—seat belts, sewers, pasteurization. It wasn't luck that gave Cate and Brian a 99.2 percent chance of living past five years old versus Vera's 50–50. But some of this has been led by greed. By the industries that benefit financially from the enforcement of these regulations, things manufactured. By people like Matthew Barbery selling "progress" for profit.

"Let's start in the back where the vats will be and work our way out," Vera says. "Emma, can you knock down this part for us?"

They work. The day is hot, and whatever overnight cool had lingered in the barn through the morning is thoroughly baked off by noon. After several hours of pulling rotted drywall and collecting debris, the rented dumpster is almost full. So much unnecessary and ineffective insulation and room divisions that had been added over the years, all gone. Vera's pleased to see it go and watch the old barn reemerge.

She finds herself impressed by Cate's and Brian's work ethic. Emma's and Faye's, too, though they're clearly flagging in enthusiasm by the early afternoon, such is the fate of a volunteer. They were hoping to find vintage treasures in the walls they could display in their soon-to-open antique shop in Kingston, but alas.

Around three, Cate declares they all deserve a swim.

"Oh, thank god, yes please," Emma moans. "My hands are freaking killing me. Look at them." She opens her palms for everyone to see the four red blisters forming on each. Faye kisses them one by one.

"I'm going to stack the good boards we can reuse against the other wall," Brian says. "They won't be in the way there when the vats are hooked up."

"Good idea," Vera says. She moves to help then realizes one of her boots has come untied. She squats down and beads of salty sweat roll off her forehead onto the old floorboard, splatting in small stars as she loops the laces.

"Do you want us to help, too?" Cate asks her husband, who has begun to move the boards behind Vera. Brian says no, he's got it. Cate says something about changing into a suit, getting more seltzer. Emma is asking Faye about grabbing something from their car. Vera decides she'll stay to help Brian anyway. Some of these planks were once held by her father. She doesn't want anything original accidentally winding up in the dumpster.

Vera finishes double tying her knot. Suddenly an awful crash and clattering surrounds her. She screams, shrill and choked, her body an explosion of panic and adrenaline. She covers her head with her arms, bracing herself for the avalanche of rocks and darkness. She blacks out.

*

"Is she—"

"Vera!"

"Give her some space."

"Vera, can you hear me?"

The voices are above her. She can't will herself to move or open her eyes.

"Get her some water!"

"Hold her up!"

At some distance, Vera feels herself being jostled, her head set onto a lap of limbs. The light behind her eyelids is fluttering as figures move around her. The light—there's light. Vera opens an eye, another.

"Vera! Oh, thank god! Are you OK?" Cate's upside-down face asks as the world returns around her. Vera smells sawdust and sweat, feels Cate's hands on her temples, the heat of the day.

"Babe, get out of her face, let her breathe," Brian directs.

Cate leans back and Vera sits up, holds her knees loosely.

"Steady there, not too fast." Cate holds a hand against Vera's back in support.

"I'm sorry," Vera says.

"Oh my god, don't be sorry, you fainted!" Cate tells her. "You, like, screamed and collapsed into this ball."

"*I'm* sorry," Brian says, coming around to where he can see her. Emma and Faye are standing at a nervous distance behind him, anxiety painted across their faces. "I pulled a board from the pile and the whole thing fell over. I thought it hit you but it didn't, did it? You just—"

"Nothing touched me. I'm not hurt. It scared me a little, that's all," Vera says and forces herself to stand despite her still blurry vision. She brushes the sawdust off the seat of her pants and shoulders.

"You sure you're OK?" Cate asks as she picks more sawdust from Vera's hair. The concern in the air is thick. They'll be watching her now, more closely than before. What kind of person freaks out like that when some wood falls over? What *else* is weird about her?

"You don't have to worry about me, I promise," Vera tells them and smooths her hair from her forehead. "Really. I got startled for a second. It's hot, we're all a little hungover. Let's go for that swim."

Reluctantly, everyone else heads into the house to change. Vera walks to the creek. She pulls off her boots, steps out of her jeans. She makes her way barefoot down the rocky bank and walks straight into the frigid mountain water in her T-shirt and underwear. Her muscles seize and her breath is briefly stolen as she dips under, the loud rush of the water surrounding her senses. It's painful and refreshing. Centering. Over the years she's adapted to the norms of showering nearly every day, but nothing feels as good or right as this.

With her body submerged but her face above the waterline, she looks up at the tree limbs latticed across the sky. The wide green leaves oscillate gently in the high breeze, the sun shines through them and turns their shapes nearly neon. Vera feels her heartbeat in her ears.

Reversible, she thinks to herself for the thousandth time this week, and she tries to focus on the feeling it usually brings her—filling her like helium, lifting her up. But all she feels now is agitated, nervous, suspicious.

Vera doesn't quite believe it.

She wants to, so much, and a part of her maybe does. That she could die. That she won't have to live for hundreds of more years accumulating more and more close calls, falling apart like this at every loud noise or hug that's too tight. The fear always dragging along behind her, lurking, waiting, never quite gone. But there's no part of her that trusts Lydia yet. Vera wishes her brother wasn't being so blinded by his infatuation. She can't imagine how messy their breakup will inevitably be one day. What is he thinking? Sure, Eli has always loved love, falling in and out of it all the time, constantly in giddy pursuit or mourning the inevitable end. He seems to enjoy the full life cycle of a relationship. But this is different. With Lydia, there is no it-was-nice-knowing-you-see-you-never-again breakup. Not even till-death-do-us-part. Surely he knows this. Can't he get his kicks some other way?

She thinks of Thursday. Of Paul, on this creek. She left so abruptly, but she had to. *She* knows better than to muddy these waters. Especially when things are only going to get more complicated from here.

Vera sits up and runs her hands over her face. She feels shaky and spent from her outburst. She'll stick around for a bit of a swim to show them she's "OK" then she'll go back to the cottage. She'll say she has a headache, they won't push her. They'll worry about her together over dinner a little then return to the more pressing concerns of their own lives. The cidery, the shop, harmless gossip about mutual friends. A few hundred feet away Vera will tuck herself in bed. Mozart and those expired Vicodin pills she found in her duffle yesterday.

"Howdy, neighbor," a familiar voice calls from downstream and pulls her from her reverie. Vera sits up out of the water to see Eli, rod in hand.

"Hi," she says and lifts herself from the creek onto a warm, flat rock. Her T-shirt sticks to her body. Her pale legs are covered in goose bumps. He ambles up in his waders. "That a new five-weight?" she asks him.

Eli always has the best gear. More than he could ever need, but occasionally Vera finds herself jealous.

"Couldn't resist this guy." He holds it out, looking upon it with admiration. "Where's yours?" He scans the bank for Vera's rod.

"Just swimming. I was helping Cate and Brian with the barn."

"That's awful nice of you."

Vera shrugs, the sun warming her again already. "Kind of amazing to see Pa's handiwork still standing."

Eli nods. Vera's about to tell him more but he looks up at the bank where the others must be approaching.

"Hey Eli!" Cate calls out then makes the necessary introductions to Emma and Faye. Small talk is exchanged about the warm weather and the barn and the couple's soon-to-open antique shop.

"To be honest we were hoping to find a knickknack or two behind the barn walls," Faye admits. "Cate got our hopes up with all her talk of mid-century modern hand-me-downs and super vintage games found in their cabinets."

"I love antiques," Eli says. "A bit of a collector myself. Mostly vintage cars and motorcycles, but I'll have to come by when you're open and check out the goods."

"Please do!" Faye says, an excited glint in her eye.

"You feeling better?" Cate asks Vera.

Eli asks what happened.

"She fainted," Emma says, and Vera can sense all their eyes on her again.

"Just a little heatstroke." She splashes water across the tops of her thighs. "Nothing some creek water can't fix."

A silence hovers for a count as the water gurgles around them.

"So you fish, too?" Brian finally asks Eli.

"I do, do you?"

"No, but Vera does." Brian looks at her and she forces herself to not shirk from the eye contact.

"We should hit the creek together some time," her brother tells her.

"Sounds fun," she agrees, playing along with the charade. They know they need to hold off on publicly hanging out just the two of them for at least a little longer, but they've made plans to go next week after their first day of work in the lab.

"Before I go, I'm glad I ran into you all—I wanted to let you know we're doing a little work on the houses. A small team is bringing some electric to code, setting up the office, repairing the exteriors. I hope it won't be too noisy."

Cate thanks Eli for telling her, says she's sorry, she didn't even think to warn him that they were starting demo in the barn today.

"Oh, no worries. Well, you all have the right idea with a swim! Anyone else as hungover as I am?" Eli jokes, then they all bid each other goodbye and watch him walk upstream, steady and graceful. Not in the least hungover.

"I think he likes you," Emma says to Vera once Eli is around the bend.

Vera smiles and shakes her head. "I'm not interested."

"Well *I* am," Faye says, and Emma turns around with a look of surprise. "What? I'm gay not blind. He's objectively very fucking hot."

"OK, maybe we stop *objectifying* the new neighbor," Cate whispers loudly over the rush of the creek as she pulls at the bikini strings around her neck. "Especially when he might still be within hearing distance? Some of us have to live next to the guy for the foreseeable future."

10

July 2014

The next Wednesday, Vera's "Saturday" off from ranger duties, she reports to the lab for her first day of work with Eli and Lydia. She's jittery from lack of sleep—nights had been getting a little better for her until suddenly they weren't again after the barn—and she's anxious to see what the lab work holds for her.

There has to be a cover for Vera's role in all this. A ruse that can bring the ranger neighbor around frequently enough without drawing unwanted suspicion. They've decided on a botany project. An intense re-wilding of their acreage with native plants to encourage more sustainable forests and better pollination for bees and butterflies. It will require lots of sampling and studying first. Everyone already considers Vera an outdoor expert being a ranger and a good gardener, and everyone knows that the rich love the conservation of things—their money, their land. Hopefully, no one will blink.

Vera knocks on the front door. Something in the upper-right corner catches her eye. She looks up and finds a security camera.

Lydia opens the door and steps aside within the foyer, no greeting.

"Good morning," Vera says, irritated by the petty snub.

"Have you ever worked in a lab before?" Lydia asks as they enter through the second door. She hears both doors automatically close and lock behind her, a whoosh and clack, like a spaceship's airlock.

"I cleaned a veterinary office for a few months once."

"Well, please only touch what I've told you to. The key is to avoid contamination."

"Yes, ma'am," Vera agrees and salutes her then stops midgesture. "What—how—"

"Matthew flew in a team for me. Incredible, right? Don't let anyone tell you money can't solve most problems."

Vera's eyes keep scanning the room for something familiar. For the dusty, empty shelves or the counter or the old table she was expecting to see. Instead, she's standing in a brand-new sea of bright white walls and cabinetry, shining stainless steel. She'd noticed a handful of trucks parked here over the week, but she'd taken Eli at his word, that they were updating a few things. Not building a state-of-the-art lab right under their noses.

"I believe you're the older one between the two of us anyway," Lydia says and winks, just like Eli does, except it's a facsimile of it. Vera doesn't follow. "You called me ma'am," Lydia clarifies.

How much money does it take to make something like this appear in ten days?

"How old are you?" Lydia asks.

"Two hundred and thirteen," Vera answers, still gobsmacked at the scene around her. "You?"

"A lady never tells."

This snaps her out of her impressed stupor. "Seriously?"

"One hundred and eighty-seven."

So Lydia was born in 1827. Like Vera had figured, she and Eli and Ma were already gone. They missed her birth by one year. Vera realizes now is the time to ask about two other key parts of Lydia's biography she's missing.

"When did you leave? How did you know?"

"I left in 1863," Lydia says as she ushers Vera to a bar-height stainless steel worktable. "The war was on. I felt excruciatingly underutilized dragging unwilling farm children through multiplication exercises, so I left and went down to New York City to train as a nurse. I worked my way through field hospitals during the war then—"

"You were thirty-six," Vera interrupts, wanting to make sure she's collecting the facts correctly.

"I see you're good at basic arithmetic. Surely, we'll be able to put this skill to use in the lab."

Vera doesn't bite. Instead, she asks, "You weren't married?"

"Not then."

"One black coffee, one almond milk cappuccino!" Eli calls out as he enters the lab from a back room.

Not then?

"Thank you, darling," Lydia says as she accepts the small cup with both hands then kisses him on the mouth. Vera forces herself to not look away. When Eli resurfaces, he holds out the mug of coffee to his sister. He's flush with such joy. Even in the harsh fluorescent light of the lab he looks so warm and alive.

Vera takes her mug. "But when you left town, did you do it because you knew something was wrong with you?"

"Oh, Vera, I was a thirty-six-year-old 'spinster' schoolteacher who preferred the company of books to anyone else in town, *everyone* thought there was something wrong with me!" She laughs lightheartedly, like this is some cheery cocktail party anecdote, not the origin story of a hellish, lonesome existence. "I thought we covered this already at Stan's."

"Not exactly," Vera says as she watches Lydia put a possessive arm around Eli's waist.

"No, when I left here for my nursing training I wasn't displaying any noticeable symptoms so I had no idea," Lydia begins again. "Though in retrospect it seems obvious my biology was altered here. It somehow didn't cross my mind as a possibility until I heard Eli's story—*your* story—"

"The ax," Vera says.

It had taken Vera, Eli, and Ma months to place the nagging suspicion that something was off. Vera had considered bringing it up with Ma but couldn't fathom how to begin. She couldn't even articulate to herself what had felt different recently, she just knew that something *was*. Then one spring morning in 1826, Eli's ax slipped as he was splitting firewood for kindling. As always, he was using his left hand to set the wood on the chopping block, his right to swing the ax down. An easy rhythm, his left hand always in the clear in time. But on one particularly hard piece of maple, the blade bounced and skidded, then cleaved straight through the flesh of his left hand down to the bone. Vera heard the cry from the barn, where she'd been feeding the horses and bolted out to find him clutching his hand, thick red rivulets cascading onto the ground. The doctor would have to be called. She'd bring him inside to Ma and take a horse herself.

But by the time Vera got Eli into the house and sat him in front of the woodstove, he lifted his hand to show Ma and there was nothing. The blood from the wound remained, smeared across his skin and shirt. But the gash itself had disappeared.

Suddenly it clicked, coalesced, all the minor incidents with her own body over the past few months that pointed toward the same impossible conclusion. She told them. Ma, it turned out, had stories, too. A nick with a blade, a stumble that should have scraped or bruised, her chronic joint pain mysteriously gone.

Vera was the one to go into the kitchen and get a knife. A small slit across her thumb. Ma and Eli both gasped as she did it. But not one of them made a sound as they watched it vanish in seconds.

They were lucky Lotte was visiting her parents that day.

"You told me it was a horse," Lydia says, dropping her arm from Eli's waist and turning to look him in the face.

"Did I?" he asks, unconcerned.

"Yes, you said a horse kicked you and cracked your skull then your mother found you—"

"Oh, I must have mixed two different times together. Sorry, babe."

Lydia looks more than a little perturbed. "So what is it then? How did it happen?"

"Like she said." He lifts his chin toward his sister. "I was kicked by the horse later, after we'd already figured out something freaky was going down."

"What about you?" Vera asks Lydia, slightly irritated at her brother for being capable of forgetting something as monumental as this, and just as irritated at his new girlfriend for taking him to task about it.

Lydia shakes her head, as if the situation were water she could rid herself of like a dog, then begins. "I didn't understand the extent of my condition until I was mortally wounded in Cold Harbor in '64 yet—"

"Incredible," Eli jumps in eagerly. "We're in Texas sitting on our asses and she's out in the middle of the Civil-freaking-War dodging cannon fire and dragging soldiers off the field to fix them up in—"

"We were hardly sitting on our asses," Vera interrupts. They were mining and serving at the tavern in town, and it was bleak and very hard work. Though in truth the more Vera learned about the war in its aftermath, the more she felt like they *had* taken a backseat. Naturally this is not the kind of thing anyone else would normally know about them. What parts of history they chose to sit out on the sidelines. It always seems so much clearer decades after the fact, hindsight being twenty-twenty and all. But when you're in it, what's ultimately going to happen doesn't always feel so inevitable, the path forward not always so clear. Risking your neck for others not always so tempting, especially with a condition like theirs.

Still, Vera doesn't like the idea of Lydia thinking any of these things about her or Ma or Eli.

Lydia looks to Vera then back to Eli, her expression frustratingly neutral. Vera feels tricked into being defensive.

"I know, but—" Eli looks at his hands and spins a ring on his middle finger then turns to Vera and asks, "What'd you do with my finger by the way?"

"Your finger?" Lydia says.

Vera buried it in her garden, very deep and near the marigolds so the usual critters wouldn't dig it up.

Eli shakes his head with a smile and kisses his girlfriend on the lips again. "Never mind."

"Enough with the ancient history!" Lydia says. "Vera, let's get as much blood as we can before you get any caffeine in your system. I want to run your samples through the density gradient centrifuge immediately to compare with ours, see if we can't start identifying similarities in unusual protein expressions that might point to our RNA or DNA. Any other substances I should know about?" She holds out her hand for Vera's mug.

Vera takes a long drink of her coffee then sets it down on the counter, wonders if Lydia has ever had a warm bedside manner. She thinks of the many ryes she had last night so she could sleep, the Vicodin she washed down to try to turn it all off, but decides not to mention any of it.

"Nope."

In a backroom, Vera sits in a reclining chair and Lydia begins to draw her blood.

"What do you do for memory training?" Lydia asks a few minutes later as she swaps out yet another full bag of blood for an empty one. This will make four? Five? Ten?

Vera doesn't answer. She's become so far away, wouldn't be able to stand up if she wanted to. A well of panic begins to rise inside her.

"I've put Eli on a daily regimen of neuroplasticity exercises, aka memory games, and we've already seen a substantial improvement in his short-term memory retention in just six months." Lydia flicks the bag. "Isn't that right, honey?"

"Vera's always had a better memory than me." He's behind her somewhere, or above. She's amazed he's in this room. It's been so long. Everything is so long.

"You're a pretty low bar in that department, Eli darling." Vera feels a hand on her shoulder. "We'll run those tests later today on you and establish your current baseline."

"Hmm," Vera says, or thinks she does. A tide is pulling her away.

"How many of these do you need right now?" somebody asks. They are being purposefully quiet or her ears have gone dull.

"A few more."

"Maybe it's enough for now?"

Another touch on her shoulder.

"Vera?"

She cannot answer.

"She's out."

"All the better. I'll take as many as we can get today. The caffeine won't affect the blood samples, not the parts I'm looking at. Do you want to fuck?"

A laugh.

"I'm serious. Not *here*, back there."

Her brother whispers something she can't hear.

Vera sinks further into the oblivion.

*

At sunset, Vera emerges from the general store.

"We could probably get a few casts off if we hurry," Eli says, squinting west down The Road then over toward the creek they'd originally planned on fishing after today's work.

"I'm a little wiped," Vera says, when really she's reeling. Exhausted, depleted, still burning from the inside, her body working desperately to keep pace with the recent destruction of blood and tissue wrecked upon it by Lydia over the past eight hours.

It was unlike her usual deaths and healings. Long, relentless. Tedious. No quick flash of nothing, no freeing feeling of that brief untethering. It was like struggling to swim upstream, against the current. It was like drowning. As both of them watched on.

It was much too much like the desert.

"You good?" Lydia asked her a few times, and Vera could only nod with her eyes clenched shut. But she nodded.

She will not be the weak link in this chain.

"You should go without me," Vera tells her brother as she puts a hand on the porch's railing to steady herself.

"I might."

She lifts her other hand in a wave and walks down the steps and into the grass, trying to hide the stiffness in her gait.

"You did great today!" Eli calls after her.

She lifts her hand again but doesn't turn around this time.

"Wolven—" he calls out and Vera pauses, twists to face him in the dying light. He falters, pushes his hair back with both hands. "I think Ma would be proud of us, don't you?"

Ma wasn't always the way she was by the time she left them. In fact, she didn't become religious until well after she became immortal. Didn't turn to the divine in her grief over Pa or the end of their lives as they knew them. Her spiritualism came on slowly. An ember, a flame, some smoke. It would seem to go out only to start back up again somewhere else later. The Quakers, the Mormons, the snake handlers, the seers. It always felt fleeting, which suited their lifestyles. In retrospect Vera realized she'd assumed her mother was simply seeking companionship in the baptisms, choirs, Bible groups, and charities. Especially because she never asked Eli or Vera to join her. Had she been finding the answers to the questions of their particular existence, wouldn't she have wanted to share that with her children? Or maybe she tried and they'd refused each time, engulfed in the immediacy of their lives as they were. The horses and whiskey and card games, the odd jobs and brief affairs, the getting by and by and by.

Eventually though, Ma stopped starting over and began to bring her growing collection of spiritual convictions with her to each new place. Her dedication to God—it was always the Judeo-Christian, almighty father figure—grew in fervor with each dinky, whitewashed church she entered.

It was when they were working in a desolate mining town in West Texas during the Civil War that Ma became convinced this was a punishment, or at the very least a test.

"The war?" Eli asked as he smoked his pipe, adding more dust to his incorruptible lungs.

"All of it," Ma answered.

But for what none of them could ever quite reconcile. Had they been particularly bad? People are notoriously terrible judges of their own character, but really now.

Besides, while their lives were hellish, surely this wasn't hell. Limbo *maybe*. But not hell. This was all just too . . . unremarkable to be hell?

When Ma's spiritual devotion turned to obsessive charity, Eli and Vera were frankly relieved she'd found an outlet. The soup kitchens, orphanages, reservations, military hospitals, the lone man down on his luck sleeping in the street or in the barn with the animals. Eli and Vera chose to ignore the nights she came home unusually late, limping, the telltale pink of a freshly healed gash on her face. It was easier to live their own lives. To not consider that these horrible men who their ma had tried to help were probably their own drinking buddies, their fellow miners and bartenders. Vera knew more of it than Eli did. She herself had been murdered three times before Ma finally left them, nearly raped many more. But she'd become a better shot over the years and more precise with a knife or a broken bottle. Some were merely maimed, others, yes, she killed. And so Vera was afraid, god she was afraid, that she would have gone and murdered every last one of those men who'd hurt Ma if she'd have let her. She knew Ma would have told her to turn the other cheek, to rise above. So she didn't ask. She never asked.

"I haven't known what Ma thinks for a long time," Vera tells her brother now.

"Right. She—never mind. We—you did rad today, Wolven. I'm glad we're doing this. It's been too long since we were in on something together."

"Almost fifty years," Vera says.

"I guess I'm saying it feels right to be here with you, you know? I've missed you."

"I'm glad you're here now, too," Vera says and she means it, even though underneath what she's said is a tangled, grievous churn of other feelings she has about him and the time they have and haven't spent together. Feelings she certainly doesn't have the energy to wade into tonight.

Her brother's face relaxes a little, now that he's heard what he wants to hear, just like she knew it would. She waves and leaves. Hears the pneumatic click of the front door sealing behind him as he returns inside.

Vera crosses the meadow, her eyes pulsing bright spots. No, she realizes, she's seeing fireflies. Hundreds of them glowing on and off, on and off, bobbing just above the high grass. She stops to behold them. Her own body pulsing in time.

"Reversible," she whispers aloud. A promise. A lighthouse offshore.

The day is fading swiftly now from warm dusk to the grayed shadows of night. She walks past the barn, toward the house and cottage, her limbs stiff and burning. She spots the silhouette of Cate in a chair on the front porch and steadies herself for more talk.

"Aren't they incredible?" Cate asks, standing, and Vera agrees then bids her good night.

"I've been wanting to say thank you again for your help in the barn the other day."

Vera stops walking. "My pleasure." Because it was. To shore up Pa's work. To preserve something when the rest of the world seems bent on destruction.

"You know so much about this stuff! It's incredible. And it's made me realize how little I know and how much I'm going to have to hire out and—"

The tone of Cate's voice is leaning toward an ask. A few sentences later it arrives: Could she and Brian pay Vera to help them renovate the barn?

"Yes," Vera says. She doesn't need to consider it. She'll help with the barn. She'll fill more of her daunting hours. Stay busy. Bide her time until she gets what she needs.

"Oh my gosh, Vera, thank you! What have I done to deserve you?" Cate squeals and bounds down the porch steps, enclosing her in one of her frequent hugs. Vera braces herself, puts an arm around her landlord, gives a single pat, then pulls away.

"But I don't need the money."

Cate tries to insist, but Vera knows it's halfhearted. And it's fine. She doesn't need the cash. She makes more than enough with her forest ranger salary for her small life. Isn't saving for any future this time.

"Well, even with your *insanely* generous offer, I think I've got to take on other investors," Cate says then lowers her voice to a whisper. "These guys are obviously loaded but I feel like it's way too awkward to ask them, right?" She nods toward the general store.

Vera shifts her weight to her other hip. She doesn't want to talk about money or Eli and Lydia. She wants to get home and get through the rest of this burning alone.

"But maybe Stan would be into it?" Cate continues. "Would you come pitch him with me next week? I mean, now that you're our head contractor!"

"Sure, but can we—I've got to get to bed. It's been a long day."

"OMG, of course!" Cate says with enthusiasm then cocks her head sideways. "Are you feeling OK?"

Vera nods, paints on a smile. "I'll survive."

11

July 2014

"If you didn't 'gram it, it didn't happen," Ranger Lopez says as he holds open the door for Vera.

"We nearly lost someone off a cliff in Joshua Tree who was trying to take a picture of themself—"

"A selfie."

"A what?"

Lopez snorts with laughter. "It's called a selfie. Van Valkenburgh, are you messing with me?" He shakes his head as he follows her into the building.

"Rangers! Welcome to Hunter-Tannersville Elementary!" says a cheery young woman in black slacks and a blue sweater. "I'm Ms. Donovan. We'll have you sign in with the office right here."

Vera and Lopez take turns with the nearly dried-out ballpoint pen and sign their names, the date, their arrival time, and the purpose of their visit on the printout tucked into the plastic clipboard. The elderly secretary accepts it back with a stoic nod.

Out west Vera didn't do many school or camp visits as part of her job, but here the team is smaller, so all the rangers rotate. Some of them grumble about having to "babysit" and talk Smokey the Bear, but so far Vera has enjoyed the few youth-focused events she's participated in. Kids are earnest and honest, the little ones especially. They take things like fire safety, species endangerment, and litter deadly serious in a manner that only someone who will live with the consequences or is still innocent of heart can. She respects this respect of theirs.

This morning they're presenting to all thirty-eight campers in kindergarten through fourth grade in the shiny, echo chamber of the gymnasium. The crowd is rowdy and excited though it's hardly nine in the morning. It's taking a few minutes to get the projector to properly sync with their park-issued laptop—so much technology is helpful yet still incredibly tedious and hiccup prone, no matter what it is. Lopez fusses with it, skipping through the slides. Vera's eyes catch on the photographs of last winter's rescue drills.

Ice axes and ropes. Orange toboggans. Those shining marathon blankets. A helicopter.

"Lopez, you handle the drill parts, OK?" Her chest tightens.

"Ugh, this stupid dongle," he says as he continues to fuss with different cords.

She looks at the screen again. There's Lopez, wrapped up like he's the rescue target.

"You heard me? I wasn't there, so I think you should be the one to teach them about the drills."

"But you did rescues out west, too, right?"

The whip of the helicopter's blades. The shine of that blanket.

Right away she knew her left leg was broken and both arms, too, twisted and crushed under the boulders. No matter how much she struggled, she couldn't wrest herself free. Couldn't see anything in the total darkness in which she was buried. The constant burning as her body tried to heal but couldn't under the weight of the rock. A pulsing fire inside her. Waiting and waiting. Her growing thirst and hunger and fear.

"Lopez can you please—"

Vera can't get the rest out of her mouth.

"There we go!" Lopez cries as the slideshow finally appears on the large screen. There's a round of oohs from the audience. "All right, let's get this show started." He picks up a microphone, turns it on to a gush of static. "Good morning future rangers!" he calls to the sea of children and gives them a salute they all return in fashions both solemn and silly.

Vera looks out into the dimmed gymnasium. She steadies herself, pushes the memories back down along with the bile in her throat. Puts her hands on her hips and salutes them back.

They've got a good cop–bad cop routine they fall into easily where Vera is the straight man to Lopez's antics. He's much more comfortable around children than she is, perhaps extra eager to practice his mix of humor and care with his own on the way now. It certainly helps that it's only been about twenty years since Lopez himself was a kid, one who also gathered in gymnasiums like this and was taught how to sit "crisscross applesauce" and raise his hand for questions. It's been more than two centuries since Vera was a child, and even then, despite the fact that it took place hardly twenty miles from here, this was decidedly not her childhood experience. Vera never went to school. She was a kid on a working farm in the early 1800s, and a girl at that. Besides, the one-room schoolhouse in the valley where Lydia eventually taught wasn't even built until she was fourteen and already too old for it. Everything Vera has learned she's learned by doing—by watching and copying, picking up bits as she's gone along. She didn't learn to read and write until she was in her forties. She still accidentally spells certain words the old British way on occasion, still harbors a soft spot for the floral formality of yore over the strange hybrid of corporate speak and casual eagerness of today's written word.

The presentation continues. They talk about forest fires. They talk about litter. They talk about what to pack for a hike, what to do if you become lost. When the slides about last winter's rescue drills appear on the screen, Vera steels herself.

The children are audibly wowed.

"I know this looks fun and cool, but rescue drills are serious business," Lopez says. He continues, but to Vera, his voice begins to drift into the distance. The whine of the enormous, dimmed lights grows high-pitched in her ears and her heart is hurrying. She tries to concentrate on the feeling of her feet on the floor, she unlocks her knees. Her vision is fuzzing out on the edges.

It was a relatively mild, 4.2 magnitude earthquake a few dozen miles from the park that triggered a small landslide in a remote cluster of boulders where Vera happened to be, alone. Wrong place, wrong time.

When they finally found her—a no-show at work after three straight years of clockwork reliability, her car tracked down in one of the park's lots—Vera didn't know how long she'd been trapped, time having lost any linear shape in the darkness and searing pain. There was the groan of a machine. There was the mix of voices shouting. The piercing light when she finally emerged, filthy but shockingly unscathed. Blood crusted and dried from injuries healed before she was even on the stretcher.

Unbelievable you weren't hurt, they all said. *A miracle*. And Vera forced herself to agree with them aloud, then hid from their reasonable questions under the guise of shock both real and convenient.

"Snow, rain, the cold, it can—"

Lopez is still talking. Vera keeps her eyes open to the light of the gymnasium. *I'm OK*, she tells herself. *I'm OK now*. Then she feels something on her arm and startles, comes to. Lopez is looking at her.

"Isn't that right, Ranger Van Valkenburgh?"

She nods vigorously despite not knowing what he's just said. He goes on.

"Rattlesnakes, earthquakes, mountain lions, avalanches. Every region has its dangers. But the biggest danger of all? Is being unprepared." Lopez lets his advice sit heavy in the air for a moment.

But what could have ever prepared her for any of this?

"OK!" Lopez clicks to the next slide and a photograph of a man holding a large trout appears. "Who here likes to go fishing?"

At the end of their presentation, they field questions. A few aren't about their ranger jobs, but they answer them happily nonetheless— *What's your favorite color? Do you have a pet?*—and of course some aren't questions at all.

"My dad says girls shouldn't be rangers because they aren't strong enough to carry big men like him out of the woods," says one little boy.

Lopez begins to answer before Vera can.

"Well, tell your dad we hope he never gets lost in the woods and has to be rescued by Ranger Van Valkenburgh and proven wrong." A few oohs rise from the back of the room where the older kids are sitting. "I'm only kidding! But seriously, our team—"

"My mom also says so," the boy continues. "And she says girls shouldn't be cops either because nobody respects a lady cop, but my uncle Paul says you're probably stronger than you look."

Vera realizes where she's seen this child before: jumping off tables at the chicken barbecue.

"Thank you, Jayden, I think that's enough," says a camp counselor, a hand on the boy's shoulder as she firmly pushes him back into a seated position. "I believe we have time for two more questions. Who has a question for these fine rangers? Remember, a question ends in a question mark!"

*

"I'm guessing Uncle Paul is *fishing* Paul, am I right?" Lopez asks once they're back in the parking lot.

Vera shrugs. He raises an eyebrow, and she gives him a gentle smack on the arm then spots his wife across the lot holding the little orb of her growing belly in two clasped hands.

"Your date awaits."

"Baby!" Lopez cries and dashes the last few steps to her side, links his arm into hers.

Vera has met Jenny three times now, all in parking lots—once at a trailhead at the end of a workday, once at headquarters, and now here. She's warm and frank, and she and Lopez are clearly in love. Vera understands why his family adores her, signs of destiny or not.

"Jenny, you look great," Vera tells her, knowing what nearly every uncomfortable pregnant woman wants to hear regardless of how her body is reacting to growing a second life. Vera thinks most pregnant women do in fact look a specific kind of beautiful. It's the bounty of it, the necessary strength. Sometimes though, the sight of a pregnant woman makes Vera irretrievably sad. Not because she's mourning some lost chance at having children of her own—she's never wanted them and is grateful that a side effect of her condition appears to be infertility, not to mention a lack of menstruation. It's the somber fact that there inside that warm womb is another soul she will inevitably outlive.

"Ah, do you like the nice green pallor of my skin? Morning sickness is doing wonders for my complexion!" Jenny jokes then hugs Vera hello. She smells like vanilla. Lopez says she was beautiful before and just as beautiful now, if not more so.

"Is he this much of an ass-kisser at work these days, too?" Jenny asks, and at this Vera laughs because Lopez has in fact turned into very much of an ass-kisser at work, ever since he decided there's a real possibility for a promotion.

"Oh no, I forgot the freaking computer!" he says, panicked.

"It's probably still in the gym," Vera assures him, then he dashes off, calling over his shoulder that he'll be two minutes, he's sorry.

"You can explain to Dr. Lin it was your fault if we're late again!" Jenny shouts after him.

As they wait for Lopez to return so he can accompany Jenny to her checkup, there's a break in the clouds and the sun bears down on them, the heat of the asphalt reflecting back. The warmth replenishes Vera. Her panic in the gym feels far away now. She asks Jenny about cravings, the nursery she heard they're starting to put together, possible names.

"Enough baby talk," Jenny interrupts her abruptly, and for a moment Vera is taken aback. "It's all anyone wants to talk about! *That's* what's turning my brain to mush, not the baby. Tell me something fun. What are you doing this weekend? Who are you sleeping with?"

Vera smiles. She likes Jenny's candor, and is relieved that she isn't turning out to be the jealous or paranoid type. The existence of platonic friendships between men and women is maybe one of the more radical changes Vera has experienced over her lifetimes. But even now they're still treated as anomalies, as delicate balances, always in danger of tipping just too far into the intimate and right into bed, even by the most supposedly progressive people.

"I'm sorry to disappoint you but my big weekend plan is to work my shifts, and I'm not sleeping with anyone at the moment."

"Not anyone or not anyone who's technically available?" Jenny presses, her voice lowered, playful. "Is he married? I won't tell."

Vera looks over Jenny's shoulder at the school's front door.

"There's no one," she insists as she smooths her uniform shirt into her pressed pants.

"Is it a 'she'? I don't care about that. My college roommate was gay."

"There's no one, really," Vera insists again.

"Bullshit," says Jenny with a sly smile.

"It's not, I promise."

"Then I guess you've just got that look."

"What look? Like I enjoy affairs with married men?"

She doesn't. Marriages seem hard enough and Vera has never liked the idea of ruining them for people during their relatively short time together. There are plenty of other fish for the taking.

"Like you know something the rest of us don't," Jenny says. They hold their eye contact until they hear the metal clank of the double doors.

"Found it!"

*

That evening, Vera meets Cate and Stan at Antonio's Pizza & More as planned.

"We'll have one with mushrooms, onions, and green peppers and for the other, let's do your white pie with sausage," says Stan, ordering for the table.

"You want sausage on the large Snowball?" the waitress clarifies, her pen frozen above her folded pad.

"Yes please, Darlene."

Darlene doesn't blink her heavily made-up eyes. Vera never liked it when people used the name on her tag either when she was a waitress.

"Vera's a pescatarian," Cate reminds Stan.

"Are you? Forgive me! Scratch the sausage. But we'll have three more margaritas please."

Vera puts her hand on top of her barely touched drink. "I'm good." She's still reeling a little from the assembly. Besides, she's the designated driver and needs to make a show of staying sober.

"Nonsense. You'll be finished by the time she comes with the pizzas, better to order now," Stan insists as he shoos Darlene away with a smile and wave.

"OK, we should probably get through the business part of this meeting before I drink too much," Cate says, unrolling her silverware from a paper napkin. "I have to confess, I'm a little nervous."

Stan smiles. He's enjoying the formal attention of being pitched to by Cate and Vera, even in a place as informal as Antonio's. Most of the tables with children have left, now that it's after eight. A few young, local couples are at the back bar. Women in tight jeans, low shirts, ironed hair, and lots of eyeliner. Men in jeans and their clean sweatshirts, their clean baseball caps, as opposed to the ones they wear to work. They place coasters over their unfinished beers and take smoke breaks outside together then return and laugh loudly at inside jokes like this is an extension of their living rooms. Most weekenders only come for takeout, as the restaurant is neither cool nor quaint but rather, the awkward middle reality that makes up most small-town establishments. Stan fancies himself both urban and country enough to hold his own in between here. The location was his suggestion.

"So as you know we've started doing some work in the barn ourselves, but there are a few tasks that are a little beyond our DIY skills, which means we've got to hire out, *so* we're looking for investors." Cate's turned pink already. She breathes in. "Naturally you were one of the first people who came to mind. You're a social hub of the community and you are, forgive my French, rich."

Vera watches Stan tighten the corners of his mouth to hold back a smile. He reclines, putting an elbow over the back of his chair.

He thinks he's got his cards close to his chest, but Vera knows immediately: he's going to invest.

Good.

"Koreans have a system for this kind of community lending," he says before Cate can continue. "It's called *keh*. Everyone puts money into the group pot and takes turns being the recipient. It's one of the reasons the Korean-American immigrant community is so successful at small business."

"Did your parents run a business?" Cate asks. "Or, do they?"

Stan laughs and waves a hand like he's batting away the idea. "Honey, my parents are Ukrainian Jews from suburban Pennsylvania."

Cate's eyebrows shoot up. "What?"

"I'm adopted, I never told you? You're running verrrry light background checks on your investors I see."

One hour, two pizzas, and three margaritas later, Stan agrees to invest fifty thousand dollars. Cate is ecstatic, Vera, frankly, a little shocked at the sum.

They finish their pizza and sip on the dregs of their drinks. Cate and Stan gossip lightly about the town as the leftovers congeal in the to-go box on the fourth chair at their table. Pete and Judy got a new woodshed they painted to match their house, which is cute, but it's installed awfully close to The Road, the plows might hit it in the winter. Wanda is getting that knee surgery she's been putting off for years next week and is going to spend her whole recovery up here instead of down in the city. Phil's been drinking a little harder than usual but seems happy, they probably don't need to worry.

"Did I tell you Lydia saved my life?" Stan says then takes another pull of his margarita.

"What?" Cate gasps. Vera stills herself.

"At Summer Friendsgiving she told me to get this mole on my neck checked out." He presses a hand to the back of his neck where he has a small bandage. "She said a shape and color like that could mean it was cancerous."

"Holy shit, Stan! Was it?" Cate cries.

"It *was*. I'm telling you, Lydia Kirke is a saint." Stan rubs his neck and his eyes go watery.

"Vera?"

Vera lifts her head to find Paul and his friend from the Fire Department BBQ, George.

They exchange hellos and George is introduced. They compare favorite pizza toppings and agree that the margaritas here are dangerously good. It's all very normal and polite.

Good, maybe Vera didn't make things strange between them on the stream the other week after all.

"Dangerously good margaritas? You're telling *me*. I just agreed to invest in her cidery!" Stan says, and Cate reddens visibly. Sensing his misstep, he puts a hand on her arm and says he'd have done it sober, too, he's joking, obviously he was joking.

"Paul told me about the cidery, that's cool, congrats," says George. Paul smiles at Cate and tucks his hands in the pockets of his EMT uniform pants and Vera finds herself triple checking there is no wedding ring.

"Thank you!"

"I also heard my godson was kind of a dick to you at the ranger assembly at camp today," Paul interjects, turning to Vera and surprising the entire table with this announcement.

"Oh, well—kids, it's fine," Vera stumbles. She feels certain everyone knows what she was just considering.

"'Kind of a dick'? Do tell," Stan presses. Cate tilts her head to the side, curious, as Vera hurriedly explains the basics of the scenario, leaving out the fact that George and his wife don't think she should have her job and that Paul apparently once said Vera is probably stronger than she looks.

"Kids say all kinds of dumb things they don't mean," announces Stan, who is, as far as Vera knows, childless.

"Kids say all kinds of dumb things they hear at home," Paul says then looks to George who appears momentarily shocked. "What? It's not throwing you under the bus if you said it and believe it."

Vera, Cate, and Stan all wait to see how George will receive this kind of razzing from his friend.

"I don't mean any offense," George says to Vera directly in a voice much softer than she was expecting. "I just—I'm a big guy, you know? And there's a lot of big guys out there and I—I'm not trying to be sexist, I swear I'm not a sexist. But—if I got hurt when I was hunting, I'd want the person coming to rescue me to be able to carry me out if they had to, that's all. Nothing personal."

"I promise, you don't know what I'm capable of," Vera says and while it's true, she meant it like a joke, or some kind of comfort. Instead, it's hanging there between them like the threat it also is.

The pause is filled with the ambient noise of the restaurant—a waitress talking, silverware on plates, the rumble of the radio—then George laughs heartily, like it was a joke. The others join.

"When does hunting season begin?" Cate asks.

"Musket and bow don't start for deer until November first, then it's regular open season on the twentieth."

Cate says that's good to hear because she and Brian want to harvest from the abandoned orchards that are on state land that used to belong to the house's acreage.

"You don't have enough apples on your property?" asks Stan, worried about the prospect of his investment already. Cate says they do, they totally do, they just thought it would be fun to find wild ones as well.

"Actually, we probably have too many. We're going to need help picking them once they're ready in September, do you guys wanna come? I'm gonna send something out to everyone—what're your email addresses?"

"You coming?" Paul asks Vera and Stan. Or maybe just Vera. She's the only person he's looking at.

"Of course they're coming!" Cate says.

Paul pulls a pen from his chest pocket and writes his email address on the corner of an unused napkin then passes it to George.

"Hey Vera, maybe we can hang out again before apple season, like on the creek?" Paul asks and everyone else stills. "I promise I'll let you catch more than one next time." Vera nods, feels her cheeks warming. "I'll give you my number." He takes his pen back from George and writes it on the corner of a different paper napkin then scoots it across the table to her.

"We should hit the road. The kids are hungry, and Jocelyn will think we stayed for margaritas if we take too long," George jokes. Everyone follows his cue and says their goodbyes. Vera purposely doesn't watch Paul walk away but instead drains her drink. As the straw slurps the last loud gurgle she looks up to see Cate and Stan watching her expectantly.

"I'm sorry, you guys are going to hang out *again*?" Cate asks, playfully shoving Vera on the shoulder. "When was your first date?"

"It wasn't a date. We were fishing."

"Well, next time is definitely a date," says Stan, tapping the paper napkin with Paul's phone number on it several times. Vera swipes it and puts it in her back pocket.

"I'm not interested," Vera says. Always her refrain. When she isn't. When she can't be.

"He certainly is," Cate says, giddy at this turn of events. "Vera, embrace it. You're the hot new single girl in town!"

"Lydia's the newest," Stan says, making it obvious he finds Lydia attractive.

"Lydia's not single," Cate corrects him. "It's still Vera's turn."

"All right, enough already," Vera tells them and looks out the window, where she manages to catch sight of Paul in his white truck, also looking in one more time. His eyes alight, then he's gone.

12

July–September 2014

"It's always so exciting when young folks are interested in history," Sue says as she opens the door to the municipal building for Vera, Cate, and Eli.

The Town Hall is in a former school building, repurposed in the eighties to house the offices of the supervisor, clerk, historian, and building inspector, plus a meeting room for the various town councils. It's squat and rather ugly, made of bricks with a tall flagpole out front, and it looks amiss among the white farmhouses, but it's well taken care of. Tidy and mulched.

Sue is not only an auxiliary Fire Department volunteer, she's also the town historian, for which she receives about a thousand tax dollars per year to add to her Social Security. Vera can see Cate doing mental calculations, trying to decide if she, too, would like to do something like become the town historian for a thousand dollars a year. Now that she thinks opening a business has made her a more integral part of the community, Cate is suffering from an intense case of Newcomer Enthusiasm. Today, she's here to gather more antique photographs, which she says will add local authenticity to the decor of the cidery. She invited Vera along, having pegged her as someone with an interest in "old things," too. And when Cate picked her up from Eli and Lydia's porch after a morning of lab work—just indexing their first groups of water and soil samples they'd separately collected over the past week, no more personal biospecimens required for the moment thank god— Cate invited Eli as well on a hospitable whim, and he agreed.

"Could be cool to learn about these other Van Valkenburghs," he said with a quick eyebrow raise before hopping into the backseat of Cate's station wagon.

"I've always been an appreciator of old things," Sue says now as she ushers the three of them into the carpeted, drop-ceilinged room of the office she shares with the town clerk.

"Me, too!" Cate agrees, following behind and gabbing for a bit about her love of old photographs and interior design that melds vintage with modern.

The four of them settle around the desk where Sue has already laid out several boxes of pictures, postcards, and other documents. Vera picks up the town's Bicentennial Celebration Calendar. It includes interviews with elderly residents and "traditional" recipes for pancakes and venison casseroles; 1802–2002 it says. As if the first two years her family toiled here don't count. The constant erasing. She nudges it toward Eli and points at the date. He winks.

"It's a lot, right?" says Sue, clearly proud of the amassed collection. "But wait till you see this." She holds up a finger then retrieves a paper from the stack. "When I was looking for little doodahs from The Road, I also pulled up the old tax maps and deeds for your place, Cate, aaaand coincidences of coincidences, Beverly was right—it *was* owned by a Van Valkenburgh!"

"Really?" Cate gasps, genuinely astonished and momentarily at a loss for words. Sue holds her sun-spotted hands together, so delighted to have been the one to deliver this fun news.

Vera puts on a face of pleasant surprise. "Wow," she says, rather lacklusterly, but Eli delivers enthusiasm enough for them all.

"Dude! How cool is that?" Sue and Cate cluck on with him—What are the chances? She knew the name sounded familiar! Vera spins the page around so she can read it herself.

It goes backward in time:

2013 Hoffman, Brian & Bennington, Catherine
1965 Hoffman, Joseph and Ruth (parcel split, 12 acres remain)
1926 Dunham, James (parcel split, 50 acres remain)
1874 Shoemakker, Lars
1826 Van Valkenburgh, Lotte
1802 Van Valkenburgh, Pieter

The date is wrong by two years, but there he is. Pieter. Pa.

"Ooh, I love these names. I'm one hundred percent adding Lotte to my baby list," Cate says, leaning on Vera as she looks over her shoulder at the paper.

And Lotte.

"My goodness, are you pregnant?" asks Sue, already ecstatic in the way that only someone desperate to be a grandmother can be.

"Oh god, no! I mean, one day I hope, knock on wood." Cate raps the desk with her knuckles. "Got to birth my *business baby* first."

A window-unit air conditioner kicks on and coughs out a mechanical rattle.

Eli pulls the deed across the table toward him. Vera wonders what he's thinking. He looks up at her and she smiles at him. He smiles back but it's pained.

He's thinking about Lotte.

Vera will give him the photo. She's forgotten all about it until now, stashed in her kitchen drawer. Once Lydia was here and in person and telling her yes, she is also immortal, yes, their whole condition might be reversible if they find the source, well, Vera was no longer concerned about the photo proving who Lydia really is.

It will be strange for Eli to see his young wife old, to see her next to his current, unchanged girlfriend. Then again, maybe not for him, as Eli's always been the one to keep up with friends over the years as they've aged and he hasn't, even after the box incident with Ma. Perhaps especially so. He says technology has made it easier than ever to reconnect. He's gone so far as to appear at some of his old friends' funerals and pretend to be his own grandson, basking in the nostalgic stories, the *wow you look so much like him!* He claims it's good for him. Vera can't imagine. Going to an old friend's funeral. Being remembered by anyone.

Vera flips through the nearest box of photographs, yellowing booklets, postcards, menus. She pulls out a slim leather book as the others chat on about who else once owned the house where Cate now lives, how much Sue liked Brian's grandparents, Joseph and Ruth. Vera opens it to a random page in the back, blank. She flips earlier and sees short diary entries.

July 23rd. School all day. Examinations in arithmetic tomorrow.
July 27th. A picnic for the drafted men. Am laid a-bed with a cold. Pity.

She skips to another.

August 17th. School. Muggins is the game these days. Euchre with four.
August 22nd. Washed all forenoon. Retired eight o'clock before the sun. So passeth another day.

She closes it and looks at the cover. Such soft, worn leather. She opens to the first page, looking for a year or a name.

When she sees it she almost laughs.

The luck of it.

"I do wish I had more time to organize it all." Sue sighs. "Things have gotten a little jumbled over the years, but I do my best. When my son, Paul, moved into the old schoolhouse last year he found *another* stash of documents—"

"Have you started digitizing things?" Cate asks.

"Oh, sweetie, I can hardly handle my email account. In fact, I believe the town gave me an address for my position as historian but—Georgia, have you seen that Post-it with the log-in anywhere?"

Sue, Eli, and Cate all look to the town clerk's desk behind them, and for the second time in a few months, Vera swipes something that doesn't belong to her.

Two hours and many photographs later, Vera, Eli, and Cate stand in the church's cemetery under the shade of a maple tree. There are only a few dozen headstones in the small grassy yard, so it doesn't take them long to find the one they're looking for. Eli squats down, and the daytime crickets near him hush.

LOTTE VAN VALKENBURGH
b. 1799 d. 1874

Where were they then? Missoula? Nevada City? Mormon country?

They left Lotte behind because Lotte wasn't like them. They spent three months watching her. Every cut or bruise silent evidence stacked against her. Eli held out hope for his wife the longest. But after Vera had an uncomfortably close call in front of Lotte with a scythe scrape that instantly healed, Ma insisted it was time to go.

"We don't want to wait until it's too late," she reasoned. And while Vera knew Ma was right, she thought she recognized a certain eagerness in her. Not just to be rid of Lotte—for Vera could not deny she, too, felt some relief at that prospect despite the circumstances—but to outrun another feeling. Another person. Someone who could not follow if they tried, being as they were, buried in the yard.

For the first five years of running, they thought they were simply miraculous healers. It didn't occur to any of them until later that they might no longer be aging either. Six years passed, seven, it started to settle in. This other piece of it. So much more dangerous. Somehow they had believed that while they might survive all manner of accidents or illness, time would eventually come for them the way it comes for everyone. The rules changed as they'd understood them. They had even more to hide now. Had to pick up and leave even sooner. Five years max, three better.

Over the decades they've speculated. They've wondered if maybe they *are* aging, just at a pace so slow it's hard for the human eye to notice. Perhaps they've had a new ache, a freckle they're convinced wasn't there before.

Two hundred years later, they cannot lie to themselves this way anymore. They are freaks, medical anomalies, tortured souls in permanent limbo, and they are doomed to leave and be left behind forever. Because that's the obvious cruelty of their situation, the grotesque truth of immortality. Eli, Ma, Vera—they are *always* left behind. Even when they are the ones supposedly moving on. Everyone they have ever known has grown and aged and lived and died—everyone except each other—all of them gone. Forever. As they trudge on, the same. Forever.

Vera resists the urge to put her hand on her brother's sloped shoulders.

In 1874? They were in Utah. Ma's first real foray into Mormonism. Eli banking hard on the transcontinental railroad. Vera at work in yet another tavern.

Lotte back home, dying.

"You really think there's zero chance you're related to his Van Valkenburghs?" Cate asks Vera, kneeling next to Eli.

"My grandparents came from Holland," Vera says. As always, she'll stick to the truth, even if it's only a sliver of it.

Cate purses her lips in disappointment. She wants her friend to be an optimist, to be the kind of person who believes in kismet and fate. She fans a fly away from her head.

Vera walks over to another row, examines a large obelisk that says DUNHAM. Like Brian's grandparents, it appears they were another couple so in love they died within weeks of each other. That, or it was the flu. Vera wouldn't be surprised to find other headstones here with dates from the same month. Simple viruses could spread quickly and devastatingly back then, wiping out whole portions of a town in a matter of weeks. She's seen it more than once. Should have died from it more than once, too.

Vera touches the diary, still secure in her waistband underneath her T-shirt.

"Let's get out of here," she says.

"Sorry, do graveyards creep you out?" Cate stands and comes to Vera's side and links her arm into hers. Vera allows herself to be steered to the stone fence and wrought iron gate. "I kind of love them but I get it, dead people are freaky. Do you believe in ghosts?"

"No," Vera answers, because she doesn't.

"Do you, Eli?"

"Absolutely," he says, still kneeling in the grass at his wife's grave.

"Me, too," Cate says as she opens the gate and its rusted hinges squeal.

Eli waits a moment longer, wipes his face of sweat or maybe tears. Then finally, he stands.

They drive the mile home with the windows down. Cate sings along to something pop-y Vera doesn't recognize while Eli nods his head to the beat in the backseat and looks out the window. He is morose, but in a way that only Vera can tell. She can see it in his irises, in the slope of his shoulders, the way he cradles his own hands.

Cate however is happy. She has a new box of old photographs to scan, an original copy of a cider recipe from 1892, and plans to pick up the antique cider press from Beverly's basement this Sunday after Beverly and Sue return from church. Her dream is happening. The cidery is becoming more and more real with each passing day. Cate is a woman with a tangible future and a mere wisp of a past.

Eli asks to be let out at the post office. Vera says she also needs to check her mail.

"I'm sorry you didn't find any cooler stuff," Cate says through the open window.

"Oh, it was plenty interesting," Vera assures her. She's excited to show Eli the diary, to show Lydia. To be the one who found it and secured it. LYDIA KIRKE, 1863. Showing up with the same name was risky on Lydia's part, especially when she knows she's had her photograph taken here and left behind records of herself like this one.

Then again, who would ever suspect the truth?

When people lie to you, you never think it's because they're secretly immortal. That is, unless you are immortal, too, in which case the suspicion might occasionally consume you.

Early on in this, about fifteen years in, somewhere out in Missouri, Eli became convinced one of the other ranch hands was also deathless. He had to be all but physically restrained from asking and confessing.

At the time, Vera outwardly scoffed at Eli's obsession along with Ma, but just the year before she had also privately persuaded herself that one of the other maids where she worked was immortal as well. Vera saw the woman slip on some soapy hardwood floor and take a long, terrible fall down a set of stairs that surely should have broken something. But instead, the woman had stood and scurried off, completely unscathed.

Vera watched her closely in the following weeks, which in retrospect almost certainly contributed to the woman's jumpiness that Vera then concluded was evidence of a secret. Anna was her name.

Right before Vera and her family were due to move on, Anna died of cholera. Their boss was surprised but genuinely touched by Vera's visible mourning. Vera was grieving Anna, yes. But really the loss of what could have been. Someone else who would understand.

Yet it wasn't joy Vera felt when she figured out Lydia Kirke was like them. It was a disconcerting concoction of panic, curiosity, validation, and dread. Her brother obviously felt something totally different upon the same discovery. Was his devotion to her instantaneous? Is it only growing?

Cate drives off and Vera turns to her brother.

"I'm sorry about Lotte," she says even though it's not precisely what she means. Sorry that she died? No. Sorry that Eli wasn't there when it happened? Maybe. He slows his pace toward the post office steps.

"Lydia says Lotte never remarried." His voice is its normal volume but Vera can hear the bruising beneath. "Thinks she made money renting the fields out and sewing stuff for people."

"I guess they knew each other," Vera ventures, delicately.

"I hoped so, too, but Lydia says no. Lotte was like thirty years older than her and apparently kept to herself after we—" He stops walking and turns to face Vera, looks her in the eye. "We should have brought her with us."

"Eli, you know we couldn't have," Vera counters automatically.

How he'd begged for Lotte to come along, even after their plan was already in motion. "But she's my *wife*!" he howled as Ma and Vera were surreptitiously packing supplies in the kitchen the night before they left, Lotte asleep upstairs, and his cry was so loud Vera had lunged to cover his mouth with her hand lest he keep hollering and rouse her.

"It was too risky," Vera says now, echoing exactly what she and Ma had told him then.

"I'm so sick of lying to everyone!" he says, and suddenly all the years are held in his eyes. Eli, the life of the party, finally tired of his favorite charade? Vera is not so sure she believes it.

"Well, you don't have to lie to me. I'm the one person in the world you can always tell the truth to," she says because she still can't help but try to cheer up her brother.

His face doesn't brighten, doesn't lighten.

"And Lydia now, too!" Vera doesn't like saying it, looping Lydia in as one of *them*, but she will for the sake of this argument.

"You know what I mean."

"Isn't that what we're aiming for?" Vera presses, kicking lightly at the gravel of the post office's two-space parking lot with her sandal. The midday sun is picking up in intensity now. "If we find this, won't we be able to live out in the open?"

Vera understands this only as she says it. She's been so focused on how the source will allow her to die that she hasn't considered this other possibility.

A life out in the open?

It feels like stepping off a cliff. Too much gravity. A free fall with a bottom she can't see.

"I know," her brother says, impatient and irritated by any offer to help him feel better. He rubs his hands over his face then pushes back his hair. "It's what Lydia says, too. We won't have to hide anymore or run anymore blah blah blah—I want that, I really do," he says and the way he insists so plainly makes Vera feel all the muddier. "It's only going to get harder, Wolven. The improvements in facial recognition alone should be scaring the shit out of us."

"We can always hide," Vera counters. "The world is enormous."

"Says the woman who's never even left the country. Trust me, it's getting smaller, it's not like it used to be. We can't just change our names and relocate a hundred miles away."

"When did you switch back to Eli?"

"When we moved. Lydia, too. Matthew thought we were insane, but we told him it was for more privacy from Silicon Valley. It's kind of sappy, but really it just felt wrong to come back here as anyone but our true selves. And it'll all be out in the open soon enough. Matthew still calls me Nick sometimes by accident." Eli shakes his head. "It's going to be hard. A lot of people are going to be disappointed in us."

"For what?"

"Well for lying to their faces for two hundred years for one thing," he says a little too loudly, and Vera finds herself shushing him, looking out the periphery of her vision for possible eavesdroppers. "And for dicking around for centuries. I mean really, what do we have to show for ourselves?"

At this Vera bristles, feels the sweat dotting on her forehead.

"You're still on that?" she asks him.

It had started as campfire chatter, a long day of free climbing in the park behind them, their hands chalky but already healed of their scrapes and blisters. They were feeling happy and outside of time and the drudgery of their daily lives in that way that nature can do for anyone, immortal or not.

"Do you think Ma was right?" Eli asked, apropos of nothing other than the fact that Ma almost always came up between them when they got together.

"About what?"

"About us wasting our lives."

"Jesus, that's not exactly how she put it," Vera said and laughed, but it was forced.

"It was pretty damn close."

She didn't correct him again because he wasn't wrong. Still, she bristled at the implied accusation. That this might be something he believed now, too.

"I'm not wasting my life," she said, sitting up from her camping chair, a dangerous ember of anger heating within her. "Look at what everyone else is doing. Sitting around watching TV, setting the earth on fire for their own greed and convenience and leaving it to their grandchildren to figure out. You have the same expectations for *them*, Eli?"

"I just think we could be doing more," he insisted. "Like, I'm glad I made a boatload of cash once I finally got a real foot in on Wall Street, and god bless my early Apple stock—I donate like crazy now! But this bizarro life we've been given? It's totally an opportunity to do something deeply radical and I think we're kinda wasting it."

"Come on, don't give me this crisis-of-conscience crap right now," she told him. She meant for it to be harsh but loving in the way this kind of talk can be between siblings, but instead it came out rough. Rough like maybe how she meant it. She didn't fool herself into thinking being a ranger was particularly noble, but what the hell was *he* doing to make the world a better place, jet-setting around, collecting motorcycles, occasionally donating to some "cause"?

"I'm allowed to change," he said, sitting upright, too, the orange light of the campfire catching in his eyes.

"I never said you weren't."

He scoffed, snorted. That irritating sound someone makes when they think they are being willfully misunderstood, when they want so badly to dismiss you and your judgment but can't. Vera felt its condescension and vulnerability all at once in her own nerves. The way someone who knows you so well can get under your skin. Two hundred fucking years.

"You don't like it when I change," he continued.

"Where is this coming from?" she asked and again, it came out harsh.

"Never mind," he said, like he always did when things got too heated, and she let it go. She didn't want to fight. She passed him the bottle of whiskey instead. They wound up laughing about old times. That guy Shane from the Dakotas who could imitate anyone with spooky perfection. Their first successful fur trade with those three measly beaver pelts. Their neighbor Otto out in Nevada with the new Model T they almost wrecked that one joy ride.

Still, as they readied themselves for their tents that night, Eli announced he was going to have to leave a day early, tomorrow afternoon.

Said he had some kind of meeting that couldn't be missed. Vera didn't ask about the details, and he didn't offer any because it didn't matter if the meeting was real or not, he had decided to leave, so he was leaving.

In the morning, up first and alone, Vera went to scout one last place for them to climb before he had to go. Then everything changed for her.

"Let's not get carried away worrying about something that might not even happen," she tells him now.

"Oh, we're going to find the source. It is absolutely going to happen."

"What makes you so sure?"

"Wolven, you don't know Lydia Kirke."

*

Back in her cottage, Vera opens the diary.

Lydia Kirke, 1863

Her last year in town.

The majority of the leather-bound notebook is blank. Only the first handful of pages are filled with faded cursive. She reads quickly.

July 20th. Strawberries for supper. Retired late after reading. (The Woman in White.)

July 21st. Joseph lost three fingers in the corn crusher. Everyone coming around there.

July 23rd. School all day. Examinations in arithmetic tomorrow.

July 27th. A picnic for the drafted men. Am laid a-bed with a cold. Pity.

August 2nd. School all day. Compositions & geography. Mary might have the will to take over for me. I shall ask soon.

August 7th. Word of Aaron Dunham dead in battle.

August 8th. Terrible headache. Wind blows a perfect hurricane.

It's hardly a diary. Where are the confessions? The illumination of her heart's true desires?

Vera realizes she is looking for proof of something. That Lydia is lying. That she is bad. She wants so much for Lydia to be bad.

> *August 11th.* Shoemakker baby very ill. Must call on them again tomorrow.
> *August 14th.* Baby Lars much improved. Family very gay. Sanitation works wonders. Pamphlets helpful already.
> *August 17th.* School. Muggins is the game these days. Euchre with four.
> *August 22nd.* Washed all forenoon. Retired eight o'clock before the sun. So passeth another day.
> *September 5th.* Much rain. Roads are dreadful.
> *September 15th.* Greenbacks collected. Many farewells now everyone knows of my leaving.

Vera's impatience builds as she comes to the final entries. The pages whisk harshly.

> *September 20th.* Last days of school. Best behavior all around. Little Ed brought flowers.
> *September 26th.* Lotte mended calico dress no fee. Showed me newest gift. (Dominoes.) Made sworn to look for Eli on her behalf. Sent off with apple & good wishes. Lotte one of few I might miss.
> *September 27th.* Wagon to Woodstock tomorrow.

*

The next week, Vera returns to the lab. It sounds different, a constant rustle. Then she spots the row of cages.

"Rats?" Vera asks as she removes from her bag the small bottles of water samples she was tasked with collecting during this week's rounds.

"*Mus musculus,*" Lydia says without looking up. She's in goggles and blue rubber gloves, using a pipette to transfer what looks like blood from a small machine into a row of vials. "The North American house mouse but a progeria model, aka rapidly aging. We'll use them for xenograft transplants eventually, but for now we need something on which to test my reverse-engineering."

"We're not testing it on ourselves?" Vera asks.

"Obviously not," Lydia retorts. "We need mortal specimens to detect if there's a change. Our biology is already altered."

"So this isn't the kind of thing where we, say, take a sip from the source and it's reversed?" Vera feels immediately embarrassed and vulnerable voicing her theory aloud.

"I suppose that's possible, but there's no way to know until we have the source in hand, and besides—" Lydia looks at Vera quizzically through her goggles for a moment longer than is comfortable. "That would be a little risky for us, no?"

Vera has only taken herself to the edge of the void twice since Lydia and Eli moved in a few weeks ago. Both times just to scratch her unscratchable itch. A compulsion almost as much as a desire to end it all. She stopped with her own spring water experiments the moment they arrived, her exertions feeling small and ridiculous in comparison to this operation.

Vera looks down and opens her bag rather than maintain eye contact with Lydia.

"Of course," she agrees. "So, where's Eli?"

"Running? Fishing? Going for one of his motorcycle rides?" Lydia lists Eli's hobbies as if they are those of a silly child.

Vera takes out the last of the bottles and begins to arrange them in a tidy row, labels with geographic coordinates facing out. She feels a little stupid and annoyed, which perhaps explains why she decides to change the subject to something equally dangerous.

"Your family's store was next to our house, or, Lotte's house," Vera begins. "What was she like after we left?"

There's the briefest of pauses in Lydia's movements, then she continues to transfer samples with her pipette. A low rustle comes from the cages behind her.

"She kept to herself. I didn't see her much."

"Eli said you told him she rented the fields and was paid to do other people's mending?"

"That's right."

"But she never remarried?"

"Not when I was living in town."

"Did she ever talk about us?"

"Never," Lydia answers quickly, decisively.

Vera feels a chasm open between them, a wall coming down.

"You can leave those there and head out, I'll get to them later," Lydia says, finally looking up from her vials and meeting Vera's eyes.

"You don't need me to—"

"I've got this today, thank you."

Lydia refocuses her gaze on the machine in front of her. Vera is about to set the last sample on the counter but leaves it in the bottom of her bag instead, and walks out.

In her cottage, Vera takes the diary from her kitchen drawer and flips to the end again.

September 26th. Lotte mended calico dress no fee. Showed me newest gift. (Dominoes.) Made sworn to look for Eli on her behalf. Sent off with apple & good wishes. Lotte one of few I might miss.

"Liar," she says aloud to no one and tosses the diary back into the drawer.

It's too hot to fish, the trout lethargic and hiding in their shaded holes. She goes into her bedroom and pulls a pair of ripped shorts from the laundry basket, then rummages for her sewing kit to mend them before realizing she doesn't have the patience for that kind of fine motor skill right now. She decides to head to the backyard and attack the weeds in her garden instead.

Dirt accumulates under her short nails. The loamy scent of soil fills her senses and mollifies her anger. One hour, two. A sunburn sears into the back of her neck, then burns again as it heals away. She thinks about the variety of fruits and vegetables available at everyone's fingertips these days—in gardens, grocery stores. Still astonishing to her. Sure, some of it pales in comparison to what it used to be, so much produce genetically modified to be bigger and shinier and to survive the long trucking required for supermarkets. Berries are the worst, most of them tasting vaguely like dirty water. She misses real bananas the most. But still, the bounty of it.

On her last row, Vera reaches under a billowing head of Bibb lettuce to clear some clover and a wide-eyed field mouse darts out from underneath. She covers it quickly with a cupped hand, feels its soft fur against her palm as it frantically tries to escape from its sudden cage. Slowly, she tightens her grip around the creature until she is holding it, the small body thrashing and wriggling.

Vera needs to test the water samples on her own first before turning them over to Lydia.

She opens the sliding back door with one hand and holds the distressed mouse in the other. Her bag is still on the kitchen counter. She crosses the room and reaches into it, pulls out the one sample she didn't leave at the lab this morning.

A straw? A bowl? A cage of some sort? She needs the mouse to drink, then—

Then?

The realities of this plan arrange themselves in her mind. The deaths. Not her own.

"Damnit," she whispers. She sets the bottle on the counter then returns to the back door and reopens it with her elbow, the mouse still in her hands. She crouches in the grass and unfurls her dirt-encrusted fist. The little creature skitters away into the meadow, free once more.

Vera will just have to test the samples on herself before handing them over to Lydia. It doesn't matter if it's "risky." In fact, she very much hopes it is.

She stands and looks out at her garden, notices the apple tree next to it isn't leafed-in like the others in the rest of the orchard. It's scraggly and old, probably too far gone to fruit anymore. She feels a pang of something irritatingly close to guilt.

If Vera *does* find the source and if it *does* allow her to end it all, then Lydia will have the source, too, and Vera knows for certain now that Lydia can't be trusted.

But Lydia won't be my problem anymore then, she thinks defiantly. Nothing will.

*

The bright arc of summer passes and settles into fall. Vera works. With Lopez on the mountain walking trails. With Cate and Brian in the barn doing carpentry, plumbing, and electric. With Lydia and Eli in the lab giving blood and tissue, and out in the woods collecting water samples to analyze. Vera secretly tries each sample first on herself before handing them over. As always, she survives. She completes the daily memory exercises Lydia has prescribed. She goes to Pete and Judy's barn dance. Has dinner at Lopez and Jenny's every other Friday. She fishes with Eli. Has sex with a waiter in Woodstock, with an arborist in Hunter, and both times thinks of Jacob, of Paul. She doesn't call Paul. She doesn't give Eli the photograph of his dead wife and his ever-living girlfriend. Doesn't give Lydia her diary either. She is productive, blunting the sharp parts of herself with work, and for the first time since arriving, she begins to sleep through the night occasionally. She is almost tempted to think she could be happy here one day in the way she was in Joshua Tree before everything happened. That this happiness might be even more meaningful because she is finally home, and with her brother no less. Fishing, building, gardening. *I could die*, she thinks again and again and occasionally it lifts her gently like a balloon.

But there are still dark, unfillable holes within her. She still wakes screaming sometimes. She is still who she is.

13

September 2014

Vera steps up the creek bank into the meadow and sees at least five cars' worth of people have already arrived to help pick apples today. She didn't mean to stay on the water this long, but there was a hatch and the brookies were rising for anything she tied on—apple caddis, Parachute Madame X, you name it—and the satisfaction of pulling in nearly a dozen back-to-back was too much to walk away from. Especially with only a few weeks left in the season to be on the tributaries.

She crosses the meadow of goldenrod and purple asters to the house and cottage, her cold, bare feet feeling weightless on the soft, flat grass after the constant nudge of the current over the rocks, so slippery and uneven.

"Hey, Ranger!" Vera looks up to see it's off-duty Lopez in jeans and a plaid shirt with Jenny, Bill, and Wanda.

"You came!" Vera says, glad that Claire had insisted she extend the invite to them as well now that they've been spending nonwork time together.

Bill, hands on his hips, a gray American flag T-shirt belted into long denim shorts, asks if she caught anything.

"Not much," Vera says out of habit, even though Bill doesn't fish.

"Eli said the same thing!"

Wanda gestures toward the empty basket on her hip and asks if Vera is going to help pick.

"Yes, gonna set down my rod and come right back."

"What happened to your waders?" Bill asks. His concern feels fatherly and genuine.

"Nothing," Vera answers with a shrug. "Sometimes I go without them. It's called 'wet wading.'"

"It's called *crazy*. That creek is freezing!" Lopez jokes.

"Girl, you are something else," Jenny says with an appreciative smile.

Vera changes in the bedroom. By the time she comes out, more cars have arrived. They're parking on the side of The Road now, technically a violation in this town but that's mostly a safety concern during plow season and that kind of snow is still about a month off, which is either too soon or too far, depending on how you feel about winter. To Vera it's too soon. Fall's always felt like the most fleeting season. A holdover from her farming days. Each leaf that tumbles bringing you that much closer to frozen ground, to a finished harvest. What you've got now is what you've got for the year, and that's that.

But it's late September, peak apple season here, and Cate and Brian have gotten lucky with the weather for their community harvest. The kind of day that feels seventy in the sun, just the littlest bit nippy in the shade. A blue sky so solid and saturated it seems unreal, the mountains around them ablaze in orange and red.

Everyone is milling about under the orchard branches. The ground beneath the first cluster of the trees nearest to the barn has been covered in crinkly blue tarps to catch the apples they are shaking down. A few neighbors have brought their own ladders, their wives beneath them worrying aloud about stability. There are six long metal pickers spread among the groups, all currently wielded by men over fifty.

Vera notes Eli, Brian, George, and Jocelyn working together. She spots Paul with Wanda, Bill, and Stan and turns to join her brother but Stan calls her over.

She's been avoiding Paul all summer because the sight of him makes her ache. She rounds every creek bend quietly in case she has to retreat. Never parks where she sees his white truck.

Has never gotten around to throwing out his phone number either.

"Here I am, on the hook for sweat equity as well!" Stan says as he shakes a branch. At least twenty apples fall down on the tarp in a small thunder of thuds. Stan's only pretending to be grumpy about it. He is clearly proud of his investment as he'll tell anyone around willing to listen.

Over the past two months, Cate has rustled up another twenty thousand dollars from the other folks gathered under the trees here today. The highest investment after Stan's being ten thousand from Nancy, the rest a collection of buy-ins from one hundred to one thousand dollars for promises of discounted cider and general VIP status for life. With this extra money they bought the remaining equipment and got the new septic installed. The space is shaping up quicker than Vera thought it would.

"I've never picked apples before, this is fun!" says Wanda, all cheer as she collects the fallen ones into the large basket.

"It's a perfect day for it," Paul says, stretching his arms out into the sun and revealing a small stripe of skin between his T-shirt and jeans. Vera looks away.

"I'm starving. Think they'll mind if I eat one?" Bill asks as he reaches into the pile. Both Wanda and Stan smack his hand at the same time.

"Don't eat the profits, rule number one, Bill!" Stan reprimands.

"I told you to have a sandwich before we left, sweetheart."

"I wasn't hungry then."

"I've got a sandwich in my truck if—" Paul begins to offer.

"Nah, I'll be fine. Look! Jeff's having one. Hey Jeff! Don't eat the profits!"

They all laugh.

Their group fills three baskets easily then slows considerably once everything within standing height has been shaken or plucked. Vera climbs up the trunk and out onto the spindly branches. She sends down a second storm of shining red and green globes. Paul climbs the limbs opposite and does the same. She tries to avoid watching him, but they catch each other's eyes.

"Makes you feel like a real monkey, right?" He shakes the branch and does a startlingly good imitation of a monkey's hoot to the entire group's delight.

When every apple is collected that hasn't been pecked by a blue jay or some other winged pest, Vera hops down and is quickly reassigned by Cate with Paul to another tree then another. In this way they rotate through the entire neighborhood, catching up with different people about the fall colors and fishing season and ranger work. About grandchildren, TV shows they're watching, who's considering renting their place out on Airbnb the weekends they aren't here, there's money to be made if this trend of young people coming to the Catskills continues, whoddathunk?

Vera also finds herself passively collecting information about Paul, absorbing the answers to the questions other people have asked. He's an only child. He went to college in Syracuse. He takes his mother, Sue, to church every Sunday but doesn't consider himself a believer. He likes to cook but hates to bake. He's single.

All the while, Vera climbs. She pulls, she hoists, she hangs. She's missed rock climbing in the six months since she's come home. But how she's missed climbing trees so much more.

None of these are the original trees from the orchard Pop planted. Even the oldest, best-kept apple trees can last only a hundred years or so, but it's the same place. Her orchard. New trees have replaced the old ones a few at a time, but it's kept living. Like a body continuously replacing its cells. This orchard is different but the same. As Vera is different but the same.

Pa would have loved the idea of all this, she's sure of it. A cidery in his orchard, his barn being restored, the village coming together to harvest like this. Ma, too. She would have come out with spruce beer and hand pies. Instead, it's Cate with cans of flavored seltzer and granola bars, Brian directing people with full crates into the barn.

People are always the same, Vera thinks as she surveys everyone from her perch in the branches. Their problems, their desires, their conflicts, their needs, always the same. Technology alters the particular details of commerce, communication, exploitation, and hope, but people on the whole remain unchanged and this is how Vera has felt for a while now.

But today, up in an apple tree of her own again, warm from the sunshine and labor, from the easy glow of good company, the conclusion feels less dire to her than it usually does. Is it so bad that everyone is connected like this? The same across time? They toil, they try to make their mark, however small it might be. They build something and hope it will last long after they die. This is also what Vera could want, right? She could choose to believe that the work she's doing with Eli and Lydia will help others after she's gone.

It's continued to nag her. Ma's accusation. Eli's. What *doing something with your life* looks like. Most days she can dismiss it. Believe herself above the fray, held to a different set of standards given her circumstances.

Most days.

Vera picks the tops clean of every single tree in the orchard. She and Paul are the last ones standing. They shuffle the remaining crates to the barn as everyone else congregates around the beer and chips and cheese on the back patio of the house, where a fire has been lit to ward off the coming evening chill. The group is happy in that way you can only be after a few hours of physical labor with visible results. The chatter rises to a new jolly pitch outside the barn. Together, Vera and Paul dump the last basketful of apples into the enormous crate inside.

"You're an apple picking machine," he says as he brushes his hands against the thighs of his pants. The barn is warm and filled with the scent of sawdust and ripe fruit. Woodsmoke from the bonfire outside drifts in.

"You're not so shabby yourself," Vera says, stacking her empty basket with the others.

Paul's radio crackles. He takes it off his belt, puts it to his ear, then turns it down.

"You gotta go?"

"Nah, it's up in Windham. Something routine and I'm not on duty. I just keep a listen on things in case they need extra help."

"EMS or fire?"

"Both," he says and sheepishly unclips a second radio from the other side of his belt.

"You always wanted to be an EMT?" Vera asks, reframing the question she's often asked about becoming a forest ranger.

"When I was little, I thought I wanted to be a doctor," Paul says and sits down in a folding chair against the wall. Vera follows suit next to him. "I went off to medical school and everything, but it wasn't for me."

"Medical school sounds hard."

"That's not really why I quit," Paul says.

"Sorry!" Vera feels her cheeks flush at the stumble. "That's not what I meant."

Paul smiles, unoffended.

"It's what a lot of people thought when I came home though. That I couldn't hack it in the *real world*."

Vera waits to see what else he has to say. Doesn't want to put her foot in her mouth again.

"It's prestigious to be a doctor or a surgeon, and I'll admit it, I got caught up in the idea." He looks to the ceiling like his old self might be there. "I had a lot of plans and things I thought I should be doing—going to med school, getting married, buying the house with the yard and the two point five kids, you know?"

Vera nods, despite the fact that she has evaded these traditional pressures. That they've evaded her, for better or worse.

"But it turns out I like the small potatoes chaos of being an EMT in the middle of nowhere more than all that. This is a great place, you'll see."

"I do already."

"I'll shut up about myself now." He gives his own cheek a pretend smack. "Why'd you become a ranger?"

"I couldn't hack it in medical school."

Paul guffaws, and Vera's chest warms from the sound.

"Really though," he prods, and the way he looks at her.

"I like the outdoors."

He tilts his head as if to tell her, *Come on now*.

"I was a little listless for a while. Then I met a ranger, and she seemed happy, so I thought I'd give it a try."

"Listless?" he prods.

About ten years into the new millennium, Vera spent a spell in the desert of southern Nevada trying to dissolve. She needed to see how much of her endless time she could get through in a state of less-than-being. She meditated. She starved. She slept. She waited. It was physically painful and excruciatingly boring. But Vera is nothing if not stubborn, and she managed to pass most of 2009 in a state of near vegetation until finally one morning she couldn't help but stand up, eat the expired peanut butter in her bag, and begin to be industrious again. Building, mending, planting, tending.

It felt no more noble to opt in to life than it had felt to opt out, but it was at the very least less horrifically dull.

She was squatting there, deep in Nevada state land where no one remotely sensible ever went, and was come upon by a park ranger one day.

"You don't want to be out here," said the young Black woman whose badge read LINCOLN. Vera found herself wondering if the woman's great-great-grandparents were once enslaved and chose this name after escaping or being freed. She felt time surround her, expanding and contracting. She felt small and insignificant despite the fact that she had already lived longer than anyone else she'd ever met besides Eli or Ma.

"I'm OK," Vera finally told the ranger, who was surveying the camp, trying to estimate just how long this unwashed woman had been surviving in the rock and sand.

"I don't want to come back and find your body," the ranger pressed. Vera couldn't tell if it was a threat or a compassionate warning. At that point she was so deeply out of practice, her usual ability to read most people severely blunted by her isolation.

"You won't."

"Because you're leaving? Look—" The woman's voice softened, and she took a step closer to Vera, removed her sunglasses. "I've got room in the truck if you want to come with me." She pointed over the hill from where she'd emerged. "I can't leave you out here. It isn't right. It's my duty to help." She nodded to her badge.

"Do you like your job?" Vera asked, an idea quickly unfurling roots in her mind.

Ranger Lincoln laughed, maybe because it sounded like small talk and small talk seemed a funny thing to do out there.

"I do. I know it's not cool to like your job, but I do."

Eli was thrilled when Vera asked him for help securing a fake diploma, a Social Security card, a bank account. All the formalities required to not only live with government recognition but to *work* for said government. Eli has "known a guy" for hundreds of years and he took immense pleasure in big brother-ing the hell out of these tasks on behalf of his little sister. Hardly a year after she first had the idea, Vera was wearing khaki with a gold badge pinned to her chest. People saluted her. They did what she told them to do. They thanked her for protecting their national parklands. Suddenly, she was not so invisible, and while at times that made her feel unsteady and exposed, she also realized, with acute embarrassment and delight, that this was something she needed. To be seen.

And to be outside. She wasn't lying about that part.

Vera chews the inside of her cheeks. "Yeah, a little listless and invisible, I guess," she repeats to Paul, looking up at the ceiling for the ghosts of herself, too.

"That's crazy."

"What? Why?" She looks to him again.

"You seem like such a determined person. And you definitely weren't ever invisible to me." He holds her gaze in his own then appears to remember himself, looks up into the rafters once more. "This place is coming along," he declares a little too loudly.

"Thanks," Vera says, relief and disappointment churning in her now.

"Wait, you're the one renovating it?" His bright eyes widen.

Vera explains briefly.

"Next you're gonna tell me you know how to fly a plane," he says with a laugh.

"I've never been on a plane."

"Me neither."

"Really?" she asks, genuinely surprised, because at this point in her many lives she's grown used to being an outlier for this.

"Don't act so shocked, you haven't been on one either!" Paul says and bumps his shoulder into hers. Vera vibrates from the contact, a low hum.

"You afraid of flying?" she asks, since that's usually the reason someone avoids it. Vera supposes she's afraid of it, too, but not at all in the same way. It's the startling ease of it, being able to traverse the world in hardly a day. She doesn't trust it.

"Not really. I just don't travel much. I'm telling you, I'm a hellaciously boring, med school dropout glued to his radios. I go to Maine with George for a hunting trip once a year but that's about it. You hunt?"

"Sometimes," she answers, though in truth she hasn't in a while. She's always hunted for subsistence, not sport. Apparently taking something larger than a fish doesn't sit right with her these days, perhaps because of the profound unfairness of it, given that she herself is unkillable.

"You ever go bow hunting?"

"Sure," she says. It's what Pa taught her to use for smaller game.

"You wanna come out with me opening day?"

She pauses, considering the nature of the offer.

"Me and George," Paul clarifies and laces his fingers together.

"Won't he mind?"

"No," he says too quickly, blinking. He clearly hasn't run this invitation by George yet.

Eli and Lydia. Cate and Brian. Lopez and Jenny. Vera is not exactly interested in being a third wheel in *every* part of her life.

"I'll think about it. We should catch up with the others." Vera moves to stand but is caught on her arm by a warm hand.

"Sorry, it's just—" Paul lets go of her arm and grips the tops of his thighs like he's bracing himself for something. "Did I . . . offend you or something this summer?"

"No," she answers quickly. "Not at all."

"I thought we had a nice time on the creek that day but then—"

"I've been really busy," she says, and she knows how completely lame and empty it sounds.

"No, I get it, I'm sorry. I don't mean to hound you." Paul looks to the ground and rubs the stubble on his chin with his knuckles the way she's watched him do before.

"It's not you," Vera says, trying for a reasonable answer.

He looks up. His startling blue eyes now soft, almost pleading. His face so close.

"I like you, Vera. I've never met anyone like you before."

She can smell sweet apples on his breath now, and that mineral musk that belongs to only him. She feels her nipples harden against her will, her mouth open the slightest as he looks back at her. He leans in, incrementally closer, and Vera knows she won't be able to stop herself this time.

"Wolven?" A familiar voice calls from the other side of the barn and she jerks away. "Where'd you go? D'you have the picker? There's one last—ah."

When Eli comes around the bend, the surprise on his face is apparent but quickly returns to his normal, gregarious smile. "Either of you happen to know where the last picker went?"

"I think I saw it in the western row," Vera says, standing up quickly. She doesn't look back at Paul, walks hurriedly past her brother outside the barn where the day is settling into night. Pale pink and blue. The air feels good on her flushed cheeks.

"Was I interrupting something back there?" Eli asks her as he catches up. No schoolboy smirk, no playful smack on the arm. He's wondering how long this has been happening without him knowing. Recalculating what he thinks he knows about his sister's goings-on here.

"No, it was nothing." She lifts the picker from under the last row of apple trees and hands it to him.

"He wouldn't be the worst choice," Eli says, a smile forming on his lips as he begins to entertain the possibility.

"It's nothing," Vera insists again, and this time her brother does give her a knock on her shoulder, and Vera feels the ember inside her warming. That Eli sees it, too.

They return to the patio. Vera scans the crowd and spots Paul talking to Lopez. She falls in with other neighbors, and by the time she glances around for him again ten minutes later he's gone.

*

The next morning, Eli and Vera hike a little way up the mountain behind the meadow to collect more spring and soil samples at a particular set of coordinates Lydia has her eye on. Vera won't be able to take the samples home with her first with Eli here, but those are the dice she has to roll today. Mostly the two of them have been banished outside so Lydia can focus. She's been on a tear the past four days. Too deep into whatever she's working on to go to the harvest yesterday or be bothered by Eli and Vera today. Though Lydia, it turns out, has a startling capacity for focus. Eighteen uninterrupted hours at her desk sometimes. And her recall is downright terrifying. Entire data sets memorized after looking them over just once a week ago, a *month* ago. Her ability to analyze and synthesize information as fast as a computer's. Vera often feels sluggish and dim-witted around her, like life is happening in a foreign language she doesn't understand. She's more than happy to be away from the lab this morning.

"What about Mr. Mierenneuker?" Eli asks, ducking under a low pine bough.

"Oh my god, Mr. Mierenneuker!" Vera cackles at the offensive nickname they had for a grumpy landlord once upon a time. "Mr. Ant Fucker, right!"

"That's one of those words that hits much harder in Dutch."

"Where was that? Kansas? I haven't thought of him in *ages*!" Vera jumps across a boggy patch of moss.

They've been reminiscing about ridiculous things, silly things. The way they can when it's only the two of them and no one else is around for literal miles.

A part of Vera wants to tell him about Lydia and Lotte, but she can't without revealing how she knows, so she continues to hold the secret in.

When they return to the lab an hour later, ruddy cheeked, bags full, Lydia is at her desk, typing into her computer at her usual steady clip.

"Oh man, what about One-Eyed Ed?" Eli asks Vera, continuing their conversation as he pulls out a bottle from his bag and sets it on the stainless steel counter. "He was a gas. Remember the time he—"

"Don't you have a call with the Mainers?" Lydia interrupts, then takes a delicate sip of the espresso on her desk while continuing to type with her other hand.

"Oh shit, you're right! What time is it?" Eli asks.

"Seven minutes past eleven," Lydia answers without looking at a watch or phone.

"Crap crap crap crap—" her brother chants as he bounds over to the office in the back of the lab.

Vera is about to ask who the Mainers are, but Lydia answers before she can.

"Next round of investors we're starting to probe," she says, then goes back to typing behind her monitor.

Vera breathes in.

"You have another question," Lydia says, still typing.

Anticipating the behavior of others is a skill they've all developed over the centuries, but this is exactly why Vera applies it sparingly—it's very annoying.

Vera was going to ask Lydia a question about the way they're geotagging water versus soil tests in their data sets to double-check that she is in fact doing it correctly. Maybe ask if there is anything else she could be doing today, because it seems a little pointless to have Vera do data in-put when they all know Lydia is three thousand times more efficient at it than Vera could ever be.

"Hm," Lydia says and stops typing but doesn't look away from her screen.

Vera cracks her knuckles in one agitated roll.

Everything about Lydia annoys her right now. The way she pulls at a curl when thinking. Her ridiculous vocabulary. Her refusal to wear practical clothes even though she's living in the country. Honestly, who wears suede high heels when the ground is covered in mucky leaves and mud?

"What," Vera says, not a question.

"How often do you kill yourself?"

"Excuse me?"

Vera heard the question perfectly well. Alarm surges through her limbs, her ears go padded.

"When was the last time?" Lydia probes, her tone even, like she's asking Vera what she ate for breakfast, not how frequently she plays at ending her existence.

It's still less than when she first arrived, and almost always after ingesting one of the water samples first. It's been a few days since the last time—her wrists in the bath again? She should have known there'd be evidence in her cells somehow! She glances involuntarily at the closed door of the office where Eli is. Feels the full force of just how much she does not want her brother to find out she does this. Not like this. Not here. Not from Lydia.

"Vera, do you want to die?"

The electric lights buzz above them in the charged silence.

"Three thirty!" Eli announces loudly as he swings open the door of the back office. "Call's not scheduled till three thirty. Phew! You almost messed that one up, Wolven." He walks over, ruffles his sister's hair as he passes, and settles on the stool to her right.

"What'd I miss?"

"Nothing," Lydia says and returns to her typing without looking at Vera again.

Vera's heart thrashes under her shirt so hard she is certain they must also be able to hear it.

"Matthew just wrote and said his mom and sister are on board with the *People* magazine interview," Eli tells Lydia.

Vera, do you want to die?

"It needs to wait. There's no point drumming up the human-interest family angle until we have a product on the market. We've talked about this. Too much speculation too soon could expose and ruin us."

Vera continues to remove the water bottles from their bag, but she's merely pantomiming being busy, her hands moving without her.

She should have known Lydia would be able to tell from her tissue samples somehow.

"Lyd, his mom is really not doing so hot."

"He shouldn't have promised her a solution he can't deliver."

"But there's a chance we might—"

"Do *not* tell me you're feeding him bullshit, Eli," Lydia says, her voice slightly raised, and Vera finally lifts her head.

"Dude, I'm not telling him anything you haven't already told him yourself." Eli holds his hands up.

"There is a very, very, *very* small chance that if we find the source in the next few months we *might* be able to come up with a dosage that *might* stop the deterioration but it will absolutely *not* be FDA approved without—"

"Knock knock! Oooh, look at this place, how space-age!"

All three of them whip their heads around to spot the intruder.

"Cate! What a surprise! We didn't hear you knock," Lydia says, her voice straining to produce a casual, pleased pitch.

"I was outside and I saw Vera and Eli come in this way so I gave a knock, but no one heard, and it turned out it was open so—"

Cate's eyes continue to greedily sweep the lab. No one from the neighborhood has been invited here. Nearly everyone has asked Vera what it's like. As always, she answers honestly but with a key part or two missing. Tells them it's shiny, sterile, kind of boring.

Vera, Eli, and Lydia all give the room the same quick visual sweep. Computers, cabinets, refrigerators, maps, the few rows of new water samples Vera is supposed to enter into their system. The mice are in the back, their own blood and tissue samples stored in closed-front refrigerators. It all checks out. The botany work, just the botany work.

"You guys should keep your doors locked. I caught this woman wandering around the meadow yesterday before the harvest. Said she had some agreement with Brian's grandma that she could come up this way to state land, and I had to be like, OK, lady, but I'm running a business here now, I can't have randos stumbling around breaking their legs and suing me."

"You are so right," Eli says, his hands clasped in front of his chest. "So what can we do you for?" Vera feels Lydia moving around behind her, hears her turn something over with a clean click. Probably that framed picture of Eli in San Francisco in the seventies Lydia keeps on her desk. Apparently she likes his hair that way and has convinced him to grow it long like that again.

"I wanted to invite you to a little game night at our place on Saturday," Cate says, her eyes still combing the room around her.

"Excellent! Pictionary? Charades? Ouija?" Eli moves closer to the uninvited guest. Her attention refocuses on his face. Vera glances behind her and sees Lydia flipping a stack of paper facedown.

"I don't know. Brian's the one who likes games, so he chooses what to play. I'm in it for the drinking buddies."

"I believe I have a wonderful Chablis that pairs nicely with Scrabble and small-town gossip," Eli says, a hand now on Cate's lower back.

"Someone who speaks my language! So you'll come?"

They all agree at once, yes they'll come, they'll be there, it sounds like fun.

"Seven o'clock. No need to bring anything."

"Seven o'clock." Eli kisses one cheek, the other, his lips just grazing the corner of Cate's, the closeness just a little longer than appropriate.

When Cate says bye a moment later, it's only to Eli. Then the door is closed, the lock double-checked.

"I bet you kill at Scrabble," Eli says to Lydia as he returns, pointing a playful finger at her.

"Did you disable the automatic locks?" Lydia asks Vera.

"What? No."

"Then you didn't confirm the door was closed all the way behind you. Vera, this is serious! We could have been in the middle of—"

"But we weren't," Eli interrupts, and Vera feels a small burst of warmth at her brother coming to her defense like this.

Lydia stands, places a slim hand on each hip.

"Listen to me carefully," she begins, her voice shaking slightly. "We are *all* screwed if there is a breach, OK? This is not a game."

"OK. We'll save the games for game night," Vera says because she cannot help herself. It is both deeply satisfying and deeply unsettling to see Lydia this rattled. She has only been so implacable, so smooth. With Vera at least. In town, with the others, she is much more effusive with her affection, real or not. But always calm, collected.

"I don't know how you two have lasted as long as you have," Lydia says as she shakes her curls, her wonder and disgust potent. "Have you always been this care-fucking-free? Has our condition always been a goddamn joke to you?"

Vera, Eli, and Ma were in fact very cautious. Arrested only once in all their years together, 1828. They'd left Illinois in a hurry after running into a house fire down the road from where they lived. All nine inhabitants—seven children and their parents—were alive because of them, but the whole town was watching as they'd dashed in and out through the smoke and flames and falling beams.

Once everyone in the family had been dragged outside and accounted for, the crowd turned from grateful to skeptical faster than the blaze itself had spread through the wooden building. It was crazy of them to have run into the house in front of everyone, crazy to have gone back into their own house to gather what few belongings they had as the outrage grew. But it was early in their experience as immortals, and they were still acting impulsively, innocently. Still testing the boundaries of what miraculous deeds would be tolerated and what would be deemed too much.

They arrived in a small town in Missouri shaken and hungry. They'd spent the last of their money on getting there, so they ate a hot meal at a tavern and dashed on the bill. They were caught hardly a mile away and brought in by the sheriff to the station.

A day of questions, evasions, apologies. They were released by nightfall. Eli would have languished in the cell were he alone, he was so furious about the whole situation, no good deed going unpunished and all. But Ma and Vera were able to scrape up enough charm between the two of them to get the whole family released with a warning and a promise to continue on and to not pull that kind of trite robbery again.

On the surface it wasn't so frightening as far as encounters with the law can go, still it shook them. Being held like that.

What if one of them fell into a life sentence for something, what then? Maybe a death-defying escape could be made. But that would turn them into fugitives followed by a famous and impossible tale.

And what if they *couldn't* escape, and remained imprisoned, unaged, for decades?

"Baby, we're not—" Eli begins but is cut off immediately by Lydia.

"Don't *baby* me, Eli. I have spent one hundred and fifty-one years on my own and I have done just fine. More than fine! And now I have to babysit you two? Come up with these ridiculous cover stories? *Oh we're in love* and *she's a fucking teenage botanist whose help we reeeeally need.*"

Vera looks to her brother, but his face is inscrutable.

"Do you think you two are helping me right now?" Lydia demands. Her cheeks have gone pink with exertion, her deep-set eyes are wide and the vein in her forehead is visible. "Do you understand the insane amount of misdirection I have been doing to keep Matthew in the dark until the time is right?"

"You're carrying a lot for all of us, it's true," Eli says evenly.

"You two are liabilities in every sense of the word. You are walking, talking *data*, and if you out us too soon—" Lydia shakes her head again, doesn't finish her own sentence.

"What do you need us to do?" Eli asks, his tone gentle, the way Vera has heard him talk to skittish animals and friends who've had too much to drink.

"I need her to leave," Lydia says.

It takes Vera a moment to realize that she is the "her" in that sentence.

"Seriously?" Eli asks, expressing Vera's thoughts exactly.

"You and I have some things to discuss."

Vera doesn't want to be here right now, but she doesn't want to leave either. She wants to be able to defend herself when Lydia tells Eli what she's been doing. She wants to be able to tell them she had a head-splitter while fishing, or some other accident on a particularly tricky rescue at work. But it's clear she can't stay.

Lydia doesn't know anything for certain, she reminds herself. Vera never actually answered either of her questions.

Eli looks at his sister and gives her a nod.

How often do you kill yourself?

Vera stands.

Vera, do you want to die?

She leaves the water samples on the table, closes both doors behind herself securely.

Eli will believe her. He always takes his sister's side, eventually.

14

October 2014

The duck gives a stubborn quack. Vera pauses, then decides to forge ahead up the ramp to the post office. It waddles out of the way at the last second then hops off the stairwell into the wet grass.

The bell jingles as she opens the door.

"Hi, Vera!" Postmaster Janet says. "Mr. Mallard out there making trouble again? Aw, I love that little rascal." She leans over the counter to try to see out the window. "Gonna be sad to see him go once he decides it's time to run off to Mexico."

Vera opens her P.O. Box, flips through her pay stubs, her electric bill. She's still surprised to see her real name written down like this sometimes. The bell sounds again behind her.

"Hi, Georgie!"

Vera turns around and nods at George who nods back. The space is so small, hardly six feet wide, his jacket grazes her back as he passes behind her to his box.

"I've got some packages for you, too, one sec, hon." Janet walks away from the counter to the bins in the rear.

Vera can feel his eyes on her, wonders what Paul told him about the harvest.

"You all set for this weekend?" he finally asks. Vera looks up at him and sees he's still flipping through his own stack of mail.

"This weekend?"

Now he looks at her. "Opening day."

Vera figured that invitation disappeared the moment she herself disappeared from the barn.

"Forecast is calling for snow, which is wild but wouldn't be the first time out here. Make sure you suit up good."

"Oh, I'm sorry, I can't come. I've got work." It's both true and an excuse to get out of the invitation. She wants to go, which is how she knows she shouldn't.

"I thought your buddy was gonna cover for you, what's his name? He was at the apple thing, too."

"Lopez?"

"Yeah. Paul said he swapped days with you so you could come."

Vera frowns as she tries to follow.

"I see Jocelyn's at it again with the online shopping!" Janet says, back at the window, then dumps four soft packages on the counter. Vera steps aside as George says something about the little ones growing quickly. Janet agrees, her own little Hazel has already outgrown the goddamn princess dress she got for her birthday a few weeks ago, what can you do.

"Speaking of fashion, it looks like you could invest in another pair of overalls, Vera."

"They're not usually this bad." Vera looks down at the dirt streaks. "I'm in the middle of turning over the garden for the season."

It's the right weather to bed some of it down today, but mostly Vera is doing it because she needs the feel of the dirt in her hands right now. To move and work and stop the questions.

No lab work today, Eli texted her this morning after a long night of silence. The itch to end herself all the more irritating and intense now that she shouldn't do it.

Vera needs to know what Lydia has told him.

"When's the bar opening? Is the cider going to be sweet? I hate bitter drinks. What's with everyone and their IPAs, right Georgie?"

"I'm a Miller Lite guy myself."

"Probably best if you're going to drink it while handling a loaded gun. Hah! You getting ready for hunting season?"

"Gonna do bow season down here, then head up to Maine for early rifle. I got two tags up there."

"I don't know how you guys do it, I'm too squeamish," Janet says and gives a shiver. "But I *will* take some venison sausages again when you get 'em." She laughs a happy, raspy wheeze.

"You know I'm good for it, Jan," George says, then he turns to Vera. "If you're half as good with a bow as you are with a gun or a rod, we'll all be having venison sausage next week."

"I'm—"

"See you Saturday."

The bell jingles again and he's gone.

"Wow," Janet says, mock impressed. "One of the boys now."

"We'll see."

"Watch out, they'll blame you when they don't get anything. Like saying ladies are bad luck on boats. Always the woman's fault!" Janet launches into a story about her father-in-law blaming her for car trouble that happened well after she'd borrowed his Camry one time, takes a detour into another story that has something to do with a ruined Christmas tree, then ends her monologue by asking, "D'you want Cate and Brian's mail, too?"

"Sure."

"Don't tell the higher-ups! Federal offenses all around." Janet retrieves the rubber-banded bundle from the open back of another P.O. Box and hands it over. "I see you've been hanging out with the millionaires at the general store recently."

"I'm doing a little conservation and rewilding work with them."

"I hear they were with Facebook early on, or was it Google? That's why they've got so much cash. Don't know *why* they'd waste it on a place like this. Don't get me wrong, I live here, too, but shouldn't they buy an island in the Bahamas or something instead?"

Vera shrugs.

"Good-looking people can be so stupid," Janet says with a sigh.

Vera returns to her cottage. She checks the weather forecast and sees they are in fact predicting up to ten inches of snow this weekend. She steps into her garden and looks out over the neatly raked rows she's already put to bed, the weeded, leafy rows still standing. She decides the kale will be fine, she'll risk the parsley, but everything else she'll pull up.

Hardly twenty minutes later it's done. All the months of tending and growing and weeding and watering finished in a flash. The plants' lives so abruptly over.

It's too much food for one person all at once, especially one person who barely bothers to eat. She'll rinse everything and give some to Cate and Brian, some to Lopez.

Lopez.

Vera leaves her harvest in the grass and goes inside. She picks up her phone and calls her friend.

"Van Valkenburgh! Whatcha need?" Lopez asks by way of greeting.

"You heading anywhere near the mountain today? I harvested my whole garden with the snow coming, and it's too much for only me."

He says sure, he'll swing by at the end of his shift, that Jenny will be excited. "She's been craving your peppers, you got those? She says none of the store ones come close."

"Plenty."

"Alrighty. Catch you around six!"

"See you then. And Lopez?"

"Yeah?"

"Did my friend Paul ask you to cover for me this Saturday?"

"Your *friend* Paul asked if it was possible. Said you two might be going hunting. You wanna swap that shift? I could trade my Wednesday."

Vera shouldn't.

Then again.

"Yes, please."

"Of course, man. Anything in the name of love." She can hear the grin in his voice.

"All right, Cupid, it's just hunting."

"Is that what the kids are calling it these days?"

When Vera hangs up, she realizes she's smiling, too. She looks out her kitchen window to the barn, catches a glance of the general store between the trees. Feels her smile fall.

Vera walks in through the open door of the barn. Brian is raking a load of apples from the wash tank into the press as Cate fusses with something on the stainless steel table behind him. Music plays from a small speaker, but it's barely audible over the noise of the machines.

"At this rate it's going to take us, what, fifty hours to make a single— Vera! Save us! What have we gotten ourselves into?"

Cate is only playing at frustration. In fact, both Cate and Brian are beaming, hard work bestowing a glow on their skin that only appeared once progress on the cidery began in earnest.

"I harvested the rest of the garden with the snow coming this weekend. Dropped a bundle off on your porch."

"Ooh, thank you!"

"I was going to keep working on the back bar, but do you guys want a hand with this instead?"

Cate cries "Yes!" at the exact time Brian says "No."

"Honey don't be crazy, the back bar can wait," she insists. "We won't need Vera to build it if we don't have any freaking cider."

Brian shrugs and returns to his raking.

"You're an absolute saint to help us this much," Cate says, handing her a pair of rubber gloves. "I don't know what we'd do without you!"

They spend all afternoon scrubbing knobby apples clean, grinding them to pulpy pomace, filtering the liquid, and transferring it to vats to begin the fermentation. The work is as hard as it's ever been, mostly because the scale of the operation has increased by tenfold. Modern machines have eliminated certain parts of the manual labor that used to be required for tasks like this, but people are still necessary to the process. The time-saving convenience of the oven spares you from gathering wood and tending a fire but still requires someone to go to the grocery store, someone to wash and slice and roast, to serve and clean up after. The washing machine and dryer do the sudsing and drying instead of the creek and the washboard and the line. But someone still has to fold the clothes, and there are more of them than ever before, and they're washed even more frequently. All these years later and machines still need people to do so much of their bidding, so here they are, pouring and measuring, lifting and moving dials.

They work in the hum and gurgle of the equipment for hours as the afternoon passes outside. Brian grunts and mumbles along to the music. Cate quietly and consistently narrates her own actions aloud. They sweat through their T-shirts despite the cool air gushing in from the open square of the barn door.

Several hours later, the sun slanting across the meadow, Vera stacks the last of the empty crates against the wall nearest the large, open door. The birds are frantic, loud. Blue jays crying out as they flit through the orchard hunting for any looked-over apples, red-winged blackbirds swooping through stalks of goldenrod, the rough caw of a crow. It's like everyone knows an early snow is coming, that they need to stock up now.

A movement by the creek catches Vera's eye. She squints.

It's him.

"Think I'm gonna grab my rod and hit the water before the sun sets," she tells her landlords.

"You going with Eli again?" Brian asks as he snaps off his rubber gloves.

The way he says *again*.

"Do you think I'd be good at fly fishing?" Cate asks, pushing a few stray hairs from her face with her forearm. "I hear women are better at it because they cast more gently."

"Babe, no new hobbies," Brian says. "We've got our hands full."

"OK! OK!" Cate leans over to kiss him. Vera watches as his face tugs into a small smile despite himself.

Vera says goodbye, accepts a hug from Cate, and heads to the cottage where she ditches her filthy overalls for jeans, grabs her rod, and hurries down to the water.

Like the meadow, the creek is bustling with activity. Another hatch, fish jumping for everything.

She spots him at the second bend.

Vera calls his name above the sound of the rushing water once, twice. The third time he finally hears her, turns and looks. His face doesn't light up. It holds, blank, steady. Sad?

Lydia told him.

Eli knows she kills herself.

He knows she wants to die.

He knows she's been selfishly helping them look for the source just so she can die.

"Damnit," Vera whispers aloud, and the sound is swallowed by the noise of the creek.

She'll deny it. Deny, deny, deny. He has no reason to believe Lydia over Vera. Lydia, who doesn't even love him back. Who's been lying to both of them. Fucking Lydia.

She walks over, rod up, face neutral.

"They're hungry tonight," he says once she's within earshot. She nods. Just because he hasn't said something about it yet doesn't mean she's in the clear. Her brother has always eased his way gently into hard conversations.

"What're you using?" she asks him.

"Parachute Madame X. You?"

"This apple caddis–looking thing." She holds her palm open to show him one of the flies Paul made for her.

"Never seen one like this, it work?"

She nods. He picks it up to inspect closer. She looks at him as he takes in the tufts of silver and white on the artificial fly. She knows every inch of this face. The arch of his eyebrows, the slant of his nose, the eight little freckles on his cheeks. She's spent so many years looking at it. Spotting it in a crowd. Guessing the thoughts and feelings behind it. Wanting to punch it on occasion, sure, but mostly, looking at it and seeing *home*.

"You tie this one?"

Vera shakes her head no.

"You OK?"

"Yeah." She cracks her knuckles, holds her hand out for the fly, tells him she's just a little tired from helping Cate and Brian with the cider making, that's all. "I dug up my whole garden, too, with the snow coming. If you want some—"

"Look, Lydia, she—" Eli interrupts. Vera keeps her hand steady as her brother places the fly back in her open palm. She waits for the blow. "She told me something I'm not supposed to bring up with you, but I think it explains some recent behavior."

Vera braces herself, muscles tightened, no breath.

The first time Vera killed herself on purpose she was twenty-seven. She threw her body off the roof of the barn when she was mad at Ma that one anniversary early on. It was about lashing out, drama, and release, not death. She was young. This madness, it felt bearable. And like all twenty-somethings, she understood nothing of time.

She waited another forty-one years until she did it again. Until she really meant it.

It was 1868, they were in Nevada. Eli was out with friends, partaking in the usual drunken farewell festivities that marked each move for him. Ma was on her way to church to deliver a few household items they'd acquired but wouldn't be taking with them to their next stop. Vera stayed behind to pack up the last of her belongings, an excuse both Ma and Eli knew was just that—an excuse—but they didn't press.

There was nothing worse about this move than others. Nothing particularly terrible about the life she was leaving—tavern maid—or the one she was heading to—probably the same, just another hundred miles away. Vera was no more or less lonely than she'd been for years. There was nothing of note to change her state of mind that day, but suddenly, folding her sweater, by the second sleeve she realized she was *so tired*. Existentially tired. To be sixty-eight years old, like this. She could do it, she'd *been* doing it—surviving that is. But for whatever reason, on that day, in that room, the expanse of it in front of her opened like a tundra. All that time ahead of her, and it was too much. It was too much time.

She took her derringer from under her pillow and walked out the back door into the last of the daylight. Nothing pink or orange, nothing grand, just another day fading from blue to black. But her heaviness turned light. She became nervous, almost giddy. The shaky hands and heart palpitations, the short breaths.

When she cocked the pistol she hesitated, certain this time it would work.

So she went back inside. Found the paper, found the ink, found the pen. She wouldn't tell them why, but she'd tell them how. They would want to know how.

She held the note to her chest with one hand and used the other for the gun.

When Ma returned, Vera was scrubbing the last of the blood off the floor slats on the back porch.

"What's this?" Ma asked, and Vera looked up to see her holding the piece of paper.

"It's nothing." Vera opened her hand for it, but Ma flipped it over and read aloud:

"It works if you mean it."

"It's nothing," Vera insisted again then stood up. What did she care if the porch was stained. They were leaving anyway.

"It makes me pretty fucking sad to even consider it," Eli says, and Vera is whipped back to now. To the creek, to this conversation, her brother watching her closely.

Deny, deny, deny.

"Matthew's sick."

"What?" Vera asks. Eli mistakes her surprise for another kind.

"I know. I was also shocked when Lydia first told me but it's *super* early. He hasn't started to show any symptoms yet. It's more like he's a, what'd she say—" Eli frowns into the sky as he tries to recall. *"A likely genetic carrier.* But now that he's forty, he's totally freaking out."

Vera stands there, blood rushing through her veins with relief as she listens to Eli's secondhand explanation of Matthew Barbery's family medical history. How his grandpa died from whatever this disease is when he was thirty years old, his aunt at forty. His mother has just started showing symptoms at sixty, but almost anyone who hasn't died before sixty has lived into their late nineties.

"Basically, there's a fifty-fifty chance Matthew has it. It's a pretty harsh either-or," Eli concludes. "Live to a hundred or—"

"Wow."

Vera feels selfish and childish in her relief. Can't bring herself to truly understand or care about this millionaire's medical situation.

Lydia hasn't told Eli. Lydia hasn't told Eli!

"He's been breathing down Lydia's neck about bringing product to market or at least trials and, well you saw, it's a lot for her right now. She's sorry."

"She did *not* ask you to apologize for her," Vera says, because while there is a lot to Lydia that remains a mystery, Vera knows for certain that Lydia is not the kind of woman who lets another man do her bidding for her.

"No, but—"

"Eli, be careful with her," Vera warns, suddenly flooded with worry for him. Her gullible, heart-on-his-sleeve brother, who, when Vera finally dies, will be left alone with this woman.

"We're all on the same side, Wolven." She can hear the slight uptick in his voice that means he's annoyed now.

"I don't think you know her as well as you think you do."

Eli huffs, half laugh, half growl, his face now in soft shadow as the sun has set behind the ridge. "That's rich. She said the exact same thing about *you*."

Vera's throat tightens.

Lydia hasn't told him yet but she's circling it. Withholding it to use as leverage later.

She needs to hold on to Eli. Keep him on her side.

Vera switches her rod to her other hand.

"But you *do* know me, Eli. You know me better than literally anyone else in the entire world," she says, and it's the truth. Not all of it, but it is the truth.

"Don't."

"Did you know she's been married before?" A wild swing. A stupid swing maybe. Safer than anything she could have referenced from the diary.

"Please. Don't do this to me again," he says, and the way his tone is so pleading makes Vera stop and recalibrate. She lowers her voice as she steps onto a large rock closer to him. She'll be gentle. Eli's always required a gentle touch.

"Look, I know you think you love her, but what she said in the lab—"

"I *never* tell you what to do," Eli interrupts forcefully, and it snaps Vera to a different kind of attention. "I never tell you who you can trust or fuck or love or—Jesus, I can't do Lotte all over again with you."

"*Lotte?*"

"Yes Lotte! I'm sick of you hating every woman I love! Not everyone is as strong as you Vera, OK?" Eli's eyes are shining with anger. "Most people *need* other people to make them happy, and honestly? I'm not so sure it's the big weakness you seem to think it is."

Vera feels whiplashed. To have prepared for one conversation and found herself somewhere else so far away.

"I know Jacob dying fucked you up, but—"

"Don't bring him into this."

Vera needs to take control of the conversation again. Of herself. There's a tremor in her knees and the trees above them are leaning in and over, closing in on her. Everything is going dark and shadowed, fuzzing out.

"Jacob loved you! You loved him! And you *knew* it was never going to last and that sucks! But maybe his death was more of a blessing in disguise than you—"

A wave of red, a roar inside her.

"Jacob getting tossed from his horse and splattering his brains on a rock right in front of me was a *blessing in disguise*?"

She's yelling now. A bird scatters from a tree behind her in a thrash of wings. Even the swarm of gnats around them are momentarily blown off course.

Eli says he's sorry, he didn't mean it like that.

"Stop."

Jacob's eyes open but empty. His mouth frozen in a grimace. The yellow coneflowers wobbling in the soft wind as he lay there so still. So instantaneously gone. So much gone with him.

"Wolven—"

Vera's chest tightens. She shuts her eyes and tries to breathe in deeply. The scratch of rocks on rocks and the all-consuming darkness.

She forces her eyes open.

"You have had it so easy, Eli," she tells him steadily, and he looks at her like a puppy now, head tilted inquisitively, and it fills her with more rage. This part of her brother that she had somehow willfully forgotten. How dumb and lucky he can be. "You have *no* idea what I've been through," she says, even though a part of her knows it's unfair. To be mad at someone for not knowing what you won't tell them. But she's not thinking critically right now. She's raging. Deteriorating. She has so little to hang on to.

"I'm sorry," he says.

"It doesn't *matter* if you're sorry, sorry doesn't fix any of this," she huffs.

Eli tilts his head the other way. "What's going on with you?"

"You won't understand," she says and lifts her rod, turns to leave.

"Where are you going?"

"I don't need this shit."

"*What* shit? Wolven! Come back!"

Vera scampers up the creek bank and into the meadow. She doesn't turn around, keeps her eyes on the lights illuminating the inside of her old house. It emits such warmth, such comfort. How badly she wants to let herself in the back door and find Pa in a chair, Ma across from him, to be chided by them for being out at dusk alone then fed a warm meal, told a story. How badly Vera wants something that no longer exists. How badly she needs to leave it all behind.

15

October 2014

"As you can see, Offenses Related to Fire Laws were down fourteen percent and Offenses Related to Illegal Snowmobile Operation went down sixteen percent. High Peaks Rules and Regulations offenses look like they went up a whopping fifty percent but let's not forget last year we only gave out six of those tickets across the entire Preserve, so we're really talking about an increase of three tickets, nothing to get worked up about," Captain Newsman says. He trains his laser pointer on a different part of the chart. O'Donnell yawns audibly across the table, and Vera has to stifle her own.

The ubiquity of the PowerPoint presentation is undoubtedly one of the most tedious developments Vera has experienced in her lifetimes.

"I want to keep our eyes on Offenses Related to Fish and Wildlife Regulations in the coming year," their boss continues, either unaware of or unoffended by the minor insubordination of the yawn. "I know an increase of ten percent doesn't look like much, but this is the one that's taken a jump out of nowhere and if you ask me, we're only going to see more of these unpermitted amateur anglers and hunters out here as the region's tourism boom continues."

The number would have been even higher had Vera issued tickets instead of warnings to all the anglers she came across the past seven months who didn't have proper licensing. Most people didn't know, hadn't meant to be breaking a law when they borrowed the rod they found in their weekend rental and went down to the river. Or they were licensed for the month themselves but let their unlicensed girlfriend try a hand at it for a few casts. Vera didn't want to ticket these people and turn them off forever from something she herself loves so much.

Which isn't to say she was too soft about it either. She was stern when needed, even accidentally made one man cry. Still, for the most part, she takes little pleasure in the law enforcement aspect of her job. Especially little compared to some of the other rangers. It was announced this morning to no one's surprise that O'Donnell is the ranger with the most tickets under his belt this year so far.

Captain Newsmen comes to the final slide then everyone scatters for lunch. Vera was planning to find something to-go in town. She's not in the mood to be around other people, and Cate told her about a new café. She keeps replaying yesterday's fight with Eli in her mind, vacillating between self-righteous rage and embarrassed regret. But Lopez convinces her to join him in another room with his Tupperware of Jenny's chickpea coconut curry.

"This batch is spicy as hell, watch out," he warns her as he serves a portion onto a plastic plate left over from the morning's coffee-and-doughnut spread. "Baby loves chili pepper."

"How is the baby?" Vera asks then takes a bite. "Damn, that's good."

"Right? The baby's—"

Lopez's face crumples.

"Is everything OK?"

Yes, he insists, the baby is fine, Jenny is fine, he doesn't know why he's crying. He sniffles loudly, wipes his eyes, and looks up, forcing a smile as two lines of tears continue to run down his cheeks.

"You don't have to explain if you don't want to."

"There was a moment there where we weren't sure."

He's bad at articulating the particulars of it, or perhaps Vera has already grown used to Lydia's precision when it comes to science. The gist seems to be that something possibly irregular came up in a routine sonogram that prompted the doctor to recommend several follow-up tests. The waiting was agony, but it turns out everything is OK.

"Modern medicine, man," Lopez says with a shake of his head then wipes his nose on his sleeve.

Vera puts her hand on top of Lopez's and tells him plainly, "That sounds shitty." Because by now she knows that's all most people want to hear when they're in pain. That their pain is real, even if it isn't as bad as it could have been, even if it isn't as bad as someone else's.

His eyes well up again. The door swings open. Vera feels the wind of it at her back and turns around.

"Excuse me, didn't mean to interrupt the lovebirds," O'Donnell says with mock civility.

Lopez yanks his hands away from Vera's into his lap and sits up straight. His tear-streaked face goes slack.

"Fuck off," Vera says, and it momentarily stuns O'Donnell into silence as he stands in the doorway.

"Well that's not an especially nice way to talk to a coworker, young lady. Actually? This whole situation might be the kind of thing HR would be interested in."

"O'Donnell, man, come on, she didn't mean it," intervenes Lopez.

Vera stands and walks the few paces to the door where O'Donnell has defiantly remained. He smells like a deli sandwich. Onions and water-pressed lunch meat. She's known hundreds of him, thousands of him probably. She's spent centuries scuttling away from his threats, not causing scenes in places she couldn't afford to. He's hardly the worst of them, but she doesn't like watching Lopez shrink like that. Doesn't like Lopez explaining what she does and does not mean. Is, generally speaking, not in the mood for anyone's bullshit right now.

"No, I meant it, O'Donnell. Fuck off." Vera leans into the doorframe, fingers wrapped around the molding. Her figure is tiny and slight compared to his, but her eerily strong composure fills the space around her and O'Donnell takes a step back.

"Whatever," O'Donnell finally says in retort and slams the door.

Vera hears the snap before she feels it and gives a choked cry.

"Jesus! You OK?" Lopez asks, pushing back from the table.

She fumbles the door open with her good hand and brings the other to her chest. O'Donnell's face flashes with alarm.

"I'm fine, just a close call," she insists and hides her mangled fingers in her others as they burn and heal. O'Donnell's face relaxes into relief then victory as he decides that Vera isn't badly hurt, only frightened, just like he'd intended. He turns and walks down the carpeted hall. Lopez is at her side now.

"Bullshit, your fingers were completely in that doorway, let me see." Lopez tugs at her arm and she tugs back with a force that surprises him.

"I'm fine," she insists, the healing not quite finished.

"What's going on with you?" Lopez asks, so gently. Vera knows better than to say "nothing," so she reaches for the closest available truth:

"Just some family stuff."

"Your brother?"

"It's complicated."

"Never mind, I don't mean to pry."

Vera unclutches her hand and fans out her healed fingers for him to see.

"I'm good. Look, you don't need to worry about me, Lopez."

"I know but—"

"I'm serious. I know I don't look it, but I've been on my own for a while now. I can take care of myself."

Lopez smooths his already smooth hair back with one hand. His eyes are rimmed red from his brief bout of tears.

"I'm not saying you can't, Van Valkenburgh, I'm saying you don't have to. You can trust me, you know that right?"

Vera flexes her hand one more time.

"I know, I do." And although it came out of her mouth initially just to appease him, Vera realizes it's true. She trusts Lopez.

If only she could take him up on it.

An all-too-familiar agony begins to churn in her chest. So many friendships stopped in their tracks. The necessary wall up, the necessary escape and cutting off of all contact. People have liked Vera. Not everyone of course, but enough people that were she any other way, she might have had a nice life, one with friends. Work friends, neighbor friends, childhood friends. Friends to navigate the waters of change with, to confide in, to rely upon when things get hard. When she thinks about it, Eli is her only true friend, and that is not enough. Not even close.

But he's all she has.

That afternoon, the snow begins. On the drive home from work, she listens to Mozart as plow trucks trundle by. Fat flakes fall straight down, accumulating in neat piles on the tops of roofs, parked cars, patio furniture, fence posts.

No word from her brother.

Then again, perhaps he's waiting for her to reach out first. She was the one who walked away.

Still.

She sees the outdoor supply store coming up on her left. Decides to turn in.

Back home, Vera opens a drawer and finds the napkin she's looking for, dials the number from the cottage's rotary landline. It rings six, seven, eight times. She's about to hang up when it clicks on.

"Hello?" He's panting slightly.

"Hi, it's Vera."

"Vera! I was just shoveling out my truck. Got to stay on top of it for an early start. Are you coming? Tell me you're coming," Paul says.

Vera looks at her new compound bow and quiver of arrows sitting on her counter—forty-pound set, twenty-four-inch draw length, personally sized for her by the man working the indoor test range who was so impressed by her accuracy he'd called over another clerk to watch, too.

She feels her face pulling into a smile, like a warmth passing over her, the sun reappearing from behind a cloud.

It's just hunting.

*

Paul pulls up at five fifteen in the morning, right on time. He leans across the cab to open her door from the inside.

"Morning," he says as she climbs in.

"Morning."

She closes the heavy door, straps the seat belt across the bulk of her winter jacket.

"George is meeting us in the lot."

"That's what you said."

"Right."

He shifts into reverse, looks behind them, and puts a hand on the back of Vera's headrest then thinks better of it. The red of the brake lights illuminate his face. Vera turns the other way to look out the window, sees the sliver of the moon rising over her cottage. He shifts again, pulls out of the driveway, and they're off.

The dark of the predawn makes the truck feel anonymous and intimate at the same time. She wants to look at his face again but keeps her eyes on the stripe of plowed road lit by twin beams.

"So, do you have any siblings?"

For one disorienting moment Vera feels transparent then realizes this must be harmless small talk. That Paul must be nervous.

"A brother. You?" she asks though she already knows the answer from her apple harvest eavesdropping.

"Only child. You guys close?"

"Sometimes. He can be—" Vera looks out the window at the moon following them. "Stupid."

Paul chuckles.

"And arrogant."

"Tell me how you really feel!" he jokes, and something in Vera relaxes.

"And materialistic and obliviously privileged and *incredibly* naive for how old he is!" she adds.

Paul laughs again, takes one hand off the steering wheel and rests his elbow on the console between them.

"I always wanted a sibling," he tells the road. "George is the closest thing I've got."

"That's nice."

"It is. Except my mom definitely treats him like he's her favorite child," he says, no malice in his voice.

Vera unzips the top of her jacket, the warmth of the truck's cab finally reaching her.

"I like your mom."

"Everyone likes Sue. What about yours? You two get along?"

At first Ma was always their mother, Eli and Vera always siblings. New towns, new names, but they stuck to the story they'd been born into. Eventually they began to try on different arrangements. Cousins, husband and wife and spinster aunt. Whatever got them the housing they needed, the jobs. As they amassed decades together, their age differences began to mean less in experience, the triangular hierarchy of power between them fading in and out.

After about ninety years, Ma began to drift.

"Don't call me Ma anymore, call me Anika," she started to insist. But they couldn't. Purposefully didn't. The harder she pulled away, the tighter they clung. If only they could remind her what they once were together, who she once was and should still be—a mother, *their* mother—then surely she would stay.

But the finite nature of their three-person family was much too confining for the infinite mission to which Ma felt herself increasingly called.

One afternoon she declared: "We are wasting this blessing."

"So now it's a blessing, not a curse?" Eli huffed.

This was Chicago, 1917. Eli was mad because they were moving again, too soon for his liking. He had a job as a pit musician at a cabaret full of women just his type and no legal existence that might get him snatched by the new draft. The world was horrible right then, though his slice of it was fine. But Ma was gaining local notoriety for her saintly devotion to the wounded returning home. Her miraculous ability to spend days in the ward, soothing, cleaning, never eating, no one ever saw her eat. She wanted to go to the front lines. *I have so much to give*, she told them, and people began to wonder, worry, look at her a little too closely.

"You have to stop," Eli told her. He made her favorite roast chicken to soften the blow. Extra butter and thyme.

"I can't stop. This is something I have to do," she insisted.

"Ma, you can't—"

"I am no longer your mother," she said loudly, and it was a slap. The way it stung. They were stunned into silence. How badly it hurt to hear her say that. How surely the pain of it was further proof of their bond.

They weren't surprised when she didn't come home the next night. Or the night after. Still, not being surprised did nothing to protect them from their anguish.

Vera took it as hard as Eli, but there wasn't enough air for both of them to be gasping for breath.

"She'll find us again," Vera told her brother. "She's just letting off steam." As if Ma were the one who went on multiday benders.

They waited the whole war. Left a forwarding address. They saw her everywhere. In the cereal aisle, the bus, the park. Each other's faces. But it was never her. They held out hope until somewhere along the line they realized they no longer did. That their Ma had left them, for good.

"We haven't spoken in a while," Vera tells Paul now, pulling at the shoulder belt across her chest.

"I'm sorry."

"It's OK."

"I only talk to my dad once a year. Christmas. At this point I wish he'd stop, I don't know who he thinks it's helping."

"That sounds tough."

"For a long time it was. But people can get used to anything, right?" he asks, turning to look at her, his face lit up by the dashboard lights.

"It's true," Vera agrees, because it is. The fact that people can get used to anything is one of the best and yet most terrifying parts of being human. How easily we can turn the outrageous or ecstatic or horrifying into business as usual. How easily we all forget.

They drive in the dark and the quiet hum of the truck for a few moments longer.

Just then the lot comes into view, the red taillights of a parked truck glowing like animal eyes in the dark.

"Good, George is already here," Paul says as he pulls into the small, plowed area next to his friend. He turns off the ignition and the bulb above them goes bright. Vera squints in the sudden change of light.

"Thanks for coming," Paul tells her. She opens her eyes to meet his and, when they do, feels something stir inside of her. His smooth cheeks, strong nose, lips slightly asymmetrical. Suddenly Vera sees a face that's not just an echo of Jacob's but rather, one entirely his own.

"This is going to be fun," he continues. "Cold as all hell, but fun." His eyes crinkle into a smile and it makes Vera feel taut, spring-loaded.

He opens his door and the cold rushes in.

*

Vera curls her toes to try to bring some feeling back to them. She wants to take her gloves off and blow on her hands but doesn't want to be the first to stir.

The sky is a bright white right now, a mirror of the forest floor blanketed in snow. Six inches fell last night. It's nearly silent. The deep, padded kind of quiet that comes only with snow cover and a lack of wind. She can hear Paul breathing through his nose beside her in their covered deer blind, a faint little whistle. She heard George cough once about half an hour ago from his elevated tree stand a hundred feet east. They can see him from theirs, a pop of bright orange in all the white and vertical lines of pine.

They didn't spot any tracks on their way in, but Paul and George both agreed this was to be expected. The deer cross from below through the creek to come up the mountains. Sometimes you can catch them on their way down, but that's usually just opening day for rifles, when the hills are full of hunters taking shots and scaring them around.

Vera visually sweeps the creek up and down. Nothing. She's about to cave and take off her gloves when she feels a hand on her forearm. Even through all the winter layers she experiences a small but undeniable thrill at Paul's touch. She looks up, follows his eyes across the water, relaxes her own gaze so she can pick up on movement and—

There! A buck. About thirty feet from the stream bank, making its way toward them. She looks again and counts seven points on its antlers, each several inches long, plus a gnarled little nub on his left side. Fair game. Paul nods to her and she shakes her head, signals no, he should take it. He doesn't insist twice, threads the arrow, points it at their feet as he pulls the bowstring back, then raises the sight to his eye. Holding in position, he follows the buck with his arrowhead as it pokes its way closer.

It crosses the creek quickly, daintily. Comes straight up the bank hardly fifty feet from them, then turns sideways showing its full flank. Paul could not have asked for a better shot. She hears him exhale slowly and wait for a break between heartbeats. Then the *thwump* of the released arrow vibrates the air around them.

It's a good shot. The buck staggers and tries to scamper away. It hops a few dozen feet then falters, falls over with a thud, and lays there. Vera looks up and turns to Paul.

"Hells yeah!" he says to her with a grin then stands and shouts, "Georgie! Get your knife!"

Paul slings his bow over his shoulder and steps around Vera. He shimmies down the ladder, then runs the best he can through the snow to his kill. Vera feels happy for him, and happy for herself, now that she won't have to spend the whole day in the cold waiting, shivering, putting off having to pee. Maybe after they field dress the buck and leave the guts for the coyotes she'll go back to Paul's, help him hang it, have a celebratory beer, see how long George stays.

She knows she shouldn't, but.

Vera slings her bow over her shoulder and takes off her gloves. She warms her bare hands with her breath as she watches Paul hustle to the buck.

"That a seven-pointer?" she hears George say as he catches up to him.

"You know it!"

George slaps his friend on the back in congratulations and together they hurry to the animal.

Vera steps out backward down the ladder of the deer blind.

"All right, let's see. I'll take the—oh shit!"

"What the fuck!"

Vera drops the last few feet into the snow and looks out just in time to see the buck up and hopping off in great gallops. Ten feet away. Twenty feet. She moves to ready her bow and quickly calculates—she could get it, but she'd have to shoot over their heads and besides, she doesn't want to be the one to finish Paul's kill. She'll let them try. If they miss it, they can all track it. It'll leave a trail of blood in the snow. Together they'll find it easily enough.

Paul readies his bow and shoots. George shoots. The *thwung* of their releases echo into the air briefly, the arrows disappearing into the snowy forest. They reload and try again. The buck bounds farther uphill until it's finally, entirely out of sight.

16

October 2014

Vera tries to get out of game night at Cate and Brian's, but Cate isn't hearing any of it.

"We need you! It's a numbers thing," Cate pleads through the phone.

Vera is not looking forward to being in the same room as Eli and Lydia right now, and besides, she's exhausted from the day's exertions.

They spent all morning tracking the buck. The trail was easy to follow for the first few hundred feet, the blood bright against the white snow. But it tapered off and the tracks must have joined with another set because eventually they found themselves going in circles to no avail as the mood sagged from urgent to confused to very disappointed.

Vera couldn't help but feel it was somehow her fault, even though she knew it wasn't, even though Paul and George didn't say anything of the sort.

At two o'clock they called it and headed home. Paul dropped her off in her driveway, but the minute he pulled away Vera got into her own car and headed back out to continue the search. She shouldn't care so much. She's hunted plenty before, still fishes. Yet she just couldn't stomach the idea of the injured buck staggering around the woods in pain and fear, alone.

She found all five arrows, but not the buck. She returned just before sunset.

"Let me clean up first."

"Yay!" Cate squeals. "See you soon."

Vera takes a scalding bath. It requires immense self-control to leave the razor where it is on the ledge.

How often do you kill yourself?

She tries to turn the faucet hotter, but it's already on maximum.

I'm sick of you hating every woman I love.

She picks up the razor and throws it across the bathroom. It ricochets off the tile.

When Vera arrives at the house, Eli and Lydia are already there, snuggled on the couch. Lydia is cozily tucked into the nook of Eli's arm, wearing an expensive-looking camel-colored sweater dress, and the little scene instantly elevates Vera's pulse.

"I'm sorry, I've come empty-handed," Vera tells Cate as they hug hello, aware of Eli's eyes not on her but peripherally attuned.

"No worries, girl. I'm just glad you came!"

Stan enters the living room from the kitchen, saying something about pinot noir to Eli, and a moment later there's a knock on the door. Vera considers how long she has to stay to be considered polite. An hour she decides.

"Vera, would you grab that?" Cate asks as she takes her coat. Vera opens the door.

"Hi again."

It's Paul. Quilted work jacket zipped up to his chin, hands in his pockets, hair combed back and wet from a shower. He looks so clean and pure. For a moment Vera stands dumbly in the doorframe.

"May I—"

"Sorry! Come in." She steps aside.

"Paul! So glad you could make it!" Cate says then flashes Vera a quick, conspirator-y grin.

"Thanks for having me," Paul says as he stomps his snow-crusted boots on the welcome mat.

"OK, that's all of us," Brian announces.

"How was hunting?" Cate asks, taking Paul's jacket.

"It was good. Well—we didn't get anything. *Almost* bagged a buck but it turns out I just grazed it."

"Paul took a great shot—"

"Should have let you take it," he says to Vera then turns back to Cate. "But I'm heading to Maine tomorrow with George. Hopefully we'll have better luck up there."

"I've got the cards set up here," Brian says, so they all head over.

Everyone is corralled around the coffee table in front of the woodstove, settled into the couch, a few chairs, some pillows on the floor. Cate serves drinks as Brian explains the rules of the game. They dutifully listen then take their turns with their hands. As they play, the conversation is friendly, if not quite fascinating—weather, work. Vera is conscious of her every move right now, every word. Conscious of Lydia's performative warmth to everyone else and subtle coldness to her, Eli's geniality but slight trepidation, Paul's bashful looks. Conscious of the fact that they are all inside her house. Eli's house. Their house. She glances at the burn mark on the floor a few feet from her, thinks again of setting down that pan of hot corn cakes. Time wobbles, then holds.

She can coast. She can do this. A few more rounds of the game then she'll go back to the cottage.

And what? Lie awake in her room with the lights on?

Vera downs her mulled wine, and it scalds her throat a little but not enough.

Drinks are refilled. The group calibrates together after the first two rounds of the game, the laughter becoming a little looser, everyone's posture relaxing. Everyone's but Vera's.

"Getting a dog your first year after leaving the city is a country cliché," Stan declares as he puts down a card for his turn. "Go ahead and take up ceramics while you're at it."

"I know but they're so cute! I promise I won't start pickling and knitting, too," Cate insists as she refills Vera's glass to the brim with the fresh pot of mulled wine she's just retrieved from the kitchen.

"We always had dogs growing up," Paul says. "Labs. They're great if you take the time to train them."

"And that's the problem! No one ever does!" cries Stan as he holds his mug out for more. Cate tops him off, promises she and Brian will train it. Says they'll have to because you can't have a badly behaved dog running around a place of business.

"You ever had a dog, Vera?" Cate asks and Vera realizes that Cate can tell she's far away.

"Just one, a long time ago."

"What about you Eli?" Cate prods. Everyone turns to face Eli.

"Dash. He was a stray we took in—"

A spotted English setter Eli started feeding on their back porch in Oklahoma. They eventually let him inside and he was everything a dog can be. Loyal, excitable, kind. He followed the three of them for all of the 1850s and when Vera found him one summer morning under the front stairs, stiff and cold, it split her down the middle. No more dogs after that, she decided. Her life already had more than enough goodbyes.

"I prefer cats," Lydia interrupts. "They're smart, significantly more independent than dogs, and can easily live twenty years if well taken care of." No one says anything, and Lydia recalculates. "But I'm sure your dog will be adorable! What will you name it?" she asks Cate, then blows on her mug. So delicate, as if her tongue wouldn't grow back if she'd burned the whole thing off. Vera watches Eli's hand trace small circles on her shoulder.

"Maybe something nature themed? I don't want to have a human name for the dog and then wind up with a kid with a dog name. Like, 'Here's my dog, Daniel, and my son, Lucky.'"

"I don't know, Lucky Hoffman? Don't toss that one aside too quickly, it could work," Eli says, and the rest of them laugh. Vera tries to not grimace. Her eyes track over to Paul and he's already looking at her, like he's trying to figure something out. She turns her gaze down to her cards.

"I like Hunter," Brian chimes in, and no one is sure what to say. It seems obvious Cate will have the final word on what to name their pet.

"That's kinda nature-y too," Paul offers with a smile and shrug.

"Well, anything's better than Cupcake," says Stan.

Cate laughs with her hand over her mouth. "I'm telling Nancy!"

Stan says go ahead, Nancy knows he thinks her dog's name is stupid. "I call it Cinnabun whenever I'm over for martinis to provoke her. She loves it."

"Nancy or the dog?" Paul asks, and this time Vera nearly chuckles with the others.

"Vera, it's your turn," Brian says, the only one of them eager to continue the game.

Vera plays a random card. She could probably win if she tried, she's good at cards. Then again, Eli's the real card counter between them. He puts one down, and Brian nods approvingly.

When it's Paul's turn, he plays one then says, "This place is beautiful."

"Thank you!" Cate coos, obviously pleased with the compliment. "If we were loaded I'd have gutted the whole thing when we moved in and made it all big and airy and open concept but I'm so glad we didn't. I love it this way now."

Even the hypothetical gutting of the house makes Vera wince.

"It's brilliant you didn't. This place has so much character, I mean look at these floors," Stan says.

"And these beams have got to be original," Paul adds, squinting up, and they all follow suit. "You can see the marks from how people used to hand hew logs with adzes before sawmills."

As everyone else tilts their heads up, Vera glances at her brother, who has also involuntarily looked her way.

"Excuse me one sec," Vera says, standing quickly.

"Ladies' room?" Cate asks. Vera nods. "There's one off the kitchen and one at the top of the stairs."

Vera feels Paul's eyes on her as she walks away. Eli's and Lydia's, too.

The bathroom is in what used to be a linen closet. Vera turns on the faucet and waits for the water to warm then rubs her face in big circles. She flushes for effect, washes her hands with soap, and considers how tedious it used to be to go to the outhouse, to shuttle commodes.

People have no idea how good they have it these days.

Vera leaves the bathroom and is about to go downstairs when she sees the door to her old room is ajar.

She takes one step, another. The floor creaks, right where it always has.

Part of her expects to see her bed and quilt and pinecone collection, her boots under the dresser, the old doll Ma sewed with the red apron and lopsided braids.

A chorus of laughter rises from downstairs. She pushes open the door and braces herself.

Clothing. Lilting piles of sloppily folded sweaters, stacks of jeans and dresses. Vera stumbles over a pair of high heels and catches herself on a rack of coats.

It's Cate's extra storage. City clothes she doesn't wear here. Vera's childhood room now a closet for someone else's overflow.

A feeling akin to shame rises in her throat. For wanting to find something of herself, for being disappointed not to. She wants so much right now, too much. And Vera can't want things. Because she can't have them. Peace, a life, a death. Vera needs to rid herself of these desires. Rid herself of everything.

She needs to go home. She'll stay for another round then confess she's exhausted, pretend she has an early start tomorrow. They don't need her for this game no one but Brian wants to play. They don't need her for anything.

Vera backs out of her old room and closes the door. She steps over the creaky board and heads down the stairs toward the living room.

"Now that everyone's back," Brian says, holding up his cards. "Stan, I think it's your turn to—"

Suddenly the lights cut out and all the machines in the house give a static sigh as they power off. The room is instantly dark save for the flickering orange of the woodstove's glass front, which illuminates everyone's faces just enough to see each other's surprised expressions.

Vera lets out a gasp and grabs the sofa's arm as everyone else giggles in the dark.

"Ooooooh!"

"Oh no!"

"Yay!"

She feels her chest contracting.

"Hang on, I'll call the electric company and report it," Cate says. She pours the rest of the mulled wine evenly between Stan's and Eli's mugs then disappears into the darkness with her arms in front of her.

Vera tries to steady her breathing. She squeezes her eyes shut then opens them wide, looks into the woodstove, the flames, the light.

"You OK?" Paul asks quietly, suddenly behind her, and she jumps a little. Smiles tightly and nods, can't bring herself to speak yet.

"So much sexier without electricity," Stan says, settling into a pillow on the ground. "We should all live by candlelight more."

"Candlelight is overrated. I'd always choose a life with electricity," Lydia says firmly from the couch.

"Not a romantic I see," says Stan.

I'm OK, I'm OK, I'm OK, Vera tells herself as she continues to look into the flames of the woodstove, conscious of Paul's eyes still on her. Her limbs tingle and the back of her neck and head feel electrified.

"Nothing romantic about hundreds of thousands of children dying from preventable diseases before refrigerated vaccines," Lydia counters.

Lydia is right. But Vera wants to tell her to shut up, to tell everyone to shut up and find more candles, find more light. Even if she weren't already panicking, she'd want to shut down this conversation. Over the years she and Eli have informally developed a policy of never dipping into games about a past that's only hypothetical to everyone else around them. It's dangerous territory. *What era would you time travel to? Were people smarter before the Internet because they had to remember things? Would you have been an abolitionist and hid runaways? Would you have known to buy a brownstone in Brooklyn back in the sixties as an investment?*

The only thing worse is speculation about a future just as hypothetical, so far away is the year 2090, 3090. Flying cars, a burning Earth, everyone living under one Google Nation. Even people with children—people who will theoretically have descendants living through these end times—are oddly disconnected from their predictions, be them good or bad. It's best avoided entirely, but here's Lydia gearing up to go head-to-head with Stan.

THE FOUNTAIN

"I'm just saying—"

Vera's ears have gone cottony again and she can feel her heartbeat in her whole body. She closes her eyes.

"You sure you're OK?" Paul asks, crouching next to her. It's EMT Paul at her side now she realizes. He knows she's not well.

"The phone doesn't work, duh!" Cate says, reappearing. "It's digital."

"I've got a rotary one in the cottage! I'll go call for us," Vera says and bolts upright. She has to get out, out, out.

"I'll come with," Eli volunteers, and Vera leaves with him, unable to conjure the words to keep her brother away.

The wind howls through the valley, mingling with the guttural chug of Eli and Lydia's generators running next door. Usually it comes from the west, but tonight it's whipping in from the east and the light flurries are steadily accumulating into more and more inches. Such an early winter. Such a sudden winter. Everything changing in just a day.

The cold air is a relief on Vera's cheeks. They hurry down the dark line of the driveway and into the little cottage.

For as much time as they spend together, none of it is in Vera's space, and she feels momentarily exposed as she watches the flashlight on Eli's cell phone travel over her few possessions. He hasn't been inside since that first night three months ago. She reaches for the landline on the wall of the kitchen. Her hands quiver.

Vera turns her back to Eli and fishes out her notebook of local numbers from the drawer beneath the phone, pushing aside her derringer and Lydia's diary, then quickly closes it shut. She dials her way through the electric company's automatic menu, relieved to have a task she can focus on.

It's OK, you're OK, it's OK, you're OK.

"You have any extra flashlights?" Eli asks. "We have some at our place but—"

"Hall closet," Vera answers. She can feel herself realigning, now that she has a small, concrete mission to complete. An operator comes on the line.

"Good evening, this is Central Hudson, how may I help you today?"

Vera reports the outage, gives the address. The tired-sounding woman confirms that it is in fact down throughout the entire area.

"A tree musta taken out a wire somewhere. Pretty big storm coming. I have no information on restoration at this time, ma'am. Is there anything else I can help you with today?"

"No, thank you."

Vera hangs up, hears Eli open the closet, and remembers too late.

"The hell is this?"

The samples.

"A work thing," she tries. But she's shaking again. When was the last time she ate? Soup the night before? After the whole day out. What happened to keeping it together? She's spent *centuries* keeping it together and now everything is deteriorating, falling apart, boiling up.

"No," her brother says. "This is stuff from the lab. These are water samples."

She doesn't move. Can't.

He returns to the living room, the beam of a flashlight shining ahead of him on the worn brown carpet.

"I got the same kind of bottles for myself. I was looking for the source before you came," she says. Let him think they're leftover from that time.

He steps closer.

"Why?" he asks, and it's harsh. He's mad at her right now. So mad at her for everything she said on the creek the day before yesterday. For who knows what else.

"Same reason you and Lydia came looking for it," Vera says, but her voice is weak and unconvincing. She can't do this right now. She squeezes her eyes shut and opens them again in a desperate attempt to get more light.

The darkness.

"Oh sorry, did Matthew Barbery also tap you as an investor for his longevity company? Or was it as a researcher? I must have missed that."

"No—I—I was looking for me."

"Why."

"I don't know!" She's yelling now. Breaking. Nothing's holding.

"Whoa, whoa hold up." Her brother steps closer to her. She backs away, bumps into the dish rack on the kitchen counter, and startles as it clatters, lets out a strangled little yelp.

"Wolven, look at me. What is going on with you?"

She looks at him, her brother, gentler now. He wants to know, so sincerely. He wants to help. She wants to tell him, but she cannot form the words. Everything stuck. He steps closer, puts two hands on her shoulders, stoops down so they're eye to eye. The flashlight dangles off his wrist and sways back and forth, the sterile blue light sweeping across their faces making strange, angular shadows. So much darkness behind him.

"In the desert—" she starts, but it's all she can get out before she crumples.

He catches her just before she hits the floor, leans her against the kitchen drawers, then lowers her slowly onto the cold linoleum where he crouches next to her.

She sobs. Wet and guttural and bottomless.

"It's OK, Wolven. Let it out. It's OK."

He tries to hold her but she pushes him off.

"Whoa—"

"There was a landslide," she says and takes in a ragged breath. "I got—" Her voice catches again but she pushes on. "I got stuck in the rubble and—"

"Holy shit! When? Where?" His eyes are wide and alert. He's instantly in emergency mode, as if this problem that's already happened is something he can retroactively fix.

"At the end of our trip," Vera says, and she feels a heat in her chest. An anger growing.

"For how long?"

Apparently, when the medics lifted her out and into the light, she called one of them Eli. She doesn't remember doing this, but she believes it because in those first agonizing hours—days?—she had been able to push through the pain of being trapped because she knew her brother would come looking for her soon. After all, she'd left a note.

Scouting one more spot for us to climb two miles north. Be back by 9 a.m.

On the stretcher in the rescue vehicle, suddenly lucid and very scared all over again, the medic asked Vera who Eli was. An emergency contact she wanted to call?

"He's nobody," she said. Because apparently that was who she had become to him. Somebody he could so easily discard. Nobody.

"Wolven, how long were you trapped?" Eli prods her again, a hand on her shoulder. She shakes him off once more.

How could he not have looked for her?

"Four and a half days."

At this her brother gasps.

"You left me," Vera says in a harsh, horrible whisper.

Any longer than that and they wouldn't have been able to chock it up to one of those lucky but still physically possible "miracles." Any longer and—

"Fuck!" Her brother rubs his hands over his face, and she sees that he's crying. "I—goddamnit! I can't do *anything* right! I—" He sucks in a sob. "It was Lydia!"

Vera's face shows her confusion. *Lydia?*

"Not her *fault*, it's *my* fault. I'd just met Lydia and I wanted to tell her the truth about us, but I knew I had to ask you first and I screwed it all up!" He's rambling, anxious to confess, to clarify. "It went *so* bad when I tried to bring it up with you that night and you got so mad at me and I knew you were going to say no if I *really* asked, so I completely wussed out and didn't ask, I just left. I saw your note but I left. And Jesus, you were—" His voice cracks here again.

"I made it out."

"But I'm supposed to *protect* you! You're my little sister! It's *my* fault!"

It is.

It isn't.

Vera puts her hands on his shoulders and his bluster deflates, his body sags.

"Wolven, I'm so sorry."

"It's OK," she tells him, because it has to be.

They have to go on. They always do. Together.

He pulls her in all the way for a hug. He smells like the mulled wine they've been drinking, his fancy cologne. She feels him inhale deeply then out. They're quiet for a full minute, two.

"You really wanted to die after that? That's why you came home?" he finally says into the top of her head, and all she can do is nod. He holds her tighter.

Vera feels her rage receding. Relief begins to fill her slowly. A syncing, a realigning. A warm comfort she hasn't felt in too long. To be with Eli again, fully. Her family. The only person in the world who truly understands her. The only person who truly loves her. Not always well, not even close, but always.

They stay there long enough that she can eventually make out the faint thump of his heart with her head against his chest.

"I won't tell Lydia about the samples," he finally says.

"OK."

"But get rid of them. Even if you don't trust her yet, you can trust me, right?"

Again, she nods. She is so exhausted now. The early start, the hours in the woods. These years accumulated together like thick snow. Lydia feels far away. It doesn't matter what she thinks or knows now—Eli knows she came here to die, and he still loves her.

A loud knock on the hollow front door rattles the cottage and scares them apart. They look through the window's square to a face.

Vera scuttles up quickly and opens the door. "Sorry! Long wait on the line but it's in," she says. She hears Eli getting to his feet behind her. She pushes her hair back from her forehead. Her body heals quickly enough that her face probably isn't puffy anymore, but there are still tears on her cheeks and in her hairline. She gives another wipe and says, "The operator said it's probably a tree down somewhere."

Brian stands there silently, trying to make sense of what he's seen.

Eli steps forward and puts a hand on his shoulder. "We should probably start drinking all the beer in the house before it gets warm, right?" And with that he gives his neighbor a slightly less than gentle push out the door.

*

Back in the house, candles are lit and the mood swells. People love to survive something together. Eli gets his fiddle and plays like the virtuoso he is. Vera sings along—an old mining tune from their West Texas days they pretend they both happen to know. There's laughter, no more card games. Vera finds herself next to Paul. She leans into him and he puts his arm around her shoulders, smelling fresh out of the shower still. His laugh is deep and delighted. Even Lydia appears to be having a genuinely good time sipping and humming along, giggling with Cate and Stan and Brian.

Vera allows herself to lighten with the relief of all that release—the tears and the truth—and to be carried out on the tide of revelry as the fat snowflakes pile up outside, stacking high along the window ledges.

Lydia is the first to say they should get going. Stan offers to drive Paul home, but Paul protests, says the old schoolhouse is too far out of Stan's way, especially in a storm.

"You can sleep on my couch," Vera says, and everyone agrees, like it's the only sensible solution. Like a couch will be involved.

"You sure?" Paul asks, quietly enough as if it's just for her, even though it's clear now everyone has been waiting, rooting.

"Absolutely," Vera tells him.

Coats are bundled. They all tumble out the front door into the steady snow, their laughter swallowed by the rumble of Eli and Lydia's generators. Goodbyes are bid. Vera and Paul hurry through the sideways flurries to the cottage.

Inside it's dark and cold.

"I should have lit the woodstove when I came to call it in," Vera says. "Let me get some more—"

As she turns, she bumps right into Paul. There's a half second of stillness and then they are upon each other.

His lips on hers, their tongues, hands all over each other. They grab madly at their own coats, struggling with sleeves, unwilling to separate their mouths and miss one moment of this. Layers finally off and on the floor, Vera grips Paul's muscular shoulders, his firm ass. Touches him everywhere she's only allowed herself to half-look. His mouth is everything, this kiss. God, why did she wait this long? She presses up against him and feels the length of him pressing back.

Lips still on his, she pulls him over to the couch, pushes him down, straddles his lap. His cold, strong hands reach under her sweater and run up her spine then slide back down to grip her hips. He tastes like minerals and the sun. She puts her fingers under his shirt, moves them up his stomach, the light scratch of his chest hair. He leans forward and she hurries off his shirt, feels his nipples taut from the cold and excitement. He lifts her sweater over her head, no bra, her own nipples freed. He takes one in his mouth and she lets out a small gasp.

If they were ever going to stop, that time has now passed.

She unbuttons her pants, and before she can reach for his, he slips a hand into her underwear and everything concentrates right there, that electric nub. She gasps again and he puts his other hand on the back of her neck, looks her in the eye. He rubs her in slow, deliberate circles and she doesn't look away. Keeps her gaze on his, only darkness around them.

After a moment he pulls her face to his, brings their lips back together. His mouth is even better than before and they begin to hurry again. She feels him over his pants, pulls at his buttons, but he holds her off, still rubbing her as their mouths search each other greedily. Time dissolves and they are here, only here, heat building, pleasure rising, until suddenly, so quickly, she can no longer hold back, that wave cresting over her, thunderous and quaking. She moans into his mouth as she pushes into his hand for more and more and more and finally enough.

As the wave subsides, Vera returns to her other senses. She can hear herself panting lightly, feels the warmth of his skin against hers. Paul slides his hands out from her pants.

"Was that . . . enough for you?" he asks. She takes his head in her hands, kisses him again, now more languid, exploratory. She holds his bottom lip between both of hers, traces the angles of his freshly shaved face with her thumbs, can feel him beneath her, still eager.

Now is normally when she leaves. She stands, but instead of buttoning up her pants, she takes off her boots toe to heel, and pulls her jeans all the way down. She steps out of everything. It's still dark without any artificial light around them, but their eyes have adjusted, and she watches him taking in her naked form.

He reaches for his belt, button, fly. Kicks off his shoes, tears at his socks, all the while not losing sight of her, his eyes locked on her body. Again, Vera doesn't look away. He grabs for something in his pants' pocket as he slips them off, then opens the square foil with his teeth. Vera doesn't need to use a condom but now is not the time for explanations like that, so she steps forward, takes it out of his hand and into her own. He leans back against the couch, still watching. She straddles his legs again, both of them naked now, and takes her time as she rolls the condom over him. He bucks involuntarily.

She lifts herself above him and hovers for a moment, brings her lips to his.

"Vera—" he begins, but whatever else he wanted to tell her becomes unintelligible noise as she lowers herself onto him.

*

In the morning, Vera wakes alone to silence. She gets out of bed, puts on her thick, tattered robe, and walks out into the living room to stoke the woodstove. But it's already roaring, the heat filling the room.

On the kitchen table she finds a note.

Wanted to wake you but you looked so peaceful. Radio called me in. Don't think I can make it back here before I'm off to Maine with George tonight. Dinner at my place when I'm home next Tuesday? Wish I could stay.

17

October 2014

Three days later, the power is still out, and Cate is beside herself, unable to work on anything that requires a computer, which turns out to be 99 percent of her work now that the cider is bottled and aging.

"I'm losing my freaking mind," she tells Vera Wednesday morning, arms crossed. She's standing on her porch in the same leggings and sweater she's had on since Saturday night. The property's well can't pull water without electricity, so no one's had a shower or flushed without a bucket since that night either. Vera has had plenty of experience with circumstances far more rustic, but it's clearly taking a toll on Cate.

"Let's go to the Diner, the power's back on over there," Vera says. She's not due at work for another three hours and knows she needs a hot meal before heading out to the trails in these conditions.

"Ugh, I shouldn't, I've basically eaten only ice cream and cheese since the power went out. Didn't want it to spoil."

Vera considers telling Cate to pack her perishables in a cooler with snow and keep it on the porch, to only open the fridge once or twice a day when they absolutely have to. But she knows this isn't the type of helpful thinking people in a mood like Cate's want to hear.

"We'll go for a walk first," Vera says instead. Cate moans about having to do cardio in the freezing woods, but she's already moving inside to gather her things.

They cut straight through the smooth white meadow and across the iced-over creek into the pines. Vera lets Cate talk about the hoops the Department of Health is having her jump through for their water treatment system, about Brian's snoring when he isn't pacing around like an insomniac. About how great Emma and Faye's vintage store is doing, they were in a *Vogue* Top Ten list. How that new place in Phoenicia is painted the exact shade of green she already chose for the cidery's branding but it's a bakery so it's probably OK, right?

Cate is anxious and disproportionately strung out. As her voice carries through the pines, Vera lets her own mind slide around time—climbing up the hillside as a child to help collect the sheep for sheering, leaving with Eli and Ma that morning in 1826, tracking the blood from the buck with Paul and George just a few days ago.

Wish I could stay.

Me, too, Vera thinks, and the clarity feels startling.

Vera is sick of leaving.

Vera wishes she could stay.

Not for Paul—that night was ecstatic, but she hasn't completely lost her mind. For herself. There was a time when she thought she would never see these woods again. How deeply grateful she is to be in them now.

What if she didn't have to leave?

The thought begins to bloom inside her. A reaching, gnawing, tender thing sprouting roots around her heart. For the first time in almost two hundred years she is home, and for the first time ever she might be able to stay. These woods, her woods, she could walk them for centuries more.

No. She doesn't want any of it the way Lydia is offering—the international attention, the scrutiny. The commodification of this extremely dangerous condition.

But what about just one quiet lifetime more?

Vera, do you want to die?

Yes, she tells herself. Of course she does! Of course she does.

She can die here. *That's* what she wants. That's what she means by stay.

Right?

"*OMG*, a deer!" Cate cries, startling Vera from her reverie. She looks up. There's a buck, hardly thirty feet away. It stands elegant and still, only its tail twitches left right left right as it watches them with its large eyes. Vera holds her breath waiting for it to bound off, counts seven points and there, a gnarled nub on the left antler.

Paul's deer!

So it did survive. *Good for him,* she thinks and relief floods her with warmth.

"It's not going to charge us, is it?" whispers Cate. Vera smiles, takes her friend's arm in hers, and shakes her head no. The three of them stand there like that for another twenty, thirty seconds. Then the buck swishes its tail one last time, and continues downhill alone.

*

At the Diner Vera orders pancakes and Cate gets a Reuben with salad and fries.

"You'll have some, too, right?"

As they wait for their meals, they watch the other lunchers' plates appear in the kitchen window announced by the ding of a small metal bell. The place is decidedly calmer than it was all summer and fall, when it was swarming with city tourists. It's not a regular diner, not like the ones Vera has worked in. It's a little fancy, modern. Lopez calls it "hipster" in a way that sounds like both a compliment and maybe a dig.

"We share a clientele," Cate explains. "But I think we're also gonna get more locals to come to the cidery who think this place is too much or whatever."

Vera nods.

"For example, locals like . . . Paul?"

Vera's eyes follow a plate of eggs and home fries in a waitress's hand as it's delivered to the booth two down from them. When she looks back at her table companion, Cate guffaws.

"Jesus, Vera, I'm trying to be discreet. It is not my forte, so can you please spill already?"

Vera can't help but smile. "It happened. It was nice."

"Nice? I am starving for details! All I think about is the goddamn cidery. Indulge me in a little escapism!"

"It was—really good."

"*Really good.*" Cate sighs exaggeratedly, folding her arms. "What am I supposed to do with that! You know, Brian and Paul used to play together."

"Really?" Vera asks, relieved at the slight change in topic. After years of every kind of secrecy, she's never been one to kiss and tell.

"They played together in the summers when they were little. But not that much. It probably won't shock you to hear Brian was an indoor kid." Cate clasps her hands over her paper place mat menu as fifties doo-wop blares above them. Of all the music Vera has heard over the years, she would have never guessed that these songs would be the ones with staying power.

"He says Paul's always been a nice dude, even when most kids were douchebag teenagers, so. I'm excited for you!" Cate continues as she fusses with her bun. "A little local romance is better than whatever weird thing you've had going on with Eli."

"Eli? No."

"Brian's the one who's convinced you guys are having an affair."

Vera is about to ask Cate how long she and Brian have been together. People always get distracted once they start talking about themselves, but Cate continues. Brian isn't the most astute social observer, she agrees, but come on, Vera and Eli are clearly close, and it's not like plants are *that* fun. He's sexy and rich, believe her, she understands. "Girl, I literally *dreamed* about that goodbye kiss he gave me in the lab."

"It's not like that with us, I promise," Vera says, and she knows how much it sounds like she's hiding something. Which of course she is. She always is. It's just never the something anyone thinks it is.

Cate holds up her hands and says no judgment. She took Brian right from under his ex's nose. "You two have an easy vibe about you, it's sweet. And Lydia obviously hates you, no offense."

It stings to hear, even though it shouldn't.

"They won't last though," Cate adds breezily, and Vera's attention narrows. "He's clearly a project for her."

Vera feels a rush of validation followed swiftly by an aftertaste of fear.

She doesn't want to be right about Lydia using her brother. Lying to them.

Vera must be wearing her thoughts on her face because Cate asks, "You don't think so?"

"Oh, I don't know."

"I overheard her hounding him about doing his *memory exercises* at game night after he couldn't remember whose turn it was. Like he's some feeble old man on the cusp of dementia." Cate rolls her eyes. "Everyone thinks they want to tame a bad boy until they remember it means turning into his mother."

"Who had the pancakes?" a waitress asks, now at their side. Vera raises her hand.

"Hey, why does he call you Wolven?"

Wolvenwelp is the Dutch word for "wolf cub." The wolves who circled the house those early days. Eli used to tease that they were drawn to her cries when she was a baby. Over the years it got shortened to Wolven. Like all nicknames it means nothing and everything all at once.

"It's just a joke," Vera tells Cate. As she pours maple syrup over her pancakes, she decides to switch tactics. "I've been meaning to ask, and feel free to say it's none of my business—"

"Girl, you *live* at my business and are literally *building* my business, you are allowed to ask me anything you want. Shoot."

"Why did you turn down their offer on the house?"

"Whose offer?" Cate says, then takes a massive bite in the middle of her sandwich. Blobs of corned beef and sauerkraut drop onto her plate.

"Eli and Lydia's. Fountain's."

Cate stops chewing and frowns, then starts chewing again quickly, nodding her head along as if that will speed the process. She swallows.

"They never made an offer on our place," she finally says.

A crack, a fissure. Vera is pretty certain Eli isn't the one lying. Or Cate.

"I must have misunderstood."

Cate wants to know who told her. *She* didn't say anything like that, did Eli say they did? Some other neighbor? That's weird, that's really weird.

She's working herself into a froth again.

"It's not like you guys would have sold anyway," Vera says, trying to bring Cate back down. This was the whole point of hanging out, to unwind the poor woman a little.

"Oh my god, I would have sold in a fucking *heartbeat*!" Cate wails loud enough for the egg eaters two tables down to turn around.

"But you've got the cidery now," Vera says, much more quietly.

"Fuck the cidery! I would have—"

Vera watches Cate's eyes zone out into the middle distance as she imagines her alternate path. The sale, the money, moving somewhere else. Back to Brooklyn? To somewhere different entirely? What other lives for herself is she conjuring and mourning right now?

Hardly three seconds later, Vera sees Cate return to the present. To her debt and her small town, her brewing cider and half-finished renovation. This life she's supposedly so pleased to pioneer, the roots she claims she wants.

"I'm sure I misunderstood," Vera says again and cuts at her pancakes.

"How we doing over here?" the waitress asks, having returned, coffee carafe in hand.

Cate gives a little shiver then puts on a smile.

"It's delicious as always!"

The waitress nods and walks away. Vera takes a large bite.

"No, you're right," Cate says. "I wouldn't have sold. This is where we're supposed to be, this is what we're supposed to be doing." She picks up her sandwich again. "Did I tell you we're thinking about naming ciders after locals? I wanna do Postmaster Janet for one of our first runs, you think she'd be down? I think she'd be down."

"I think Janet would love it."

That evening, by the time Vera finishes her shift, the power has finally returned to the valley. She takes a hot bath. Out of habit, she scans the ledge of the tub for her razor, remembers tossing it. Decides she doesn't want to tonight anyway, the usual itch feeling far away. Then she remembers it doesn't matter anymore if she does or doesn't do it. Eli knows.

He knows everything and he still loves her.

Vera also knows she shouldn't feel ashamed of what she does. She herself has certainly never judged anyone who has died by their own hand. Has felt no special communion with them either though. But that's because they are as distant to her as everyone else in the world is, existing in a parallel, untouchable reality she, too, was once a part of. But the act of it, even if it is exactly that—merely an acting out of something without tangible consequence—has felt like a betrayal to Eli ever since Ma left them. To even pretend that Vera, too, would leave him alone in this world.

And yet he knows now. And yet he's still here.

Because he has Lydia?

After the bath, she puts another log in the woodstove and leaves its small iron door open so she can listen to it crackle and feel its warmth. The boiler rattles off, having made enough heat to be caught up. In the new silence she hears indistinct yelling coming from across the way. She cocks her head, closes her eyes to listen harder. It's Cate, then Brian. Mostly Cate.

Her phone dings. She walks over, makes sure to not look out the window toward the house.

It's from Lydia.

Bonfire at our place tonight?

Then another.

No work, just play.

*

"Really? 1969?" Lydia asks, leaning forward in her Adirondack chair. Her face is flushed and curious in the light of the flames.

"Hells yeah, that's my favorite year!" Eli says. He sits up in his chair so he can gesticulate more widely. "The Beatles were still together,

Janis and Jimi were still alive. There was Woodstock! It was awesome! All the war protests, people came together, man. Stonewall? For god's sake, we landed on the freaking moon! What's not to like about 1969?"

Vera slinks deeper into her chair, resettles the soft blanket over her lap. She can't help but bristle a little at her brother's answer. He's listing all the things that at the time made her feel like everything was moving too fast, like life was speeding up but with no final destination. The world had become loud and crowded, violent on a scale more terrifying than it had ever felt before. All the stakes were higher. It was exactly why she wanted to retreat back into the land.

It was also the year she and Eli finally went their separate ways.

"Of course you were a hippy," Lydia says conclusively, though not entirely dismissively. "Vera?"

1825, Vera answers in her head. Pa alive. All of them still mortal, together.

"I'm gonna guess 1895," Eli says, pointing at his sister. "We built that groovy cabin with the wrap around deck in Montana, and the fishing was out of this world."

Vera smiles, doesn't correct him. That *was* a good year, too.

"1874," Lydia answers her own question. "I completed my first formal nursing degree at the New York Training School at Bellevue Hospital. It was truly radical for the time how dedicated we were to Florence Nightingale's emphasis on sanitary knowledge, technical skill, and ward time. All very standard now but quite cutting edge back then. I'm still proud of us. OK, OK—" She downs the rest of the whiskey in her glass and holds it out to Eli for more. "An invention you could never go back to not having."

"Am I allowed to say something like 'my espresso machine' instead of 'penicillin' and not get in trouble?" Eli says, and both Lydia and Vera laugh.

"OK, fine. Then I guess mine is nail polish. It's so vain and pointless, but I love it." Lydia holds her manicured hands over the fire's light to admire them. Then she pushes up her sleeve, reaches into the flames, and moves a log. The scent of singed flesh briefly fills the night around them.

"Synthetic fishing line," Vera answers and downs her glass so her brother can pour her more, too.

"A thing you wish you could do," Lydia prompts.

"Get a tattoo!" Eli answers decisively. Lydia pulls a face.

"Darling, people who die at a mere eighty regret their tattoos."

"I got one once," he says, ignoring his girlfriend's observation. "Or *tried* to. I was with these motorcycle buddies and we were in some after-hours spot on Venice Beach and I figured fuck it let's try and oh my god the guy's face when it kept disappearing!" Eli shakes his head and laughs, and because this story is safely in the past, Vera can laugh, too. She looks to Lydia, who seems to be smiling despite herself.

"What did you want?" Vera asks.

"I don't know, to look cool?" Eli answers.

"No, I mean what did you want for a tattoo!" Vera clarifies and again they laugh together.

"You know, I don't remember!" More laughter, more whiskey downed.

"I wish I could pierce my ears," Lydia says, touching her lobes. "Clip-on earrings aren't the same."

There's a brief silence before Vera realizes they're waiting for her answer. *What do you wish you could do?*

Stop living like this, she thinks, but it doesn't seem right to say.

"Age just enough so that I'm never called 'young lady' by a man ever again?" she finally answers, and Lydia guffaws and grabs her forearm.

"My god, right? How old is that? It's not thirty-six, I tell you!"

They drink and drink and drink, trying to outrace their bodies.

Several hours and several bottles later, they are still outside in Eli and Lydia's yard, circled around the fire. The clouds have dissipated to reveal a splatter of stars. A waning crescent moon rises above the silhouetted pines that sway in the wind like shaggy, gentle giants. It's cold but they are warm from the fire and managing to maintain their inebriation—are absolutely smashed to a degree Vera hasn't been in decades—and no one wants to pump the brakes.

They are crossing a boundary, digging a tunnel together, going deeper. It's cathartic to talk about everything they normally work so hard to hide. To toss it around in the open instead. Eli and Vera have indulged in brief bouts of this over the years, but there's something different with Lydia around. She asks better questions. She allows them to have different answers.

Remember life before matches?
Remember corsets and stays and those horrible crinolines?
Where were you when JFK was assassinated?
What about Abraham Lincoln?
When and where was your first car ride?
How many people have you slept with?
What friends' descendants have you kept an eye on?

"Favorite immortal indulgence," Eli prompts as he fills their glasses from the fourth or maybe fifth bottle he's retrieved. No one is counting now.

"Cigarettes," Lydia answers without hesitation.

"I've never seen you smoke," Eli says.

"Like you said, it's an *indulgence*."

"Free solo climbing," Vera tells the moon. Chalky fingers, forearms exploding from the strain, no ropes. Damn the desert, it can't take climbing away from her.

"Taking any drug I want," Eli adds. "Hey, you guys wanna do 'shrooms? I think I have some in the house somewhere, let me—"

Lydia pulls him back down and he plops into his chair with a glassy-eyed grin.

"Person you miss the most," she prompts.

"Jacob," Vera says without pause and Eli grunts in approval.

"Ma, Pa," he answers.

"Well, now I look like an asshole for choosing an old boyfriend," Vera says, and they all laugh. They swirl in their intoxication, in what makes them the same together but different from everyone else.

Is this what Eli was talking about? Could it be this easy? To trust each other? Just lean into it. Don't fight Lydia, Lydia isn't going anywhere. She's *not* Lotte, she's not any of the others. She's family now. She has to be.

I should give her back her diary, Vera thinks. *Pretend I just found it.*

Their laughs settle and Lydia answers her own question.

"Cecelia. I was her nurse until smallpox took her. She was eleven, but smart as a whip. She could have been someone."

They're somber, still. Lydia's eyes well, or maybe it's the light.

"I'm sorry," Vera tells her.

"Not your fault," Lydia says. There's another pause, then she adds, "Cecelia was the first person I told."

"About being—" Eli doesn't finish his sentence, instead, gestures at the three of them in a vague circle, the night so dark around him.

"She was dying," Lydia says, her words sliding together. Vera looks up at the moon again, and it's moving even though it's not, just the way her eyes are seeing it.

"Is that cruel?" Eli asks, not as if he's judging, just genuinely uncertain.

"It didn't feel like it at the time. She was excited, it was our secret." Lydia takes another drink. "I told her I was going to figure out how to give it to everyone, the good part. Healing. No more pointless death."

"And look at you now," Eli says and grins, victorious. Lydia raises her head, her eyes wet, wet for sure, and gives a reluctant smile back.

"You tell anyone else?" Vera can't help but ask. What if she had told Jacob? Would it have changed anything?

"Only a few. They were all on their deathbeds, it was safe." More silence, time sluicing by them. Then she whispers, "I needed to be seen."

Lydia retreats deeply into herself then, gone from the bonfire, from this whole plane of being. Vera thinks again about how alone this woman was in all of this for so long.

Then Lydia resurfaces and asks Vera, "You ever tell anyone?"

Vera shakes her head no. Lydia looks to Eli.

"Just you," he answers, then leans over to kiss her on the mouth.

Lydia takes another drink, passes Eli the bottle, then asks the flames: "How many people have you killed?"

Eli swallows and snorts. "Like on purpose?"

"Three," Vera says, and her brother swings around to face her.

"Really?"

"They were assholes!" Vera slurs. God she's drunk. "They were all trying to kill me! It was self-defense. Really!" She's protesting strongly, not because she feels guilty but because it's true. They were each horrible men, horrible strangers who thought they could take Vera's body, her life. The sheer number of times she's had to defend herself.

"What about you?" Lydia asks him, and Vera knows the answer before he says it, knows his softness. What he hasn't had to know.

"Me?" Eli asks, gloved hand over his heart. "None." He turns to his girlfriend.

"I haven't kept count."

Eli stands up again. He looms. "Like it's too many to count?"

"Says the man who's slept with at least three thousand women and a few dozen men." Lydia waves her hand at him, at the swirling smoke.

"Yeah, I've had consensual sex with a lot of people over the past two hundred years, but I didn't *murder* any of them. Did—"

"They were all bad, too," Lydia interrupts. Her voice isn't raised, but it's firm in a way Vera's only heard pointed in her direction before. Never at Eli.

"Like they were all trying to kill you?" he clarifies. He's shocked, completely shocked at this whole thing.

"Eli, you have no idea what it's like to be a woman in this world," Lydia says with finality.

They're silent again for a moment. Just the low whoosh of the flames, a log settling.

"But things are better now, right?" he says. So gently, like a little boy.

Lydia looks at Vera and suddenly, in unison, they explode with laughter. Their cackles carry up to the constellations.

*

Vera opens her eyes and briefly doesn't understand where she is.

A bed—a luxurious bed. A pale wooden dresser, an overstuffed white chair. A large photograph of Jimi Hendrix onstage at Woodstock against a dark green wall.

Eli and Lydia's.

She sits up. She's naked, her clothes in a puddle on the thick carpet, as if she'd simply vanished there. She spies an open door to a bathroom so she rises. Shiny blue tiles, an enormous bowl of a tub, a double-headed shower, fluffy towels. Late morning sun comes through the giant skylight. She decides to take a shower, hot water still feeling like a luxury after a few days without it.

Standing in its stream she combs through the night and feels tender, a little exposed. Did she say too much? Ask too much? There are pockets that are slightly blurry. For example, how she wound up sleeping here.

After her shower she dresses in yesterday's clothes, makes the bed, leaves the room, and finds herself at the top of the stairs.

Their house is beautiful, out of a magazine, a movie. The furniture oversized but somehow perfect, fabrics an unexpectedly pleasing combination of different textures, colors, and patterns. Vintage, antique, modern. Framed art and shelves of not just books but also ceramics, small statues, silver knickknacks. Carpets layered upon carpets. It's all so much warmer than Vera would have ever guessed. Eli's interior design style, while decadent in spirit and expense, tends to run toward minimalist in that high-end-architect kind of way—only one couch in a room, but it's the size of a small car and costs just as much. As for Lydia, well, Vera's realizing she's assumed Lydia's style would match her lab—cold, functional, sterile—but she was very wrong.

"Oh good, you're up," Lydia says behind her, and Vera swings around to see her standing in a silk pajama set and matching robe, espresso cup in her hand. Her hair is loose at her shoulders, and she has no makeup on. She looks older than she usually does, the fine lines around her eyes and the corners of her mouth more visible, but a certain kind of pretty nonetheless.

"Thank you for letting me crash here," Vera says, slightly nervous in a morning-after kind of way.

"No, thank *you* for staying. Apologies about bullying you into it last night. We don't have the opportunity for many visitors we can be our true selves around. Coffee?"

Vera follows her host past laden bookshelves and remembers looking at them last night. Lydia saying she's read them all, offering it as a library Vera can borrow from anytime she wants. Lydia being . . . *nice* to her.

In the kitchen, there are shining stainless steel appliances, glowing marble countertops, and tree-dappled sunlight. Framed paintings of woodsy landscapes, a giant ceramic bowl filled with a ridiculous number of lemons.

"French press? Chemex? I could pull an espresso if you'd prefer."

"I usually have instant if I have anything," Vera says, and she's not lying, not trying to highlight the differences between them but honestly doesn't know what to choose. She's not even sure she understands what the options are.

Lydia nods and proceeds to fill the enamel kettle from the tap that extends out of the stove's backsplash. A faucet just for pots and kettles, imagine.

"Eli went for a run," Lydia says over the gushing water.

"Oh?"

She turns off the tap. "He likes to sweat out the toxins. I've tried to explain that our bodies do an unusually magnificent job of this on their own at a cellular level, but." She shrugs, like this is a little tiff they have all the time. The intimacy of it.

They are building a *life* here.

One to continue after Vera dies.

Lydia turns the burner on for the kettle, reaches for a coffee press then a pale green mug, and sets them on the countertop. A phone dings on the other side of the room. She glides over, reads it, and gives a little irritated sigh before setting it back facedown.

"Fountain stuff?" Vera ventures, feeling emboldened by last night.

Lydia looks at her and Vera knows she's making a calculation. To tell or not to tell. Then again, maybe it's a performance of inner debate designed to make Vera think she's about to confide in her.

"Matthew's been kneeling on my neck a bit about speeding things along."

"He's sick."

"Eli told you," Lydia says, doesn't ask. Vera nods. "He's fine. There's a fifty percent chance things will take a tumble at some point within the next ten years, but he's coming up on a milestone birthday, so he's being a little anxious about the whole thing and acting like *I'm* the one dragging my feet, standing between him and his cure."

Vera says nothing. It's the surest way to make other people say more.

"We're moving as quickly as we can," Lydia continues. She has models running twenty-four seven. She's already isolated some key telomeres and might have found two proteins that seem to be uniquely overexpressed in all three of them. They are a small and relatively homogenous sample set, but having Vera here as a surprise third specimen did increase their data possibilities enormously.

"I wish we could find your mother already." Lydia sighs with a shake of her head, like she's talking about an outdoor cat who hasn't come home for dinner yet, not Ma. "Eli says she had joint trouble that disappeared, yes?"

"I think so."

Lydia explains that she's most frustrated by the mystery of the radical regrowth their bodies are capable of, but also by the possibility that the change—whatever it is—might reverse preexisting conditions.

A question appears in Vera's mind and she silently scolds herself for not having thought to ask earlier.

"Do you have any living family?"

"No," Lydia answers. "My parents were their parents' only surviving children who lived long enough to produce offspring. My siblings' lines died out within the next generation. Fevers, infections, accidents, the usual."

Vera is about to say she's sorry when Lydia cuts her off. "It's unlike anything I've ever studied, our condition."

"It's magic," Vera says, not really meaning it.

"Magic is just science we don't understand yet," Lydia counters decisively. She tightens the sash of her silk robe, says if they could find the source it would blow the whole thing open. "What we need is a time travel machine," she concludes.

"Sounds lucrative."

The kettle whistles and Lydia walks over, continuing to talk as she prepares the coffee. "I wish I could go back and watch us, cross-reference our patterns and habits. It was here. Whatever did this to us, I am one hundred percent certain of it." She pushes the steaming cup across the countertop to Vera, who accepts.

"Thank you." She takes a sip. It's outrageously delicious.

"I was hoping your boyfriend found my old papers at the schoolhouse."

Vera takes another sip, steady. Remembers her drunken revelation that she should give Lydia back her diary—did she also say something about it aloud?

"I'm not sure I'd call Paul my boyfriend," Vera says to deflect.

"Irrelevant semantics." Lydia's looking at her in her unsettlingly intense way.

"Sue said he gave a bunch of things he found to the historical society," Vera offers, struggling to keep her voice from lilting up into a question, a dead giveaway that she's feigning casual.

"I've already looked at what Sue has." Lydia pours some coffee into her own tiny cup.

"Have you asked Cate? She's got a bunch of old documents from the woman who owned this place before you."

"Really?" Lydia's interest is thoroughly perked. Vera explains what Cate told her about acquiring the photographs, the ones she saw Cate scan.

"It's worth asking," Vera says. It is, Lydia agrees, and then they sip in silence.

How would that diary help? Vera wonders. It was hardly illuminating. The only remotely interesting parts being the facts that Lydia knew Lotte well enough to think she'd miss her and that Lotte thought Eli was still alive.

Vera wants to ask Lydia why she's lying. Did she actually go looking for Eli at Lotte's behest? Is she . . . jealous of a dead woman?

"Who were you married to?" Vera asks instead, and Lydia looks up from her coffee.

"When?"

"When you—you said you were married once?"

Lydia tucks an errant curl behind her ear and gives a little humph. "Oh, I've been married many times."

Vera's never been married. Can't imagine a version of her lives where she has been, especially not many times.

"Many? Why?"

"Money of course," Lydia answers, like this is a thing Vera already knows.

"But—"

"Some of them were old and left it all to me when they died almost immediately after our nuptials. Others were strikingly stupid, so it was easy to make off with it. Don't look so shocked, Vera. Surely our unusual circumstances have forced you to make calculations like this before, no?"

Vera nods yes because she has to.

Lydia sets down her coffee.

"Listen, I know it's been a slightly bumpy start for the two of us," she continues, and Vera holds herself still. "But Eli's right. Even setting aside the research, the three of us are very lucky to have found each other. This is not an easy world in which to be alone."

"It's not," Vera agrees carefully. "But we both found our ways."

"Us kind of women always do," Lydia says with a wink, and something about it makes Vera shiver.

18

October 2014

The post office is crowded, as it always is just before noon when it's about to close for the day.

"Everyone in at eleven forty-five. Come on people, you had all morning!" Janet complains loudly from behind the counter, but they each know she enjoys the bustle.

"Junk, junk, junk," says Stan as he slips catalogs and unopened envelopes into the recycling receptacle. "Bills, bills, bills. Can't you arrange something more exciting for me, Janet?"

Vera closes her P.O. Box as the bell on the door jingles again.

"Well, isn't this the place to be?" Paul's mom, Sue, says as she enters the small room full of neighbors.

"The height of high society on The Road!" Stan adds, and a few folks laugh while others continue about their business of sending and retrieving mail.

"People, you have twelve minutes left, so do what you gotta do and get out. Don't make me late for Hoagie!" And at that everyone smiles, charmed that their postmaster delivers the mail with the white husky from the house across the street in her passenger seat because he likes car rides, and she likes dogs.

"How are you, Sue?" Vera asks as she squeezes past her toward the door. She smells like baby powder and tea.

"The cold is hard on my arthritis, but I can't complain." Sue lowers her voice a little and adds, "I hear you and Paul have plans next week." No one looks over, but Vera can feel every pair of ears tune in her way.

"We do. He's making me dinner once he's back from Maine."

"That's right! He's making vodka sauce pasta," Sue confirms. "I told him he has to make a salad, too, women like salad. What do you like for dessert? I think he's baking brownies. They'll be from a box but they're good, I taught him how."

"That all sounds delicious to me," Vera answers, realizing Sue thinks this is a first date. That she's trying to say she approves, to let the whole neighborhood know she approves.

"Sounds delicious to me, too," says Stan, and he raises an eyebrow at Vera on his way out.

"Christ, people, you aren't even going to *pretend* to not eavesdrop?" Janet admonishes them all as she comes around the counter to straighten the display of priority envelopes. "Get your gossip somewhere else! Nine more minutes!"

Vera says her goodbyes, ducks out the door, and heads down the ramp into the autumn sun.

The early snow has melted. There are only a few yellow leaves left on the tops of the tallest maples now. The rest blew off and floated down to the grasses, where they curled and dried, rolling into crispy piles that got smashed and soaked under the first big storm. Foggy clouds hang heavy on the maroon mountain ridges, and the fields are all wet and pale straw. The air smells of woodsmoke and mud.

Vera has about twenty minutes until Eli's expecting her to pick him up. They're scouting out a possible backcountry skiing spot just north of here. They'll hike it, maybe clear a few logs, put it on the mental map for later in the winter. If she waits the twenty minutes here, the corn bread sitting on her front seat will get cold, and she knows Eli likes it best hot, like they both did when Ma used to make it. She hasn't baked a loaf of it in decades, but the recipe came back to her the way certain muscle memories can. It's a nice thing to do. Bake your brother corn bread.

It's *not* nice to continue to hide his girlfriend's diary. Especially when she's looking for it.

It's also decidedly not nice to lie to your boyfriend's sister.
Did she ever talk about us?
Never.
Vera can't place why Lydia's lying about Lotte. Can't decide why Lydia told her about using her exes for money. Was that supposed to make Vera trust her more?

The guttural roar of an engine turns the heads of Vera and the rest of the exiled post office attendees standing outside. A small, sleek car growls as it speeds past them down The Road. Half the crowd shakes their heads as they watch it disappear until a screech of brakes pulverizes the air and the car speeds back in reverse before coming to an equally abrupt stop in front of the post office.

The passenger window lowers, and a silhouette leans over, one hand on the steering wheel. The driver asks something inaudible above the chug of the engine. Donald Filson, always in his neon MOUNTAINTOP CONTRACTING sweatshirt, walks up to handle the situation.

"Twenty-six?" he asks after a moment of listening, then stands upright again, looks across the street, and tries to spot a house number on any of the nearby buildings. "I don't—what's the name?"

Vera can't hear the driver's answer, but she knows. She walks up behind Donald and leans down.

He looks just like his pictures online. Tanned but smooth, coiffed but a little purposefully rugged.

"You looking for Lydia Kirke?" she asks.

"Bingo!" He smiles and points at her with a finger-and-thumb pistol.

"Why didn't you say so?" Donald reprimands the man, unwilling to relinquish his role as local liaison. "They've over here."

"Here?"

"No, here—"

Vera lets the men confuse each other for a few moments longer as she notes the buttery leather weekend bag in the front seat of the car, the new smartphone, the half-drunk bottle of green juice, the pack of opened cigarettes.

Here is a man who has hedged his bets but is ultimately convinced that time will not come for him because there might in fact be a solution.

Finally, she intervenes. "I was about to head over there myself, I can show you."

"Well, isn't this my lucky day?"

Vera wants to bring him to Eli and Lydia's house, not the lab, but that's not where they are this morning. She parks next to Eli's car, Matthew on the other side. When he emerges, he lets out a whistle.

"1964 Jaguar E-Type? Hot damn."

Vera shows him to the front door of the old store, walking slowly, hoping they've been spotted. She wants to give Eli and Lydia as much time as possible to hide anything that might need hiding. This man knows more than most people about what goes on in this building, but certainly not everything.

He takes his bag out of the car and slings it over his shoulder, babbling jovially about the lack of cell service, the dismal road conditions, the jet lag that usually never gets to him but he had to fly commercial instead of private, not even first class. He slept horribly.

"I'm sorry, I'm such an asshole," he interrupts himself and extends his hand. "I'm Matthew Barbery." He says it in such a way that makes clear he's used to being recognized.

Vera keeps her face placid as she pulls the warm corn bread against her chest with one hand and extends the other to shake. "Vera. You in town long?" She slows her steps even more. Maybe they've seen the cars and are prepping now.

"Not sure. Kind of a surprise visit."

"I didn't know Lydia liked surprises."

He laughs, genuinely pleased by the observation, then squints at her. "You guys friends?"

"I'm bringing her and Eli some corn bread," Vera says by way of an answer and holds out the wrapped loaf as evidence.

"I cannot believe they live here," Matthew continues, taking in the modest facade of the lab. "No offense, it's just not at *all* their style."

"They live in that other building next door. They work here in the old general store."

As Matthew takes in the structure, a memory of the first time Vera came to the building falls over her vision. She and Ma were on their way to the Bakkers' to return a farm tool they'd borrowed when they saw the highly anticipated store had finally opened for business. There were barrels in the window and sacks of flour and sugar stacked high. When they pushed the door open it sounded with a little bell. Inside, everything was neatly arranged. Vera felt overwhelmed by the sheer abundance of it all. Excited yet simultaneously afraid that things were changing too quickly, at a speed that outstripped her own natural pace. Little did she know how long that feeling would follow her, all the way back to these steps.

Matthew hops up the last of the walkway and gives an enthusiastic and rhythmic knock on the front door. Vera strains to hear any hint of noise behind the walls, even though she knows she won't be able to through the soundproofed foyer. He steps back and looks up at the second-floor windows, knocks again, no longer looking to Vera, now that she's fulfilled her role of delivering him to his destination.

He's underdressed for the weather in his thin sweater, clearly anxious to be inside already and get on with whatever it is that's brought him here on his unannounced visit. The scent of artificial cedar and bergamot wafts off his body and through the cold as he moves about.

The door opens without a sound and the frustration on Lydia's face is obvious. She does not attempt to hide it but rather declares, "Matthew! You know I don't like surprises."

"That's what she said!" he cries, pointing at Vera and grinning like a proud child.

"Let me tell Eli you're here." Lydia closes the door swiftly in their faces. Matthew laughs disingenuously, attempting to cover his embarrassment in front of Vera. He shifts his bag farther up his shoulder and looks around, as if something more interesting might be happening somewhere else nearby. Vera stands very still. A crow calls overhead.

A moment later Eli returns.

"Duuuuuude!"

"Duuuuuude!"

Big hugs and back slaps, come-in, come-in! Eli delivers the welcome

Matthew was clearly expecting. Vera takes a step toward the front door and catches her brother's eye as he gives an almost imperceptible shake of his head *no*.

"I'll be off now. See you around," Vera says and begins to walk away.

"Wait!" Matthew calls, turning around, his arm draped over Eli's shoulders. "What about your corn bread?"

"Corn bread?" Eli asks, his head cocked to the side.

Vera feels stupid and extraneous, excluded and vulnerable.

She feels very much like a little sister.

"Dude, she made you corn bread! This place, man. So. Fucking. Quaint! You should have seen the crowd at the post office when I rolled up. I'm going to be the talk of the town!"

*

Matthew Barbery *is* the talk of the town for the next few days, just not in a particularly flattering way. Everyone who sees him—outside the post office, cruising motorcycles down The Road at high speed with Eli, jogging in expensive performance gear, and asking about the nearest place for a smoothie—feels their interaction with him confirms their belief that money makes you stupid. That California is full of ridiculous people whose power is disproportionate to their real-life skills. All the suspicion that surrounded Eli and Lydia upon their arrival, which they've managed to subdue over the past few months, is starting to rise around them again like a fog.

Vera feels alternately protective of then annoyed by Eli and Lydia as she goes about her ranger duties and her life at the cottage. Her usual shifts at the lab come and go without so much as a text from either of them. A week passes. Matthew's car sits prominently in front of the general store, and it feels like a taunt. She rakes, she stacks firewood, she cuts the rest of the garden down. She scrubs the cottage clean, repairs a cabinet, finishes the back bar at the cidery. Lopez is too busy taking Jenny to prenatal appointments and setting up the nursery to hang out after work. Paul is still in Maine. Cate is swamped with a last-second freelance project she's taken on to float some bills. All the weekenders she calls are out of town. Even Stan is too busy for a drink or a meal.

She wishes she could quiet her mind. The momentary peace she thought she'd felt after telling Eli about the landslide, after Paul, even after the bonfire—she can feel it fraying again.

Day Eight of her exile from all things Fountain, Vera is invited over to Cate and Brian's.

"We're on a classics kick," Cate says as she makes room on the couch for Vera. *Citizen Cane, Psycho, A Streetcar Named Desire.* All movies Vera saw in theaters with Eli when they first came out some fifty-plus years ago, but she'll watch them again. Anything that won't feel like waiting.

They're hardly halfway through *Casablanca* before the layers of Vera's different lives become too much for her to bear. Mending sweaters with Ma in front of the woodstove right here in this room, the packed theater in North Dakota where she and Eli first watched this film, sitting here on this couch now with her landlords. Sometimes her lives catch up with her like this all at once. It's happened before, but it's rare and has always been easy enough to shake when all she did was move forward, never looping back to the same place. But now, here—

"I'm sorry I'm more tired than I thought. I'm going to head out," she says.

"Is it too boring?" Cate asks. "Old movies can be so slow. D'you want to watch something else?"

"No, it's a great movie. I'm tired, honest."

"You sure?"

"She said she's tired, babe, let her go," Brian says gently, and Vera feels grateful then irritated that of all people Brian is the one who understands her best right now.

Vera stands quickly before they can ask her more and her knees bang the coffee table, knocking over their mugs of tea.

"Sorry!"

They all lunge to pick up the overturned drinks and move wet magazines, cards, and domino tiles. Cate says it's OK. Brian leaves to get a kitchen towel.

"Hand me that will you?" Cate asks, gesturing toward the wooden box splayed open on the floor. Vera crouches, reaching, then stops as her eyes scan the inscription on the inside lip of the lid.

I will always love you.

"Where'd you get this?" Vera asks.

The box is identical to the one Eli bought for a girlfriend back in . . . Nevada? Vera remembers giving him a hard time about having it inscribed like that.

"Not the nicest thing to promise someone you know you're going to break up with eventually," she told him, half jest, half genuine warning. It was maybe twenty years in to their new lives. She'd already seen him cycle through plenty of women by that point.

He shrugged her off, bought it anyway. Vera never thought about it again.

"The dominoes?" Cate asks. "Came with the house. Emma and Faye say they're legit from the 1800s. Pretty cool, right?"

"But it's impossible," Vera says, not meaning to say it aloud.

"Why do you say that?" Cate asks, a tinge of hurt at the edge of her voice.

Vera runs a finger over the cursive words.

"Vera?" Cate prods.

A coincidence? Something she's misremembering?

"Vera?"

"I'm sorry! I—I'm just out of sorts today."

Cate gently removes the box from Vera's hand. "Go get some rest, girl."

Back in the cottage Vera pours herself a heavy rye and takes Lydia's diary out of its hiding place. She flips through the entries to get to the last one:

September 26th. Lotte mended calico dress no fee. Showed me
newest gift. (Dominoes.) Made sworn to look for Eli on her behalf.
Sent off with apple & good wishes. Lotte one of few I might miss.

Eli was sending Lotte gifts. And lying about it, this whole time. Vera is dumbstruck.

It's not the most enormous lie. And her brother has always been generous to a fault when it comes to gifts, especially with women. Even when money was tight there was always enough for a flower, a ribbon, a pocket mirror for someone else. It wouldn't have been the smartest choice to keep sending things to Lotte, but Eli—well.

She looks up from the diary.

What else does she not know?

She's told herself they're keeping her at a distance right now to protect their work. While the town can believe a ranger is helping with an extensive conservation project, Matthew, who understands at least some of the true nature of Lydia's research, would be worried about the proximity of any outsider to his company's work. Vera intellectually comprehends this, but she does not like it. Does not like how easily replaceable she is to Eli and Lydia. Does not like this glimpse into what the future will hold. More Matthews buzzing around town talking about "disrupting death," altruism mixing with greed to create a noxious power. The weight of the world's attention pressing on this little town. The whole thing built upon a pile of lies. She looks through her window, where the bright ring of the moon glows, and realizes with a vicious start:

I've been fooling myself.

It's been so easy to pretend that this is how it might be. Hiking and skiing with Eli, a little lab work here and there, some fishing, the occasional party at Stan's, some affection with someone kind like Paul. The gentle rhythms of what could pass as a regular life. It's stupid, so naive and stupid of her to ignore what has been coming this whole time.

Yet that's what she has always done. As much as she's avoided looking backward into the epic fields of her past, she's spent just as many years averting her eyes from the future. It's too long, too much of the same, and now that it could all be different, well, she doesn't like how that looks either.

How could she have not imagined that something like the earthquake could happen to her? How could she have not imagined that nothing is ever as it seems, even with the people you love?

Then again, no one really does. These are just a few of the numerous possibilities people never consider when they play What If You Could Live Forever. Everyone's answers are always lists of the many things they would do, the places they would see. It's never: *Learn to disassociate from my body so I can pass the time in case I am trapped somewhere and unable to move for years on end but cannot die.*

Never: *Learn to give up on love because I will always outlive everyone I meet.*

Never: *Learn to leave home again and again and again until nowhere ever feels like home.*

Suddenly the cottage is too small to bear. She needs to get out. She pushes through the back door in a rush.

The air is cold and dry. No soft clouds of condensation puff with her uneven breath. The lopsided orb of the not-quite-full moon is luminous enough that she could read a book out here. Everything feels sharp—the light, the cold bite of the few remaining piles of snow, her mind. Her shadow cuts a precise silhouette on the ground. She can see her frayed braid, individual fingers carved in black against the brightness. The stars above pierce through the fabric of the sky, they flicker and taunt in their clarity, distance, and scale. What are light-years to Vera? How many of these stars showing themselves have already died?

She thinks she hears someone say her name but doesn't see anyone.

Does she want to die? She *thought* she wanted to give herself to the earth if she could. There would be such ecstasy in the relief. Yet there's never any relief. That's the cruelty of it. No pause in forever.

"Vera?"

She looks again but still sees no one.

Her memories are talking to her now. Her thoughts are scrambled, something irretrievably damaged and loosened by time and the landslide, further mangled by returning here, by the stress of it all, by Lydia's stupid memory exercises. Her body doesn't age, but something is happening to her mind. She's slipping and it will keep getting harder and harder to hold on. Harder and harder to tell herself she wants to. It's getting worse, all of it is getting worse. She would give each year she has to someone else if she could. Bestow them like golden gifts to the people who are robbed of theirs. To the ones grieved for being taken too soon. The ones who would make something beautiful and worthy of it. There are people who would do so much more than she has.

But that isn't how it works. Vera has nothing she can give.

A wind cuts swiftly across the meadow and the cold burns her bare, prickled skin. She gasps. Realizes she's barefoot and without a jacket. It hurts, but it centralizes her pain and for that she's perversely grateful.

The human body is so unprepared to face this world, she thinks as she looks up at the sky. But so is the rest of her—unprepared. Then again, who could ever be prepared for anything as stupefying as infinity?

Something grabs her shoulder and before she has the capacity to consider it, Vera turns around and uses the attacker's momentum to throw them to the ground. She jumps back, fists up, ready to fight the man, the gun, the knife, the bear. Centuries of defending herself too deeply ingrained in her body to be erased by the muddied heaviness of her mind.

"It's me, it's me! It's Brian!"

Vera sees the figure crouched in the snow. Sweatshirt, snow boots, plaid pajama pants. Hands over his head.

Vera comes to fully. "I'm sorry!"

She helps him upright, her heart speeding from the surprise. Once standing, he takes a step back and looks at her with that familiar wariness. The kind that usually means it's time to go soon.

"I'm sorry," she says again. "I didn't know it was you."

She'll soothe and distract, explain away the bizarre, the impossible. Like she's always done. But he's already suspicious of her—

"No, it's my bad." He brushes the snow off his pants, clearly embarrassed. "I couldn't fall asleep and went to get some water and I saw you out the window and—everyone says don't wake up sleepwalkers 'cause you'll scare them."

It's an acceptable explanation. Vera nods and shrugs. The wind has stopped and they stand in the moonlight, considering each other. She can tell he's working up the courage to say something more.

"I've been wanting to explain—" he finally ventures, looking into the night behind her then the ground, unable to hold the eye contact.

"I didn't tell Cate about the offer because I really wanted to make this work." It takes a moment for Vera to find the thread.

The Fountain's offer to buy the house.

"I was worried she'd say yes and then we'd have to move back to the city, and we'd be at square one again and I—" He trails off and shrugs, toes some frozen mud with his boots. "We were having a really rough go of it in Brooklyn, and Cate was super anxious and depressed. But when we moved out here everything got better, especially once we decided to do the cidery and I just—I didn't want to go back to the way things were."

So he hasn't pursued his suspicion of her. Maybe thinking she was having an affair with Eli was enough of a distraction, maybe sleepwalking can cover the rest. He has no idea what's going on with her. Just as she's lacked the ability to understand him either.

All these billions of little stories of suffering. Everyone alone in their pain, no one knowing each other's truth.

Vera feels a small pang of empathy for the embarrassed man in front of her. Like a light bell that rings out bright and clear. But it's quickly muffled by the heavy cloak of her own agony.

Hers is worse.

It is so much worse. A torment of mythical scale for a mere human and that is the flaw. That is the big, jagged crack that runs through the whole of her existence—

Vera is immortal, but she is still human.

"We should probably get back inside and—holy shit are you barefoot?"

Vera doesn't bother to look down, suddenly emboldened in her hopelessness, Brian's wariness of her no longer so dangerous. She turns toward the house and cottage.

"It won't kill me."

19

November 2014

Despite the subzero temperatures of the polar-vortex currently swirling through the region, Lopez is absolutely radiant with joy during today's trail rounds, and it's managing to rub off on Vera. The twenty-four-week appointment went perfectly, the nursery is painted a beautiful mossy green, his mom found his old christening dress and it's hanging now in the baby's closet, making the whole thing feel that much more imminent.

"Those little armholes are going to be filled with our baby's arms, it's *wild* Vera! It's like, I know this, I've always known this baby is real, but it's *really* real now if that makes any sense?"

"Sure it does," Vera agrees.

"And the socks?" Lopez grabs at his heart and his gloves make a padded thud against his jacket as he pretends to stagger back a few steps down the trail, which has stayed snowy at this high elevation despite that first melt in town. "They're literally the cutest things I've ever seen in my entire life."

"I bet you were a cute baby." Vera imagines him shrunk down, his cheeks chunky, his same eyes wide and curious.

"Gerber baby material for sure," Lopez agrees, proud and playful, taking a few jogging steps to catch back up. "My mom still has my baby photos hung in her hallway. What about you? Have you always been so skinny and suspicious?" He gives her a punch on her parka.

"I was a very ugly baby," Vera says, though she has no idea. There are no pictures of her. No drawings. No one around who would truly remember.

Lopez guffaws.

"People came from far and wide to behold me," she continues, because it makes her feel better to amuse him. "The World's Ugliest Baby."

They laugh then settle into amicable silence again as they climb the remaining half mile.

Their last stop of the day is the Hunter Mountain Fire Tower cabin. Someone reported that hikers or perhaps a bear broke in, so they are going to check it out and properly secure it once again.

When they arrive, the door is locked and there's no evidence anyone has been inside since the two of them closed it up this fall. Maybe it was a prank call, maybe a miscommunication. Normally this kind of fool's errand would annoy Vera, especially in weather this bad, but she's been so desperate for distraction that she doesn't mind.

"Should we go up?" she asks Lopez, nodding to the fire tower. "Would be a shame to miss the view when we've come all this way."

He says all right with a grimace and their boots clang with each step on the winding metal stairs, Lopez leading the way at a jog. The wind roars, and what little of her skin is exposed to the elements is completely numb. The tower shakes with each gust. At the top, they take in the expanse of snow-crusted pines, the smooth gradations of thick gray clouds that cover the sky.

"It's beautiful," Lopez says, and Vera nods in agreement because it is. It's viciously cold, well below zero with the windchill, but it's gorgeous. Still, they should probably get going. She'll be fine—frostbite, hypothermia, none of it a threat—but she needs to act like it's a concern. Needs to think of Lopez, too.

"We should head down."

"One second, I have—" Lopez looks out and around, suddenly bashful. "I have something to ask you."

Vera feels like he's going to propose. A ridiculous prospect and not at all a possibility, but her heart flutters in anticipation of whatever it is.

"Jenny and I have been talking and we were wondering, would you be the baby's godmother?"

Good Lopez, sweet Lopez. Vera is flooded with a warmth of appreciation for him and joy at seeing herself through his eyes—Ranger Van Valkenburgh, a person who deserves something like this.

But who he sees is not the real her. And she'll be gone soon enough, either far away from town or dead if things go according to plan. She can't be someone's godmother.

"You can think about it, you don't have to answer now. It's a big ask, I know!" He's babbling because she's taken too long to answer, and he's mistaken her silence for her not wanting to do it.

"No, Lopez, I am *so* honored," she begins, moving closer to him.

"It was just an idea, you don't have to—"

Suddenly he slips on an icy patch. His arms windmill to catch his balance but he bangs against the railing behind him. There's a loud crack. He moves out, beyond where the railing should be, where the railing just was. Vera reaches, but he's an inch too far.

He falls.

Vera doesn't think, just acts. She leaps out after him in a swimmer's dive. She wants to minimize her air resistance, beat him to the bottom. His arms flail like he's drowning, his dark eyes are wide as they lock on to hers, but he doesn't cry out. Vera feels gravity pull at her insides as they soar the sixty feet down.

She grabs his shoulders with two hands and forces a spin so she can land between him and the ground as time performs the trick it always does when something dire is happening. It slows and expands, suddenly elastic and untrustworthy, or maybe generous as it offers you the gift of seeing, *really* seeing, what's in front of you, right before it all might end.

And what does Vera see?

A friend's life she wants to save.

That she will have to disappear because surviving a fall like this without so much as a scratch will be too miraculous to sit well with anyone, and he will have seen.

That it's all OK because it's time to go. It's time for her to leave here once again.

Vera hits the packed snow first. The broken railing pierces straight through her right side as her skull and spine shatter against the snow and ice, the pain already bright white through her entire being when Lopez slams on top of her a fraction of a second later.

They lay there without moving. Vera lets the agony spasm through her body, then the warmth of healing. The sky above her is a solid, untextured gray. Minutes pass.

The moment she's able to use her arms she rolls Lopez off her as carefully as she can, more pain pulsing through her body. She would rather keep him stabilized in case he's broken his neck or his back, but she needs to get moving. She sits up, feels heavy and wrong, throbbing.

The railing is still in her.

She grabs at it from behind and gives a tug, but it only sears her, doesn't come out. She screams from the pain, feels the contents of her stomach climb up her throat but holds it back. She reaches both hands behind herself again and gives another pull as hard as she can then blacks out.

*

When Vera comes to, the burning is gone. She's cold now, shivering violently. She bolts up and leans over Lopez where she rolled him off next to her.

There is a lot of blood and she can't tell how much is hers. She scans him up and down quickly. His leg looks wrong, it shouldn't bend that way.

"Lopez!" she says loudly and gives his cold cheeks a few smacks, but his eyes remain closed. She unzips his jacket enough to slip her fingers onto his neck to check his pulse and there it is, faint, but there, thank god. She yells his name again, unzips his jacket all the way. There's no blood but at least four ribs have broken. She zips him back up, works her hands down his legs and sees the red snow around the lower half of his body.

"No, no, no," she says. Not an artery. Not that artery. She grabs at him and feels it, his thigh bone, out where it shouldn't be. The moment she makes contact with it he gasps and his eyes shock open wide.

"Lopez! Stay with me!"

They close again.

"I fell," he says, his voice soft with weakness and wonder.

Vera moves quickly. Sheds her jacket, pulls her belt off for a tourniquet. He screams as she tightens it around his thigh and his eyes roll as he lifts his head, the patch of snow beneath him red there, too.

"Stay with me Lopez, stay with me!" Vera demands as she fumbles with her satellite phone, numb fingers, adrenaline racing. She'll call in a medical evacuation. If someone's on-site the helicopter can be here in fifteen minutes, can get him to Albany in another twenty-five. She doesn't know how long they were both out, but it couldn't have been that long, a few minutes maximum, the sky is the same. There's a chance, he has a chance, he could make it.

"You're going to be OK," she tells him as she dials, though the moment it comes out of her mouth it feels empty and untrue.

He's going to die.

"You jumped," he says, and his eyes close once more.

"I did." She gives his cheeks another smack with one hand. His eyes open again and hold on to hers. "I jumped for you, I got you. I—" He's listening, following, staying with her. She has to keep talking. "I'm OK, I got lucky I—" The operator comes in and she reports her coordinates. Lopez's eyelids flicker up and down and he mumbles as Vera talks. The red snow around them continues to spread. Vera shouts what she can into the phone, what injuries she sees, the list mounting, the probability of Lopez's survival diminishing with every word, every second.

When she hangs up, he's out again. She wraps her bloodied and torn coat over him, gives his cheeks another smack, and then he's here, awake.

"You have to take care of the baby," he tells her.

"I'll be her godmother, yes, I want to be her godmother, please!" Vera says as she continues to tuck him in, the wind blasting through her thin uniform shirt.

"And Jenny."

Vera shakes her head no and forces a smile. "No, no, I don't have to take care of Jenny, you're going to be OK, Lopez. The evac is on its way, ETA five minutes," she lies. It's ten minimum, probably more like fifteen. She looks down at the mess of blood and snow and feathers from her torn jacket and sees with shattering clarity just how unlikely it is that he will make it to Albany. That he'll make it past the next few minutes.

It was our secret.

"Are you OK?" he asks her, still looking out for someone other than himself.

"I'm fine! Totally unscathed, I—" she begins, but now that she's faced with it, she hesitates how to explain. "I'm different, Lopez. I can't—I can't get injured."

He closes his eyes again and winces.

"You can't die, too," he tells her. "The baby needs someone."

"She'll always have me, Lopez! That's what I'm saying, I—I can't die."

Something lifts. She is no longer cold. His eyes open once more.

"You jumped."

"I jumped because I can't die, it's this, this *condition*. I'm—" There's a momentum now. "I'm *old* Lopez, I'm two hundred and fourteen years old because I can't die."

"You can't die," he repeats and his eyes glass over, focus, glass over again.

"I was born here, this is my hometown, November sixteenth, 1800. You always knew something was strange about me, you *knew* it."

He squeezes her hand, and she squeezes back. "I knew it?" he asks and he sounds like a child, so small.

"You knew something was different, that I was hiding something, Lopez you're a good one! You're so smart and kind and—"

His eyelids flutter again and the wind roars. "You can't die," he repeats.

"I can't die," she says, so firmly. Out loud. The truth.

"I'm going to die."

"No, you're not!" She puts her hands on his cheeks and leans over him, her own vision blurring from her tears or her injuries or both. The wind picks up and she crouches over his body to protect him from the gales, to do whatever she can for him in these final moments.

"I'm going to die," he says again.

Suddenly, Vera realizes it's not the roar of the wind she hears but the blades of an incoming helicopter.

She looks up. There it is, like an enormous dragonfly. The roar grows, the wind rushes harder. The helicopter wobbles as it lands.

Paul is the first EMT to jump out as it touches down. Snow whips around them like a sandstorm.

"It's his head! And his ribs and his right leg! I made a tourniquet but—"

Paul does the quickest of triages, holding Lopez gently, asking if he can feel this or this, his bedside manner still tender despite the fact that he's yelling to be heard over the blades of the helicopter. The other two EMTs appear at his side with the orange stretcher. There's a flurry of motion as they swoop in, and Vera steps back and nearly stumbles over the piece of railing behind her. They strap Lopez in with a neck brace, a back brace. The other two carry him off.

"Let's go!" Paul yells to Vera, and he begins to follow Lopez and the rest of his team to the helicopter.

"I'm OK!" Vera hollers back. Paul stops and turns.

"You're covered in blood, Vera, come on!" He holds out his hand.

Vera shakes her head. No examinations. She got lucky once. Twice? She rubs her hands together and feels the dried blood stick and flake off. She hasn't cleaned herself, hasn't thought any of this through. The gusts from the helicopter are picking up again.

"I've got to shut down the site!"

Paul comes closer, his hand extended. "Vera! You're wasting precious seconds for him!"

"Is he going to die?"

"We don't know, Vera, come on!"

"Just go!"

Vera turns and hunches against the wind of the blades. She expects to feel Paul grab for her, to drag her with him, but there's nothing. The roar grows louder, moves above her then away, the drone fading, becoming more and more distant until it's finally only a ringing in her ears.

She stands in the middle of the red snow.

Then she picks up her jacket and runs.

Vera flies down the mountain, full speed, thoughts banging with each pounding step.

He's alive, he's alive, he's alive.
He's dead, he's dead, he's dead.
I told him, I told him, I told him.

Her lungs feel burned from the cold, her limbs exhausted, but she pushes faster and faster down the trail.

She's supposed to be waiting for Captain Newsman, maybe the police. There are statements to be given and an area to be cordoned off. But she might have changed everything, might have fucked it all up forever. She can't wait there for them. She has to go.

He's alive, he's alive, he's alive.
He's dead, he's dead, he's dead.
I told him, I told him, I told him.

*

"What do you mean you told him?" her brother asks.

"That I can't die, that I'm old—I don't know, everything! He was *dying*!"

"Whoa, whoa, OK." Eli puts an arm around Vera and pulls her from the front porch into the hallway of the house.

Lydia calls from deeper inside their home asking who it is. It smells like dinner. It's so warm. So normal. Eli hollers over his shoulder that it's just a neighbor, then he looks back at Vera and says firmly but quietly, "No one will believe him."

"But they might!" Vera babbles on about how Lopez saw her jump after him, how she has no wounds, not a scratch, but her blood is everywhere up there with his, how she refused to get in the helicopter with Paul.

"No one will believe him," her brother repeats.

There's a chorus of laughter from another room and Vera realizes Matthew is here, at the house. She hears steps, Lydia's voice coming closer. She freezes. Eli moves in front of her.

"Just a little neighborly—" he begins, but when he realizes it's only Lydia, he drops the act. "Her partner knows."

"Holy shit, Vera, look at you," Lydia hisses. "What the hell happened?"

She's smeared with blood and dirt, her jacket is leaking white and red-stained feathers.

"Get out of the—in here." Lydia pulls them both into the dimly lit living room.

Eli gives Lydia the outline of events, quickly, quietly—Lopez falling, Vera jumping, Vera telling Lopez the truth about herself before the helicopter arrived. Lydia's face stays blank as she processes.

"I think it's fine," Eli concludes. "No one's gonna believe what somebody in that much pain thinks they saw or heard, right?"

"Let's hope he dies," Lydia says.

"Don't say that," Vera spits, a white-hot wrath raging within her. "I don't want him to *die*. I jumped out of a fucking fire tower to save him—"

"You better hope he dies, or we are all in for an absolute shitstorm of scrutiny!" Lydia whispers hoarsely, her bracelets jangling as she points at Vera.

"You are such a hypocrite! *You* told people!" Vera says loudly enough for both Eli and Lydia to look over their shoulders toward the rest of the house. Eli puts a hand on Vera's arm that she shakes off. "Isn't this whole fucking thing supposed to be about saving lives?"

"Yes, but *systemically,* not one at a time," Lydia growls. "Jesus, Vera, you'd rather save *one* guy's life than millions of others? How selfish are you?"

"Lydia," Eli warns.

Vera is boiling.

She could kill Lydia right now.

"Look, I've been meaning to float a new scenario," Lydia begins again, more calmly this time, manicured hands primly clasped together. "If this situation goes south, or if this whole enterprise is simply too much for you to bear, Vera, I *do* have the capacity to put you into a medically induced coma until—"

"What?" Vera balks.

"Shh! Just hear me out! We'd wake you up soon as we have everything sorted—"

"Are you fucking serious?" Vera interrupts.

Eli puts a hand on each of their shoulders and tells them, "Let's not get ahead of ourselves here."

Vera sees herself locked in a stainless steel coffin, a series of tubes inside her. Lydia turning the dials up and down for decades. Centuries. Trapped.

"Never," Vera says.

She turns to leave but her brother grabs her, asks where she's going.

"I don't know," she answers, because she doesn't know. To the cottage? To wait until someone rounds her up? To pack? To leave?

"Go home, clean yourself up," he tells her. "You ran down the stairs after he fell, that's the story, nothing more."

"I ran down the stairs after he fell," she repeats.

"You ran down the stairs after he fell," Lydia echoes him.

"Who ran down the—holy crap, ranger girl, are you OK?"

They all turn to see Matthew Barbery, a dinner napkin in his hands.

"Vera's partner had a terrible accident on the mountain," Eli explains.

"Oh shit, is he—"

"We don't know yet. Vera came because she needed—" her brother begins but clearly can't come up with a plausible lie.

"Never mind, I've got it," Vera says, anxious to be out of this house now.

"Is that blood?" Matthew asks.

"Vera, you go home, clean yourself up, and give us a call if you need *anything*, OK?" Lydia says as she puts an arm around her, and it takes monumental self-control for Vera to not shake it off. The whole performance of concern such a farce.

A medically induced *coma*?

"He'll be OK," Eli tells Vera as Lydia opens the door. Vera doesn't normally like to be lied to, but right now she loves her brother for doing just that.

*

Vera is chewed out for leaving the site but forgiven.

"I can only imagine the shock you were feeling," Captain Newsman says, holding his ranger hat against his chest, his silver hair shining in the night. Vera nods.

"You want to come in?" she offers but doesn't open the door of her cottage any wider. She assumes he won't take her up on it anyway, his truck is running in the driveway, the headlights illuminating them both where they stand.

"No, thank you," he says, he should be getting back to headquarters. There's several hours of paperwork left ahead of him. "I've got your statement, I'll let you know if we need anything else from you but for now, you should rest. I mean no offense, but Van Valkenburgh, you don't look well."

"I'm OK, I promise."

"I'm no psychologist but listen, this is going to shake you up a little, OK? Even if Lopez pulls through."

Vera asks what the doctors are saying.

"He's still in surgery. His wife is—"

"Oh my god, *Jenny*, I should go—"

"No," Captain Newsman says firmly. "You need to rest. They won't let you in until tomorrow's visiting hours anyway. Get a little shut-eye, maybe have yourself a whiskey—just one to take the edge off. You got a friend you can call?"

Vera nods, but she knows she won't call anyone tonight.

"You've been through a lot this year. That landslide situation alone was enough to make you move across the country and change your name."

Vera opens her mouth to say something. She's never spoken to Captain Newsman directly about it. She kept it out of her interview, didn't want it following her here. Her former boss must have said something to him in the recommendation process.

She feels exposed, and it must show on her face because Newsman says, "I'm not asking you to explain anything about your personal life to me. I'm just saying, go easy on yourself, kid." He ducks his head forward and sets his hat back on. "Like my wife says, you gotta put on your own oxygen mask first, OK? You won't be a help to anybody if you aren't taking care of yourself, too."

*

Vera pours herself the prescribed glass of whiskey, sits down at her kitchen table, and finally lets herself cry.

She usually disappears. She moves, she changes her name, she loses touch. It's becoming harder to pull off, but she's no longer a fan of faking her own death to kill the trail. It makes people feel too bad, and besides, there's always the inevitable complication of there not being a body.

After their initial disappearance, Ma preferred the open-and-shut nature of a clear "death" if moving on quickly and quietly wasn't possible. She argued that closure was the easiest way to keep people from looking for them once they were gone, said it was kinder to everyone they left behind. For years Vera had to decide with Eli and Ma how to disappear, all of them leaving together at once, then with just Eli. But for the past four and a half decades she's been on her own and has been able to keep it simple. A ghost who becomes a ghost.

Vera pours a second glass.

She'd been ready to disappear, to give it all up to save Lopez. She should feel valiant, this proves she's a *good person*, doesn't it? That when push comes to shove, she *is* willing to use her power and endanger herself for the sake of someone else?

Instead, she feels even more like a fraud.

It isn't a sacrifice to throw herself off a fire tower. She knew she would live—she always does. And it isn't a sacrifice to run away from her life because that's *also* what she always does. Jump, fall, run, run, run.

She'd been looking forward to having a bigger garden this spring. To tasting the cider she'd helped make, to returning to the creeks with her rod and reel with Eli, to Pete and Judy's annual barn dance. To her rounds with Lopez, to helping Paul and George with the chicken barbecue. To doing it all at least a few more times, a few more years.

A third glass. A fourth. Faster now.

No, she realizes with renewed agony—she's been looking forward to doing it *once*, all in a long row, for many years, about sixty to seventy more to be precise. To growing old here. Living a real life here.

What awful irony to have returned for death only to find herself now longing for this exact life, no longer possible in any way. None of it ever possible. Absolute infinity ahead of her. The gruesome loneliness of it.

She pours herself a fifth glass and downs it. She stands up, sufficiently wobbly now for at least the next few minutes, and walks down the short hallway to the bathroom, turns on the tub, and rummages in the medicine cabinet, shaking orange pill bottles. No. Her body aches from putting itself back together but she wants to rip it apart. She needs to obliterate herself. She needs an explosion.

She sits on the toilet and pulls at her socks. Her limbs feel distant, unattached. The room tilts and swirls.

She hears a noise, a knock maybe, and pauses. She strains her ears to listen over the running water. Nothing.

The sound again.

Probably Eli. She doesn't want to deal with him anymore tonight after all. Doesn't want him in here apologizing on Lydia's behalf. *Oh, she didn't mean it when she said Lopez should die. She didn't mean it when she said she's thought about eliminating you.*

Would Lydia put her in a coma against her will? The thought makes her nauseated and prickly all over.

She pulls off one sock but can't get the second past her heel.

It will never be just me and Eli again, she thinks, and feels the weight of defeat.

She walks back into the kitchen, sock flopping, bracing against the hallway with one hand. No one's at the door's window. She finds her derringer, holds it at her side. She enters the bathroom, her vision tilting, time bending into itself.

The fall.

Jacob's eyes.

The desert.

The ice.

The rock.

The blood on the snow.

The darkness.

She sits on the toilet lid and squeezes her eyes shut.

It's too much. All of it, too much. And there is no way out. She is always falling, always trapped.

A bang on the bathroom window startles her enough to let out a strangled scream. She's shocked back to the present—the fluorescent light above the mirrored medicine cabinet, the filling tub about to overflow. She looks at the steamed dark square of window and sees a pale face.

"I'm coming in!" Cate shouts through the pane and disappears.

Vera stays on the toilet as she hears her front door open, hurried steps down the short hallway. The bathroom door swings wide.

"Vera, are you OK?"

"I ran down the stairs after he fell," she says dutifully. That's the story.

Cate turns off the tub and Vera finally registers how loud it was when it was running.

"Let's—OK—can—"

Vera closes her eyes as she listens to Cate moving around her, talking about getting cleaned up.

"I think I need to leave," Vera says and opens her eyes. She needs to leave. If Lopez survives—what does he remember?

"I'm just gonna take this—"

Cate gestures to the derringer in Vera's grip on her lap. Vera lifts the gun and Cate holds it with two fingers like it's too hot, does something with it, goes somewhere. Vera's vision comes in and out again. Her eyes are open, now closed. Her pants are being removed, gently, the stubborn sock. A shirt over her head.

"Can you step in for me? That a girl."

The water is warm, pure.

"OK, that's good. Looks like none of the blood was yours."

"I ran down the stairs after he fell."

"That's what you said. He's so lucky you were there," Cate coos as she pets Vera's hair with a delicate hand.

"I'm going to be alone forever," Vera says apropos of seemingly nothing, but the stitching around her has ripped.

"No, you won't, you're a total catch. You have so much time."

Vera grunts, eyes still closed.

"Besides, I think Paul is very into you."

"He doesn't know me." The room is whirling around her but already slowing down some.

"Whatever, that's the exciting part, when everything is new and it's all possibility." Cate rubs something off Vera's face with her fingers, cleans her own hands in the bathwater. "He wouldn't have sent me over here to check on you if he didn't care about you."

"He's just doing his job," Vera says, but there's an ember of something small within her that she can feel again.

"Listen." Cate readjusts herself on the ledge of the tub. "I'm going to lay out some facts and you're just going to have to accept them, OK?"

Vera opens her eyes.

"I need verbal confirmation."

"OK," Vera grumbles.

"Fact one: Paul likes you." Vera opens her mouth to protest but Cate interrupts before she can begin. "Nuh uh-uh. Fact two: you are an amazing friend."

A liar. A freak.

"But—"

"No buts!" Cate says and tells her to think about how much Vera has helped her with the barn and the cidery. All the apples she's picked and the hours she's spent with the machines, all the renovations she did practically by herself. "Everyone loves you, Vera. Even Brian, who's a total fucking grump. He went out to get you when you were sleepwalking. And he was so worried Eli was creeping on you he was all ready to, like, defend your honor and beat him up or something!"

At that Vera manages a smile and a snort.

"Lydia hates me."

"She's just jealous. She doesn't hate you. She also texted me to come check on you."

"She did?" Vera sits up a little. Her buzz is waning.

"Yeah, which is weird, now that I think about it. How did she know something went down?"

"Probably saw emergency vehicles on The Road," Vera suggests and hopes it sticks. Cate agrees yes, that was probably it.

"Can't get away with anything without the neighbors noticing," Cate jokes but sighs in such a way that shows she also means it. "But for reals, Vera, you're an amazing friend. You saved Lopez's life today."

Vera moves to contradict her.

"Nope! I've watched a *lot* of medical dramas, and if he made it all the way to Albany and through surgery then he's going to be fine."

"Those shows aren't real."

"Listen." Cate tilts Vera's face up, hands cupping her cheeks, and looks into her eyes. "He's going to be OK. Can you say it?"

"He's going to be OK," Vera says, and she feels a tear spill. Cate rubs it away with her thumb, holds her there.

Everyone Vera has ever cared for has died. Everyone except for Ma and Eli in her whole hellaciously long life. This one shouldn't hit any harder. And yet it does.

Something cracked in the desert, kept cracking when she came home, and it's awful.

Letting yourself care for people.

Letting yourself think your life can be something more than whatever it already is.

"He's going to be OK," Cate repeats, and Vera allows herself to briefly taste the optimism, the possible future where Lopez wakes up from surgery and is OK, and for a moment it feels so warm and right.

Until she remembers the problem with him being OK.

*

A shrill ring. Cate and Vera both startle from open-mouthed sleep on the couch. A muted daylight filters in through the small windows. Vera stands stiffly and hobbles to the phone on the wall.

"He's awake," Jenny says. She rattles off some medical jargon, the procedures he endured. He's damaged but alive. "It's a goddamn miracle," she says, and Vera hears her begin to cry.

"Jenny—"

She sniffles and stops herself. "He's asking for you."

20

November 2014

Jenny hugs Vera when she enters the room, pressing the firm ball of her pregnant stomach against her. Over Jenny's shoulder, Vera sees Lopez, who is varying shades of pink and purple, swollen and wrapped. She can hardly tell if his eyes are open. She hears the rustle of someone standing and realizes there are four other women behind her. Jenny releases her.

"Guys, this is Vera."

His sisters, his mother. They nod and smile wearily. His mother walks over with her hands out, takes Vera's in hers. They're plump and warm.

"Thank you," she says.

"I didn't do anything."

"You saved my life," Lopez says, and they all turn to face him.

Jenny steps toward the door and puts an arm out for the others to follow, says she'll give them the room.

Vera waits for them to leave. The door closes with a heavy click. Her limbs are buzzing. She turns to Lopez again, arranges her face to be as blank as she can muster.

He knows.

He struggles to sit up farther and winces. Vera comes over and helps him, props the pillow higher behind his neck. "This OK?"

"It's OK," he says and settles. "I mean, I'm pretty fucked-up, Van Valkenburgh." She nods, waiting to see precisely what he means.

She has enough clothes in her car to start over. Some cash. Lydia's diary and the photograph of her with Lotte, too, her derringer—she didn't want any strange evidence left behind. It will be her sloppiest exit—she had to pack quickly and discreetly when Cate was there—and they will be in pursuit. Lots of people, depending on how big the story gets. Lydia is right, it will be a shitstorm of scrutiny. Gone are the days of only needing to make it over the border to Mexico. She'll have to retreat deep into the woods somewhere. Maybe Eli and Lydia will help her hide. It might be in their interest, depending on how much of a connection anyone is able to draw between her and them, her and Fountain. Maybe it will damage their whole operation, or maybe it will invigorate it. *See? People* can *live forever!*

"Like not going to walk without help for months fucked-up," Lopez continues. Vera nods.

"I'm so glad you're alive." She takes his hand in hers, and he squeezes it back.

"I thought I was going to die."

Vera nods again.

"I swear I saw you jump after me."

She doesn't move.

"And you told me you couldn't die."

Locked in her own body.

"You said you were two hundred years old and—" He closes his eyes again tightly, the pain. Vera asks him if she should get a nurse.

She'll get a nurse and keep walking.

"No." He sucks in a deep breath through his teeth. "You said some seriously weird shit, Vera."

She'll have enough of a head start. Even if he begins to yell, no one will have the authority to stop her and hold her in the hospital. She hasn't done anything wrong.

"Did you mean it?" he asks and looks at her pleadingly. She can feel herself blanching. She's taking too long to answer again.

Just tell him no.

"I know I've got the concussion of the century right now, but I distinctly remember you telling me—" She stands and looks out the window, doesn't want to face him when he says it. "You'd be the baby's godmother."

She turns back around.

"I know, I know, people agree to crazy stuff when they think it's the end, but can I hold you to this one?" he asks her, his smile returned.

Vera sits on the edge of his bed and takes his hand in hers again.

"Yes, I meant it. I meant every word."

*

Vera drives the hour and a half straight back to Paul's.

His truck isn't at the schoolhouse but she turns off the ignition anyway. Then she hears an engine behind her and looks in her rearview mirror. She gets out.

"I was just at your place," he says as he climbs down from his truck. His breath puffs in clouds, his lips are pink. "You weren't answering your phone."

"I was in Albany."

"It's a fucking miracle, right?"

"It's what they're saying."

He takes her in his arms. He smells like snow.

"You scared me for a second," he says into her neck. "When we got the call, they told me it was rangers and I thought—I thought I might never see you again."

"I'm here now," Vera says, and it's true, and it's the best she can offer.

Inside his house they become bodies together. Safe, alive, and voracious for each other.

After, they lay side by side, their pulses slowing once more, limbs heavy with satisfaction. Their hands touch, a few fingers linked. Vera feels warm, properly warm for the first time since coming down the mountain. Paul sighs, and she looks over to see his eyes are closed, his lips parted in a faint smile. It makes her grin up at the ceiling. She settles her head higher on her pillow and takes in her surroundings.

The place is tidy. Sparse but not cold. It's a single large room—kitchen on one end, bed on the other, living area in the middle with a green couch, a coffee table, and a TV stand stuffed with books. There's a small woodstove near the front door. On the walls, a clock, a framed map of the Catskills, and one large taxidermy buck head, its neck turned as if trying to peer out the window.

"You hungry?" Paul asks, rolling onto his side to face her.

"Yes," Vera says, suddenly ravenous. She can't remember the last time she ate.

"I had big plans to make you my favorite vodka sauce pasta tomorrow but—"

"That's what your mom said."

"My *mom*?"

"I ran into her at the post office the other day."

Paul shakes his head in gentle disbelief, and his hair falls over his brow. "Sorry, she—I hope she didn't freak you out."

"Not at all," Vera tells him. "She just loves you."

"She does," he says, and his conviction of it is so simple, so pure, something catches in Vera's throat. When was the last time she felt unquestionably loved by her mother?

"Let me see what I've got," Paul says with renewed enthusiasm, and he launches himself out of bed. He pulls on the boxers he'd tossed to the floor and pads over to the kitchen, opens the fridge, a high cabinet.

Vera looks around the room again and remembers—this was the schoolhouse. She never stepped foot in here before now, having been too old to attend when it was built. But it gives her a little shiver, thinking of all the time Lydia has spent in here. She pulls the covers up over herself.

"Grilled cheese and tomato soup?" he asks.

"Perfect."

A few minutes later, it's ready. They eat standing over the kitchen island in their underwear. It's salty, delicious, hot.

"Wait, how was Maine?" Vera asks in between bites.

"George got a nine pointer!" Paul says, so cheery, so able to be happy for his friend. "To be honest, I was having a hard time concentrating." The way he smiles makes Vera flush. She has the ridiculous thought: *I feel young.*

"I love that look."

"What look?" she asks, afraid of being transparent.

"That one you were making before I made you self-conscious, sorry." He laughs at himself then elaborates. "You're so... serious sometimes." She must balk because he tells her, "It wasn't an insult! I like that, too—that you're serious. I like all of you, Vera."

For the moment, she allows herself to pretend that it could be true.

"I like you, too."

At that, Paul leans across the small island and kisses her on the mouth. Salty lips. She wants to get back in bed with him. Or clear the counter right here.

After a moment of kissing, he pulls away and asks, "You ever had a close call like this before? Had to pronounce a death on the job?"

She nods, thinking not of her work as a park ranger, but the dozens and dozens of other deaths she's been near over her lives. The few she's caused. Jacob.

"Everyone tells you it gets easier, but it doesn't," Paul says.

"No, it doesn't."

Paul takes the grilled cheese out of Vera's hand and sets it down, pushes the plates and empty bowls to the side. Vera lifts herself onto the counter, wraps her legs around his waist. They kiss deeply, hungry again, urgent. Suddenly Paul pulls away and looks out toward his driveway. Then Vera hears it, too—wheels on gravel.

"Shit, hang on." Paul disappears into the bathroom behind them, reappearing quickly with a flannel robe he tosses to Vera on his way to the bedside to pick up his discarded pants and shirt. As he hops into the legs of his jeans, Vera slips on the robe, cranes her neck around to try to see who it is, but their vehicles are blocking the view.

"You expecting someone?" she asks.

"It's Lydia."

"What?" Vera says even though she's heard him just fine, and then she sees her, too, wrapped in a sleek wool coat, high-heeled boots.

Paul opens the door before she knocks. "Lydia, how are you?"

"I'm well, thank you," she says stepping in, the cold air entering with her.

Paul stammers through something polite as he closes the door at her back. Offers to take her jacket, to get her some water or tea.

"No, no, I'm sorry. I know it's a little uncouth to drop in like this, but I've been looking for Vera." Lydia's eyes settle on her and Vera's skin feels mildly electric.

"Everything OK?" Paul asks Lydia.

"Oh yes! I just wanted to check up on her after what happened, and she wasn't at home or answering her phone so—"

"I'm fine. Lopez is going to be OK, too," Vera says firmly, hoping her tone can communicate the information Lydia is in fact looking for—that they're all going to be fine, that Vera didn't mess things up for Lydia. That Lydia should leave.

Lydia looks Vera over in her intense way, calculating something, and Vera feels briefly more naked than she would if Paul's robe fell off of her. Hunted.

"Thank goodness!" Lydia says brightly after a beat. "Oh, thank goodness!"

"Yeah, the whole thing's kind of a miracle," Paul agrees, looking between the women.

"Are you two in the mood to celebrate?" Lydia asks as she puts her hand on the doorknob. "Matthew wants to take us out to that new place Cate was raving about, Bone and Root?"

Paul looks to Vera. The way he's waiting for her response—she knows he'll decline if she asks him to, but she also knows he wants to go.

"What time?" Vera asks.

"Seven."

"Sure," Vera agrees.

Lydia says that's wonderful, then takes an unabashed look around the room. "I love what you've done with the place," she tells Paul, then swiftly leaves.

The door closes, he turns to Vera.

"You want to meet him that badly?" she asks before he can say anything else.

"Oh god, no! But my mom and Bev will kill me if I don't go and report back."

The relief makes Vera smile. She walks over, kisses him.

"He's unbearable," she warns.

"I can't wait."

*

"Orange wine is the new rosé," Cate tells the table. "Trust me."

"You heard it here first!" Matthew says, and he raises his glass. "Now if I may propose a toast."

Everyone stops themselves from drinking the sip they were about to take.

"Only if it's quick, I can't tell you how badly I need this drink right now," Eli says, and they all chuckle.

"As you know, I'm in the business of miracles," Matthew begins. Cate is rapt, Brian willing enough to listen. Lydia has her head inclined in some kind of uncharacteristic deference. The restaurant's low candlelight gives everyone a healthy, luminous glow. "Most simply put, I want to save lives."

Paul squeezes Vera's thigh under the table. Matthew has very much been delivering on being as insufferable as she warned.

Glass raised, Matthew continues. "I believe that the work I'm doing with Lydia will save many lives—my own especially!" he adds jovially and more people chuckle. "But it's important to remember the boots on the ground." At this, he turns to Vera and Paul's part of the table. "To the fine, humble folks who put their own lives on the line every day in the service of saving others."

The condescension is syrupy, but there's an honest compliment somewhere in there, too.

"To Vera and Paul!"

"Here, here!" Eli says and they all clink glasses and drink. Paul gives her thigh another squeeze under the table, and it warms her whole core. She sips the wine. It's acidic and strange, faintly carbonated.

"Fascinating," Eli says, swirling the glass. "Is that beeswax I'm tasting?"

"Yes!" Cate cries and gives him a flirtatious smack on his arm. "It's aged in beeswax vessels, OMG you can *taste* that? Your palette is bananas."

Eli raises his eyebrows playfully.

"This place is darling," Matthew declares as he mops up the last of the artichoke appetizer with the one small corner of sourdough toast that remains. He leans back. "I like the whole reclaimed-wood thing they have going on, and the portraits? Nice touch."

Everyone turns to look at the row of thrift shop–looking oil paintings of farm animals and vegetables. Cate lowers her voice and tells the table Emma and Faye think the general minimalism of the place is less a matter of taste than evidence of a lack of it, but Cate disagrees, thinks it's just right.

"I do agree however that the ampersand in the name is very five years ago," she finishes with a whisper.

"They opened this week?" Brian asks. He dips his finger in the wet wax of the small candle on the table between them and the flame flickers. Last week, Cate clarifies, then rattles off the various blogs and other publications in which they've already been featured.

"So the Catskills are the new Brooklyn? Should I be investing in more real estate here?" Matthew asks, his tone joking, but there's an avarice in his voice that can't be fully cloaked.

Vera watches as the restaurant's sole server delivers entrées to the table two over from them. As he walks away, the woman holds her phone above her plate to take a picture. Vera scans the rest of the room and realizes two other people have been watching their group, only to look away at her glance.

She feels a flash of panic—so many years of dodging dangerous curiosity—but then remembers that Matthew is relatively famous.

"I've got the farro salad here," says a voice appearing at their side. A tall, skinny blond man in an apron is holding several plates across both arms.

"That's me!" Cate says, pushing her silverware aside.

"And the pork chop—" Paul raises his hand. Vera's mouth waters. She hasn't eaten meat in years but still craves it when it smells this good.

"Which means you must have the mushroom farfalle," he says to Vera as he sets the last plate on the table. "I'll be right out with the duck and harvest medley."

"Are you Eric?" Cate asks the man. The candle's warm light bounces across her excited features. Vera notices Cate has put on a full face of makeup for the occasion.

"I am. I'm the owner, nice to meet you." Hands on his slim, aproned hips then one outstretched to shake. "My wife's in the back—"

"Emily, right? Sorry! Such a stalker move. I've been following your renovation on Instagram."

An equally tall, raven-haired woman appears bearing the last of the entrées. "Speak of the devil!" her husband says. Emily smiles at everyone as she sets down a plate.

"Thank you so much for coming," she tells them, serving Brian first then Matthew last of everyone. Perhaps they're trying to act unimpressed to save face or to make him feel more comfortable. From his frown though, it's apparent Matthew would appreciate more fanfare.

Everyone digs in except Cate, who chats with Eric giddily, Emily having returned to the kitchen. They talk about their operations, their moves from Brooklyn, the adjustments to country life. They sound unable to decide upon the proper narrative. Is the work they pursue easy or difficult? Well received or battled against? An earned balance or an exciting overextension of effort?

"Brian grew up here," Cate says.

"Summers mostly," Brian corrects, but Eric doesn't seem to hear.

"Oh, that's awesome. Local clout goes a long way," he says, hands back on his hips. Vera notes a tattoo of a radish curling up his inner forearm. "Emily and I weren't sure if we were gonna be chased out of town by the locals—ahhhh, the New Yorkers are coming!" He fake screams in a whisper and Cate and Brian laugh knowingly.

"Paul's actually from here, too," Cate adds, remembering just a little too late. Eric opens his mouth to say something but is cut off by Matthew.

"I unfortunately understand a thing or two about accidentally scaring the locals." They all laugh for him, a little uncertain. Paul gives Vera's thigh another under-the-table squeeze.

"I'm sorry, I should let you guys eat!" Eric says with finality. "I've stranded poor Emily in the kitchen."

"You'll have to come by for a cider!" Cate offers, perhaps forgetting that there is no cider to speak of yet.

"For sure! So glad we got to meet Catskills Cider Co! Thank you everyone for coming!"

They tuck back into their meals. Eli says it's outstanding, Lydia moans in approval. Brian declares it's the best duck he's ever tasted.

"I have one more toast," Matthew says, and Vera assumes he's not used to losing the room the way he did just then. The table looks up, though only Brian reaches for his glass. "Tonight is also a celebration of something else. Lydia, may I?"

"You may not," she answers. The others laugh but Vera senses the strain, something darker.

Lydia's afraid.

Matthew tells her to relax, they're going to find out anyway, why not let them be the first to know? It happened in their very own little town, they'll be famous for it soon enough.

Lydia sets down her fork and knife. "Matthew don't—"

"Lydia has created the world's first immortal cell."

It doesn't land with the splash he was hoping. Everyone looks perplexed at best.

"Like vampire immortal?" Paul asks.

Vera's pasta now tastes like clay, but she keeps chewing quietly.

"Well, I do believe it can be exposed to sunlight and hasn't grown pointy little fangs yet," Matthew begins, smiling at his own joke. "But generally speaking, yes, am I right Lydia? I don't think I'm exaggerating here."

"Technically it's a neutrophil, which is an immune cell subtype," Lydia answers, hands clasped in her lap. "Most can survive for two days maximum, but we've isolated a set that has been surviving in a cell culture dish for five weeks, which in terms of neutrophils is practically an eternity."

There's a brief pause as everyone attempts to digest the science.

"So cool!" Cate finally says.

"But everything is still very much in the early research stages! So, Matthew, darling, we shouldn't be getting *too* excited about what we think we have or haven't seen."

Vera and Eli exchange quick glances. He gives her an almost imperceptible shrug.

So Eli didn't know about this either.

Has Lydia really reverse engineered an immortal specimen already? She's made it seem like without the source, that kind of thing would take years of experiments, not months. Then again, Lydia could have been actively keeping their expectations low. Could have even surprised herself with how quickly she's been able to accomplish this.

If it's true, this is huge. And probably not the kind of thing to announce to an entire table of people you just met at a tiny restaurant full of eavesdroppers.

"Come on, let's be optimists, just for the night!" Matthew insists. "A man fell several hundred feet off a fire tower and lived to tell the tale. Good news is in the air! Do you think they have champagne here?"

"I think I saw a pét-nat from southern France on their wine list," Cate says, scanning the table to see if there's an extra drink menu around.

"Ah, this would be a moment for Dom, but we'll work with what they have. What's the proprietor's name again, Aaron?" Matthew cranes his neck to look around the restaurant. "Where is he?"

Vera goes through the motions of the rest of dinner at a distance. It takes excruciatingly long. She keeps thinking she'll be able to follow Lydia to the bathroom and grill her, but Lydia never gets up. Vera can't even secure eye contact with her the entire meal. When Matthew orders an espresso after dessert has already been cleared, Vera wants to scream.

Finally, the check is presented and there's some performative arguing over who's going to pay until Matthew clicks down a heavy black card and declares dinner his treat.

In the chilly parking lot, Paul walks Vera to her car. She climbs in and closes the door, starts the ignition, and lowers the window. He leans in, and kisses her deeply. For a moment she almost forgets everything else around her.

"I really can't convince you to stay over?" he asks after they pull apart.

"Tomorrow," Vera tells him. "I still haven't been home since the hospital—"

"Tomorrow," he says. Then he puts his knuckle under her chin and lifts it for another kiss.

As he walks away, Vera rolls up the window, pulls out her phone, and turns it on. The screen alights with missed texts and calls but she ignores them all.

"Meet me in the lab," she tells her brother when he picks up. "Bring her with you."

⁂

"I had to give him something," Lydia says before Vera even speaks.

"What did you give him?" she asks as she sets her go-bag on the worktable. She didn't stop at the cottage, came straight here.

"He's been pressuring me like mad all week. You heard him, Eli, he was threatening to bring on another scientist."

"We could have made it work," Eli says, ever the optimist.

Lydia barks a single, ugly laugh. "How? Do you understand what we have here?" She gestures to the lab around them.

Vera asks again what Lydia gave Matthew, though she's more and more certain she already knows.

Lydia huffs and puts her hands on her hips, defiant. She juts out her chin and Vera notices her lipstick is fresh. That she reapplied it to come argue with her here.

"It was only *one* set of your culture dishes," Lydia tells Vera.

Vera takes a step toward her and asks, "Why me?"

"Come on!" Lydia says, throwing her arms in the air, her bracelets jangling. "You told Lopez the whole fucking deal on your own accord, and now you're going to come for me because I gave Matthew one lousy, totally anonymous cell?"

"It's pretty risky," Eli says, shifting his weight side to side, like he's always done when nervous. "Not to mention unethical."

"Unethical my ass. Why do you care, Vera? You'll be dead soon enough once we solve this thing anyway. Isn't that the plan?"

"What?" Eli asks. Vera looks at him, and he frowns. Her heart constricts.

"Oh, I'm sorry," Lydia says with mock sincerity. "Have you not told him you've only been playing along so you can finally die?"

"That's not—" Vera begins, but her words are too tangled to come out. The buzz of the lights above her feels oppressive.

"Of course that's why you're doing this!" Lydia interrupts and takes a step toward her. "You're a coward, Vera. A selfish coward. It's disgusting and I'm tired of pretending otherwise."

"I'm not a coward," Vera says, but the quiet of her voice betrays her.

"Yes you are!" Lydia yells. "What have you made of this time you've been given? Who have you helped? You haven't even had the guts to live a ridiculous life of hedonistic pleasure! This is your chance to finally *do* something and you're too selfish to—" Lydia cuts herself off with an exasperated sigh. Like explaining this is a waste of her own endless supply of time. "Do you want to die?" she asks Vera plainly.

Vera looks to the ceiling, her eyes filling.

The years. The pain.

"Wolven, is it—true?"

"I told you," Vera says to her brother, desperation creeping up her chest. "In the cottage. I told you about the earthquake and—"

"Yeah, but that was why you first came here, not why you shacked up with us and Fountain, right?" He looks boyish again. Hopeful. Scared. "You weren't *pretending* you wanted to help other people just so you could—" Eli doesn't finish his sentence.

Vera looks away. It's too much.

"Disgraceful," Lydia says.

"It's not disgraceful to not want to live like this!" Vera yells, heat suddenly in her throat. The rage, the despair. The complete unfairness of it all. Why them? Why not Pa? Why Lydia but not Lotte? Why? *Why* be put through any of this?

"Wait, how did you know?" Eli asks his girlfriend. "I didn't say anything." And the small show of loyalty gives Vera pause.

"It must be in my samples," Vera says.

"No," Lydia counters.

Not the answer she was expecting. Reality so slippery around her right now. "But—"

"Oh, Vera." Lydia sighs. "It's written all over your fucking face."

The buzzing floods her ears now. Her blood, her pulse. Fear and shame and rage.

She feels a hand on her shoulder. Her brother's, heavy and steady. It threatens to unravel her.

"You had no right to use my body," Vera says, and it comes out wobbly.

Lydia throws her hands up in exasperation. "I did what had to be done, OK?"

Vera feels the momentum of this entire operation like a riptide right now. An unconquerable current that has stolen a part of her she can never get back. But it was always going to happen like this. She knew it. She knew this whole thing was bad news. This woman. All this, just a small taste of what's to come. Being the human experiment. Why did she ever agree to any of it?

For it all to finally end.

Vera's resolve returns. She takes another step toward Lydia and feels Eli's hand on her shoulder holding her back. She looks Lydia directly in the eye. "Is it reversible?" she demands.

"Lydia, babe, I think you owe Vera an apology at the very least."

"No. I did what had to be done for *all* of us."

"I don't need your fucking apology," Vera says, shrugging off her brother's hand, so close to Lydia now she can smell her perfume. "I asked, is it reversible, or have you been lying about that, too?"

Lydia shakes her head with distain. "Obviously I cannot be one hundred percent certain, but yes, I'm ninety-nine point nine-nine, all right? Now let's call it a day and—"

"Babe?" Eli begins, still calm. He steps around Vera, doesn't look at her. She wonders if he even can. "Whatever Vera has or hasn't been doing, that was a pretty big choice you made without consulting us."

"Eli, she's been *lying* to us this whole time!" Lydia cries, curls shaking. "Besides, it's my research."

"It's *my* cell!" Vera yells.

"Don't be such a child! There's absolutely no reason for Matthew to believe it's *your* cell cultures he saw. I—"

"They're yours?" a voice asks from behind her, and they all whip around.

Matthew's eyes are ablaze. From the drinks, the revelation. He steps out of the foyer, where he must have been listening, and into the lab.

"Bro! You need something?" Eli asks cheerful but tight. He moves toward him, putting his body between Vera and the intruder. "We told you, we'd be right back."

Lydia says something about Vera taking her conservation work very seriously, that she had an idea after dinner that just couldn't wait. Then she asks Matthew how he got in.

"I reset the security when I arrived. I knew you were hiding something from me, Lydia, and I was right. I thought it was the cell and that we were all good now, but a whole *person?*" He looks Vera up and down. It's unabashedly predatory. "Is she really—"

"I think there's been a pretty big misunderstanding," Eli says as he puts both hands on his sister's shoulders and begins to steer her to the door past Matthew. "Vera was just dropping off some—"

"Dude, don't lie to me," Matthew tells him, truly disappointed that his CFO, his investor, his friend, would treat him like this. "I heard it all."

Lydia claps her hands together. "Matthew, I know this is a lot to take in at once."

"This is fucking insane," he says, giddy now.

Lydia continues, using her lecture voice. "Yes, Vera is the first person ever to successfully—"

"Lydia's immortal, too," Vera interrupts. All heads swing to Vera, then back to Lydia.

Lydia laughs, high and false.

"I know we all accidentally jumped the gun on revealing your identity at such an early stage, Vera, but let's—"

"She is," Vera insists, then has an idea. "Look!" She reaches for her go-bag on the table, rummages hurriedly through the sweaters, the envelope of cash. She pulls out the photograph of Lydia and Lotte on the front porch of the general store and holds it up for them to see.

Lydia asks if that's supposed to be her, still pretending to be dubious, lighthearted.

"Lotte?" Eli says with a gasp and takes the photo from Vera. He leans in closer. Matthew peers with him, looking at the picture, then back at Lydia.

"She could be your twin," Matthew says.

But he's unconvinced.

"And this!" Vera says, yanking out the diary. Lydia startles.

"Where'd you get that?" she demands and lunges for it. Vera pulls it closer to her chest and turns around, frantically flipping the pages.

"Right here! It says 'Lydia Kirke, 1863'! And the photo, the back of the photo, has her name on it, too. This was her family's place! The general store!"

"Vera, this is absurd. I'm not—"

"Do you see it?" Vera asks Matthew, coming closer to him. She can smell the wine in the sweat that's beaded on his forehead. "Do you believe me? She was born in 1827."

Eli looks up from the photograph, returning to the present clusterfuck.

Matthew's eyes have gone foggier. You can all but hear the gears in his brain turning as he tries to process the tsunami of information. "Lydia, is it true?" he asks her.

"Of course not! Vera is understandably upset. Like I said, we jumped the gun a little on the permissions front and she's probably, *understandably*, a little terrified of being the face of all this alone, right? It's OK, Vera. Nothing will leave this room until the time is right. We have your best interests in mind. We're all here to protect you while we do what's best for the world."

Vera reaches in her bag again and pulls out her derringer.

"Oh shit," Matthew says excitedly. "Are you going to show me how you can get shot and survive it?"

"No. Lydia will."

There's a bang, and the bullet passes straight through Lydia's chest, shattering a row of beakers behind her. Matthew screams. Lydia staggers a moment against the countertop, blood blooming around the hole in her blouse.

Then she rights herself.

"Vera," she says calmly, her voice thick with hate.

"Holy fucking shit," Matthew says, his hands on his head. "Holy fucking shit, holy fucking shit, holy fucking shit," he chants as he hops up and down then bursts into a strangled, maniacal cackle. "You two are going to make me a fucking bajillionaire!"

"This isn't what it seems," Lydia tells him through clenched teeth.

"This cannot get out," Matthew says, his tone swerving into ominous now. "No one else can know. You cannot leave. You two cannot ever fucking leave my sight again."

He points at Vera with one hand and at Lydia with the other. Everything in Vera recoils.

To be trapped, with this man, in who-knows-what conditions.

Vera looks at Lydia and sees her face contorted in a terror that matches her own.

There could always be something worse than the desert.

Suddenly someone is upon Vera. She braces herself, then quickly realizes it's Eli. That he's taken her gun.

He holds it straight out at Matthew. "I'm sorry."

"Dude!"

The lab reverberates with a second shot.

Matthew crumples to the ground. A smooth puddle of red begins to expand beneath his head, his face frozen in surprise.

"Shit," Lydia says decisively in the quiet.

"I had to," Eli whispers.

"Shit shit shit," Lydia repeats, shaking her hands out like she might be able to shake this whole situation off.

Vera goes to her brother, takes her derringer out of his grip. He's still looking at Matthew.

"Eli." When he doesn't turn to her, she moves his face with her hands. "Eli?"

His eyes are glassed over, under a frozen distance.

His first.

She remembers hers. Throwing up in the alley after, the way the man's body twitched as the life left him. How those three seconds ran on a terrifying loop every time she closed her eyes for months.

It doesn't get easier.

"You did the right thing," Vera tells her brother, a hand on his back.

"I killed him," he says plainly.

"This is not good," Lydia insists from the other side of the room, the panic starting to palpably rise in her.

"You did the right thing, Eli," Vera says again, her brother now staring at Matthew's lifeless body. "Who knows what he would have done to us?"

"We need to fix this," Lydia says, her voice strained.

"Just give us a second. We will," Vera tells her.

"How?" Lydia demands.

"We'll get rid of him."

"How?" she demands again.

"There's only one way," Eli says, finally looking up. "We burn the whole thing down."

*

Half an hour later, Eli's plan is in motion despite Lydia's protests.

"This can't be the only way," she says from behind him as she wrenches closed the caps on the emergency sprinklers. "We're going to lose so much data!"

"We have backups," he says as he continues to pour gasoline across the countertops from one of the large red containers he keeps on hand for his motorcycles.

"Not of our samples!" she cries.

"Then you'll take more later! That's not the problem right now, Lydia!" Eli yells, and Vera realizes this is the most furious and scared she has ever seen him in two hundred years. "Somebody might have heard those shots and somebody is going to notice that Matthew is missing and *somebody*—"

"All right, all fucking right!" Lydia yells back at him, then picks up the other gasoline container and starts erratically dumping gas on the ground, her heels now soaked, her blouse still stained red.

Vera continues to pour from her own canister, her boots crunching on the broken glass, the smeared blood.

"Eli! His face?" Lydia asks, incredulous.

Vera looks over at her brother, who is dousing his friend in gasoline.

"He needs to be completely incinerated or they'll find the gunshot wound. I thought you've *done* this kind of thing before," he snarls. But he sets the canister on the floor and folds Matthew's hands across his chest, pauses, looks down at him. Vera looks away. Hears Eli pick up the canister and start pouring again.

They set the lab aflame.

Outside, in the cold dark, they wait behind a thicket of bare forsythia branches tucked under the maples that run between the lab and the barn. They should go home, change their clothes, and pretend to stumble out confused with the rest of the neighbors. But they need to make sure the whole thing catches. They need to make sure no volunteer firefighters get hurt.

"This is incredibly stupid. We're going to get caught," Lydia says.

The windows glow orange from within. The scent of acrid smoke begins to fill the night air around them.

"Cate's probably called it in by now," Eli says.

"No, she sleeps with earplugs and an eye mask, it'll be Brian if anyone." Vera blows on her hands. They reek of gasoline.

"The whole thing needs to go up," Lydia says, craning her neck above the bushes. "We cannot have people digging around—"

"They won't know what they're looking at," Eli interrupts her as he pulls her back down. "It's just Matthew. *He's* what needs to—"

Something inside the building bursts with a loud bang and the flames in the old store begin to lick the windows.

A horn sounds, long and low.

"Damnit," Vera says, because it's the volunteer alarm, and it's too soon.

"Come on, come on, come on," Eli whispers like this is some kind of match and he's rooting for his favorite team in overtime.

One minute, another, another, the fire gaining momentum as the three of them crouch in silence. And then the Volunteer Fire Department is here, leaping off the engine, hoses and hats. Vera sees Paul and her insides tense. She looks at Lydia, red nails in her teeth, then to Eli. He's looking at the photo again.

"Lotte knew you weren't dead," Vera says to him. "You were sending her things. She told Lydia."

Eli looks up.

"What?" Lydia asks, incredulous.

"It's in your diary, the last entry. You say Lotte told you she thought Eli was still alive."

"I never—"

"Don't lie to me, OK? I've read it," Vera says and recites the entry from memory: "'September twenty-sixth. Lotte mended calico dress no fee. Showed me newest gift. Dominoes. Made sworn to look for Eli on her behalf. Sent off with apple and good wishes. Lotte one of few I might miss.'"

"So you *did* know Lotte?" Eli asks his girlfriend.

Lydia breathes in to defend herself, to lie, then deflates immediately.

"Well, now you've done it, Vera," she says.

"Me? You're the one who's been lying about knowing Lotte and setting out to look for Eli!"

"I wasn't looking for Eli. We met by chance and I had no idea who he was until he told me."

"But you *lied* to us—"

"Because I didn't want to break your brother's heart, OK!" She says it so loud, but at this point the fire and the hoses and the shouts from the volunteers are louder.

"What are you talking about?" Eli asks her. He is still shook, stunned. The gun, the gasoline, now this.

Lydia tears at a nail with her teeth. Her curls are wild. She's shivering in her filthy blouse.

"Lotte was waiting for you," she finally says to Eli, her voice gentler than it's been all night. "The gifts you sent—she thought you were telling her to wait for you."

Eli's face contorts.

"No one believed her!" Lydia says. "These gifts she would talk about getting in the mail from you? You coming back for her?" She shakes her head, looks up into the starless sky then back at Eli. "We all loved her. We just thought she was a little crazy from the grief."

No one speaks. There are shouts and the crashing and crackling of the building being consumed by flame.

Lydia lied, but—

"And the waiting." Eli says. "I made it worse." His tone flat, factual.

"Maybe," Lydia says, no will to lie anymore.

Vera looks at her brother, absolutely crushed. The mess of the past hour weighing upon him, the past years. The missteps, miscalculations.

And Lydia, head hung. Everyone trying, trying so hard and failing. Always failing.

"Can I have my diary, please?" Lydia asks Vera, and opens her hands to receive it.

"I don't have it."

She turns. "Eli?"

"I don't have it either."

Another explosion, one that shakes the earth beneath them. They all look at the building, the second floor aflame.

"Don't lie to me right now."

"I swear on my life I don't have it," Vera says, her hands up. Eli shakes his head, too.

"I *need* that diary. It has the key, I know it. I know it in my bones." Lydia stands and begins to pull off her heels.

"Lydia, no!" Eli says, but she's already taken off.

Lydia dashes barefoot through the patches of iced over mud and snow toward the burning lab, her skirt and bloodstained blouse billowing out behind her. Eli stands but doesn't move his feet. Together they watch as George spots Lydia and tries to stop her from entering, but he's too late.

"Lydia!" someone screams.

She runs through the open side door into the orange glow and billowing smoke, the flaming, growling monster of a building.

The volunteers wave their arms, drop their hoses, and shout wildly. One of them moves to follow her.

Vera stands. Runs.

She reaches Paul just as the next explosion breaks, tossing everyone backward onto the frozen grass, piles of people knocked down, knocked out.

As Vera lays there against Paul she hears an unearthly, agonized howl coming from the lab.

The kind caused by a scalding thrum felt as no longer a person, but millions of unconnected pieces, ripped apart and in pain forever and absolutely ever.

A never-ending cry.

What they've wondered and worried. Plan B.

21

November 2014

Despite her many deaths, Vera has never had a funeral. She's never drawn up a plan for others to follow either—burial versus cremation, these flowers not those—because none of her fantasies of dying have ever included anything about what happens *after* she dies.

At first glance she believes that's because she won't care if she's finally dead. She'll be released into the nothingness, all the strife and joy and humanly concern immediately vaporized, end of life plans included.

But standing here now at Lydia's funeral, shoulder to shoulder between a silently crying Cate and a stoic Stan under the latticed shade of the leafless maples with two dozen other neighbors, Vera wonders if in fact it's because she has never thought anyone *else* would care. Because after all, funerals are for the living left behind. For the grievers. For the people who need a moment to process the otherwise stark punctuation a death brings. Before. After. Here. Gone.

Who has ever cared when Vera Van Valkenburgh has died?

"To close, Lydia's partner, Eli, will read something by one of her favorite poets, Emily Dickinson," the white-haired pastor says, then he steps aside and folds his hands with solemn decorum. For a flash, Vera sees Preacher Janssen instead—Lotte's father—with his combed-back hair and skin as pale as his daughter's, his appearance so obviously betraying the fact that he never spent a day in the fields. Vera wonders briefly who presided over Lotte's funeral here, her own father surely gone by then.

Eli moves to the head of the crowd, his broad shoulders cutting a precise silhouette of black against the milky, winter afternoon sun. He pulls a card from the inside pocket of his jacket, looks at it once then back up at the huddled crowd.

"This poem is called 'Unable are the Loved to die.'" He pauses, then recites from memory:

> "Unable are the Loved to die
> For Love is Immortality,
> Nay, it is Deity—"

Eli's voice hitches as he says "Diety" and Vera feels her own throat constrict, feels the taught focus of the crowd in her brother's hands.

> "Unable they that love—to die
> For Love reforms Vitality
> Into Divinity."

The silence after is heavy and soft, the wind entirely stilled. No one moves, hypnotized by Eli's recitation, by thoughts of their own inevitable deaths. A blue jay's cry cuts above somewhere behind them all, a quick, lone call, then nothing. Another. Vera looks at her brother and realizes:

He is truly devastated.

When he wipes an overflowing eye with his finger the spell breaks, everyone now moving to dab their own. To blow their noses, shift their weight to the other hip. Stomp their chilly feet in the cold, wet grass of the small graveyard.

"Thank you for coming today," Eli tells them as he tucks the unused card back into his jacket. "And for welcoming us to this beautiful little valley. Lydia has left too soon, but her love lives on with all of us."

Vera notes her brother's precise wording, how he never outright says Lydia is dead. It jolts her out of the present funeral reverie back into their harsher, smaller, shared reality.

This funeral is a sham.

Vera's blood quickens as she angers at the empty showmanship. The wringing out of tears for someone who's currently on a plane, very much alive. She must flinch because Cate takes her hand and squeezes it. Vera squeezes back then lets go. Looks away from her brother and scans the crowd—Pete and Judy, Wanda and Bill, Paul and Sue, George and Jocelyn and Beverly, and so many more, everyone so solemn.

"Thank you, sir," Eli says to the pastor, then he returns to his position in the front row of the small crowd.

According to the press, Matthew Barbery's funeral in San Jose was a who's who of young tech and venture capital.

It was also real.

Eli wanted to go, whether for appearances' sake or out of genuine remorse Vera couldn't tell, but Lydia was still in a very bad way and so, he wouldn't leave her side.

She'd been blown apart, burned to near ash. A mangled collection of charred bones and cooked organs. None of the Fire Department held out hope of rescuing her after the explosion, and she was lucky for it. They all were. Though for two whole hours they didn't know—Eli and Vera hovering outside, looking as genuinely distressed as all the other neighbors who'd appeared, worrying, *Was Lydia dead?*

Or just as bad: *Would Paul and George and the others find her impossibly alive?*

Once the building had been dampened down to hissing wet ash and mangled steel, Eli gave his statement to the police—they came home after dinner, Matthew and Lydia went to the lab to discuss work, Lydia returned to the house to get something, and then it happened. She must have run in to try to save her friend. It was a suitable explanation. No reason to expect foul play. A lab full of all those chemicals, such an unfortunate but not unheard-of accident. A real shame the sprinkler system malfunctioned.

Eli and Vera waited hardly ten seconds after the last flashing light pulled away—Paul's truck, he was so reluctant to leave Vera after this stretch of horrible close calls but she insisted—then they dashed back into the debris, ducking under the yellow caution tape, scraping through the ravaged mess with their bare hands. Their nostrils filled with soot, their fingers filthy and numb from the wet and cold of it.

After twenty silent minutes of searching, Vera heard Eli wretch. She looked up from where she was digging and saw him hunched over, on his knees, wiping his mouth with his sleeve. That's when she knew he'd found her.

Eli allowed his sister to help him carry what remained of Lydia inside and up to their bedroom, but the moment after they lay her down, Vera was banished. She knew she should have insisted on staying. She could help her brother, help Lydia. But in truth it was too gruesome even for her. The gore and stench of it. The horrible little wheezing, wailing sound coming out of what was once Lydia's mouth. And the conflicting mass of feelings swirling in her own gut. The relief and rage. Lydia's comeuppance. Any hopes for Plan B as a viable exit for Vera thoroughly dashed.

It took two days for Lydia to fully heal. Once she was recovered enough to talk, she and Eli made plans together, which he relayed to Vera during her one short visit. In the coming weeks he will convince Fountain's remaining investors to sell him the land. He'll then sell to a shell company of his own, level what's left of the general store, and rent the house at a fair rate to a nice family while he and Lydia ride it out for fifty to seventy years somewhere far away and beautiful like Uruguay, maybe Greece. Lydia will keep trying to reverse engineer what she can. Keep trying to remember something, anything from her past that the three of them share that could be the key. Then they'll return to try it all over again after anyone who would remember them has died. Arrive with new identities but the same quest. It's a setback, yes, but they do have the time.

The pastor concludes the service. Eli drops a handful of ceremonial dirt onto the ceremonial grave. The miserable crowd collects around him, cooing their condolences, and then they disperse. Car engines starting up roughly in the cold. No memorial party. She wouldn't have wanted the fuss, Eli told them when they tried to protest.

Cate links her arm into Vera's, and together they join the last of the crowd as it files out.

"She was so young," Cate says. "Not even forty, right?" Vera doesn't say anything, nods.

"And so brilliant," Stan adds. "Think what she could have done if she'd only had more time."

"I have," Vera says and hopes the darkness hasn't crept entirely up her throat.

As Cate and Stan continue to bemoan the supposed loss of a dazzling mind, Vera watches Eli a couple dozen feet ahead of them as he shakes Pete's hand and receives a hug from Judy. As they get into their car, he turns heel and walks briskly down The Road toward his house.

"I'm just going to make sure Eli's OK to be alone right now," Vera tells them.

"That's a good idea," Cate agrees. "If you or he need *anything*—"

"I will, thank you," Vera interrupts, then hurries her steps to a light jog.

He beats her to the house, closing the door behind himself without looking back, though Vera's certain he felt her following. She walks up the stairs and knocks. The wind shifts and she can just make out the bitter smell of burned rubble.

When he opens the door he hesitates, like he might not open it all the way for her.

"My flight's in three hours," he says.

Vera says she won't take long and steps over the threshold, pushing past him.

Everything has been boxed. All the life and warmth of the home packed away into cardboard cubes. How quickly it can all come apart. She follows him through the hollow house into the kitchen.

"I'm sorry," she says, for the hundredth time this week.

"Stop saying that, it wasn't all your fault."

"OK, I'll stop."

She watches him as he rummages through the large leather bag on the countertop. He won't look at her.

"The funeral turned out nice," she says.

"I'm glad Lydia didn't see the flowers Cate brought. She hates lilies," he tells the contents of his bag.

"I'm surprised you went with a headstone after all. What did it say,

1979? I think you shaved a year off what she normally told people. Very—"

"What do you want, Vera?" he asks, and it pierces her, to hear him use her given name when it's just them.

"I want you to stay."

"Well I can't, can I?" He zips up the bag with a ferocity.

"Just a few more years, what's the rush? We can keep looking, you and me."

He shakes his head, says Lydia needs him.

"Lydia doesn't *need* you, she's basking in the sun on an island somewhere in the Ionian Sea, isn't that what you two settled on? *I* need you."

Eli puts both his hands on the counter, lets his head drop. When he looks up again, he meets his sister's eyes, and something has given way.

There he is, her brother.

"You were only ever doing this so you could die," he says quietly.

Vera doesn't know what to say. Because it's true. But not the whole truth, not really.

"Did you ever believe it was a good idea?" he pushes. "Did you ever think about helping *other* people with what we were doing?"

"Of course I did! I—I was pretty fucked-up Eli. I *am* pretty fucked-up."

"We're all fucked-up, Wolven!" he roars, his anger deep and sudden. "You think I haven't offed myself a thousand times? You think I've chosen some of the world's most dangerous hobbies just for *fun*?"

Vera falls silent again as she rearranges what she's thought she's known.

A new tint over everything.

Eli also wants it to end.

The motorcycles and drug binges, the skydiving and helicopter skiing. She's always figured he's been chasing an adrenaline fix, his tolerance forced higher and higher. That it's all been *fun* for him.

"This is some seriously heavy shit, and that is exactly why we have to turn it into something!" He slams the counter with his hand for emphasis and it makes her jump. "We can't carry this forever for no fucking reason!"

"I know!" she screams back, because screaming is all she's capable of right now. The rage, the loss. She's never been this mad at him in her whole life. Never wanted something of him so badly either.

Eli pushes an errant lock of hair out of his face with both hands. He says he doesn't have time for this, he needs to go to the airport.

"You need to stay, Eli, this is our *home*. We're finally home and you're just going to leave me here, alone?"

"You don't have to stay."

"But I *want* to stay, that's what I'm saying."

"Then stay! Keep looking for the source. Keep killing mail-order mice—"

"That was Lydia, I only tested the water on myself."

"Jesus, Vera, you're willfully missing the point!" He shakes his head and hoists his bag over his shoulder. "You have to stop turning yourself into the victim! OK, maybe I've had it easier than you, but you've had it plenty easier than this would be for a *lot* of other people." Vera stills at the shameful truth within the accusation. "You're always so set on seeing the worst of this instead of seeing what could be." He pauses, lets out a breath. Vera releases her own, realizes she's been holding hers, too. "I'm leaving. I belong with Lydia right now. I'm trying to actually *learn* something from my past, don't you get it?"

"She's not Lotte."

Eli huffs and Vera feels so small.

"Will you ever come back?" she asks.

"Of course we will, we talked about this."

"It's never going to be the same again, is it," she says, and it's not a question. She feels the expanse between them.

Eli turns and walks through the house back toward the front door and Vera follows him. He opens it.

"Things are always changing. You can't stop change," he tells her, and the symmetry of it makes Vera's knees momentarily weak.

The steps of their bungalow in rural Oregon, 1969.

"Come with me to San Francisco," he'd said back then, his bag across his shoulder, his hair so long.

"I can't," she'd told him.

"You don't want to," he'd countered, and the way he looked at her, like he was hurt, too. Like she was the one leaving him.

Has she been telling herself that story wrong as well?

"I love you, Eli," Vera tells him now.

That day he told her he loved her, too. That he always will.

This time he doesn't say anything. Doesn't even look back as he leaves the door open behind him and walks down the porch to his small, fancy car. Black suit, broad shoulders. A silhouette she'd know from one hundred miles away, one hundred years away.

Vera doesn't follow him as he tosses his bag in the front seat and ducks into the driver's side. As the car roars to life and backs out of the driveway, she stands in the doorframe of the house, her limbs impossibly heavy.

Five minutes, ten, twenty, an hour later Vera leaves. She closes the door behind her, the click of it so final.

*

Despite the cold, Vera is sitting in a folding chair under the scraggliest apple tree, looking out at her winter-dead garden.

She hears a knock on her front door. She rises, walks around the side of the cottage, and finds Paul looking in the kitchen windows.

"Hi," she says, and he jumps.

"Jesus, you scared me." He smiles a little and a small part of her wilts within.

"I was out back making plans for next year's garden," she says, though all she's really been doing is staring into the middle distance thinking, *It's over*, again and again and again.

"Can we talk?" Paul asks, his demeanor suddenly nervous.

Vera's organs sink.

"OK."

Inside, they take off their jackets. She offers him water, he declines. They settle at the kitchen table. He laces his fingers together and Vera watches his hands, the hands that will never touch her again.

She's spooked him, her proximity to tragedy. Or he's come to his senses and realized Vera is an obliterated, awful mess no sane person should ever go near. It doesn't matter. He's gone. And she needs to be going now, too.

"I don't really know how to say this, so I'm just going to come out with it in one go," Paul begins.

She'll leave at the end of the month, pay through the rest of her lease even though she'll be gone. She'll start over. Again. She can do this, she's done this so many times before. This is what her life must be, how dare she ever hope it might be more?

Paul breathes in. Vera braces herself for the impact.

"I know the fire at the lab was arson and I'm pretty sure you were involved, but no one else suspects any of it and I'm not going to say anything to anyone because I'm assuming you had a very good reason."

Vera coughs once into her fist as she tries to absorb the magnitude of what he's just told her.

He puts a hand up like a traffic cop.

"I'm not asking you to tell me anything. In fact, I think it's probably better for the both of us if you don't say a word about any of it to me right now."

Vera holds herself still.

Paul looks at her, pulls her hands from across the table into his own.

"You're unlike anyone I've ever met, Vera Van Valkenburgh."

She looks down at their hands, can't bring herself to meet his eyes because this doesn't change anything. She's still going to have to leave. If not right now then four years from now, or six, maybe ten if she's extremely careful. And it will still be four years of lies, six, ten. Of hiding, of staying in place but really running, always running from the truth, and she can't do that to him. He deserves better.

"I wasn't going to say this part," he begins again. "But now that I got the other part over with, maybe it won't be so bad."

"Paul—"

"I think I'm falling in love with you."

A curtain parting. An open door. A chance, a new chance.

"Paul, I have something to tell you, too."

22

September 2015

Vera has three fish tucked into the front pocket of her waders. They were jumping for everything today. Especially the new number she tied for herself last night, a silvery little wisp she was hoping could imitate everything from a stone fly to an injured cricket. She must have pulled in twenty trout this afternoon. Brookies and browns, all of them longer than her forearm. When she gets home, she'll grill the browns she kept with lemon and salt, some parsley from her garden. She'll give one to Cate and Brian and another to Stan after all their shifts are done.

She pulls herself up and over a partially eroded section of the creek bank, extra careful to point her rod tip high and away from anything it could snag. George accidentally snapped her three-weight last weekend when they were on the stream together, so while that one's out for repair she only has her five-weight to work with, and she's not going to be rodless for a single day of this glorious early fall fishing. She's been hoping to get Lopez out with her on the creek this season, too, but between his responsibilities as lieutenant and as a dad to baby Harlow Vera Lopez, he's happily much too busy for fishing.

The creeks are running high from a wet August. The grass is green, but the trees are starting to turn yellow and orange on the tops of the mountains again. Some of the apples in the orchard have begun to redden and plump into what's looking like another remarkable harvest for a second year in a row. The sun's setting earlier now. It disappears behind the mountains completely by six thirty these days, but the hour before is always liquid, golden, and stunning. Everyone on the cidery patio taking out their phones, trying to capture the elusive magic of the valley.

Vera keeps to the tree line on the eastern edge of the property as she walks back to her cottage. To be spotted in waders with a rod by the dozens of drinkers would mean that many more people knowing about her favorite holes, and some things are best kept secret.

At her back door, she unlaces her boots, steps out of her waders, hangs them up on their peg, then breaks down her rod and lets herself in.

"My fly worked! They were wild for it!" she says as she enters, holding out her three fish, but the cottage is quiet. She scans the room—mail on the table, a gallon of stain for the new kitchen cabinets she's making, which Paul said he would pick up for her after work. She looks out the front window and sees his truck, puts the three fish on a plate in the fridge, then walks over to the pile of mail—an electric bill, a political campaign postcard, next month's mortgage statement.

Cate and Brian sold her the cottage this summer. It was Cate's idea. She proposed it on a whim around a backyard bonfire one night in early spring, but it stuck, sounded more and more reasonable the more they discussed it. A tax break for Cate and Brian plus some much-needed cash, a place of Vera's own she could renovate to her liking. They carved off three acres for her, including her garden, the site of what was once Pa's grave, and access down to the creek, the original Van Valkenburgh plot shrinking one more time.

Later that night in bed in the cottage, Paul asked her if this meant she was going to stay. She took his face in her hands, told him, "You know how much I want to."

It was the truth. And they tell each other the truth now.

He's catching up on her stories. Two hundred years of experiences don't get told all at once. But it's a revelation, to have someone other than Eli or Ma or Lydia know about her. This revelation of being fully seen by someone and to have that someone stay.

He treats her with kindness and curiosity, wonder and awe, though it hasn't been entirely easy. As much as Vera likes not having to hide her true nature from him, a part of her misses having the secret to herself. She has given him a piece of her she can never have back. Besides, it will take more than a few months to demolish the walls she has built so carefully around herself over the centuries. And while she has plenty of time to get used to this, Paul only has so much. He knows that she will have to leave in a handful of years. They've talked about moving together, bringing him along—to Wyoming, Alaska, maybe Patagonia, he could learn Spanish, his EMT skills are transferable almost anywhere—but this place is his home, and he will get old.

There is no simple solution for them.

So they're taking it day by day, each step a choice, made together. What they share, what they don't. By all appearances, Paul lives at the cottage. The bedroom closet is half full of his clothes, his favorite pans and knives have migrated from the schoolhouse to her kitchen. Even his taxidermy deer head has been hung prominently near the woodstove. But it's only Vera's name on the deed, and he still owns the schoolhouse.

There is no road map to follow for two people like them. No one whose advice they can really ask. But he says he understands the choices she's made so far—to run, to return, to be dubious of Lydia and Eli's vision. Understands these choices as well as anyone who isn't living them can. And this is no small thing for Vera.

She closed on the cottage July ninth. That night, at Paul's nudging, she called Eli, but the number was disconnected. She figured he'd call her the next day from his new one—it was their anniversary, the one of leaving this place—but for the first time ever, he didn't.

Vera flips through the mail again and realizes she missed a note in Paul's precise handwriting:

Grabbing a drink. Find me if you're in the mood too. x

She puts on her shoes then walks the hundred feet from her front door to Catskills Cider Co.

"The usual," she says to Brian then sits on a stool at the very end, her mouth already anticipating the crisp relief of a fresh pour.

Brian, it turns out, is really good at making cider. And Cate is really good at making any publicity good publicity. She rode the waves of that winter's press circus around Matthew's and Lydia's deaths gracefully. Managed to use it as an opportunity and somehow not come out looking like a selfish vulture but rather a concerned, loving community member.

They opened in June. Everyone in town, Vera included, has been stunned by the cidery's popularity, by the scope of the coverage that's outlasted any interest in the local tragedy, by the number of people who are willing to drive all the way down this dead-end road to have a taste. Early naysayers didn't take long to rewrite history and claim they'd been supportive all along. Early supporters wear it proudly like a badge. Villagers still grumble about cars that drive too fast, but people have to grumble about something.

"We just tapped Janet's Sour, you wanna try that instead?" Brian asks, a white dishrag over his shoulder.

"Definitely."

"That's the one with the quince? It's crazy tart, so delicious," says the young woman sitting a stool over. Vera smiles back. It's a good crowd for a Thursday night. The long bar is nearly full. Stan is chatting up Wanda and Bill plus another couple she doesn't recognize at the other end, and at least a dozen other people are outside on the stone patio that faces the mountains. Paul is probably in their favorite corner seat out there, just hidden from view.

Brian returns with a glass of pale yellow cider. Vera takes a sip and nods. Of all the recipes, this one tastes the most like cider used to.

"You did good."

"Our first aged batch should be ready by the end of the month. I want to try it now but I'm gonna wait, make sure we get the most out of the bourbon barrels in the process."

"I'm excited to try that one, too." Vera stands. She picks up her glass, smiles at Brian, says cheers to the couple next to her, then walks to the open barn door.

"Vera!"

Cate is waving her over to a table by the far wall, a tray of empty glasses balanced in the other hand, branded denim apron tied across her waist. Vera takes a few steps toward her smiling friend before the woman seated at the table turns around and stops time.

The golden light, the noise. It all stalls, stretches, collapsing, expanding. Then Cate is talking again.

"This is who I was telling you about! Vera, this is—I'm sorry, I didn't catch your name."

Ma laughs. "That's because I didn't give it to you, honey."

"And I've been talking at you for like half an hour! OMG, I'm so rude, sorry, I get excited when people want to know about the history of this place. Vera's a nerd for it, too—ooh is that Janet's Sour? It came out amazing, didn't it?"

Vera can only nod.

"Take a seat," her mother says. She pats the empty chair next to hers with one hand.

"Hunter! Down boy!" Cate reprimands as she shoos away the bouncing pup who's come upon them. "I'm sorry, I have to go. Brian is going to kill me if I don't finish collecting the empties."

"Thanks for chatting."

"Thank *you*! I'm sorry I was such a bitch last year when you—"

"Don't worry about it, honey."

With that, Cate leaves and Hunter trots after his owner, his tail wagging high behind him.

Vera sits down and feels a warm hand on her own under the table. She squeezes it back then lets go quickly, takes a pull of her cider to steady herself. Ma pushes a piece of blond hair away from her own face and looks into Vera's eyes.

"It's nice to meet you."

"You, too."

Vera's heart flips in her chest, up into her neck. The primal need to clutch her mother—Ma! here!—threatens to overtake any sense of decorum.

"Have you been here before?" she forces herself to ask.

"I've been coming to the area every year for a while now. There's something I like to keep an eye on."

It clicks. The hiker Cate told them about last year who had an old agreement with Brian's grandparents. The "trespasser" Cate was convinced would sue them if she got lost or fell.

Ma takes a sip of her cider. "You like it here?"

"I can't bring myself to leave." They look at each other, taking in what time has and hasn't done to them. "Where have you been?" Vera asks. It's not something she'd ask a stranger, but it could maybe pass for normal conversation if overheard. She needs to know.

"Oh here, there, all around. I specialize in being where no one else wants to be. Ebola wards for example. I was just in Guinea."

Vera keeps her eyes on Ma, who looks at her daughter, then past her, over her shoulder.

"I heard about the accident next door. Cate said you all were friends?"

"Yes."

"I'm sorry."

"I didn't know Matthew well, but Lydia and Eli—" Her voice catches in her throat.

"Would you like to take a walk with me before the sun sets?"

Vera leaves her drink on the table, follows her mother out of the barn onto the patio. The last of the day's sun burns orange across the meadow. A group of chickadees flutter from bush to bush. There's a bonfire going in the pit outside and the smoke drifts up and out.

Vera looks at her mother. She's never seen her in clothes this modern. Water-wicking pants, hiking boots, a thin, puffy, purple layer. She looks younger than she remembers. Then again, forty-six is young now, comparatively speaking. Vera's eyes keep scanning her, trying to make sense of what she's seeing.

It's really her.

Ma looks toward their old house, and Vera follows her gaze.

"You're the ranger who lives in the cottage, then?"

"I am."

"I saw your truck parked there last year."

Such a near miss. It makes her ache.

"Would you show it to me?" Ma asks.

"The house?"

"Your cottage."

"Of course."

They cross the patio and Vera hears her name.

It's Paul. He's changed out of his EMT uniform into jeans and a Catskills Cider Co. sweatshirt. His cheeks are flushed pink from the sun. He looks handsome and happy to see her.

"How'd your new fly work out?" he asks eagerly as he scoots down the bench to make room for her.

"It was great, I—" She looks at Ma and can't finish her sentence.

"I'm Paul," he says to Ma, his hand extended over the table. Ma shakes it.

"I'm Ani, nice to meet you. I'm going to borrow Vera for a minute before she sits."

"Sure thing," he says to Ma then looks back at Vera, who is no longer capable of fully masking herself in front of him. "You good?"

"I'm a little surprised to see her," she answers honestly. "It's been a while."

"You guys go way back?" he asks the women, and only Vera knows what he's really after. She nods. He sits up straight. "Ani you said?"

Ma says yes, and Paul takes a large drink from his pint of cider. He knows Vera's mother's name is Anika.

"I'll have her back in a few," Ma tells him as she hooks her arm into Vera's and gives her a gentle tug. Vera nods to Paul like, *It's OK,* and she and her mother step off the patio into the grass.

They cut across the meadow, the feeling of her mother's sturdy arm linked in hers so familiar. When they pass the back of their old house, Ma looks up at it but doesn't slow down.

"Have you been inside?" Vera asks. "I mean, since we left?"

"Many times," Ma answers, and Vera feels a small jolt of shock. "I knew the Hoffmans, I knew the Dunhams before the Hoffmans, I knew the Shoemakkers before the Dunhams—"

"Wait, how long have you been coming here?" Vera asks as they round the corner of the house into her backyard. She lets go of her mother's arm to face her.

"Since I came back from the war," Ma says plainly, and it makes Vera's heart constrict. "I believe the first time was 1921?"

"But we made a pact to never return," Vera insists, falling back on the old logic that kept her away from this place for so long.

"I didn't know where else to look for you two."

Vera stops. Feels the earth opening beneath her. She stumbles over to the old blossom-less apple tree at the edge of her garden and sits down in the grass, leans against the gnarled trunk. Thinks this must have been how Paul felt when she told him about herself. Reality splitting, a screen coming down in front of you changing the color of everything.

Ma has been looking for them this whole time.

"Eli and I never came here. Not until last year. We didn't come together, we—" Vera starts to explain as Ma sits down next to her. How to fill her in on one hundred years of lives? "We weren't living together anymore."

"Do you know where he is now?"

Vera nods yes despite being uncertain of his exact whereabouts because she is also uncertain how much her mother knows. Uncertain how much she wants to tell her yet.

"And Lydia, she's the Kirke's daughter from next door, yes?" Ma presses, and Vera nods again. "Your brother was working with her to find the source?"

"We both were, but I—" And here Vera stops, momentarily unable to continue, too many emotions lodged in her throat. Ma takes one of Vera's hands and wraps it in both of hers, brings it up to her lips and gives it a kiss, just like she used to do when Vera was little and upset about something.

"I came back to die," Vera says, wanting to get ahead of the truth this time, her hand still wrapped in her mother's. "On my own. I thought I'd find the source and somehow be able to reverse it." The vagueness of her initial plan almost embarrasses her now. "Then Eli showed up with Lydia and they were looking for the same thing—"

"With Matthew Barbery."

"He didn't know about them or why they actually moved here. Lydia told him she needed somewhere quiet to do her research."

Vera sees the lab in her mind. The dusty, empty shelves of the general store when they first arrived, the gleaming sterile space where they worked together those four months. The flames engulfing it.

"What did you find?" Ma asks, her hazel-green eyes alight like Eli's.

"Nothing."

Ma nods solemnly, takes her hands off Vera's and folds them in her own lap, then turns her head toward the mountains. She looks so peaceful, but Vera can feel an undercurrent of emotion rippling through her, like static electricity radiating. She's thinking, calculating something.

"Lydia says if we find the spring, she can eliminate most diseases," Vera tells her.

"Possibly," Ma says, then turns back to face her daughter. "But at what cost?"

It surprises Vera, and makes her realize why she's been hesitant to tell Ma everything.

She was certain Ma would agree with Lydia, not her.

"I thought you believed we should be using this to help people," Vera says.

"There are better ways to help people than giving life-altering power to already powerful men, are there not?"

Vera has to tell her.

"Lydia also says that if we find the fountain, she thinks she can reverse it. Our condition."

"Would you do that?" Ma asks, not missing a beat.

"I thought I would." Vera brushes some grass off her knee then looks up into the branches above her. The sun is beginning to set, birds flitting through the dusk-darkening sky.

Over the past year, Vera has given up on dying. It was a false hope, she's concluded, after all the hours and hours of replaying how things might have otherwise gone. If only because that hope was too dangerous. Too impossible to justify against what else would be unleashed in the wake of her own release. Staying alive—forever if she has to—that is how she will help others. It's the only way.

"I'm sorry I left you two like that," Ma says, interrupting Vera's thoughts, and she looks back at her mother's face. Her eyes are glassy, wet. "I don't regret how I've spent my time since then, but I do regret how I got there."

Vera feels her own eyes begin to water.

"It's OK."

"It's not," Ma says firmly. "But I'm not going to make the same mistake again. We need each other. This world is not a place to navigate alone when you're like us."

"But you've done it," Vera says. World War I front lines, Ebola wards. Where else has Ma gone in between?

"I haven't been alone."

Another fissure.

"There are others?" Vera asks, and it comes out in a whisper.

"Of course."

"And you know them?"

"I do."

With that, Ma stands and begins to scale the apple tree above Vera.

"What are you doing?"

"Do you remember this tree?" Ma asks as she pulls her way up through the branches gracefully.

"Maybe?" The shape of the orchard has changed so much over the years, it's hard to place. Besides, any trees they planted should be long gone by now.

"It almost never grew any apples, maybe one every ten years. But you loved to climb it, so you wouldn't let us cut it down," Ma says from above her. "You scaled it right after we finished burying your father over there, and you found one." She reaches out to a high branch and plucks something. "Just one."

She holds the apple out for Vera to see. It's gnarled, a mottled red and green, lumpy and small, but an apple nonetheless.

"You threw it down to Eli, and we shared it, just the three of us. Not Lotte, she had gone to fetch something in the house. I remember thinking it seemed so unfair that your father was missing out on that moment—the sweetness of the apple, and of the three of us sharing it together. So unfair that he would miss all the future moments, too."

The memory returns to her. Not precisely. It's been bent and fuzzed by time, but the feeling is there fully intact. The three of them together, the fourth missing. A hole. The injustice of it. The lack of reason.

"Look."

Vera follows her mother's finger into the meadow.

It's Paul's buck. Vera can tell from the split in the antlers and the nub on its left side. Strange that they grew back this year with the same anomaly. Vera opens her mouth to explain that she knows this animal, but it starts to walk toward them and she stops.

"That's a good boy, come here old friend," Ma beckons as she pockets the apple and climbs down quickly. The deer moves forward, no hesitation, its long legs stepping across the grass with steady purpose. Twenty feet away, ten. Ma drops from the tree to the ground, and stretches out her arms. The buck nuzzles into her chest.

Vera watches in silence as her mother holds the deer, murmuring into its hide. Ma has always been the one in the family who's best with animals. The one to calm the cow in labor, the spooked horse. She must have honed her skills over the years. But still, it feels remarkable to Vera, almost unreal to see her mother holding the deer like this.

After a moment it begins to root around near her pockets and Ma laughs, takes out the apple she just picked from the tree.

"Yes, for you. The one I always save for you if it comes. Now don't you go sharing it. Good boy, good boy."

He takes it from her hand in one bite. The crunch of his chewing fills the air around them.

Ma lets go of the deer and looks at her daughter.

"Vera, it's not a fountain."

Acknowledgments

Thank you to my agent, Ali Lake, for plucking this story from the pile and bettering it every step of the way. I have learned so much from you already and am so lucky to have you and the whole O'Connor Literary team in my corner.

To my editor, Sarah Stein, for immediately seeing the love and hope in this book, and for nurturing that throughout the entire process. Your optimism is infectious and your edits so smart and considered. What a privilege to have my work in your hands.

To the whole team at Harper in editorial, design, production, sales, marketing, publicity, and beyond. This book would not make it to readers without all of you! Thank you.

To my early readers. You were each so generous with your hard-earned writerly wisdom and your time—time you could have spent writing your own gorgeous work! My gratitude for you all runs deep. In alphabetical order: Stephanie Danler for holding the door open to others behind you and for your meaningful encouragement. Jen Doll for the millions of drafts and the long, inspiring phone calls. Isaac Fitzgerald for the kind words, shared ciders, loud laughter, and even occasional tears. Dominique Johnson for your impeccable memory and astounding thoughtfulness. Jo Piazza for your boundless generosity, unfailing frankness about the business of writing, and fellow feral parenting. Aimee Pokwatka for your oh so sweet enthusiasm and support at such a key moment. Ashley Rubell Burkholder for your curiosity, our two-person book club, and your near mystical belief in the power of art. And Emma Straub for your support, your sincerity, and your enthusiasm that's as bright and playful as your fashion.

To Jami Attenberg for creating the *1000 Words of Summer* community where this book began, and to Tracy Kennard who lovingly bullied me into trying it then sticking with it. Tracy, I wish you could have read the whole thing, but your keen eye was with me the entire way and will stay with me forever.

To Kelly Farber for your unparalleled publishing insight with which you are so genuinely generous.

To my Good Art Friends for all the support throughout the oh so many steps that happen before, during, and after the actual writing of a book—Jen Doll, Maris Kreizman, Glynnis MacNicol, Kate McKean, Carolyn Murnick, Jo Piazza, and Michelle Ruiz.

To David Scieszka for expertly weighing in on the science of longevity.

To all the historians who have taken the time to preserve and make accessible the diaries, letters, and other artifacts through which we can peek into the past.

To forest rangers everywhere, especially those here in the Catskills. I took some liberties with your line of work in this piece of fiction, but I hope my sincere admiration and respect for what you do comes alive in this story as fact.

To my Catskills community—none of you are in this book, but all of you are in this book! What I mean is, I could never have imagined this fictional, loving, silly, and uniquely textured community on the page without having lived one in reality with all of you. Thank you for welcoming me and Steven all those years ago, and for your continued support of us, our family, and our art.

To my Spruceton Inn guests. I cannot fully express how wonderful it is to resurface from writing to check you in, pour you a beer, and chat. Your support has made so much of my writing life possible—thank you. I love to share this place with you.

To our Spruceton Inn Artist Residents. You've thanked me for giving you space and time to create, and I thank you for giving me endless inspiration, and for welcoming me into your artistic worlds.

ACKNOWLEDGMENTS

To the oh so many teachers who dug deep with me into reading and writing and thinking at Berkeley Carroll, Pitzer College, and beyond. I'm ridiculously lucky that there are too many of you to count.

To every writer whose words have changed the pathways of my brain, my heart, my life.

To the librarians and booksellers who've put these words into my hands.

To every friend who's asked how the book is coming along and loved and encouraged me in your own way. You know who you are.

To my in-laws, Kathie and David Weinberg, for your curious questions, deep support, and generous grandparenting. Not to mention the raising of Steven!

To my dad, Jon Scieszka, for reading rough drafts of your own work straight off a yellow legal pad for my bedtime stories. For the gajillions of hours you've spent reading so many things I've written, from grade school projects to high school essays to multiple drafts of this very novel. You have shown me what it means to be a writer who engages with the world with an amused and curious heart. Bonus points for the fly-fishing insight and bottomless love.

To my mom, Jeri Hansen, for your singular style, infinite encouragement, and deepest of love. You taught me by example the importance of listening to your truest self. I miss you terribly.

To my kids, Amina and Felix, I love you. Thank you for the wonder and for always reminding me what life is really about. You are each an inspiration.

To my husband, Steven Weinberg. You make art fun, you make art meaningful. You make life fun, you make life meaningful. I love you.

And to you, reader. Thank you, thank you, thank you.

*

If you or someone you know is struggling with suicidal thoughts, confidential assistance is available through the Suicide and Crisis Lifeline by calling or texting 988.

About the Author

Casey Scieszka is a born and raised Brooklynite who has lived in Beijing, San Francisco, Fez, and Timbuktu where she was a Fulbright Scholar. In 2013 she and her husband, artist Steven Weinberg, moved to the Catskill Mountains and opened the Spruceton Inn: a Catskills Bed & Bar, which runs an annual Artist Residency hosting world-renowned painters, bestselling authors, and Pulitzer Prize and National Book Award finalists.